SAFFRON YELLOW

Saffron Yellow

ANTHEM PRESS
An imprint of Wimbledon Publishing Company Limited (WPC)
First published in the United Kingdom in 2016 by
ANTHEM PRESS
75–76 Blackfriars Road
London SE1 8HA

www.anthempress.com

Original title: *Safran San*
Copyright © İnci Aral 2011
Copyright © Kalem Agency 2011
Originally published by Kırmızı Kedi Publishing, Istanbul, Turkey
English translation copyright © Melahat Behlil 2011

A CIP record for this book is available from the British Library.

ISBN 978–1–78308–449–4

This title is also available as an ebook.

SAFFRON YELLOW

İNCI ARAL

Translated by Melahat Behlil

ANTHEM PRESS

About the Author

In *New False Times*, published in 1994, I had turned my perspective and literary interest to the experiences of my people and to their disorientation and disintegration due to loss of values. This was further developed in *Purple*, published in 2003, and *Saffron Yellow* was the third book completing the trilogy. When I started to write *Saffron Yellow*, I realized that as a writer who aims to be a witness of her times, impressions and feelings pertaining to years gone by form an essential integrity in many ways. That is why I renamed the first book *Green* and gave the trilogy the title *NEW FALSE TIMES*.

İnci Aral

"Sometimes the vapour hovered as soon as it left the mouth, dense and heavy, and brought forth another scene, the smoke and smells that gathered over the roofs in the metropolises, the opaque smoke that did not disperse, the poisonous air that settled over the bituminous streets. It wasn't the floating mists of memory nor its dry transparency, but the charred remains of burned lives that covered the city like a scab, the sponge swollen with vital matter that no longer flowed, the congestion of the past, present, and future that froze existences calcified in the illusion of movement."

Italo Calvino
Invisible Cities

1
Autumn

He had returned home from London that evening. It was late at night when he opened the suitcase he had brought home, assuming it was his own, and saw that it was someone else's. Although he went through the contents with the obsessive attention of a pervert, he wasn't able to find any sign or any clue to the identity of the owner.

The contents clearly showed that the suitcase belonged to a young woman. The plain clothes of good quality formed an attractive contrast with the seductive underwear. A pair of 38-size dark brown flannel trousers, two shirts, one white and one pink, a brand-g-string set of light lilac lace, two other similar sets, one black and one white, a few pairs of stockings, a gray and pink silk scarf, a belt, a tiny black skirt, a pair of classic black shoes with low heels – size 38 – in a plastic lined shoe bag. The length of the trousers indicated that the owner of the suitcase was about 1.70 m tall. The cosmetics in the small toilet case were expensive and of good quality, the silver jewelry in the velvet bag was beautiful. There were two thick gold rings which were exquisite: one embedded with a ruby and the other with an emerald.

When he set out the pieces of jewelry on his bed, he noticed that there were still some pieces jingling in the bag. As he emptied the bag on the bed cover, a handful of old coins fell out. Sixteen silver coins…

Was this surprising? Volkan wasn't sure. However, he could guess that the rings and the coins were very valuable. One saw the likes of these articles only in museums, amongst ancient artifacts. A suitcase was certainly not ideal for carrying around objects such as these.

Nonetheless, it was also possible that they were fakes. But if they had historical value, they were − particularly the coins − pointing at a reverse voyage contrary to the customary route. Perhaps they had been taken out of the country to be sold and had been returned for some reason. They might also have been gone in a greater number and come back less. Whatever the reason, it was rather daring to keep them in a suitcase. On the other hand, a suitcase could be less conspicuous, more practical than hand luggage. Volkan had no experience in these matters.

He wondered about this absent-minded woman who couldn't keep track of her hidden treasure. What was she like?

He always kept an identification card with the company letterhead in the outer compartment of his suitcase as a precaution against such confusing situations. It would be better to wait a few days for the woman to call before making a loss claim to the airline. He couldn't decide. The suitcase could prove dangerous. There was no need to look for trouble, to put oneself in jeopardy.

He wondered if he were waiting at the threshold of a detective story about to be written. He was alone in his room in the office. Compared to the usual clatter, it was a calm afternoon. His tastefully decorated office which resembled a huge living room was on the fifth floor, carefully protected from the outside world. When he stood at the window, he could see the vehicles, the people, the bus stops, the junctions and the traffic lights far below, all making him dizzy. There were times when he panicked and wanted to descend to the street as soon as possible and mix with the crowd. But what he felt in this room was privilege and power. A virtual power far above the army of people moving about like ants down below!

He sank into his armchair. He looked at the screen in front of him showing the chart of the Cosmos Investment Holding's areas of activity. Financial transactions, consultancy for the stock exchange and multinational company funds, buying and selling and managing of assets and real estate on a large scale...Mediation in the marketing of private and public real estate to be privatized...Always and definitely a large profit...Vulgar realities and villainous situations...

An important sale was to be finalized the following day. The details had to be reviewed once again. Certain esteemed gentlemen were to be persuaded and the situation wrapped up safely, then it was to be discussed who would be bribed and how much, and documents would be signed mutually. This was Volkan's job. He had been doing the same thing in the name of someone else, continuously enlarging its scope over the past five years. He never thought about what he had done, he was always busy contemplating what he had to do. And this had made him bold and courageous.

When he was still new with the company, he would see himself as a wizard of mathematics after each successful transaction. Negotiating over reports and graphics, creating unforeseen advantages for the company and analyzing commission reports quickly were things he was good at. However, his biggest success lay in his warm, convincing attitude when dealing with people. The most important thing that brought quick success in this business was to look sympathetic and trustworthy, as well as having experience and a sharp mind. Even though nobody trusted one other, they felt that it was necessary to act so, and it went without saying that a person had to be sympathetic and experienced. Volkan believed that he had been born gifted. It was never a problem for him to listen to people with undivided attention and courtesy while keeping his patience and composure.

An air pump was droning somewhere close by, stopping and starting again. He got up, walked to the window and looked down. The weather was uncertain, it was raining slightly – a weak autumn drizzle. The tops of the trees in a garden on the other side of the road glistened in the rain. He looked at the building's front garden decorated with shrubs and natural rocks resembling statues. He felt dizzy. He tried to empty his mind, to fill it with the rain, the trees and the wind. But the noise of the air pump continued. They were digging the streets again.

He had slept very little the night before. More and more could he sleep only with the help of pills or alcohol? Sometimes, just as he was about to fall asleep, he would start with the feeling that he had stumbled and was about to fall down a horrible ravine or that it was imperative he should not fall asleep. A subject, a word or an event he had hardly dwelled upon during the day would come back as an important midnight ghost and occupy his mind. All details and indifferences became extremely important; anger, hate, all emotions were sharpened.

The same thing had happened, and as if taking advantage of an occasion for staying awake, he had spent the whole night thinking about what sort of a woman would be the owner of that titillating underwear and that fragrance which had settled on the clothes in the suitcase. Not being able to sleep, tossing about in bed in the dark room had clouded his mind and stupefied him totally.

He had stopped dreaming a long time ago. Sometimes while dozing off, he saw tiring negotiations, pretentious sentences, figures, complicated and bankrupt stock exchange boards. Hotel rooms without bathrooms, finding himself barefoot or naked in crowded avenues, infected splinters digging into his skin…Always an effort, hastiness, an anxiety…Once he had dreamt that his penis was electrified as he was about to have sex with a woman he didn't know; his instrument had given out sparks and made short circuit. It was to be expected. He hadn't been with a woman for a long time.

The phone rang. A lady inquired about the "switched suitcases." Fine, put her on!

"Volkan Bey? This is Melike Eda. I have your suitcase. I hope that you have mine."

"I do have a suitcase, but there is no name tag. I was waiting for you to call."

"Shall I count the stuff inside so that you can be sure?" A playful laugh.

"Are you thinking that there could be a third one? Wouldn't that be too much confusion?"

"You are right, it would be too much. But I will still tell you, I had some jewelry in a velvet bag."

"That's right. I had to go through your bag to find out who it belonged to."

"How shall we make the exchange? Would you like me to send your suitcase to you or shall we meet?"

The voice on the telephone was alive, bright, vibrant like an echo and most enticing. To meet? Yes, why not? The driver could have settled the matter but there was a secret invitation in the happy tone of this sweet voice. He tried to picture the woman but he couldn't.

"As you like. Naturally if we meet, we will be solving the problem directly. What shall we do?"

"You tell me, Volkan Bey."

"Where are you?"

"On the Anatolian side, but I plan to go over to the European side today. I will drop by and leave you the suitcase. It's the Cosmos Plaza, isn't it? Will you be at your office in the afternoon?"

"I'll be expecting you."

He put down the receiver. He felt badly shaken. The woman's voice had been like a strong current. It had enveloped him, spun him around and dropped him. It was rude to ask a woman to come to him but the conversation had developed that way, or perhaps the woman had led the conversation in that direction. She was right; hers was a mysterious suitcase and valuable enough to be anxious about. She was after her little treasure that she couldn't leave unmentioned. That was why her voice was full of excitement and conciliation.

I hope she is as beautiful as her voice, he thought, I need an angel from paradise to fall in my arms.

He was quite a brain in mathematics, but his world of dreams was full of changing shapes and images. Just as a single sign or figure was sufficient to spark off his web of thinking, a tiny image was enough for him to dream upon. Whenever he felt himself at the start of something new, he would feel a kind of joy mixed with fright, a childish excitement, or exhilaration, as if he were about to set sail on unknown waters. On the other hand, he trusted his intuition. The woman on the phone was definitely lovely and attractive. Naturally there was always the possibility of disappointment, as the chances were only fifty-fifty. He was already in possession of sufficient important data such as her height, vital stats and even underwear. He laughed.

The woman's suitcase was at his home. He sent his driver to Bebek to fetch it. He looked at himself in the mirror next to the door and ran his fingers through his hair. His large amber eyes were deep and sleepy as if he had just got up from a siesta. This look had always impressed women. It was true that he was slightly overweight, but at least he wasn't bald. He had a shock of wavy, light brown hair.

He picked up the ringing phone. It was Nilhan.

"You are nowhere to be seen. I've missed you."

"We can't seem to meet. Life is so fast. How was summer?"

"A cruise to the Greek Islands, then some Bodrum…New York in September…In the meanwhile I fell in love and made a very important discovery about myself. You'll be surprised. But now I want to ask you something else."

Nilhan was the general manager of the Turkish branch of a large American bank. She was a true authority, a wizard in banking matters. But as a woman, she was blind. She couldn't form lasting connections with men. Although she was almost fifty, she often fell into painful relationships which she quickly grew tired of.

She talked about a difficult foreign currency transaction.

"It's not important," said Volkan. "I'll talk to Harun, I'm sure the matter can be settled."

"Are you free tomorrow evening? Would you like to do something?"

"I'll be in Norway, Nil. Let's talk next week."

Ah, Nil! Some things were over, lived through without being named, without being clearly defined. Whenever Volkan heard her voice, he remembered the start of their relationship. But he missed the touch of her skin only when he was really alone and when he didn't feel the shame of a pleasure that didn't fit their present situation.

When he met Nilhan, he was twenty-four years old. He had gone to the States on a scholarship and joined a master's program in New York, after graduating from the department of mathematics at the Middle East Technical University in Ankara. He was staying at the dormitory of the university and felt that the whole world was under his feet. He had grown up and become an adult through her. Although they thought they were in love, what was between them was more akin to friendship. This closeness had lasted three long years, not with passion but with sensuality and affection. What made their relationship special was perhaps the fact that they were both far from being possessive about each other.

Making love to Nilhan was a physical state of transparency. Reaching climax was the point where possession ended. He remembered the Sundays they spent in the bedroom of the house in Honolulu. Their reckless lovemaking, like a boat sailing into open seas without ropes, full of appetite, as if it were the first time, as if they had never seen each other before…

He had long since forgotten the countless nights, obscured by weed, which he had shared with her. The rooms where they slept, woke up and whispered to each other in, where obscene words flew in the humid air. He had forgotten, but all the same these memories had remained in the place where they had been cast off.

Nothing dragged on without forming a habit. For a long time now, there had been nothing between them except a feeling of familiarity. In the time that had passed, there had been other lovers, other anxieties, different lives. They had both changed a great deal, but Nilhan's transformation had been extraordinary.

Before sending her to Istanbul as the Turkish representative of the bank, they had recreated her from head to toe in the States. That slightly plump woman with wide hips had been replaced by a perfect beauty. Her excess fat had been removed; her cheekbones, her nose and her chin had been remodeled by expert hands according to ideal measurements. Volkan was now able to recognize her only by her eyes. She was still attractive in spite of her age. And she was elegant even if an emotional immaturity appeared behind the unhealthy expression on her face when she talked about her lovers. The self-confidence provided by her high position had made her distant, cool and difficult to please. However, it could not be denied that her position had a big role in keeping younger men at her side, even if it was for short periods.

She became a member of high society shortly after she started living in Istanbul. This had not been by choice but by letting matters take their own course. She was seen in exclusive parties, lived in a seaside mansion in Yeniköy with butlers and bodyguards, rode around in Cadillacs and cruised the world in the yachts of famous industrialists. In spite of all this, her life was listless and isolated. Loneliness was waiting to engulf her in the decorated rooms of that huge mansion which was a prison she had created herself.

A keen intelligence, an overwhelming abundance and a deadly loneliness! What sweet consolation! What majestic hopelessness! All of a sudden, Volkan smelt a whiff of decay and felt a similar pain; he was filled with a longing for purification.

This longing had started in the months of spring when he realized he had become a stranger who looked at his own life as if he were looking at someone else's, a stranger who approached his work, his environment and everything else with cynicism and found it all very boring. And it looked as if this would continue until he was able to clarify his reason of existence and what he expected from the future. This was a tiresome process. He knew well what it was to fall into an abyss after asking impossible questions. A darkness would settle inside him, becoming denser and bursting suddenly, overwhelming everything.

He saw himself in the mirror near the door. A bruised William Hurt in a light colored, wide-cut suit...The same childish, seductive smile, the same blondness, but rougher, more conceited...

How did he look to others?

Like someone who had forgotten where he had come from, someone with a complicated story and a shady future? Or an attractive young man who had a totally satisfying life filled with solid successes and an impressive and mysterious image?

Satisfying? A general definition, a distant assumption…

Success? An abstract thought you could never be sure of.

In any case, when he woke up in the mornings, he found it more and more difficult to remember who he really was. Behind that image of the so-called happiness, there was a burning discontent. An incomprehensible feeling of failure which he couldn't manage to shake off. He felt a soiled drabness, and an uncontrollable loneliness which seemed to be growing within every day.

The door opened and Harun came in. His large, teasing blue eyes set in his wide face were alive with laughter. He held up his hand to Volkan for a high five. Then he fell into one of the armchairs in front of the desk. Volkan felt like a member of a large secret organization. This was a familiar and beneficial feeling, even if it wasn't able to keep him away from the turmoil, madness and filth of the world.

"Bravo, you did a great job once again," said Harun. "Frankel called. He was in a very good mood. The sale has been finalized."

Harun was the founder, the brain, the biggest partner and the boss of Cosmos Investment Holding. He was heavier and less shapely than Volkan but he didn't care. Whenever the occasion arose, he would say that he was born large and that he was hefty even as a young boy.

"What news of the others? What happened in London?"

"It's as I told you on the phone. They want to think about it. Just a bargaining manouver…Actually they are bursting with joy. The stuff is cheap and valuable. They know very well that if it weren't for us, it would go to someone else for three times as much."

"We have to be careful. If the press or someone else gets a whiff of this deal, it could lead to complications. The guys are clever, they are thinking of partnership with us because of the long-term concession."

"A local partner would guarantee the deal for them. It would be good for us, too. The risk we will take is low, but our chance of winning is very high. What's more, we will be the ones to decide on the details of the partnership and sale."

"So? Is something bothering you?"

"There will be a lot of tremors when the deal is done."

"Never mind. It'll blow over. Let's look at it this way: we are businessmen. Let those who are selling the country think about what's good for it!"

He looked at Volkan through a mask of cool objectivity. This was the secretly mocking expression of someone who believed that his flawless indifference and intelligence protected him from all evil. His condescending smile was a message which seemed to mean "Nobody can slow me down!" and it was meant for everyone, regardless of whether they hated him or loved him.

Some leftist dinosaurs and the antiquated so-called patriots saw Harun as a conman, an unprincipled, bloodsucking conspirator despicable for his greed of money. However, in the liberal money market, those who made money from money knew the value of the slightest indication that he uttered. The success and intelligence he had shown in the first financial crisis he was faced with had turned Harun into one of the most important figures of the financial sector while he was still a young man. In the years gone by, Cosmos Investment had acquired international importance and had started to draw attention with the successful negotiations it had finalized especially for important clients from the Middle East. Those who showed the greatest interest in the mediation services of the company were opportunists and financial players who had dealings with the government and bargain-seeking foreign investors who were watching the privatization furore with greedy eyes. Harun's arms were long, and his methods of gathering secret information and closing deals were as productive as his activities at high levels.

"I'll be going to the meeting at the stock exchange," he said, looking at his watch. "Foreign exchange is in a critical state. And in the afternoon, I have an exquisite, private appointment." This meant "I'll be at my bachelor's pad." His weakest point was women. However, he was also capable of twisting them around his finger and casting them away whenever necessary so that he could have a clear head. He made no room for defeat.

He had inherited from his mother the eyes that glittered with a merciless cunning and the extraordinary regularity of his features. This woman who was the plump, pink-skinned, bashful wife of a scrubby moneylender dealing in illegal foreign exchange in Tahtakale, had been transformed into a motherly sultana who walked through the corridors of the company proudly covered in furs that made her frame look more bulky. Unfortunately, the blond good looks she had passed on to her son were too effeminate. After becoming a businessman, Harun had probably learned to cover this softness of his structure – which carried the risk of being misunderstood – with an impressive austerity, a frightening coldness.

In spite of his bulkiness, he lived at a galloping, breathless pace. Volkan had also been running with him for five years toward an unknown destination. He was presented to Harun by Nilhan with profuse praises after he had returned from the States. He certainly hadn't let his ex-lover down.

In that period, the notions of law and justice had lost their validity, empty words had been replaced by newer and emptier words, colors had faded and everything had become invisible in a great cloud of dust. The wind was blowing directly from behind Harun. Volkan didn't even have to jump. They hit it off well.

As soon as he went out of the room, he heard Harun shouting at someone in the corridor. He was very good at keeping his employers at a distance by a disturbing expression of contempt. Although his university education was nothing special, he had been spoiled by his rise through the ranks of finance and the success he had gained as a young man. He knew how to behave like a true street hawker when necessary. He was also very good at putting people down with unexpected outbursts of rudeness and obnoxious behavior if he felt they had overstepped the bounds of a relationship.

Volkan always backed him. He showed no anger or indecision on occasions which were contrary to his personality and beliefs. He never criticized Harun or revealed what he really thought about him.

He stiffened like someone frightened of pain. Why? Was it because he wanted to be successful at all costs, to be preferred over others, to have money and to believe that he was lucky? It was three o'clock. If there was nothing important such as an appointment or a meeting, three o'clock was a time he didn't like being at work. He sifted through the mail his secretary brought him. He worked until 5:30, waiting for the phone to ring. He didn't have an appointment and he didn't have to hurry anywhere, but for some reason he was impatient. He remembered that he had forgotten to talk to Harun about Nilhan's problem. It was a delicate, complicated matter. All the same, he sent her an e-mail telling her they would settle the matter the next day.

It was getting dark. He watched the smoke of his cigarette rising through the air and remembered a beach on the ocean far away. He could almost see the clouds over the sea lose their silhouettes and turn gold. He heard the sound of waves crashing and felt Nilhan's naked skin rubbing against his own.

As Melike Eda paused at his door and smiled at him, Volkan found her even more attractive than his wildest expectations. He stood up, watching the young woman walk with a spring in her gait and a smile on her lips. She was tall, slender and pretty. She was wearing a faded pair of jeans, a V-neck brown sweater with a somewhat deep V-neck, and a lovely necklace made of colored beads. She was without pretension, direct, natural. She shook his hand.

"I better not sit down, I'm already late, I don't want to keep you any longer," said the young woman.

"Oh, no, please, do sit down."

He showed her to a seat. They sat by the window, face to face, as she reached out to the flowers on the coffee table and lovingly stroked the colorful chrysanthemums. He was impressed by how quickly she seemed to overcome the distance between them. It was an intelligent and refined tactic to gain time.

"How beautiful they are. I love these flowers," said Melike sweetly. She turned her eyes away from the flowers and looked at Volkan as if she was trying to understand what sort of person he was. Before he could avert her eyes, they had been gazing intently into each other's eyes. He felt loved and caressed by that look, he was confused.

"I thought of you as being much older," said Melike. "I was surprised when I saw you. You are very young!"

Her shining eyes looked sincere and friendly. Volkan found himself thinking that lately he was moved easily by any kind of emotional demonstration. As he responded to the woman's seductive smile, he felt confused, not knowing what to say.

"You are just as I imagined."

"Is that so? You must be a person with strong foresight."

"You have a lovely voice. It kindles one's imagination."

"Thank you. I apologize for this mix-up. I don't want to detain you, you must be busy," repeated Melike. "Is my suitcase here?"

She had long, wavy, dark brown hair with red highlights down to her shoulders. Her dreamy, large, dark eyes reflected shyness, an apprehension she was trying to hide. Her classical Greek nose gave her face a regal air.

"I like to be detained at the office by matters which are not about business," said Volkan. "Don't worry about your suitcase. I have it brought here. There it is." He pointed with his head to a corner of the room. His own suitcase which Melike had brought back was by the side of the desk. The two suitcases were ditto identical.

In their excitement they shared the blame, as they discussed who had been the first to pick up the wrong suitcase.

"I was extremely absent-minded yesterday. As I'm afraid of flying, I had taken a pill. I was almost in a stupor, believe me," said the young woman. "You weren't very angry with me, were you?"

"No, no. It's my fault. I was tired and distracted. It's no problem, and anyway, this mistake became a reason for us to meet. We chose the same suitcase. Do you believe in coincidences?"

"Yes, sometimes. And you?"

"Me, too."

Looking at her was a joy, a sweet pleasure. She isn't a timid woman; she certainly isn't stupid or awkward, either; she is a straightforward, sincere person, not someone to be ignored, thought Volkan.

Her face was a flawless oval. Her strong self-confidence and naturalness could be felt in her smile. She had put on a light lip gloss. Her mouth was shapely, delicate, one of those mouths whose kiss tasted of water! As she spoke every word carefully, the enthusiasm in her voice reminded him of a little girl who hadn't yet lost her joyfulness. Her gaze gleamed with the light reflected off her red fringe, while she tried to keep away from her face an obstinate tuft of hair by frequently throwing back her head and arching her slender neck.

"You know who I am and what I do, but I know nothing about you except your name," said Volkan.

"I have a shop in Kadıköy. I deal with antiques and design jewelry," said Melike. She added, "I buy and sell antiques, and I also design jewelry based on those pieces. Are you interested in the subject?"

"Yes, a little. I can't really say I understand much. What I really like is the art of painting."

"I used to paint at one point, I'm actually a graduate of the Academy of Fine Arts, but when I started my jewelry business, I could not continue painting."

Volkan decided not to mention the pieces he had found in her bag. There was no reason to bring up the subject if she didn't ask. On the other hand, he had to find a way to assure her that her treasure was in its place. He asked what she would like to drink.

"I must confess I went through your belongings to find a clue about your identity. Then I put everything back," he said, trying to reassure her. He waited. "To tell you the truth, you have some extraordinary jewelry. I believe most of them are antique pieces. You are lucky that your suitcase didn't fall into the wrong hands."

"None of what you have seen is original, but you are right all the same."

The secretary served tea and withdrew.

Volkan guessed she was lying. He smiled. He knew how he looked when he smiled. A marked patience, some sadness and trustworthy intelligence. The female race preferred unaffected, intelligent and trustworthy men to strikingly handsome ones. Their eyes met once again. Something passed through him, a soft, fragile current! Melike bent her head over the teacup.

She had to be in her early thirties. Every so often, a hidden worldly wisdom reflected in the darkness of her black eyes and tiny wrinkles appeared at the sides of her mouth when she laughed. Her whole being exuded mature femininity and freshness. With an inviting look, she said, "I would like to show you some interesting pieces if you come to my studio."

"You are very kind, it will be my pleasure."

"If you'll excuse me now, I have to go over to the other side of town, and I better leave before the traffic gets bad."

"Do you have a car?"

"Yes, it's no problem." She got up and walked to her suitcase.

"I hope there is no more mix-up or we would have to meet again," said Volkan. "It would be a pleasure to see you again but I would not want to worry you."

As soon as he spoke, he found his words inappropriate but they had already been spoken. Melike laughed.

"It is not necessary to confuse our suitcases for that, Volkan Bey," she said.

"You are right. Friendships can be born out of such occasions. Let's meet again whenever it suits you."

Melike thought for an instant. "Of course, why not?" she said. She looked at him as if she was looking at a naughty child and laughed again.

Volkan realized that he had been more audacious than he would have expected of himself. He blushed. This young woman had crossed his path at a very unusual time in his life, and he panicked at the idea of losing her. He was about to fall into the huge web of weariness and depression. He had freed himself from taking passion too seriously but he had missed the excitement of his early youth, the echoes of a past hidden in the ruins of memory. There was a feeling of urgency in him.

"Oh, how could I forget, I'm having an exhibition of my jewelry in ten days," said Melike. "I would be very happy if you can come." She took out a visiting card and an invitation out of her bag and held them out to him. Her voice was distant, a proud tone.

"I will try to come if I'm in town," said Volkan.

"Well, I have given you a lot of trouble, good bye."

"On the contrary, it was a pleasure. If there is anything I can do for you, please call…anytime…"

He wrote his phone number on a card and gave it to Melike. He felt like touching her soft silky skin, caressing the sunburnt line which could be seen through her open neckline, and kissing the soft groove that her collarbones formed on her neck.

This wasn't a rough sort of passion. It was more of a remembrance, a revival with a heavy dose of affection. He was almost grateful to her for having picked up his suitcase. He rang the bell and asked the attendant to take the suitcase and accompany the young woman to her car.

He looked at her as she walked down the corridor. Her body was gracefully voluptuous, her hips were high and round enough to inspire erotic dreams.

But these were ordinary things for him.

He had learned not to trust his eyes where women were concerned. What struck him most was the confusion he had fallen into, although he was an experienced man. He had lived with upper class women trapped in relationships which explored all areas except that comfortable place where reciprocal shortcomings were accepted. A woman like this, completely at ease with herself, someone who looked what she really was...What a surprise!

He went back and sat at his desk. He looked at Melike's card:

KULPANTİK – Melike Eda Sezer – Tel...Web site...E-mail...Address...Second-hand dealer, he thought, a second-hand dealer. Suits me fine, that really suits me fine!

2

Just before leaving the house, Melike Eda looked at herself at the huge gold-framed mirror at the entrance of the living room. She spread her lipstick on her lips by rubbing them together. She looked beautiful in spite of her pale face and the gloominess of her dream. Even though her hair was carelessly disheveled, her gaze was soft and humid. For some time now, she had abandoned herself to the comfort of maturity. Her light blue t-shirt peeking from her black velvet jacket had JUST IMAGINE, printed on it, almost a contradiction. The telephone rang as she started walking to the door. She hesitated before picking up the receiver. It was Şahan. His voice was tense as if he were going to break news of a terrible accident.

"We have to talk, Eda."

"I'm about to go out, what is it, what's the matter?"

"I have to tell you something, have you got five minutes?"

Once again, Melike felt anger mixed with pity. When they met three months ago, she was so much in need of forgetting herself, of having someone to hang on to, that she had thrown herself into this man's arms without thinking too much. Şahan was a complicated, yet ordinary man who had never been loved. At the beginning, his attempts at hiding his incompetence had angered Melike. However, after a short while, the feeling of pity took over. He was so boring that sometimes she would get tired just by looking at his face. During their last argument, she had stormed out of the man's mediocre, untidy house banging the door behind her and they hadn't spoken for two weeks.

"Look, honey, I want to be honest with you. I was a fool. I feel terrible. Can we meet tonight?"

"No. We are through," said Melike.

"We did not take such a decision, you on your side…"

"Please, Şahan, I'm in a hurry."

"OK, look. We must meet again, because it's not something I can tell you on the phone."

Always the same story thought Melike wearily. Always the same song.

"I'm hanging up. Tell me quickly whatever you have to say."

"I slept with someone, a woman who knows how to do it."

Melike sat on the nearest chair. The cup of coffee she hadn't finished in the morning was still on the side table. She picked it up and took a sip from the cold coffee without thinking.

"Good, I'm happy for you."

"I love you, Eda. I don't think this will last. She is a silly girl, a student. You know how it goes."

There was a silence. A moment of injury…Melike tried to picture the girl; she had to be one of those stupid little bitches. One of those skinny girls with long, black hair and large tin earrings hanging from her ears, in tight pants, her belly showing…Stupid clod, she thought. She was filled with endless gloom. Since when was honesty the same as audacity? What sort of brain arrest had she experienced in thinking that he was a human being?

"Are you trying to make me jealous? I don't even care. Don't worry about me, okay?"

"Are you sure? I can end my relationship with her right now."

"What does this have to do with me? I wish you a pleasant love life. Enjoy it!"

"Please wait! This is an accident. I expect you to understand. Perhaps I was looking for a place to unload all the negative energy in me after our phone conversation last week, I really don't know. That is, if our relationship gets better again...and that depends on you..."

"First of all," interrupted Melike. "I don't like the word 'relationship.' It's empty, meaningless. Second, all flights have been canceled due to an accident. Third, I don't love you because you are an absolute..."

"Ass," she finished her sentence silently. She banged down the receiver. She was upset rather than sorry. That man was department manager in a company. He had first struck Melike as someone who had learned his lesson of manliness by heart. But he received negative marks from her on the first test. On the first night she slept with him, she realized he would be good only as a stopgap arrangement and she soon lost the desire to make love. He was filled with an excess of male pride and self-confidence, but he was so quickly aroused that he ejaculated within a minute. According to him, Melike didn't like sex, she didn't consider it a part of love. Furthermore, she wasn't relaxed during the act and didn't know how to have fun!

She hadn't made an effort to change the man's superficial opinions. There was nothing worth fighting for.

They had gone on holiday for a week early in September and she had seen that he was a penny-pinching bumpkin, from his underwear to his dancing. He would get upset when paying the bill, turning red, indicating that he had found it too high and didn't want to put his hand in his pocket. There is no need to count, she thought. These things get uglier over time. A woman could see all these faults and still love a man. She could love him madly, without logic, embracing his loose manners, his snoring, his false teeth, his provincialism, and in spite of all his failings, could love him as he is, his true self, his essence, because he is who he is. Furthermore, essence was not something the other party had to have; it concerned us.

She felt a great loneliness and the helplessness of not knowing which words would explain her feelings. This was an ordinary, proper, clean ending. Her attempts at opening herself up to people had always been cut short like this.

Ever since she was ten years old, she had lived her life with small ups followed by big downs. Later, she understood that falling, just like disappearing, also meant falling away from the shallow judgment and gaze of other people, that it was liberating. This was at least a consoling thought.

While walking to the car park, she regretted not having taken her raincoat. The sky was dark and it was drizzling. The sultanas in the flowerbed in the middle of the lawn looked fresh. They didn't seem to have been affected by last night's storm.

At Altunizade, she turned in the direction of Beylerbeyi. She blinked a few times, then opened her eyes wide and went slowly onto the main road. It was as if her eyesight had weakened because of her anger. Luckily, the traffic was not too bad as the windshield wipers crisscrossed across her windshield with a slight squeak, her thoughts also jumped from place to place. One could have several thoughts at once and yet not realize this when arranging and transforming them into words. The truth was that there wasn't much that would tie any man to any woman.

She had gone through adventures, superficial, shallow affairs, through days of rapture, negation, recklessness and indifference...She had blindfolded herself with her own hands, and at one point she had been trapped between impassable mountains and had come very close to falling off a cliff. She had experienced great, painful separations; the ways of the world had become clearer after each separation, and she had come to terms with her pain. Her claim of her injured state was what kept her from going mad altogether, keeping her more or less sane.

The suicide six years ago of the only man she loved had been a turning point in her life. After the tragedy, she had embarked on a long journey to understand herself. She found out she had been desperately hopeless at the time when she was with Nedim and that she was living the wrong life. She hadn't shaken off the doubt that she had worsened Nedim's illness. If only Nedim could have had some hope in the world, if only he could have opened his door slightly, he could have hung on to her. That had failed. Their love had been condemned to be unsatisfactory.

What the young man had kept alive was the dream of a chaotic lost love, not one of harmony. He had created moments of excitement from the passing of a cloud – from a window left open, from the wings of swallows, from a rusty key. He had been charting the deserts on the moon and was searching for a new planet where he could live *without* participating in anything, because he didn't believe in the future of his love for Melike, or of himself or the world.

Melike felt that delicate pain again, the remnant of a pain mishandled by time. Nedim had been right. He was a loser, and he was being realistic when he said that the number of losers would multiply incredibly. Many people had turned into flattened objects of daily use, had become silent, feeble or cowardly and gone out of circulation. Melike felt like a blank piece of paper with a signature that didn't belong to her. She remembered that period with a helpless feeling of loss. Nedim, with his sharp, ironic intelligence, was a stubborn rival who sparked Melike's thinking. He was the fastidious supervisor of her unhappiness. Perhaps their bonding had turned into love as they could compromise only on certain points or in momentous flashes of lightning.

She first went to Kadıköy, to the foundry. Nothing had been delayed, the man had worked well. There were one or two pieces still to be cast but he would have them ready for the exhibition.

In the beginning, Melike produced replicas. They were so good that one could hardly tell them from the original. Then she started getting bored. Preparing replicas was too static, monotonous, a concrete and detailed action. It was essential to take tradition as a starting point, as a solid foundation on which to build other forms and interpret them differently. These were loading points, determiners that fired her memory, but it was the actual process of creation that really attracted her. This was where art started. The childlike exciting process of creation…

Giving life to the forms inside her head, transforming them into objects and rendering them independent and alive had become an obsession with her now. She saw the world of objects and of the living as intertwined, like mixed abstract forms. Figures of Anatolian civilization carrying the essence of their time, carpet motifs loaded with connotations, the simplicity of Ottoman architecture were all indispensable data for transforming concrete into abstract forms. However, what really created magic was embedding the old forms within the new.

She couldn't find a parking space in front of the hairdresser's. She parked the car in one of the side streets and walked. She was only going to have her hair fixed. Her fingernails were in a bad condition but as she was going to be working until the exhibition, she wanted to have a manicure on the last day.

She left the hairdresser's in a hurry when they were through with her hair. She had planned to finish some shopping and then go to her uncle's seaside mansion for tea. It wasn't the best day for relaxing over tea, but she would tell her uncle about her last trip and ask for his advice on the layout of the exhibition.

Niyazi Bey was a well-known expert of antiquities and an antique dealer. He was the one who had drawn her into the antique business, taught her the fineness of art and guided her toward making jewelry. As Melike was living through the last pages of her personal history of failures, her uncle had lifted her from the ground and put her back on her feet, giving her a chance to forget the past. She owed him a life.

Melike bought some skimmed milk, yoghurt, muesli and fruit from the supermarket. A sleepless night had left with a slight headache.

She had woken with palpitations in the early morning. The trees in the garden of the housing complex were rustling in the wind. Little monotonous taps at the window gave the impression that there was someone outside. When she got up to look, she saw that a branch of the linden tree outside her bedroom had been broken and was leaning against the window, touching the windowpane with every gust of wind. The garden, dotted with outdoor lamps, appeared velvety soft under the full moon. She drew open the curtains to let the moonlight into her room and returned to bed, remembering the dream she had been having.

She was in the shop. She wasn't selling antiques or jewelry, she was trying to sell the dreams those objects had adopted. As far as she remembered of her dream, it was not the jewelry that was valuable, but the secret dreams it represented. Good and bad, positive and negative dreams…It was hard to guess what sort of a secret each piece of jewelry or object contained. That is why shopping was difficult and took a long time. Sometimes a stone, a color, a form or a design would inspire an unlikely feeling, but wouldn't give itself away entirely, because the important thing was not to know. Not to know but only to hope…

She swore at the taxi that passed by, blowing its horn. She quickly returned to her dream. In fact it wasn't clear if I was the buyer or the seller, she thought, because the customers were insisting on selling her some invisible things as well. It was a long dream, tiring as if it were a difficult task, lasting for hours…More based on knowing without knowing rather than being tangible…Toward the end of the dream, she left the shop and mounted a strange horse standing outside. Strange because it was a wooden horse, decorated with rustic dyes, tassels and beads, and it was impassive and alive at once. It even had a name: Slavery! It was a good-natured, soft-hearted wooden animal. The expression on its face was something between laughing and crying. It had bent down and taken Melike on its back. Then she had wandered around as though they were in a strange city, far from home, looking for a place that would accept her and her horse, taking refuge in dingy hostels and wards crowded with women. They were all either too noisy or too sordid to stay in, or were places without barns.

She often had such strange dreams. Perhaps these were unsent letters, unconscious exercises in soul-searching, because hers was a memory made of cryptic messages. She usually didn't try to unravel the mystery; she couldn't see herself as a tomb raider. Her distant past had been lost since an unknown time, and she preferred to believe that what she knew about her past was not more than what was known to a stranger. However, when she dreamed, her numb memory would stir and everything – except those that could be labeled sweet – and the humiliations and regrets would come back stronger.

The creaking stairs of a house in a small town, ash-colored days, the strange, angry, crazy face of a stranger, a trampled sky was coming back…almost…

Almost…So much time had passed since those nights, those rooms, the screams, the chills, the beds and the bodies, one could never be certain that they had really existed. No feeling, no inclination, no mistake, no cruelty, no hate, no mercy – alive or dead – nothing was certain now.

"To pity is easier than to hate!" That was what Nedim had written. But this was a hasty judgment. It was impossible to name certain feelings. They were all buried so deep in dust that the best thing was to let them be, and to forget. However, the eye of dreams could see in the dark as well, and truth glowed for an instant before disappearing into the pitch-black background.

Just like in her childhood, she sometimes saw herself among skeletons that would be shouting, crying and burning in planes crashing onto mountains, because fire, sin and mourning had gnawed at the deepest part of her body. She had carried on her shoulders that horrible, assumed childhood, rejecting it at the same time. That childhood was never inspiring neither her joys nor her sorrows…That was why her inner line of continuity was broken and everything had long ago turned into a boring present time.

Perhaps this was the surest way of staying alive: killing all illusions about the past and the future.

She descended to Beylerbeyi from the foot of the bridge. Her uncle lived with his lover in a biggish seaside mansion guarded by armed men. His lover Hayali, was a man of thirty-five or forty, and as far as she knew, had studied medicine. He was an expert in historical artifacts, someone who was well known and consulted in the market.

His real name was Hayati. He collected old figures of the shadow plays of Habitat and Maragos, and also produced them himself as a hobby. He had a workroom on the ground floor of the mansion that he also used as study.

Melike had hated him at first sight. It wasn't really hate but a sort of fear, or a flinch. Hayali had looked at her with a vulgar sparkle in his eyes, as if scorning her for being a woman, belittling her. You might think that he desired her and found his desire disgusting at once. His expression had upset Melike. She later came to the conclusion that he scorned everyone, even her uncle, with an obstinate defensive energy.

Although she didn't like to run into Hayali, for some reason she was always overtaken by an absurd excitement every time she saw the young man. Perhaps this was created by that secret conflict between them. Melike looked at Hayali with the same secret hate, violence and repudiation as he bore toward her. It was as if they mutually saw each other's invisible faces and fearing that wanted to destroy each other.

Nevertheless Hayali was better at hiding his feelings than Melike. He possessed a natural and feminine ability to act. He cunningly played the beautiful, tasteful, loving, generous, courteous, art-loving, intelligent, distinguished, balanced, composed lover to her uncle. It was as if he was doing all he could do to silence the demanding spirit of the old man, to cancel the age difference of twenty-five years and disparity of status between them, and to annihilate his willpower.

Some time ago, he had brought into the house a so-called relative of his as a secretary. This girl, Işıl looked like an adolescent boy. Her body had no curves. Narrow hips, barely any breasts, a long neck, a proud clear face and very short straw-colored hair. Because of her seemingly ambiguous gender, she evoked strange feelings in Melike which alternated between pity and apprehension.

She was afraid that her uncle would be hurt by these two. Not that any of them complained. One could guess that there had to be a kind intense of sexual communication and balance between these three people living together. Melike hadn't seen an open indication, it was just a feeling. One reason for her hatred for Hayali was the possibility of the young man's awareness of what she continuously carried in her head: the tiring sexual connotations and richness of images concerning this threesome. Sometimes she saw in his eyes or his mocking, seductive smile a hint that gave away his awareness on purpose.

She turned into the narrow lane that led from the main road to the house. One of the guards who opened the gate showed her to a parking place. She left the key in the starter. Hayali's four-wheeler was in its place, he had to be home. Melike shuddered with disgust.

The garden was still fresh with autumn roses bathed in rain. The ivy on the sidewall of the house and the purple flowers of the passiflora plant which had covered the gazebo were enjoying their last days of glory. The lavender-hued sky and the hesitant sighs of the gray-blue sea created a feeling of melancholic loneliness.

Melike Eda went to the back of the house amid dog barks. She saw adan Hanım waiting for her at the open door. They saluted each other.

"It's your bad luck Eda Hanım, the weather is not too good. You will have to take your tea indoors. Your uncle is upstairs, waiting for you in his room."

The section which opened to the large rectangular entrance was empty and the doors were closed. The floor which used to be of flagstone was now covered with mahogany boards. The house had been totally renovated under Hayali's supervision, the year before. The exterior had been repaired and painted olive green, and some practical changes had been made in the interior.

The door to Hayali's study was closed. The poignant sound of a tambour and the smell of leather, aniline dyes and wax filtered out of the room. Melike liked workshops, so she wanted to go in to see what he was doing, to breathe that hot air for a moment. But she quickly changed her mind.

She walked toward the stairs. The shelves supported by high, elegant props all around the hall were filled with valuable Çanakkale pottery, pitchers and plates. The walls had been painted light beige. Two leather couches faced each other in front of the glass doors that separated the porch from the living room. The teak armchairs and the summer deck chairs outside had not yet been removed.

She went upstairs. In one of the wings opening to the hall and the terrace beyond, there was an antique dining table for eight. The other wing contained a black grand piano. The magnificent crystal chandelier hanging over the piano added pinkish golden flickers to the reflections of the sea on the walls and on the ceiling and onto the mirrors and the ancient Shiraz carpet on the floor.

Melike knocked on the door and entered smiling. Niyazi Bey got up from his desk with exaggerated joy and embraced her. They sat down. The black cat, Ares, got up from the cushion where he had been lying and rubbing itself against Melike's legs, gave her a courteous "welcome."

"It's been some time since we saw each other, isn't it?" said Niyazi Bey, his eyes smiling.

"Fifteen days, my dear Uncle."

"Ah…Long enough to age one…Getting old is something that damages one's self-confidence, Melike. A painful paradox for an abstract mind that constantly thinks about the noble beauty of the past."

"You aren't old, Uncle. It's more difficult for women. Look at me; before you know it, I have turned thirty-four."

Although Melike lived as if there was no beginning and no end to her youth, she had begun to worry about the years that passed so quickly. Protective creams, gels, collagen masks would become useless after a while. This could be considered an irrelevant fear for a woman who wasn't obsessed about her beauty. But it was impossible to ignore the whole thing and act as if she wasn't aware of anything. Naturally she wanted to stay young just like everyone else, but what she was really afraid of losing was the gaiety, the rebelliousness and the hopefullness of youth. What an irrelevant fear for someone who never had those things...

"Thirty-four is a good age," said Niyazi Bey with longing. "The age of being carried away by great passions."

"They also call it the age of settling down."

"That was in the past. I want you to be happy, my dear. It makes me sad to see you so lonely."

"I would have liked to make good use of your experience."

"I don't know, my dear. I can only guess what is missing in your life. I think this is a problem which arises from the conflict between the physical discomfort that your past inflicted on you and your imagination."

"I am surrounded with selfishness, laziness, vulgarity and fundamentalism," said Melike. At a time when the male race has so deteriorated, I don't know where to set my foot in."

"You expect too much. Nobody can love this way, Melike."

"Love? Very difficult to do, Uncle. As one matures..."

"You begin to love with more awareness. Naturally after a certain age, you feel sadder and more hopeless, you become more skeptical and morose but..."

This is the first time my uncle and I are talking about these things, thought Melike. She had never seen him so pessimistic before. He had to be referring to Hayali, and since he had brought up the subject, he was surely going to say more.

"You cannot invest in love," continued Niyazi Bey. "It is lived and finished by itself. You don't want it to finish but it does."

"A cool-headed approach! Are we talking about Hayali?"

"I'm trying to be logical. As for Hayali, he is a young man. Sooner or later, he will want to live his own life. He has done a lot for me. He accomplished some great things lately but I respect his feelings."

My uncle is pouring his heart out, thought Melike, so there must be a crack somewhere. She felt a vague happiness. If only this story would end before long. No, it didn't look as if it would. Hear, hear! Hayali had accomplished great things! Niyazi Bey was probably talking about the sacred door curtain of Kaaba. However, an expert in London had claimed that the curtain which had been sold for hundreds of thousands of dollars was a fake. Most probably it really was a fake and they would soon be in trouble.

"The problem is that half of this house belongs to Hayali. If a separation is the case, we both will be in a difficult position."

Melike was dumbstruck. Hadn't her uncle invested everything he had in this house eight years ago?

"I did a share transfer to him last year. There were some economical and personal reasons necessitated by our partnership," explained Niyazi Bey.

A burning anger gripped Melike. As the future heir, the mansion didn't mean much to her. She was angry because of this inhuman situation. Niyazi Bey had introduced Hayali into a special environment; he had supported him and showed him empathy. It was now obvious what Hayali had been after all along. It didn't seem possible that an experienced man like her uncle, who could be so conniving with people he didn't like, would be deceived by an ungrateful impostor.

"I know that you are careful with people who try to take advantage of your generosity. But for some reason you seem to have let go of all caution this time," said Melike.

"Ours is not an ordinary relation. I trust Hayali. But one mustn't mix love with business. I am worried because I am attached to this place; it would make me very sad to lose it."

Melike looked at the door. Why was he hiding, why wasn't he stepping forward, this Hayali guy? Was it to scheme in secret? What could be easier for a hypocrite like him to fool a weak, old man?

In her uncle's face, in the curve of his lips, there was a vague sort of outrage, a kind of wickedness that seemed to mix with goodness and a selfish grief. Melike felt a subtle change in their relationship. Her uncle had always considered her his one and only daughter, his natural partner and the only person he trusted. But then Hayali had come between them. A conceited, greedy, audacious faggot!

"Have you talked to him?" she asked.

"There is nothing to talk about; I just feel we are drifting apart."

The room they were in was more like a study or a den. One might think there was no order to the decor, it was haphazardly filled with furniture and all sorts of other objects. There was a phonograph in the corner and a jumble of records and magazines on the floor. The cabinet by the door filled with fancy bottles gave the room an air of being an office. However, this feeling was quickly dispersed by the outstanding examples of Ottoman glass workmanship filling the shelves of the cabinet. One wall of the room was entirely covered by a bookcase with glass doors, chaotically packed with beautifully bound rare books. For an instant, Melike felt as if she had been locked up in the old trunk of a second-hand dealer.

At a certain period – in the 1990s – Niyazi Bey had dealt on a big scale in smuggling historical objects, making a large fortune for himself. Now he was passing time with less important tasks which had become his hobbies. Perhaps this was all that was in his power now. On the other hand, Hayali was doing business through old contacts by using Niyazi Bey's name, and no doubt feathering his nest on the side. Melike had remained silent pretending not to know, not only because she felt this was her uncle's private life but also because she felt left out. Now she was worried for the first time.

The years of ascension for her uncle had been a time of drifting for Melike. She had divorced her husband whom she had married before she was twenty – while still a student – and she was wandering around. At times, she would open her eyes in strange beds, next to louts she didn't know; she couldn't figure out where she was heading.

Her uncle insisted she finish her education. Then he restored his old two-storey house in Mühürdar, which had a storeroom for old furniture and a shop on the ground floor, transforming it into a place where Melike could live and work; then he turned it over to her. They became partners and within a year, Melike learned to manage the shop by herself and became her uncle's trusted help. It had been ten years since they had been working together. They knew each other well and could communicate through codes and signs. In the beginning, she abided strictly by her uncle's rules, his work methods and arrangements. While she had an affair with Metin, a photographer who worked with her uncle, she found herself involved in the smuggling business. Her involvement was limited to being courier and transporting certain pieces. Naturally she had been somewhat scared of the legal implications and her conscience had not been at ease, but as she couldn't oppose Metin she had acquiesced.

In a way, she had become her uncle's protective shield, his decent public image. All I did was to recognize the system and give up what I had been led to believe, she thought. Her uncle used to argue that it was necessary to abide by the rules only when they were applicable to everyone without exception. The rules which existed but were applied only to the weak unavoidably created evaders. Breaking the law was inevitable for the army of victims and the persecuted which made up the majority. Niyazi Bey always said that one had to be somewhat savage to be able to live in this country which owed its independence to smuggling of all kinds. Everyone knew this, it was how the system was fed and stood on its feet. It would be impossible to take the slightest step if the state didn't allow it. So he said.

In order to save appearances, Niyazi Bey let himself undergo a trial a few times and even went to prison for periods of several months. Two years ago, he was also attacked by a local treasure-hunting mafia and was shot in the foot. So the real danger was not the law but the share battles, and getting rid of an old man seemed easy to some people. Hayali came into the picture at this point. He backed him and became his protector.

Was this really the truth? She thought her uncle had probably been tricked. The market functioned according to definite rules within a large network of connections which had been organized to include everyone from famous collectors to errand boys. Anyone who went beyond this, who broke the chain, was punished according to the amount of money in question. This organization did not exist in the years her uncle had started working, and Niyazi Bey more or less worked for himself at that time. In the meantime, no doubt there had been some snags, but then Hayali came along and arranged everything, a little roughly but with a delicate solemnity.

Melike felt tiny, naive and very stupid.

She had entered the jewelry business partly to escape her environment. She wanted to ward off the danger and to be independent. At that time, she had been relieved when Hayali suddenly appeared on the scene and took control of the business. She had felt relief at being left alone by the old man, intentionally or unintentionally.

He needs me, she thought. He must have seen the trick that was played on him. It was true that the man downstairs, who distracted himself with Karagöz-Hacivat figures while listening to classical Turkish music, had turned her uncle's head with his special kind of radiance, charm and pride, filling his life for two years. But now, all that seemed to be over. Melike felt that she would always be indispensable, whereas Hayali could easily be replaced by someone else. Yes, but what could she do? After waking up to all this, she wasn't going to lower herself to the point of going to Hayali to beg for mercy, even if it was in the name someone else.

Uncle…He had never seemed so helpless, so broken before. He had reached sixty-five; the lines on his protruding, wide forehead had multiplied. His green eyes were still lively, but his eyelids had creased and become saggy. Nevertheless, his slender body, his upright stance and his long legs and the feminine elegance and fastidiousness so typical of him were still the same.

Dusk was falling as the bluish light seeping in through the window on the Bosphorus was rapidly turning dark. Niyazi Bey looked at the other shore and the emerging lights of the evening which was slowly sucking in time. He glanced at the Russian tanker which seemed to be flowing close to the house, then he rang the bell and asked for tea.

"Where is Hayali? Why is he hiding from me?" asked Melike. "I can never see him when I come here."

"I don't think you two like each other very much," said Niyazi Bey.

"He gives me the impression of being an insincere, conniving person."

"No, he is all right. He only has his weak points. Furthermore, he is a narcissist. But all the same, he isn't someone who cannot be managed."

Melike was silent. Niyazi Bey looked outside with a poignant smile as if in deep thought.

"But even hate implies deep sentimentality," he said.

What did he mean? Melike flinched, what was her uncle trying to say?

"You have never fallen in love, my dear, or maybe showing your love is against your nature."

"I may not have been able to show it, but I did love someone, Uncle."

"That wasn't love. You were a child then. And the man was mad, anyway. Oh well, things of the past…In essence, Nedim was an honest, straightforward person. But as it usually happens in these cases, life went after the poor boy and made him pay."

What a commercial approach, thought Melike.

Şadan Hanım brought some homemade ginger cookies and olive pasties with tea. She served the tea and left the room.

"There was no problem with the coins, I hope."

"There was," said Melike. "The buyer bought only thirty of them. Eighteen were returned on the grounds that they were fake."

Niyazi Bey didn't speak for a while.

"It's possible. I may have been mistaken, but I don't think that they are fake," he said. Then he added, "The problem is that suspicion has gained the status of genius in our day."

Melike told him with a slightly piqued air that she had been left in an awkward position, that the man had become angry and hadn't even looked at the rings. This had been her last job anyway. She did not want to continue. Her uncle listened to her thoughtfully. Well, she was right. All the same, it wasn't a bad thing that most of the coins had proved authentic, because forgers were working with high-profile methods.

Melike thought she would never know how sincere her uncle was. These were familiar attitudes. She was sure that he had known all along. Anyway, this was the last time; I have paid my debt, she thought. She took out a small sack from her bag and put it on the table. She didn't feel she had to tell him about her lost suitcase.

On her way back home, she thought about her conversation with her uncle on affection and love.

When she rearranged her life, she had succeeded in balancing her sexual expectations and her aimless drifting. Nevertheless, she was still not far from this fiery enigma of life and death. She could not understand at all why the different manifestations of sexuality were called love. She believed in sexual love, but she also thought that sex was a simple, amusing and ordinary activity. What sense was there in censuring such a natural act, that sweet blindness with teary-eyed sentimentalities, pointless promises and painful temporary liaisons!

She was against the traditional approach to this area of private and closed originality. This was a hypocritical, underhanded, unjust understanding weighed down by public judgments and punishments particularly applied to the female race.

Perhaps in a hundred years from now, sex would become more secure, and having been converted as a whole into something totally technological, it would become sterile, healthy, uniform, virtual and definitely less fun. This way, it would be possible to live relationships which were more independent, flexible and more ordinary than ever. Even now, people's dreams about love and sex had already started to degenerate.

But was that really true? She thought of Volkan. Although somewhat overweight, he was an attractive man. There was a childish air about him in spite of his important position. Becoming the assistant director of a large conglomerate was an indication of high achievement for a person his age, and yet he wasn't presumptuous. He had openly shown that Melike had impressed him. Although he had tried to hide it, his attraction was so obvious to Melike that she felt excited as well. Even if it didn't happen very often lately, the refined attention and the secret desire of a distinguished man was something she enjoyed. Actually it was her first condition for opening her arms to a man. Whether the man was ugly, handsome, fat, thin, young or old was of no importance whatsoever at that point.

For a moment she felt a happy anticipation, then her heart sank with the hopelessness that followed. She had met the man only the day before. She had been through many short-lived adventures that had started in the same way. Now she could feel how her relation with a man would – or rather, wouldn't be – like love at first sight. Although this man was sincere and open, she knew that from her standpoint, everything would soon turn into a mock, boring game of feigned ignorance.

Would it really? Why was she so prejudiced? There was still some time until her exhibition, but if the young man did come to the opening, maybe it could bring them close to each other. She wanted him to come, because this classy broker seemed like a good man to keep in tow.

Melike returned to Altunizade. She lived in a large, airy flat in a well-protected housing complex. It had been three years since she had converted the old house in Mühürdar back to a warehouse and a shop, and had moved to this place. So many shops were opened on that street that it had become impossible to use the house as residence. She still had to pay for her new flat but that would be finished soon. The economic geography of her life was richer and more colorful than her isolated internal geography.

She changed into another set of clothes as soon as she got home. She looked at her face without makeup in the bathroom light which hardened her features. For an instant, she thought she was looking at the face of her uncle-father-stepfather, the first man to lay a hand on her, the eyes which wanted more than she could give. The girl lying in the little room in the attic, squirming as she felt the hardness between her hips and recoiling upon seeing the electrified blue of the man's gaze.

Yes but why, why was she remembering all this now?

Whenever she was attracted to a man, she felt trapped. She felt a strong urge to punish her flesh and thereby pouring out the venom inside her. She wanted to erase the past but the more she tried the more alive it became. She looked for the innocence of childhood in her own eyes but all she could find was the open acceptance of her sinfulness.

He is no longer there, she thought, without quite knowing who she was talking about. He is dead. In my memory, he turned into a nonexistent entity beyond pain.

This childless stepfather had never been her father and he never would be. He would remain the object of her scary sadness, her helplessness and desperate attempts to be saved. He would always remind her of the mortality of human skin and the insolent, flighty temporality of passion.

She heated two chicken legs and ate them with some salad. She spent a large part of her day in the studio and the shop, went to the gym three times a week and usually had some meat and vegetables for dinner. There was no guarantee that living with a single person for a lifetime – together with the burdens it would bring – would be more enjoyable and more pleasant. No, she couldn't bear a life like that, she couldn't stand it. A better, more interesting world has to start with me, but how?

She thought of Şahan. She turned on her mobile. Just as she expected, that blockhead had sent her three messages. In the first one he was saying that he loved her, and in the next two, he was talking nonsense and accusing her of being a frigid whore. Well, it was normal that the price of freedom would have this much side effect. It doesn't really matter, she thought.

She dropped her elbows on the table and looked at the empty plates. She had always envied crowded family tables, meals joyfully eaten by the whole family, children and all. All of a sudden, there were tears in her eyes. What was she going to do when she was forty, fifty or sixty? I should have had a child, she thought, rather, I should have a child. I must have a child by a man who may not be a safe port but who is at least a ship. She could almost visualize that ambiguous, tortuous shape of happiness. She cried quietly as if trying to free herself from her memories, her pseudo-conceit, her fear of being alone and the loneliness she felt while making love to countless men.

She fought back sleep until the book she was trying to read fell out of her hand. She caressed her cat Pati that had jumped onto the bed. At the beginning of next week, she was going to call Volkan to remind him of the exhibition once again. She had to try her luck. This was a handgrip, a tiny hope that would carry her to reality ...for the time being.

3

Volkan walked in step to the music along the corridor before entering the dim, humming depths of the club. As he passed, the light which filtered through the stained glass panels on both sides sprinkled him with lace-like spots resembling colored flowers.

The place had been prepared for unexpected cold weather, early rains and strong winds. Portable panels and windows which were removed during summer and opened the entire space toward the seashore had been put back.

That night, the weather was lukewarm and pleasant as if autumn would never end. The large windows were wide open to the smells of rotting leaves and the sea. The dense odors of alcohol, food and perfume were mingling with a pure breeze from the fresh air.

He walked behind the waiter along the side of the dance floor and sat at a table with a view and at equal distance to the bar and the dance floor. Although it was a weekday, most of the tables were occupied. In this club of the elite, management, service and food suited the quality, taste and expectations of the patrons. From the glasses to the armchairs, from the lamps to the mirrors, everything had been cleverly designed to emphasize expensive privilege. This was a small island hidden from the shame- and sin-filled world of crude people and the obtrusive eyes of the paparazzi. It was a kind of refuge, a place to meet, to see and remember each other, to have fun and let go. Everything seemed to breathe a slight dissatisfaction under the well-arranged lights.

He leaned back. The night outside the windows was enchanting. The copper moon rising from behind the skyscrapers on the hill and the fidgety, colorful reflections of the opposite shore on the calm, dark blue sea sparked off a feeling of eternity and insignificance. Man was transient; a moment's entity for nature, and the earth was a great sage who accepted the variability of life as a valid contrast, a temporary obligation, while poor mankind pointlessly continued to struggle with it.

He leaned forward trying to see the bar from amongst the crowd. He recognized Harun from his size. He had perched on a high stool at the end of the bow-shaped bar, with his elbows propped up on the counter, and he was talking very closely with the banker son of a famous businessman. From afar, he looked like an overfilled ice-cream cone.

Volkan hadn't been to the club for some time. The night he saw a young arabesque singer, who had suddenly become very popular amongst the elite crowd, singing on top of his voice on the stage, Volkan's hair had stood on end and he had walked out. Harun had said, "These things happen in our postmodern world, sonny boy, the guy is very fashionable these days. I'm sure he is better than that American jazz singer who was here some time ago. Come on, relax a little." But Harun always took the worst of the worse as a starting point.

He greeted a few people. He had a large circle of friends. However, when he was with people he knew or considered as his friends, he had started doubting more often than ever whether these friendships had a stable foundation or any real meaning. He disliked the way many of these people reflected their ideas, their thoughts or what they approved of. He had to make an effort not to show his disdain, and what's more, not to start unnecessary arguments.

He felt a wrenching feeling in his stomach, an uncomfortable scratching like hunger. No, he wasn't hungry. He had grabbed a bite before leaving his house. Harun had probably done the same thing. They had both been ruined by these double gluttonies and endless business dinners in the best restaurants of the world from Tokyo to Toronto. Actually it wasn't so difficult for him to lose ten kilos and become as attractive as he used to be as a young man. All it took was some willpower.

He looked at the ever-moving, undulating crowd around him. Those standing around with their drinks in their hands, others sitting at tables in the dining section, bursting into loud peals of laughter showing their white teeth, other easy-going, relaxed types who still had on their dark glasses in the dim light…Naturally people had put on their masks before leaving their homes. All dressed up and ready to look lively, pretty and healthy, to give out positive energy and to play the games which had rigid rules…Perhaps they sometimes dreamt of changing the games but never the rules. Or was it the other way around?

What ruled at that moment was the contentment of being lucky, beautiful, rich and free from being controled and pressured. The weakest and the most sickening aspects of some of these people would come to fore as the night advanced. Full of pride and confidence of their class, they would surpass their limits of consuming alcohol and drugs and reveal without any scruples the pent-up boredom they felt.

"Where have you been, my love? Have you cast a spell over me? I think about you constantly…"

He turned around to the slender, soft arms wrapped around his neck from behind, and that familiar, somewhat heavy perfume of wild carnations. Fundi!

She was wearing a cocoa-colored satin skirt which sat tightly around her lovely buttocks, leaving half of her thighs uncovered. She had combed back her hair to a bun on top of her head. Her over made-up green eyes filled half of her face. Sometimes the look in those eyes would be shadowed by sadness, but her smile was always irresistible. This tiny jet-set painter was a real wild cat…

"I'm on a love diet, Fundi. You know that I like to pity myself."

"Dieting hasn't been good for you. You've put on weight since stopping your bedroom exercises!"

"Continuous economic growth, kitten. What can one do?"

Fundi was famous for organizing exhibitions in her studio-galleries in Istanbul and Bodrum which ended in wild parties. Volkan liked her paintings, her conversation and most of all, her backside. They had made love a few times in their wild days, and he had bought a few of her pictures as a treat. She was one of the most amusing and creative women in bed that he knew. Biting Volkan's earlobe softly and playfully, she whispered,

"Let me know when your diet is finished so that we can rub off your rust. In the meanwhile, try to get a little smaller, my sweetheart!"

With the softness and agility of a cat, she rubbed her belly against Volkan's face and drew back. She had so adapted to being like a cat that she had almost mutated. As she walked away, Volkan stared at her buttocks moving harmoniously under the bright satin. It gave him pleasure to imagine filling his hands with those globes and pressing himself against her soft belly. Fundi was the best of the worst; courageous, loving when necessary, a little obscene but frank. One could pour out his heart to her – up to a certain limit – and go on a short trip with her. And that would be enough.

Almost everyone knew each other in this circle and he had met most of the women. Some of them looked interesting and profound at first sight. However, as most of them preferred to live with borrowed identities, they turned out to be shallow before too long. It wasn't easy to sharpen one's personality or quickly pour it into a personality, cast so as not to be left out. On the other hand, as their appearances had been groomed and polished with almost the same methods, they were astonishingly identical. Their blondeness, their dark tan, and their habit of flinging their hair from side to side, their exaggeratedly scanty clothes were so similar that it was almost impossible to differentiate between these women, to find and love one who was different from the pack.

The men were the same. They had lost their right to be themselves. They were now trying to cheer up their loss by their fashionable clothes, accessories and personal articles such as watches, glasses and mobile telephones. It was obvious at first glance that they spent at least as much time and money as the women did in their effort to become cool, robot-like types with their well-cut hair carefully styled and soaked in gel, their tattoos and their extraregular facial features.

The woman passing in front of him was wearing white boots that went up to her thighs. The short legs she was trying to hide in those boots seemed to be even more crooked to Volkan. On the other hand, what was amazing were her large, firm breasts which had been oiled and polished. These artificial breasts which were protruding out of her dress did not at all go well with her short, skinny body. When he looked at the face of the woman sitting in the red armchair by the lamp, he recognized the meaningless, empty visage of a woman with whom he had had a one-night stand in the days when he was still a rookie. Their eyes met for a moment but the woman was looking at him with unseeing eyes. A cold breeze passed through Volkan. He had an uncomfortable feeling of decay and regret. He swayed a little in his seat as if falling back.

A rainy midnight loomed in his memory. Flat, immobile images...A hollow, dry chest, empty breasts with black tits...A gluttonous mouth approaching the dick in her hand with appetite...

An unexpected, coarse, bitter wave of desire rose inside him. A half-hearted swelling which quickly deflated...Then he felt a strong nausea and dizziness. Whenever certain scenes from his life, some images from the past arose in his mind, he was rocked with a feeling similar to being incurably abused. This was a psychological reaction rather than a physical one, a negativity complicating the present by the useless escapes of denying the past or resorting to oblivion.

"Welcome, Volkan, you didn't wait long, I hope?" asked Harun as he settled into the opposite armchair.

"I've just arrived."

"I feel like giving that so-called banker a good beating. He expects help from me. What the hell can I do, buddy?"

"Didn't he know what would happen to him when he was robbing his own bank?"

"He didn't expect it. Well, you have to bear the consequences…"

He probably meant justice. Which justice? Ninety percent of justice was now money. Volkan remembered the incident he had witnessed downstairs at the office the month before. The legal advisor of the company was forcing a judge to speak to a video camera. He had received a two-hundred-thousand-dollar bribe from Harun to finalize a process favorably but hadn't been able to do so. He was absolutely crushed, "Forgive me," he was saying, "I couldn't do it, the other party was in the right and they were strong. I will try to pay you back in some other way. Do whatever you want, I'm finished already." He was a middle-aged man with gray hair. He was on the verge of tears, hunched up and motionless. Volkan had pitied neither the man nor the state he was in. But he had been upset, not knowing what to do, and he had felt a deep, lacerating hopelessness in the name of those who still believed in the concept of justice.

Although Harun reacted strongly to such occasional snags, he had succeeded in changing his "bad guy" image considerably as he gained a bigger place in the business world. As years passed, he had acquired a distinction, a dignity that came with money. He had learned that whatever he did, he had to arrange his business by seemingly sticking to the rules and to avoid getting reactions, and that he should carefully stay away from being in the position of acquiring unfair power, a place he could easily topple down from.

He had been quick in trusting Volkan's knowledge and experience and his ability to keep secrets and finalize deals, and he had loved him as much as he could. On the other hand, Volkan's feelings toward his boss were still not too clear in spite of the fact that he knew him well. Harun was leading Volkan to think that for a gem yet to be processed, it was inevitable not to resort to cheating and illegality in order to survive and be successful in the business world of this country. The likes of Harun were rare talents. Even if they were guilty, their confident and cool bearing evoked a mixture of respect and awe in others.

They ordered their meals and drinks. They had approached each other carefully right from the beginning. Being close in age, travelling together most of the time and their common indulgence in food had strengthened their friendship. Volkan was now in an important and responsible position in the company and his success was rewarded by company stocks; however, Volkan wasn't yet blindly dedicated to Harun. He was always on the watch, because he knew well that this ambitious and talented man also had a dangerous and dark side.

"Look, honey, I'm in a meeting. Stop torturing me, okay? Come on; mind your own business, go to sleep! Fine, fine! Is the boy back? Okay! I'll be home soon."

Harun had turned his back a little and was on the mobile phone, talking with a conciliatory tone to his wife. The image of beautiful, elegant Selda appear before Volkan's eyes. The poor girl was about to go mad. Lately she had been going around half dazed, in a state between sleep and consciousness. She was in depression perhaps because her marriage did not let her go forward on the road she had carved for herself using intelligence, full of suspicion and emotional ups and downs. She looked at the double-crossing world from behind her dark glasses which she never took off. They had a large, rosy-cheeked, thirteen-year old son who was in no way able to communicate either with his mother or with his father. Just as he was about to be expelled from school for throwing his mobile phone at his teacher's head, Harun had intervened and the problem had been solved the week before – naturally – by the termination of the teacher.

"We mustn't forget," he said turning back to Volkan, "we should tell those people beforehand that the tender is not one hundred percent sure. You never know, someone else may feed some people more than we do."

"That's not possible, man!"

"I know it isn't, but act as if it were."

Volkan realized that his attention had wandered due to distraction caused by fatigue, and he wasn't listening to the advice his boss was giving him about the meetings he was going to have in Geneva the next day. The club was very noisy and Harun was speaking about unnecessary things while he made love with his eyes to the girl, an ex-model now pop singer, sitting at one of the nearby tables.

"You're tired," he said suddenly looking at Volkan.

"Yes, what's more, I can hardly hear you."

"The night and the fun are just beginning, my friend."

The music they played at that hour was loud and very provocative. Titillating disco music made up of love-making sound effects, inviting even the most sedate to be seduced and get lusty. A woman who seemed to be making love at the microphone in a secluded place was moaning madly and her little screams filled the air.

People had started dancing again. It was a strange dance, really strange! The women were moving to the rhythm of the music by jutting out their hips, and the men standing right behind them, pushed their lower bodies forward. These movements which seemed unstudied and parallel to the beat of the music were monotonous, childish and almost bodiless. Even if they were often and accidentally bumping into each other in the crowd, nobody could meet face to face or come in direct contact with another. No one looked anyone in the eyes. Surrendering to the deafening music, they made no attempt to get into any kind of contact.

"Look at them," Volkan said. "This is the dance of loneliness, the state of multiple individuality. Both pitiful and funny ... They look like a flock of perplexed, frightened sheep stuffed into a dark pen."

"Only for the time being," said Harun. "They will soon begin to cling to each other. See that singer girl, that babe in black? She hasn't got a voice but she is beautiful. I'll go and chat with her for a while."

He went over to her and pulled her up by the arm. She started dancing in front of Harun, smiling and moving her hips.

She was blonde, tall and quite beautiful. These girls who had nothing and dreamt of having everything, what did they feel when they were with louts like Harun? Were they thinking of the telephone or shopping bills, the rent or the instalments of the car?

All of a sudden, he felt he needed to leave. Sometime ago, he would spend long nights here, eating, drinking and enjoying himself until morning. Whereas now, a ghost-like voice was calling to him from deep inside, saying "This is a stage setting, everything is pointless."

Harun pulled the girl close, whispered something in her ear, pinched her cheek and let her go. He came back, all in a sweat, sat and waved at the waiter. He wanted a drink.

"I've had enough. I'm flying tomorrow," said Volkan.

"In that case, I won't have anything either. I've already put on two more kilos this week. They are talking about a new dietician. Apparently he makes you lose weight by the method of constant nibbling, what do you say?"

"Such diets never work for me."

"I think it's worth trying. Just imagine, you are stuffing yourself every moment."

"And whetting your appetite all the more." They fell silent. Another night filled with forced conversations, questions asked and answers given just to make small talk, thought Volkan. And what did he expect? Who wanted more in this environment?

"What's eating you, Volkan? I've been wanting to ask you but never got around to it. What's wrong?"

"Nothing in particular. Important deals came one after the other. And I think I'm suffering a little from loneliness," he forced a smile.

"Why should you be lonely? You are young, handsome, a bachelor...You can have any woman you like wherever you go, whenever you want."

"I haven't got the strength..." said Volkan in a joking tone.

"Come on, you've been fast ever since I've known you. Or has your sense of touch deteriorated, eh? I've heard that you can have temporary emotional paralysis as a result of addiction to one-night stands. People dig into the Internet because of this. I think there is lots of fun, it's a remedy for loneliness…"

"Empty words, lies and pretensions…That's all." He waved his hand as if to say "forget it."

"Hey, did you see those crazy pornographic animation sites? It's you who directs everything," said Harun.

"Cold…Very cold…"

"A little, but such fantasies are good for people in every way. Sexuality is a most creative energy. The road to success and power goes through that. What I say also applies for politics. Look at the state of the country! All the people who rule us are old farts. Believe me, that's why everything is in such a bad state."

"Although it's not very clear who rules who, that is not an opinion to be ignored."

"Look here, buddy, don't get all paranoid and waste away. Don't forget, we'll see much better days. Don't lose your form now."

"Don't worry, I take good care of myself," said Volkan with a laugh. "It's just that I'm tired of passing fancies and suffocating relationships, that's all."

He generally avoided – with an instinctive fear – sharing his private life with Harun, because he was a loose-mouthed, gossipy braggart in those subjects.

"You should go for having fun, not relationships. There are some new developments in that field," said Harun, bending toward him to have his voice heard. "Here is the latest news: One of those women who know everyone – she was a secret agent or a policewoman or something of the sort – has entered the market. She employs university graduates and cultured babes. They are guaranteed to be under twenty."

"Yes, and isn't it strange, this female Bond who is famous for the parties she gives in her home, freely saunters around and uses her so-called vintage boutique as an office. And what does she guarantee?"

"Oh, I see that you are well-informed about everything. Her guarantee is the happiness and satisfaction of her clients, sonny boy. The system works well, the team is superb! There are no headaches such as police raids or scandal. There is limitless security support. For one thing, the girls work for a certain circle, for the well-known, the distinguished. The business is something like ours, high-level intermediary services."

"Come on…" Volkan gulped as if something was stuck in his throat.

"It's true. In all kinds of intermediary business there is a profit, therefore, something more or less unethical, isn't that so?"

Whatever, you provide the venue. A pleasant home environment is preferred. You sit down and talk about music, poetry, the cinema. A young babe talks to you about the film *Casablanca* or Rimbaud, *The Alchemist* or the *Da Vinci Code*…You listen to Mozart or Leonard Cohen. As you lightly touch each other and sip champagne, a romantic, intellectual atmosphere starts to develop. Excitement mounts…"

"The seller has decorated the old story very nicely. They will soon be filming the commercials, too."

"Everybody is talking about the beauty and the quality of the girls. No bad temper or sulking, no bickering, no jealousy, no pregnancy and no talk of 'let's get married, let's get divorced,'"

"Almost paradise…"

"I'm serious. They take orders according to demand. It seems there are girls trained for surprise parties and group sex. They provide an escort service and even gigolos."

"Well, those are nothing new."

"What's new are the girls! Just think, educated dolls, low-mileage, milk-drinking babes from good families, tight boys out of a picture! You just give them a call and they bring them wherever you want."

It was obvious that Harun had been making use of this service. He insisted, "Doesn't it interest you?"

"Going on a safari in Africa is what interests me more these days. Perhaps I'm not too happy with my own image."

"Hey, you're a great, good-looking guy. Or have you developed a hang-up about weight? What's more, the girl you are paying doesn't have to like you, you know that."

That was precisely the problem for Volkan; the one who paid –including every approach – was always in the dominant position. The trouble was that he was no longer sure if making love to a woman who put up with him in disgust but for the sake of money was any better than masturbation. It was unnerving to get aroused by the visual richness of paid sex and then to live the insipidity that followed. That was when he felt unhappy, inhibited, helpless and once again deadly lonely. The truth was that he could no longer go to bed with prostitutes.

"The night is long," said Harun. "I'm going somewhere else with that girl. I don't want to go home. I'm not on good terms with Selda. She keeps insisting we should get a divorce. Naturally that's impossible, it's absurd. Sometimes I feel like strangling her." He looked at Volkan as if asking for sympathy.

"Things will improve, you'll manage," said Volkan to cut it short. It was a delicate subject and there was no need for giving opinions. Selda was sick. "You lived through such periods before. These things happen. Doesn't she go to therapy anymore?"

"She does, she also has medication. Look, I mean well and I'm fond of my wife. The problem is that women have this hang-up about love. That's why fondness can't save the day. Needs change quickly, and the feeling of closeness becomes boring and tiresome with time."

"Don't scare me, I'm exceedingly emotional these days," said Volkan, surprised at his own indiscretion. "After a certain age, one looks for someone real, someone who will last."

"A lovely thought, a dream…"

"Naturally one has to find the right woman. Perhaps love may last then."

"Don't believe in love. Rookies and kids can manage, but it is difficult for people like us who have been through a lot."

"If one loses love, one turns into a sick animal born handicapped," said Volkan as if complaining.

"No, a man wouldn't lose anything. He would pull himself together, become more independent and find himself."

In the large, graded space of the club, there were partitions separated by low panels, quiet corners which would allow for more intimate relations in the later hours of the night, dark alcoves resembling theater boxes. One could see some people sitting close and others kissing. After a certain hour, the ultraviolet light which was blinking in time to the disco beat of the music had created an atmosphere for cheap, exciting escapades. But how could all these people remain without love? Had love now turned into a children's game in the world of selfishness and lies?

That was how it seemed to be. Volkan looked at the crowd with a kind of pity. All that happened in the world, the dynamics of important change, the fact that civilization was quickly drifting toward a depression interested them only from their own point of view. Their general attitude was to stay away from the misfortunes of others; not seeing, not hearing, not knowing. Their ambitions, their loneliness, their worries were special to themselves. This was the world of money. He knew very well that most of these people worshipped only money and they truly believed that all kinds of satisfaction could be bought with money. This was the only tool for love, peace, health and happiness. And naturally for freedom...

For some time now, he had stopped being curious about what these people believed in and where they spent their money, how many lovers they changed in a week, where they traveled in the world, what means they used to express themselves, which doctors, which therapists they saw. There was nothing about them that he didn't know.

There was one thing he couldn't understand. How did these people who had slept with someone many times before, whom they swapped regularly and no longer found at all interesting, could consider that person as being someone else in this environment and under these lights? With which expectations did they leave the club together at the end of the night? However, there was nothing to be surprised about. These were the constantly repeated, desperate incestuous relations of an extended family.

When Harun asked his permission to invite to their table the girl he had been dancing with, Volkan got up saying that he wasn't feeling well and he would go home to bed. He was in no mood to bear with them as it was quite obvious that this was what Harun expected him to do.

As he passed along the corridor with the stained glass windows, he thought, I must be going through a transformation. For some reason, nothing was the same at that moment as it had been three years, three months or even three days ago. His loneliness was more like the discomfort of someone who was fed up with the usual means of self-satisfaction and was reconsidering his choices. He wished his transformation could be one of enlarging, stretching his limits, and not the opposite.

He lived in a penthouse in Bebek. He got off at the garden gate and sent away his driver. The night was silent and cool; the sea on the other side of the road was dark and shiny. He felt the warmth of the wine and the taste of the cigar he had put out a while ago. He took the elevator to the top floor feeling almost spent, insensitive, aged. Of late he had been walking up the steps for exercise.

The years were passing by and cracks were beginning to appear. What had happened to that happy young man? He was thirty-seven years old. Perhaps his life would be over with a heart attack before he had turned forty. In that case, there would be no meaning to success, making money, making or not making love.

His home was nice and warm where everything was in order. The cleaning lady had polished everything. At the beginning of summer, just as he was entering depression, he had changed his house, although this wasn't at all what he had had in mind. At least he had been kept somewhat busy by this new flat he had bought, putting it through an overhaul, making alterations and decorating it to his taste. Then in August, he had traveled to Venice, Rome and Denmark on trips which were part business and part pleasure, finishing his holiday with a five-day cruise in the south. He hadn't really enjoyed that, either. He was tired by summer, his spirit devoid of love, hate or taste.

He looked over his home. There was a white buck leather couch and two black armchairs in the wide, spacious living room. The audio system and the home theater equipment had been cleverly concealed. There was nothing showy, no carelessly placed item, everything was simple and sufficient. The floor was of shiny white linoleum. On it were two small, long-haired white carpets. The only colored objects in the room were the two abstract paintings by Fundi, one over the fireplace and the other on the wall behind the couch.

He went to bed. He wasn't sleepy. The therapist he had been seeing had made no comments on his insomnia and weariness. He had continuously stayed silent and had only given him medication which had turned him into a rag mop. Apparently when there were transformations and diminutions in the chemistry of the brain, they had to be replaced! Was it that simple? He had thrown away the medicine and stopped therapy the month before. He had been going to that man to seek help in drawing himself a narrow path to pass through in the desert he had fallen into. Anticipating to be saved from the pain of having somehow lost certain things…With the hope that perhaps that thing, whatever it was, could return to him if he really tried…

He turned off the light. As he lay in the darkness embracing him, he missed having someone who would put her arms around him and hold him tight against her. He longed for the peace he used to feel in Nilhan's arms a long time ago, even on nights when they didn't make love.

Nilhan was the daughter of one of his mother's distant relatives. Her family had migrated to the States when she was four. Her father had started as bell-boy in a hotel, later working in all sorts of jobs such as selling fruit and driving taxis, and had managed to raise his two children. Nilhan had received a good education in mathematics and computer sciences and had quickly made her place in life as a talented engineer. She was working in a company in Hawaii which did research on heuristic programming techniques. It had been she who had extended Volkan's scholarship, arranged for him to go to Hawaii after New York and found him a job in a bank.

They hadn't met before. It was only after it became certain that he would be going to the States that she was remembered and mentioned at Volkan's home. Their first meeting was in New York, in a bar on Fifth Avenue one April evening. She was an average woman; slightly plump, wide-hipped, brown-haired and middle-sized. Her best features were her blue-green eyes, as amazing as the deep sea.

She was more or less ten years older than Volkan, about thirty-five at that time. She looked beautiful and impressive under the blinking bar lights. Her full white breasts, which could be seen through her partly unbuttoned shirt, were moving with an extraordinary buoyancy and freshness with every movement she made, catching his eye. Volkan was drinking seriously for the first time in his life, and as he drank, he felt lightheaded. They talked about family, university, the States and Turkey and laughed a lot. Nilhan was looking at him in the way a self-confidant woman looks at a man she likes, trying to figure out whether a relationship could flourish between them. What if it could? Since it was she who wanted it, Volkan wouldn't have any objections. But these things had to be done within a plan, a program; not so quickly, so obviously and in such a rush.

That night, Nilhan took him to her hotel saying that she did not want to be alone. Volkan's fear of doing something wrong had turned into a worry of not being up to par. So this was how things were done in the States, people jumped into bed very quickly. He hadn't had much experience, and he wasn't ready for the fact that someone he didn't know would want to touch his body. All the same, he realized that the woman needed the contact of naked skin and he yielded to her.

They continued to be together at intervals whenever Nilhan came to New York. When he finished university, Volkan decided to go to Hawaii to be with her instead of returning to Turkey.

His new life sometimes seemed like a lovely surprise. A passionate female, a magnificent landscape, an exquisite climate, beautiful parks, lovely shops, an easy life, wealth and a job which wasn't boring…Nilhan had simple tastes. She wasn't tiring and she had a good circle of acquaintances. This was advantageous and effective in her advancement.

They lived in a beautiful house with a garden. Neither of them had offered him/her fully to the other. Nilhan loosened his body, opened his fists and put him to sleep against her breast like a child. She was teaching arrogance, life and joy to a timid young man who treated women with respect. As for Volkan, he was afraid that the gratitude he felt for her would turn into a continued starvation, a deprivation and even self-sacrifice.

After three years, he had risen to a certain position in the bank where he worked. He had developed a great self-trust in his abilities, and he was sure that he would soon be a person attracting attention. However, he wasn't sure he had shown the same success at acquiring an independent "personality." In time, he started to feel uneasy, a constriction as if he was pegged down. Slight disputes, postponed or ignored discords had started to surface between Nilhan and himself. And the all-too-familiar positive emotions were no longer able to soothe his soul like before. Instead of accepting what the woman provided and placed in front of him, his growing desire was to suffer if necessary but to make an effort to keep what had been his own choice.

The problem was solved by itself when Nilhan was appointed as the financial director to the New York branch of the bank. They finished their relationship without pain, as if it were something they had expected. It was many years later when Volkan found out that her frequent visits to the central office had to do with a high-level official with whom she had a relationship.

When he thought about all the women who had been part of his life, their names came to his mind but they no longer kindled his fire. He remembered some with a sweet, warm longing, others with a silent, tired pain. There was only one name in his heart which he protected like a precious gem:

Carol. Volkan had made her believe that she was loved, and then with a rough neglect rooted in his happiness, he had smashed her hopes. Naturally Carol had done the same to him with her suspicions, her tongue bloated with anger in her tight set mouth and her darkened joy.

All of a sudden, he was taken by a feeling that the present moment and the past were flowing together as processes which affected and prepared each other. The present was taking him to an accumulated past, and the past was constantly carrying him to new versions of past situations believed to be long forgotten.

And the future? The feeling of being unraveled was keeping him from looking into the future which seemed like a faraway, empty space, a twilight zone.

He was aging rapidly like a butterfly with a single day to live.

4

Eylem got off the dolmuş at the beginning of the street. She walked down turning right first and then left twice. With the apartment buildings lined side by side, the streets resembled cement walls. They had become even narrower because of the cars parked on both sides. Football shouts, arabesque songs, the exaggerated and affected sounds of old local films blaring from television sets turned on too loud were pouring out of open windows that never saw the sun. Even the banging drums of the music shop further along the road were not enough to smother the din which confused the mind at this hour of the evening.

She had left her work place at six o'clock. Now it was almost eight o'clock. Her flat was certainly not easy to get to, but she had rented it because it was cheap and it was close to her sister's place. However, going to and from work took two hours every day because of the traffic and this was sapping her energy.

The empty street was drowned in the dull blue neon reflections of the water shop, the pastry shop and the grocer's. She saw the dark and handsome water distributor come to the door. She felt his eyes on her even after she had passed in front of him. She had moved to the apartment building on the other side of the road two weeks ago. She left every morning and came back in the evening. He was probably trying to figure out who this strange woman was. Or perhaps he was simply looking at her legs, because she had shortened all her skirts the week before.

She crossed the street, the sticky, dusty hum of the cool Indian summer evening getting louder in her ears. She was still living as a spectator and not as a participator in the neighborhood. She observed emotionally, not deeply or with understanding. She felt intensely foreign and had an annoying suspicion of being followed. Even the children seemed unpleasant, insolent and repulsive at times. She thought that the look she gave them on such occasions probably carried a certain amount of violence and she felt ashamed.

Of course she was not blind. These people were living under difficult conditions and were fighting to hang on to life. They were too busy trying to overcome their fear of loneliness by being noisy, to be compatible with the rules of civilization and to deserve their food, quietly sharpening their endurance. They were not in the least interested whether or not "the human quality, the cultural tissue of the city had deteriorated or that a strange nomadic culture of the slums had become dominant." It was true, wealth and culture made everything beautiful, whereas poverty and ignorance deformed things as much as possible. She felt in her mouth the bitterness of the dark tea she had drunk at tea break that afternoon. Her thoughts did not match the reality of her own life. These were the worries of the well-heeled. What concerned her now was the fact that it would be difficult to get used to this neighborhood filled with undeveloped, degenerate, fanatical people, where men in undershirts and women in headscarves sat at the windows and narrow balconies, and sounds of nose-blowing and throat-clearing and children screaming came from the light shafts. She would get accustomed to all this whether she liked it or not. The obligation of belonging would dominate and she would have to accept the place where she lived. For the time being, she didn't have the means to live anywhere else. For the time being? Who knew if there would be anything else?

As she opened her door, she wondered once again what her new life had in store for her. Would it be good to know? She wasn't sure. For a long time before becoming a mature person, one thought that the future consisted of a continuous spring, happy surprises, peace and illumination. One didn't think, or perhaps didn't want to think that it would also contain pain, sorrow, losses and great misfortunes.

As always, the stairwell smelled of fried green peppers, of burnt onions and of sewer. She entered her flat. She passed through the hall where the boxes with books were still piled up and entered the living room. She turned on the light and immediately closed the curtains. The most unpleasant thing about this little basement flat was that it could be watched easily, or at least, that was the impression it gave her. Fortunately it was only the living room that overlooked the street. The bedroom at the end of the corridor opened onto the unkempt back garden of the building which was full of wild weeds. Although the door with the iron bars did not give her much confidence, she planned to cut the grass outside and put a portable table there as soon as it was spring. If she didn't mind the upper back balconies full of old, rusty stuff where slave dogs barked constantly, she would have a small location where she could breath, drink her morning or afternoon tea so often.

Her fear of being watched was something she had had since childhood. For a long time, God had been a frightening force for her. That Great Being watched people from above and knew everything at a glance, even without looking, so she was very frightened of doing any wrong. Also, the world was full of sin at every corner. When Eylem was a small child, she would commit countless faults in awesome ignorance and then she would regret deeply feeling sinful. Every night, she would beg God to hear her pleas for forgiveness, and she would pray to the angels to erase the sins in her crime sheet. She understood much later that her shame did not arise from what she did but what she was; it came directly from her gender.

That is why for a long time she carried the pain of all that happened to her and all that didn't happen but had the possibility of happening to her any minute. Finally when she turned twenty, she decided to bury into the past all her sins and beliefs together with her name. Sometimes she remembered her previous name "Mutena" with an uncomfortable feeling of familiarity. But she believed that the meaning of this name – "distinguished" – which was contrary to her fate would be nothing but a long-lasting despair, so she had not hesitated for a moment to give it up.

She didn't do it legally, but by leaving the other name in the old ID and by beginning to identify herself by the new one.

The road that led from the pretentious void of "Mutena" to Eylem took almost five years. Naturally, it hadn't been easy at the beginning to create Eylem and give her a life which she saw as the key to success. The name she used in official transactions and places where she worked was still the name she had shed like a snakeskin. More time was needed until it was forgotten, totally erased. But what counted was what she called herself.

She put on her slippers, took off her jacket and hung it on the back of one of the chairs. It was now five weeks since she had arrived from Ankara. For some reason, the years she spent there seemed to have remained very far. Her sister had found this place for her and had had it painted carelessly. The small kitchen and the bathroom on the short corridor got their light from a shaft which smelt of mildew and staleness. They were both so dark that she had to turn on the light day and night.

As she had started working immediately, she had stayed with her sister for a fortnight and had acquired some furniture in the meanwhile. She had bought the refrigerator, the sofa bed in the living room and the old television set from second-hand dealers. The bed, the portable bookcase, the little rickety table and the chairs were discards from a home where her sister went to do cleaning. The first thing she had done when she had moved in was to reinforce with sticking tape the student's desk left over from the previous tenant and set up her computer. For the time being, that was her only connection with the world.

What she had brought from Ankara were her clothes and books. She had a lot of books. No matter what, she was going to put them in order that weekend. Her new job was so demanding, her commuting so tiresome and time-consuming – because of traffic – that she would come home dead tired, have a few bites quickly and would hit the sack. As she had lunch in her workplace, she didn't have to worry about eating. She usually settled for high tea in the evenings.

When she had been called for an interview, she had thought that luck was finally smiling at her. However, the hardship and stress she had lived through in the last month had made her yearn for Ankara and her old room on the third floor of an old office block in Sıhhiye, the chaotic files of correspondence and fax messages, the meatballs in bread and Turkish pizza at lunch breaks, Lale Abla's heavy perfume, the flimsy plant on the window-sill and even the shallow friendships based on little interests.

Her new work environment between the eighth and the eleventh floors of a majestic skyscraper in Büyükdere was brand new, isolated in every way, cold, frightening and something like a slave depot. The only things missing were guards with whips in their hands, glaring over them. But as there were cameras placed everywhere which were doing exactly that job, the result was the same.

It was frightening to know that one was being watched. Her face and her body became rigid like a statue the moment she walked into the office. When she went and sat at her table at the very end of the room, she felt helpless, passive, as if she was in a lifeboat with accident victims she didn't know, rushing toward an unknown destination. She hadn't yet been able to communicate with her colleagues. With their glances and their attitude, they seemed to be trying to show that she was not needed there. Sometimes she felt so bad that she had to make an extra effort not to run out into the street to shout at the top of her voice.

The main problem was whether she would be able to live on the money she was getting. At the beginning her salary – she had just realized – would not be sufficient for her to live in Istanbul by herself. She had accepted this pay partly out of desperation and partly because she felt that this jump to a large American company would be good for her career, but she was worried. Having a place of her own meant paying rent and bills out of her own money. With a rough calculation, when all her expenses had been paid, she would be left with only one third of her income. Whether she liked it or not, she would have to make do until she found a better-paying job. But the problem was that it was very difficult, almost impossible, to find a good job.

Her last four months in Ankara had been an absolute nightmare. The company had been in dire straits and when her contract expired at the beginning of summer, they had terminated not only hers but four others' as well. Eylem had waited to get responses to her job applications for months while she steeped in unbearable gloom without hope in the oppressive and unpleasant summer of Ankara.

At about the same time, her relationship with Seyit had reached the breaking point. Her problems were so peculiar to herself that she sometimes had the feeling she was doing something futile by talking to him. His deafness was most discouraging. Furthermore, he was coming by very seldom, once every few days, as if to see whether she was still alive. She wanted to get away from him, to close this page of her life forever. That was why she found herself in Istanbul without having thought much about the pros and cons.

She started making some tea. She went into the bathroom and turned on the small water heater. She stayed under the hot water until she felt her body relax completely. She left the bathroom nice and warm, exuding soap smells, and put on her sweat suit. She sat in front of the television while having a bite and trying to undo the hurt that was knotted in her throat. She didn't have to get up early the next day, she could stay in bed. She dozed for about half an hour while trying to watch a serial on television. She felt rested when she woke up. She sat in front of the computer and looked at her mail. Seyit had sent her a message:

"I thought a lot after you left. The things you told me about my personality were very offensive. I did not deserve all this

rudeness. But you are right, we are very different people. You gave the key to the caretaker when you left. Didn't it ever enter your mind to pick up the telephone to say 'thank you'? If I'm a beast, you are an ungrateful bitch, okay?! I will live a decent life with my family from now on. I made them suffer a lot because of you. I hope you will meet a great guy who will bang you better than I did. And I also hope that your great (!) goals will be fulfilled. Good luck to you and good bye!"

Eylem froze as she looked at these lines. At first, she felt a sharp, ice cold anger. "You miserable lout," she mumbled. "What a good thing I did by kicking you out!" She felt relieved. His real self had come to the surface. True, he had put a roof over her head and fed her at a time when she was penniless and desperate. But he hadn't done this out of kindness.

Yes, she had said awful things but she wasn't sorry.

Doubtless, those were not the words to say to a man who constantly bragged about his manhood, or to any man, for that matter. But one couldn't control the words that left one's mouth during a fight. The subconscious emptied itself in front of someone one had already given up on.

"What is there between us except having sex like animals? I always fooled myself into believing that sleeping with you was wonderful and fulfilling and exactly what I was craving for, that's what it was!"

Hearing all this was a complete blow for Seyit. He was stupefied, his eyes clouded over and he moved back to the middle of the room with his arms bent toward his body.

"You liar! So that's how things stand now."

"I don't love you, I never did! Do you understand?"

"Who expects love from you anyway? That's not what I wanted."

No, it wasn't!

Seyit wanted everything like a gluttonous child. His sexual desire knew no limits. This was more like gourmandise rather than hunger. He would bear down on her body until she was completely exhausted, upsetting all the defences in her consciousness, reminding her of the pain of rejection in the past.

After his lust had been satisfied, he would treat her like a sister he liked, without any jealousy. The feeling this strange man evoked in her was a kind of internal upheaval rather than disdain or disgust. She sometimes saw him as an oaf, sometimes as an unhappy man devoid of love and on occasions as a lover whom she could trust. That is why she had never been able to give him up for two years. When she woke up next to him, she would feel protected like a parasite perched under the wing of a huge bird and notice that the desolation she always felt in the depths of her soul had disappeared. Then she would smell that dreary, heavy smell of sexual intercourse left over from the night before, permeating the crumpled sheets, and she would recoil as though she was very far from her own reality.

The room where they lay was very cramped. The yellow paint on the walls, which had grown darker with humidity, had flaked off close to the floor. Everything was tiny, the bed, the wardrobe, the window and most of all, her life. On such mornings, she wished she could just fly out of that room, soar over the fields, breathe some fresh air and never come back. This cramped feeling, this remoteness and this rude man were preventing Eylem from building herself a new life, from falling in love again, from being a poet, from everything!

You can go to hell, Seyit. I was nothing when I was with you, and now I exist, she thought. I am ready to face all sorts of difficulties, chances, poetry, life and death for the merciless beauty of this world, and for myself.

When she was fourteen, she had dreamt of becoming a poet. She had a melancholic but sublime aspiration: she wanted to amaze everyone by becoming a poet. When her mother discovered the first few poems she had written, she became terrified. And when Eylem told her she would become a poet, her mother slapped her hard in the face saying, "Don't let your father hear you say that! He will most certainly kill you!"

In that household, there was no point in having dreams. As for becoming a poet, it was a totally impossible, blind wish. Being chained to the inalterable, she had been forced to become an adult once she was twelve years old. Her family never tried to understand what she thought or how she felt. They considered her a worthless object, a half-witted, undependable creature. They made her pay the price of being a girl by confining her to the house, and they watched her pass in fear from childhood to puberty.

Unfortunately being an adult did not prevent one from pain or anger; on the contrary.

Accompanied by silence and loneliness, she seemed to drift into the past. But the pain that came with these sudden falls did not last long anymore. It went as fast as it had come. Her perception of the past was limited because she had been obliged to minimize, even stop, the functioning of that part of her memory where painful remembrances were stored. Even her worst memories were under the gentle mist of possibility now. Her present reality was that she wasn't in need of anyone. She now accepted more easily that all she had lived through was part of the good things and the bad things in life.

This wasn't caused by denial or indifference. Somewhere along the way between her past and present, she had learned not to pity herself. Naturally, this had taken some training, but she had succeeded because she didn't want anybody's pity. Until she got to that point, she had been acting cocky, snotty and arrogant. She had also irritated people who were inclined to pity her. But she preferred to become the target of anger rather than feel the shame of humiliation through pity.

She was still writing poetry, she hadn't given up. Being a poet was not a profession. It was an internal effort similar to leaning over to look at one's own abyss, she knew that. That was why poets lived in shadows, a little embarrassed, timid and wary. Perhaps she loved poetry because this was how she had lived throughout her childhood.

That is another matter, she thought.

Sometimes her life of twenty-five years seemed to have been a long and difficult journey.

When she was a student, a few years ago, she believed that one was capable of preparing and setting up her own future. She was intelligent and hardworking. In spite of all the hardships and obstructions, she passed her classes regularly and entered university without difficulty. However, because of the head scarf outside her head and the questions within, she took five long years to finish. She had to repeat her second year when she couldn't enter the campus because of her head scarf. As she was left without her family support in the third year, she had to work at a "food marketing and distribution" company, becoming distracted and failing a bunch of subjects. Disowning her family had cost her a lot in life.

They were locals of a small town near Yozgat. The family had been members of a popular sect for several generations. They were fanatically religious, bigoted people. Her maternal grandfather had been the imam of a mosque until his death. Her mother used to talk to Eylem about her childhood spent in imam lodgings next to mosques, amongst graves in mosque grounds. She had told her daughter that they had become as sorrowful as they were, because they had grown up eating fruit from trees that had fed on the flesh of the dead.

Their's was a sad house, a place where life was lived as an atonement, an endless mourning, where a blind servitude, which they named love of God, was felt with each breath. Eylem was the youngest of four children. She was interested in reading. She had read the complete Koran when she was ten, and she had pored over religious stories, books, poems and interpretations of the Islam until she became a lycée student. The source of her passionate desire for reading was the independent spirit she had been born with, as well as the fear of becoming like her mother, sister and many other women she knew. She didn't have a definite picture in her mind, an ideal about what sort of a person she would become, but she knew more or less who she would not be.

His father was against her attending the lycée. As for her mother, she was used to accepting and approving without question every opinion of her husband. They spoke very little to each other. Eylem always wondered how they had ever got close enough to have four children. They probably came together hurriedly, without love, like two people who had lost their way, breaking away from each other quickly afterwards. It was impossible to imagine the opposite, because the only thing they shared was the feeling of nonexistence in this world.

They decided to marry off Eylem to the son of a distant relative as soon as she finished secondary school. She revolted. She resisted being pushed around, badly treated and humiliated. She swore to die rather than marry. After impositions and suicide threats, she was sent to her grandfather in Ankara and started attending the lycée.

The grandfather lived in a house with a garden in Keçiören with his scheming wife who was thirty years younger to him. He was a large, robust man who was almost seventy. He and his plump lady with the inquisitive eyes spent more than half the day in prayer. The woman watched Eylem's every move, and through trickery and the wish to please, she reported everything to her husband with great exaggerations. Nevertheless, Eylem was making a great effort to fit into their world. She went to school with her head covered, eyes on the ground, and wore her scarf again as soon as she came out of the school building. She helped with the housework, prayed five times a day, asking God to give her strength. But she was still scolded for unimaginable faults and sometimes got beaten by her grandfather with a broomstick. Compared to Yozgat, very little had changed in her life; oppression still continued in the same way.

Although nobody was expecting it, she passed the university entrance exam. Because of the obligation to live with her grandfather, she had chosen a branch she didn't want – economics – but that didn't matter. When she first started university, she fell in with the girls who were covered like herself and had to join their group. The girls were trying to take hopeless measures, but there was no unity amongst them. When Eylem realized that there were other formations in the background for spreading and inseminating their passionate beliefs, she broke away and became a solitary person. According to her, certain groups were using the girls as supplementary forces. She preferred being alone to being a simple object, an ornament of a concept which aimed to integrate belief with political administration. Furthermore, she was also a little afraid of her grandfather.

She was shy, and would not look at men in the eye when she was talking to them. She felt their presence instinctively, without actually seeing them. When there was one who drew her attention or showed interest in her – which happened very seldom – she would hear a thundering voice in her head, "No, you can't do that, don't even think about it! You know that they are a source of shame and pain!"

She wasn't very tall, but her body was slender, graceful and proportionate. She had long legs, high, well-formed buttocks. Her face was somewhere between beautiful and ordinary. She had a charming smile and lovely large brown-green eyes which gave her face a mysterious air. Her features might not be considered flawless when considered one by one, but there was a unique harmony and meaning in the unity of the parts that made up the whole. She was attractive and different with her white skin, black, wavy hair, her high cheekbones and her large, dignified mouth that did not deny her intelligence. However, nobody saw her beauty which was almost totally covered, hidden.

She believed that the entire visible world was the creation of God. However, she had been thinking more and more about the formalism of her concealing clothes, that they were not a detail pertaining to the essence. She had met many decent girls whose religious beliefs were strong and who yet did not cover their heads. For her, being "decent" meant being someone who was accepted and liked by everyone. These women who lived in accordance with modern times were not the slaves of anyone except God, and they were neither damned nor fit for hell. On the contrary, they were cheerful, open to love and to be loved, full of life.

As she dug deeper into the subject of covering herself, she saw how faith was interpreted in different ways, with fanaticism, and especially against women, as it passed through the phases of forming and implementing policies. In all religions, women were considered dirty, dangerous and sinful; they were devastated and used. It was easy to understand that it was her own inadequacy that left her unarmed.

In her second year, her mother died, and her father took her to Yozgat so that she would leave the university – where she wasn't welcome with her covered head anyway – run the house and help him in the shop. There was a deadly silence in the house. As soon as she saw her father's shadow in the hall when he came home in the evenings, all her blood rushed to her head, her temples started to throb and she felt she would faint, even though her father was in a more pathetic state than before. He had aged prematurely, becoming childish and he was all alone. He looked at his daughter with imploring eyes. This was a look that expected a lot of loyalty, self-sacrifice and love. However, the investment of love which was necessary for that loyalty from Eylem's point of view had not been made in the past.

Her only field of freedom, her only pleasure and consolation was reading. She had become close with the director of the town library. She first dipped into Sufism. Then she started consuming all kinds of books with great hunger. Literature, history, mythology...She was searching for herself in each page; she was discovering her internal world which was full of fears and lies. Her God was great in his endless compassion, his forgiveness, his power to guide his creatures toward the good and the beautiful. If He had created human beings in two genders, why would He differentiate as "man and woman," "upper and lower" between his creatures that He considered equal?

It was fascinating to realize that her perception was changing, that she was walking from nothingness toward herself. She pored over all she could find on the history of religions, she read the holy books. From the philosophy of religion, she went on to Western philosophy. That year, she wandered about in the limitless, endless world of thought. Later, the inexplicable sorrows of sensuality were added to the questions in her mind; they came in the form of great anguish.

It was not the religious texts, but the books of world literature that soaked her in emotions and enlightenment, encouraging her to write. Her prose was as faultless as her interest in poetry. Writing was her wish to be candid; it was not a lamentation or a search for happiness. The effort she put into reading and writing brought all her faculties together; it taught her that she was made of flesh and bones, imagination and desires. Her thinking was being released from fears and inhibitions. Nevertheless, this did not mean that her life had become light and airy. She was faced with high walls whichever way she turned to. She couldn't advance in a straight line.

So her desire to cut her ties with her family grew stronger.

In order to chase the pain caused by her conflicts, she started to write to "no one" and "nowhere." Letters addressed to nothingness...poems, dreams, diaries and impressions...Childish, candid pages reflecting her love of God and the mysterious glitter of her desires, questioning the unfinished transformation of mankind...She felt that she was now equipped with a reservoir of knowledge, and she started looking down at the world but...

She still didn't even know how to kiss!

At the beginning of the third year, she told her father that she would continue at the university. She would go back to her own life. The old man should learn how to live on his own, and if he couldn't, he should marry somebody suitable. Naturally she was accused of being a bad daughter. Her financial aid would be cut off. She didn't care. She had decided that having something to say while being bad and selfish suited her better than being meek and quiet. Actually she wasn't sure that she would get that chance, but she had to make an effort, she promised herself.

She took the train to return to Ankara. As soon as they passed Yerköy, she took off her head scarf and abandoned it to the wind outside the window. She watched that colored piece of cloth getting further and further away, fluttering over yellow fields, harvested soils and gardens; she watched it as if she was watching the life she had left behind forever.

She secured a small scholarship and a place in a girls' dorm. She started working part time for Seyit's company. She was in charge of the commercial correspondence, the accounting and the telephones. She had established a sincere but reserved relationship with her boss. At those times, she loved Seyit like an older brother. A large, dark, healthy man with hard features; not too moody, affectionate and cheerful...On some evenings, they stayed late at the office and chatted; Seyit also took her to dinner a few times.

When she started with her graduation thesis, she had already become quite restless at the dorm. She couldn't study, she couldn't sleep and she constantly argued with the other girls. The situation got even worse when her scholarship expired. For a while, she continued to stay at the dorm without permission. It felt as if the whole world had ganged up against her. She was so desperate in the middle of that huge, cold city that she couldn't resist the help and friendship offered to her in a most persuasive manner by a married man fifteen years her senior whom she had known for two years. For some time now, the man had been waiting close to her, with his nose in the air and his mouth open, waiting for the ripening pear to fall into his mouth.

Seyit gave her a room in the little ground floor flat in Küçükesat which they used as a food storage place – so that she could study and write her thesis in peace. A dim room, four meters to three meters large, overlooking a little garden with a few dried trees at the back...Nobody entered the place except the old driver and the boy who carried the goods. Eylem moved there. She enjoyed the freedom and the peace. She slept on a divan, and when she got up, she folded the covers and put them away. Her clothes were in a suitcase and her books were stacked on the floor. There was a small LPG burner on the kitchen counter and running hot water in the building twice a week. She felt liberated in that dark place which smelled of cheese, sausage, biscuits and moisture.

The depot was slowly emptied in one or two months. The boxes in the living room and those in the other rooms all disappeared. A few cheap pieces of furniture came to the flat; the living room and the kitchen were lightly furnished. The whole flat was now Eylem's. The plum trees in the garden were in bloom. She walked home from the office in twenty minutes. She was living the best spring of her life. She offered to pay a small rent out of her salary, "We'll see, don't worry about it," Seyit said.

One evening at the beginning of summer, he came to visit her. It was just a friendly call to see if she was safe and comfortable. Eylem saw him standing at the threshold with a very different expression in his face. There was only a doormat between them. A doormat to be crossed in one small step ... He crossed it and came in.

To let one's self go with the flow of time, in the direction of the wind ...

Eylem had written a story when she was fifteen years old. It was the tale of a little girl who had lost her body and whose shadow was wandering over hills and dales looking for the body which had been snatched away. The Shadow Girl was wandering by herself over sleeping towns and villages, soaring in the darkness of the night, mingling with the winds and crossing seas. Because of her search, she was constantly in motion. She was obliged to fly like the birds, alone and delicate, and always be on the move. At the end, the moment came when she was transformed into her own search. As she had already forgotten what she was looking for, she felt no pain and continued promenading her shadow without aim or memory in a borderless country of nothingness.

Eylem was reminded of this story; but Seyit had a glass of tea and went away with the air of a loving brother and without having made any advances.

At the second visit, some joking around with the hands, done as a warm-up, a few reciprocal laughs ... Something like bumping into each other accidentally while saying good-bye and a furtive embrace...

The third...Eylem accepted the declaration that he found her extremely attractive and tempting, that he desired her madly, with the same calmness she had shown while she listened to Seyit's previous offer of friendship and help. She was prepared. Seyit was sitting on the couch with his knees apart, exhibiting his desire. She quietly slid into his lap and let him undress her.

She had learned something important about her body. She wasn't cold, and somehow, she also intuitively knew how to kiss. Later when Seyit entered her with care, she felt that she had returned to her body. She put her arms around the man's back, she pressed him against herself some more and broke out in tears as if she wanted to drown her pain.

This way, the man possessed – right then and there and with unbelievable ease – this frail Shadow Girl sitting in his lap, her sweet silence which secretly told children's stories, the vague look of fright in her large innocent eyes, and then the freshness and the sweet taste of her skin, her breasts and her mouth.

Playing the buyer...With a stupid fish-like grin on his face, promising to protect her, to make her his queen...As for the seller, she thought that what seemed like cheating in this transaction was actually a way of getting even. She coolly thought that she had paid back Seyit generously for taking some pity on her. She had learned very early in life that pity was a dirty, sly feeling.

Eylem erased Seyit's disgusting letter together with the junk mail that had accumulated in her e-mail.

After all, one stumbled a little when walking against the wind.

She looked at a few web sites to check some points she had been stuck with at the office. She worked a little. The night before, she had written an essay titled "THE FUTURE" where she had poured out her heart a little; she was going to send it to a blogging site. She looked over what she had written. She wanted to be impressive both poetically and intellectually. It wasn't difficult for her to call out to young people with lives like hers, to appeal to the minds and emotions of those people as if talking to herself, because those were words which were born out of her own being and her own isolation. All the same, she worked until three o' clock in the morning, revising the text, and she finally posted it on a site she liked. She wondered what the reactions would be like. Perhaps she would anger some people, but she was sure that there would be those who would share her feelings.

She had noticed lately that there were many young people like her who had lost their perspective of the future. They were living in despair and pain, being pushed around; they were nothing. The doors were closed to the vast majority; you had to at least realize this fact in order to open them. Her effort did not come from feeling responsible for her generation; however, the less one had, the stronger was the desire to share.

She asked herself if her wish to communicate with others was due to the fact that for a long time now she had been keeping everything to herself, or was it her desire to love and be loved. Both, she replied. By sharing, she hoped to be more peaceful, to feel better and defeat loneliness. She had traveled very far from the way she had been brought up; she had been transformed into a malleable but unbreakable twig. She remembered a sentence she had written: "Sometimes I think about straying into bad, very bad paths!" At that point, she couldn't guess yet what these paths could be, because being bad was a relative concept. It could sometimes be defined as excessive obedience, and other times as rebellion. The important thing was that one should know where to find one's self again in case she got lost on unknown paths.

I also want to be seen, she thought. This was natural and was important. She wanted some people to notice her as nobody had done before; surely she had a right to that.

She couldn't resist entering her file of poems and read the last one. She had decided not to look at it for some time, leaving it to rest. She added another line and reread it from the beginning:

as my shadow sweeps past
through the misty blue of the night
like faded stars
my dreams drift away from me
jumping on the back of the wind
I don't want to go after them
perhaps I'll create new dreams
from fallen stardust
man should not lose faith in the world
because wings are flapping still
in the airy place from where the birds look down

She decided she would work some more on these lines later.

She turned off the computer and went to bed. There were voices and noises still coming from the flat upstairs. From what she could understand, the couple living there did not get along. She didn't know anyone in the building yet, and she had no intention to do so. This was to protect the intimacy of her private life and also because she did not have time for neighbors. Not being close with anyone meant not having to account for anything to anyone. Anyhow, nobody was interested in her seclusion other than the caretaker and the young woman with three children who lived opposite. In places where lives were lived in an intermingled manner, a young woman living alone still stirred the curiosity of ordinary people. When Eylem responded to the insistent questions of the woman next door by saying she had no relatives, the woman had wished her courage and prayed for her health and success. As for the caretaker, his stance was careful and aloof as though he considered it quite probable that this solitary woman would one day be the heroine of a possible scandal in the building. In the first days, he had mumbled some words like, "Is there no brother of yours?" Eylem hadn't answered him.

She was able to approach certain people with no emotion, as if they were ordinary pieces of furniture, expelling them from her life by acting as if she could not stand stupidity. However, she could not explain to herself how she had learned to do this. Perhaps everything happened as it should, all by itself.

She couldn't sleep. Upstairs, an angry male voice was shouting and swearing and a woman was begging and crying with words such as "For God's sake don't! I'll be the doormat under your feet, please don't!" The ceiling shook with the weight of something heavy thrown on the floor. The noise continued in the same tone and tempo for a little longer and then it stopped. Eylem imagined for a moment the blurred face of a woman she didn't know, her nose bleeding, her eye bruised and puffed shut. Then the face slid back further and further away and it became her own face.

She sat up in bed and waited, her heart pounding. No, murder had been avoided for the night. She quickly erased the image. After a while, she heard weak murmurs mingling with the sound of the bed creaking in rhythm back and forth. The man was raping his wife after beating her almost to death!

She put out the light and slid under the covers.

One had to scratch down to the very depths of human beings to understand them; scratch, scratch, scratch...

5

It was weekend. Volkan had a slight soreness and wished to stay home. He needed to rest but the phone which had started ringing at noon would not stop. A small news item which had appeared in a newspaper had created an uproar just before the tender, and a courageous venture was faced with the risk of turning into an unfair operation.

The news was based on the fact that there was corruption in the tender of a controversial piece of land which an unnamed local company was preparing to buy and negotiating about. This land was not legally appropriate for making touristic investments. However, Harun had made a deal with a buyer, guaranteeing that the matter would be solved with a law that was to be passed by the Parliament soon. He had the word of the government on that. However, the muck-raking of an upstart before the deal was quietly finalized was jeopardizing all the preparation and the lobbying that had been done.

The accusation was that, in order to open this land to plunder, Cosmos had tied up the deal from the inside and had offered a bribe to a company which refused to abandon the tender. This was an untrue, or rather, a simplified allegation. When Harun turned mad with rage, the company lawyers decided to send an appropriate disclaimer to the newspaper. They were condemning the publication which was based on unfounded allegations by malicious persons and provocations which didn't go beyond mere hearsay and were directed at damaging the reputation of the company. However, the agitation did not subside. Everyone who was even slightly involved in this deal had reached for the phone.

"Where did we make a mistake, tell me!" Harun was shouting on the phone. "We should have kept that impostor completely out of this deal right from the beginning!"

"All that will come out of this is just a little bit of stink. Calm down. We'll get over this in no time."

"You never know, Volkan. What are you planning to do?"

"We won't do anything. Wait and see. Nobody can corner us. You know better than me that there is no reason to worry."

The deal had been cleverly set up. There were four separate actors in the negotiations; four tycoons, every one of them more ambitious and powerful than the other. The spaces between them had been left uncertain so that anyone who decided to meddle with the game would give up after being drawn into a network of relations which became more and more complicated. Such a well-planned plot could not be destroyed easily.

The problem concerned Volkan personally, and he felt uneasy because of the nameless part he played in this deal. Actually with every problem that arose, he had lately started hating everything he did and everything that was in his life.

Besides this, none of what happened worried him.

All would end as he had planned anyway.

He pulled the covers over his head. He lay there lazily, patiently, wandering among little feelings. He called these relaxed moments in bed – which he stole from daily worries – his daydreaming sessions.

Melike was walking in now. She threw down her bag and started to undress slowly. She was wearing her lilac underwear. Her firm, sun-burnt hips were like a dazzling gift box tied tightly with some string. She had flung the yellow cover off the bed in one gesture and was standing at his bedside, slowly taking off her bra to give Volkan priority and make things easier for him…

The image changed suddenly.

Images flickered before his eyes: a sunny garden, a double-decker bus with blurred windows, a beautiful snowy night that glistened amid the thin fragments of a song, the vertiginous lights of Broadway shining in the lukewarm mist on a beautiful October evening, a red umbrella under the rain...

Women, he thought, placing his arms on the cover and listening to the sound of the rain beating against the windowpane. Women hit you suddenly with the strike of a fin. You lose one or you leave one, another one blocks your way. A new gift box, much more voluptuous, amazing, to be smelled, to be tasted and discovered.

Like Carol, for instance...

It was right after Nilhan's departure. They were chilly, piercing times...Bluebirds and blackbirds were singing in the trees, the smell of exotic flowers made one dizzy. The image of the world was one of desire.

He and Carol had neighboring seats on the Aloha Airlines flight to Maui. The girl was so beautiful and enticing that he had no choice but to go after her and fall in love with her. Just an error, an unnecessary detour, an easy harmony, a goddess half real, half illusion, a lifeboat...There was no definition to the way things went. They watched the majestic dawn of Haleakala the next day and one year later, they returned to Turkey together.

Four years that seemed like a tangled yarn ball where love-making, prolonged caresses, streets, houses, trees, seashores, kitchens, days and months were all mixed haphazardly.

Then it was over.

Happiness could be seen with the naked eye but it was difficult to describe. Whereas unhappiness was impossible to understand without touching, but for some reason, it was easier to describe. Perhaps happiness was something else. More obscure than wanting each other madly, more serene, more orderly and modest, a spontaneous emotion...Like the highest note of a symphony, a crescendo at the right place and the right moment…A surprising, silent, full ascension, something like being face to face with a situation you imagined being extraordinary.

The young woman was foreign, lost and awkward in the country of the man she loved. She was nothing without Volkan, an object which was good only for temporary pleasures. Back home, she had been a stage actress who had attracted attention and had a promising future. Here, she was a toy who made pirouettes. Sometimes she was so sad, so wrapped up in an inconsolable pain within the immeasurable loneliness of her body that Volkan would take her in his arms and pull her over himself. Then not being able to bear her hopeless, motionless slump, he would move away again.

They hadn't been able to communicate in the last few months. Volkan went with other women, but he approached Carol with compassion in order to escape the hostile passion he felt toward her. However, this attitude only increased her disappointment. Volkan was the one who had been given up, he was no longer loved, and helplessly, he was defending himself with indifference. He felt that he wanted Carol to suffer, to be completely lost, even die while still faithful to him.

He was at the peak of his career at that time and was very scared of toppling down unexpectedly. Suffering the pain of the unexplainable failure of his personal life was making him weak. His desire to live alone was mounting and he was forcing himself to look the other way even during periods of reconciliation.

She wasn't eating or sleeping properly, and lately she could do nothing without breaking into tears. Seeing her like that was no different from suddenly jumping into ice cold water. He hated the man who could not join her but said, "I love you with an ache so strong, you cannot imagine."

A person started from a certain point, walked hopefully in a given direction, but couldn't stay put in one place. Life was made up of processes, and this was what determined everything. Some things started and then they were over.

This was what happened with Carol. She returned to her country, to the place where she belonged, to her world. Volkan did not object to this parting, he let her go.

He threw off the cover and sat on the side of the bed. The pendulum of time was constantly swinging back and fro, and he and Carol were meeting again at that moment. It was once again that afternoon when they embraced and cried, happily and sadly at once. Carol was looking at him over her shoulder as she walked away. Volkan could see the condemnation in her eyes as his heart seared with pain.

He had carried in his head her image and her memory for some time. Then her image had lost its clarity, had all but disappeared. What was left of her was a slender, delicate blond shadow seen from behind frosted glass. Memories, colors, differences and estrangements...

He got up, drew back the curtains and looked at the sea. The rain had stopped. Behind the rapidly drifting clouds, the sun was appearing and disappearing like a frozen white ball. He went to the kitchen to make some tea. There were reports he had to read and charts he had to study but he didn't feel like it.

He watched a talk show while having breakfast. On these programs which were very popular, famous guests, faced by supposedly clever and insistent questions, revealed their secrets – which were not at all secret – sometimes grinning, and mostly with mock sorrow. It was evident that the downtrodden felt the satisfaction of getting even by watching the misery of the rich, the well dressed and the famous. Some people probably found consolation in knowing that they were not alone in their disintegrating lives, with their sorrows, their deprivations and their oppression, and in understanding that there was no such thing as complete happiness. Then there were the women's programs which people watched with similar feelings. These represented incomprehensible family entanglements; the most private, most secret sins and guilts were disclosed with dreadful images of exhibitionism and madness, so these scenes were even more amazing. They were watched passionately with tears in the eyes, with false anger and pity, they were applauded.

He wanted to call Melike, but as he didn't know what to say, he couldn't bring himself to do it. Perhaps he didn't want to lose the game right from the start. Melike had implied that she was free but she might still have a boyfriend or someone she was involved with. Such an attractive woman could not be expected to be alone. Perhaps she had relaxed after seeing that her little treasure was intact, so she wanted to leave Volkan behind. In that case, there would be no logic in expecting anything from her. The data at hand was not enough to write a love story for two. An ordinary mix-up, an everyday accident could not be taken any further than this. This was definitely a childish, crude dream. Temporal fancies could be rejuvenating but bearing down on to a woman from afar was the job of layabout degenerates.

He admitted he couldn't help thinking about her every now and then. This was because his restlessness wanted to fly out of its cage filled with the exaggerated feelings of sexual desire. This was a dream having acquired a shape in that woman called Melike.

The winter before – after separating from Carol – he had turned to professionally excessive ways indulging in crude, obscene, emotionless sex. His attitude toward the subject, his senses, his speed and interest were changing. He didn't want any emotion to take roots, he didn't want to be burdened, and he only wanted to let himself drift with the wind. He needed the effortlessness of vulgarity to satisfy his needs, to avoid falling into love's sticky spider's web and to bypass pain. There was no sentimentality, what did sentimentality have to do with making love!

He then saw that this kind of sexuality turned to a form of addiction, to sexual obsession in a short time. To fill the void in the depths, one felt an angry hunger whose dosage and strength were continually growing. It was as if he was having cramps and felt emptied inside; he wanted more, always more, just like a drug addict.

Besides, he was becoming more selfish and it was more difficult for him to be aroused. Compensating this fault with rudeness and violence seemed appropriate. When he saw this tendency in himself, he had a very powerful secret feeling of degradation, a desire to fall lower.

For years he had managed with great effort to fit his soul into the limits of the normal, and afterwards, as if life still owed him, he had let himself go from the top of a high cliff into the murky waters below. He constantly wanted to be punished like a dog by not being given any food or water, to make love at random, wildly as if fighting, to cry and beg and ask forgiveness for all his human weaknesses.

Nevertheless, no torture touched his skin. Then his perception told him that this was not an original experience, that it was no further than a fake affectation and that it was very dangerous.

He froze. He was guarding himself against himself.

He worked on half-done jobs drinking tea with lemon and coffee until the late hours of the evening. He carefully went over the latest reports of the business he was busy with so that there would be no snags.

His stomach was in a state of constant rebellion. He had been on a diet since the day he talked to Melike and had lost two kilos in one week. But the pain of hunger was like a torture he wasn't sure he could bear much longer. He made a choice amongst the several cold dishes his cleaning lady had prepared for him, and he decided on the "imambayıldı." With it, he had some salad without oil.

The flat smelt of cigarettes. He slid open the doors of the terrace all the way and went outside. The penthouse, which overlooked a forest at the back and the Bebek Bay in front, was enchanting with its panoramic view of the Bosphorus. One part of the terrace resembled a boat with its wooden decked floor and the half-moon-shaped seat. Another corner had been arranged as a Zen garden. There were gray-blue cushions on the seats and on the floor. He had been looking forward to entertaining his guests here during the summer, but his only guest had been his mother. He had intended to give a party before the summer was over, but as he had passed his vacation either in a hustle or traveling around, he hadn't had that chance, either. The truth of the matter was that he hadn't felt like inviting anybody.

He shivered in the cool of the evening. The trees made a rustling sound in the light breeze, a harbinger of winter. The tipsy, happy songs mellowed by the breeze coming from a nearby tavern were mingling with the noise of cars passing in the street below.

He was happy to be living as he pleased, alone but knowing how to do it. This was better and more honorable than cheaply sharing the life of someone else, whether you made it, or you failed!

He found himself to be a somewhat developed specimen of the human race. Surely some of his quests had ended in disaster but his success was more or less related to this. Quest meant desire, and desire was a great force which he felt at every step forward and even in defeat. Being a human being was the actual burning longing for life. This was the only thing that could not be overcome by forces tottering on their own lies, repressions that crushed people, deprivations and failures, because desire was a constant state of rebellion.

Was his restlessness a sign that he was losing his joy of life, he wondered. No. Everything that he possessed had stopped being attractive, that was all. Certainly they were all essential for his life, or for him to feel that he was alive, but they had become meaningless. Sometimes it was necessary for different situations, points of view and interpretations to come together and form a whole. It was then that one could notice things, wake up to the world. Just as it was for a word to have any meaning, it was essential that the first syllable be followed by other syllables, sounds and signs.

He went in. He had spent such little time in this penthouse since summer that he still wasn't at home in it. As his footsteps followed the layout of the old flat, he sometimes took a wrong turn to go to the kitchen or the bathroom. His mother had said that his home looked like a hospital; simplicity prevailed in the whole flat. The only place which didn't fit in with the rest was his study. With its bookcases covering two walls, a few paintings, a large desk in front of the doors opening to the terrace on the other side and a sofa-bed, this was the room where he spent most of his time. The interior decorator had the whole flat painted white, but he had insisted in using other colors for the study and the bedroom. He had suggested yellow for these rooms which were large and bright. According to him, yellow was an energetic, exhilarating color. However, on purpose or not, the tone was a bit too dark. Rather than yellow, it was more a metallic honey color or saffron yellow. At first he had liked it, but then according to the mood he was in, it had started to seem sometimes provocative and other times tiring and depressing. He would change it when he had the place repainted.

He clicked on the Internet as he always did when he was bored. He spent most of the night reading the economic commentary and listening to music. On nights when he felt tired, he enjoyed browsing the local blogs and chat sites which he called "the opinion of the streets" before going to sleep. He had broken away from people, from the people at the bottom so completely, that it amused him to watch a world which was a negative of his own. Actually "amused" was not the right word. Prying on other people's lives gave one the strength to hold his head up in this general environment of insecurity, pollution and degeneration. Looking at ordinary, slippery, depressing lives from where he stood made it easier for him to accept the things that happened, even if temporarily.

Young uneducated or less-educated people sometimes seemed like a hoard to him because of their banality. These people saw virtual space as the only place where they could deny their desperation. Ninety per cent of these people had no wish to search for depth or meaning in life. No novelty, no perspective to speak of, no spirit…a deteriorated, shrunken, hollow language…ramshackle opinions…clever or stupid attempts…coarse emotions that do not explain anything already known, daily blunders and confessions…cheap, shallow and ignorant…a sickening sense of humor, narcissistic pleasure and apparent indifference and yet he couldn't completely deny the attempts of these people to fit into the world without shedding their armor, to try to make themselves heard. If it weren't for this invention where people could unload themselves, where they could run and hide, general depression could have reached worse proportions.

Surely there was also a group of a certain level of sophistication. Some of them – mostly columnists or aspiring writers – displayed a sincerity that didn't require much effort. Others tried to render more effective ordinary words in general use by adopting a strict but caring attitude. There were those who lectured about forgotten or undiscovered beauties, and others who complained about being damned due to the choices they had made.

He browsed aimlessly, half asleep, as if expecting someone to appear and arouse the feeling he was waiting for. Out of the dissonant and hopeless din of a huge chorus, he was hoping to hear a single contrasting voice, one impressive note that would touch his heart and sound pleasant to his ear.

As usual, he couldn't find anything. A little humor, some inexperienced writing and a lot of blatant erotica…He got up and poured himself a glass of brandy. It was way past midnight; the drink would drag him off to sleep. Then he would finish this small nocturnal promenade in the world of people who gave away the remnants of their beings, randomly welcoming others to their dreary stories.

Suddenly he was taken aback by the lines that appeared on the screen:

THE FUTURE
To the attention of the "Nobodies"…
Please look!

I throw myself amongst you like a live bomb, right in the middle, I hurl myself!

You heard it, didn't you? You heard the explosion and you were astounded! I made it, yes, I'm the one who is shouting! Listen…

Click to continue…

I want to close my eyes when I read your writings. You are so boring with your glittery or careless, sloppy sentences, your awful singers, your stupid adorations and your banality which bears no mitigating circumstances.

I can't stand your dullness, your mental shallowness and misguided depressions. Your efforts to kill time with your fictitious confessions, urban legends and metaphysical chitchat…

You are presumably hopeless but prone to take everything lightly.

I would like to state clearly that you are cut out to be used!

Stop! Don't be in a hurry to think "what disgusting conceit, what suffocating sobriety".

I too am like you, one of the "nobodies." I am part of all that I have said.

In the mornings, tired and sleepless, I wait with you in front of a huge building for the doors to open.

We, with our patient silence or our rebellion drowned in noise, are of the same age, the same color. Our shoulders touch, we shove each other a little. From afar, we look pitiful like a herd of multi-colored cattle.

Every morning, like criminals, and frightened to be caught at our possible crimes, we open our legs and our computer cases to show that there are no bombs inside before we are allowed in.

Why am I telling you all this, you already know.

Those huge chicken coops made of glass with no windows, or with windows that don't open …Those hard rigid-strong one-man partitions that mould the job to be done …The suffocating heaviness of the air-conditioning set up according to head count and calculated breathing …

Our helplessness when all the phones start ringing at the same time …The impatient waiting as the e-mails fall into the box one after the other on a shiny screen…The communication we try to build with a language made up of furtive glances and vague signs…

We certainly know how lonely we are.

We close in on our work to prevent the settling of the pain that trickles out of limited laughs. Laughter, glances, discussions, jokes are forbidden. Nobody should touch each other needlessly. No alliance. We speak with a small voice, and with words which gradually become distant and cant. We hide our trembling knees under the desks. There are immobile observers above us, cold, like barrel ends repressing efforts of frenzy and resistance.

The solemnity and order of the office shall never be disturbed.

Spots and dust on our desks,

A silly ornament, a sterile flower, a cheeky soft drink,

There will not be.

The chains will be slackened at the ten-minute break.

A queue will be formed quietly in front of the coffee machine.

The diligent sound of the printer, scattered papers and cable webs.

Talk to courteous, rich customers with a proud elegance. However, time is limited, don't dally. Your trips to the toilet will be deduced from the sum of your working time at the end of the day. Don't drink too much water. Fill the workplace performance sheet at each hour.

We are needy, well-meaning and fragile. Crestfallen, industrious and careful, ready to resist hardships and show every effort! As long as our labor gets paid promptly and we aren't handed a pink slip!

We shall leave the office at the latest at six-oh-five as if we were coming out of ourselves. With little, sneaky grudges, empty eyes, disinfected heads…With our "nobody" loneliness and our extinguished candles…Whereas there is an endless night lying in front of us.

This man, that woman, your so-called colleague, perhaps you could go to bed with the other one who stares at you like a pig all day, just for the hell of it…No, it isn't one body plus one soul, it isn't even one body plus one body, it's not important, perhaps it would be good for the boredom or to keep from crying without reason.

Or run and buy a few things before shops close. Groping around, unnecessarily and from brands on sale…Be positive, believe in better days to come, don't worry about what you can't understand. Abide by the rules as you should. Empty your heads at the television screens fully, clearly, obscenely…

Whereas it is enough to understand just a little. In any manner…intellectually or temporarily…

You, little "nobodies," I don't know if you heard? Apparently some of our elders were amongst the rebels who once wanted to annihilate everything, the layabouts who invaded the streets, those who published and distributed silly manifestos and young people who wrote strange slogans on the walls; they later cowered and were tamed down. It is said that these want a fairer order, a more beautiful and purposeful future.

They apparently dream of a future, they are able to dream of a future!

It is very difficult to conceive, but they actually believe – even if somewhat naively – in something called the future! Perhaps there are those amongst you who remember the faces of your close ones on visiting days in the prison. You must have heard, you must have listened as if it were a frightening tale; I'm sure some of you know all the things that happened to them.

This was how we learned the ending of passionate dreams that would go nowhere!

You are saying to me, at least you have a job. But this doesn't mean that I'm not right. Most probably I'll be jobless tomorrow or the day after.

What I'm curious to know is why does the future seem so blurred and dark to us? What is going to happen to "nobodies" like us in that darkness?

Is the future in the monopoly of tycoons, racketeers, the elite, the bullies and those who are always on the side of all the governments? What if there is no place left because of this crowd, what if we can't find a little corner for ourselves in that hell?

Little "nobodies," don't be angry with me. I'm a young person but the image in my head is so blurred, I can't manage to be stupidly hopeful, good and compatible.

I hate stupidity. I hate stock exchange boards. I hate well-dressed, close shaven, sweet smelling noisy men of figures with over-polished shoes. I hate hysterical supply brokers. I hate the closed circuit stock exchange. I hate mercenary sentimentality and life insurances taken out on fraudulent policies.

I don't like the pity industry, the masters of cheapness trained from the cradle.

It wasn't willingly that I learned by heart all that I was needlessly taught. The states of the smashed atom, the kinds of tripe…it was out of obligation that I read the 27-volume history of the prophets! I am a rebel, I don't fit in with the rules of the market, I disowned forever those who hurt me.

I love sharpening my words, making mistakes which I later regret, those who are undeniably good and I love entering unknown crossroads.

All the same, I must confess that I'm not as clean as you might think.

I'm quickly becoming soiled like most of you.

I may take bad roads, very bad roads without intent.

My words are so small, so inadequate that they float around in the unbelievably heavy webs of lies, I know. That's why I'm sure you haven't understood me once again.

Listen! All those who are here by chance, all those modest people, artificial dolls stuffed with straw, sleeping princes, the absent-minded, the over-pale, the false believers or infidels. If what I say doesn't interest you, don't bother. Pray constantly, go dancing, smoke pot, have a great ball, drive fast if you can find a car, eat and drink, make love till you want no more.

You are right, I'm boring. I've wasted your valueless time.

I apologize.

But you, the others, those without connections, mute friends…Think, gather your thoughts, and if you too wish to share, tell the world your true story.

Perhaps then we can find some sort of a solution for saving the grounded ship of our future. In cooperation and with our "own means"…

Yellowspot

With a bizarre shiver, Volkan leaned back and lit a cigarette. He sat there listening to the silence of the night. He felt like a cheap instrument which printed price tags.

Whoever this was, a self-declared young person, s/he was aware of the fact that the end of the world hadn't arrived yet. Perhaps there was despair and anger in what s/he wrote but it was evident that s/he was far from being devoid of intelligence and sensitivity.

At least s/he was trying to appease his/her fright by whistling.

More that…S/he was walking naked in the storm. Only love, hate or a great desperation could make one do something like that.

It wasn't evident who and what – man or woman – the writer was. By the way s/he expressed himself/herself, s/he was trying to stir up a hornet's nest, living his/her first vertical combat. The main importance of the message was its demonstration that it was no use to plug up with rags the holes in a roof which had become like a sieve.

He went to the beginning of the young person's article and reread it. This was a text he could answer by identifying himself with it completely. From outside, he didn't seem like the right choice to reply to this message, neither as a personality nor by his place in society. However, he hadn't lost his ability to hear. Somebody was talking out there. Somebody in dire straits…Someone who believed that s/he had lost her/his future but also continued her/his belief that there would be someone in this world who would understand her/him. Perhaps s/he didn't know anything, perhaps s/he wasn't deeply aware but s/he found the strength to defend her/his existence. S/he was trying to explain what s/he had to say by lining up words one after the other, calling to her/his side all those who weren't evil or stupid. The call was woven with the words of an unskilled poet, but this did not overshadow her/his sincerity in any way. Responses that came to such an article full of adverse but justified questions would probably not help other than by blowing the flames, but that was another issue.

He quivered. Didn't he have a contribution, however small and indirect, in the stealing of that future?

No, it certainly wasn't his fault; it wasn't anybody's fault really. This was how things went. Everybody believed that progress would be made by dragging things on, and naturally everybody had to help progress! It was impossible to progress without believing in progress. Hadn't they been taught to be on the side of progress, be it with noble feelings or for personal goals?

His mind was a shambles. Perhaps his crime was silence. To obey the rule of silence ...The most convenient way of keeping secrets was pretending not to know, didn't he know that? He refilled his glass. He didn't know if he obeyed or not. The most certain truth of that moment was that he had been someone else at that time.

Suddenly he thought that he had surpassed the danger of staying silent, that he possessed – or that at least he should possess – the capacity to be as courageous as this young person. Instead of being smug and rich, he could choose to be free tomorrow. However, this freedom would have to contain a silence in connection with his past which would no doubt last for an eternity. All the same, putting his cards on the table by telling Harun all he could and even those he shouldn't would cost him a few unpleasant but fleeting hours, that was all.

He had forgotten when he last had a concept about a future which was possible, realistic, with ambiguities, hopes, anticipations, excitements causing sleepless nights, dreams, struggles and failures. What was even more painful was the fact that for the last ten years, he hadn't had the chance to wait for tomorrow with longing and passion. Some people had continuously nudged him from behind, pushing him toward tomorrow. He was living so fast that he had become speed blind. He would realize that the future had arrived only after having fallen into it, and then he settled for watching it go by in ignorance.

Fortunately one sometimes saw these things within seconds in a very short time span. Surely this was a moment of overflow.

For a while, Volkan felt suspended once again somewhere between the past and the present. Then with a feeling of future anxiety and passionate regret for the first time since his adolescence, he wished he could go back to the beginning.

Who was this person? He wished they could meet, see and talk to each other.

In a moment, he found himself writing:

"Dear Yellowspot..."

6

On Sunday morning, Eylem arranged her books. She had no bookcase. She had built a few shelves by putting wooden planks between some bricks she had taken from a construction site. She put as many books as she could on the shelf and piled the rest on a stool. During breakfast, she had decided that no matter how defeated she was, she would do everything necessary to fit into this world, because even in darkest despair, one could find lots of things that mattered.

There were replies to her article. Someone had found her exceedingly pessimistic, another was criticizing her for making such a big fuss over her own problems. If she didn't like the conditions of her work, she should take a more comfortable job. Actually, a rebellious (!) person like her should not be working in Western-style workplaces.

Someone else had given a violent reaction, saying that those who didn't believe in Turkey's future were over-nationalistic and underdeveloped people who had the phobia of fragmentation. Very few people would be fooled by the subversive efforts of a "so-called poet" with insufficient knowledge. The youth and "all the young people of all ages" were not devoid of hopes and dreams; however, these weren't the dreams of their grandfathers and they never would be.

There was another who was wiser and better bred. She/he shared Eylem's anxiety although she/he found her poetic discourse inadequate and unnecessary and her content sentimental. According to this person, the only cause of all problems was global economy. Those who continued to be dependent on this merciless source of funds would never be able to save the future from mortgage. The country, complete with all its assets, had turned into a giant pawned object. This was the only bitter truth that blocked the way of the young and stole their future. In the short run, there was nothing that could be changed with personal efforts. On the contrary, the situation would get worse and worse every day and a final collapse was inevitable. The comment ended by saying that the only way to get out of this situation and build a new future was immediate independence and socialism.

Eylem read these remarks with some boredom which she didn't find at all interesting. It was easy to believe that the country and even the world were running toward destruction. Nevertheless, people wanted something to lean on, to hope for. Yes but how? The dreams of the globalists who defended liberal economy had begun to fade, and the argument of collapse foreseen in the dialectic materialism of the leftists had come to nothing. Instead, the force which was expected to crumble had grown and become wild, taking on a completely different aspect. Hopeful ideals and principles had cracked and crumbled. As a result, it had become necessary to accept the fact that everything which defied the rules of existence would stay alive by eating and destroying those around it. This was the frightening truth which poisoned the world and created sources of income out of wars.

There was another short response. It said that if one wanted to stay alive, one had to find a way to conform to this world, obeying its rules and benefiting from the advantages of the system as much as one could. Only those who could do this would survive and have a future. The remaining misfits, those who couldn't keep up with the times, would definitely be eliminated.

She shook her head with regret. She wasn't going to start a theoretical debate on such a platform. Her interest was directed at what young people like herself felt about their future and what they experienced. These people write down their sexual fantasies and expectations in a most explicit manner, even if the language they choose is timeworn. Yet they are uneasy, timid and even gawky in expressing themselves on an inner and intellectual level. Men could not surmount their extra-bloated egos while they tried to hide their wounds seeking support from a fake story that should cover their faults. Even in situations when they hid their identity and remained anonymous. And young women tended to look down on everything reacting more and more ill-temperedly, individualistically, daringly and aggressively.

The phone rang, it was her sister.

"Why don't you come over sometime today," she said. "As you know, I can't go out. Your uncle's in a bad mood again. Maybe I'll feel better if you and I chat a little."

Her sister's place was two stops away. She could postpone arranging the kitchen until the next day. As she was dressing, she noticed that the waist of her jeans had become loose. Her ribs had sharpened, her breasts had become smaller. She had lost a lot of weight during the bustle of the last few weeks. Her face was haggard, the cheekbones were protruding, cheeks sunken and her long, thick lashes were shadowing a wild gaze. There was something strangely alien about her. I might grow wings, she thought. Then I can fly, naturally if nobody comes and tears them off!

She walked out intending to take a *dolmu* (shared taxi) but then she decided to walk. Since coming to Istanbul, she had not been bored during off-hours. There were books and magazines to read, things to write, work to do. Istanbul was beautiful, very beautiful indeed. It would be fantastic if only she had a little money.

She wanted to call her father after putting some order into her life. The answer she would get was bound to be something like "I don't have such a daughter!" or "Where the hell is you mucking around?" and there was no way of changing that. Hearing her father's voice would make her feel ten years old and guilty again. She thought it would be best to forget about it.

Sevdiye opened the door, trying to keep at bay her five-year-old son who was pulling at her skirt. The people who came to their home were so few that the children were overcome by excitement whenever the doorbell rang. The nine-year-old Merve ran to embrace Eylem. The house smelled of alcohol, food and urine. There was poverty, decay and neglect everywhere.

Şükrü shouted from inside, "Sevdiye, who is it? Is it Mutena?"

"Go and say hello to him," suggested Sevdiye.

They entered the little room overlooking the street. Şükrü – she couldn't bring herself to call him "uncle" – was on the sofa, he could lay there but couldn't get up, where he managed to half-sit. Even if one couldn't say he had collapsed, he had shrunk; an expression of helplessness and a frightening selfishness had settled in his gaze.

"Hello, how are you?" said Eylem. Coolly, without getting too close, standing…

"How do you expect me to be? As you see …"

They had married off her sister by force to this man who was a distant relative. Sevdiye was helplessly tolerating this good-for-nothing who has been tormenting her since ten years. Şükrü continually tyrannized his wife, being angry at not being loved and for the silent hatred she felt for him.

Now he was even more ill-tempered than before. The stroke he had suffered the year before was probably due to taking alcohol and drugs at the same time. He had been to prison many times for all sorts of crimes ranging from being a drug courier to selling drugs, from smuggling to assault. The scoundrel had managed to pull through each time! Now it was he who felt the pitiful resignation his wife had to suffer in the past. But Seydiye had neither any compassion nor any love for him, and she didn't owe him anything.

Although they were hard up and barely managed to survive, as soon as he had left the hospital he had started drinking knowing it was strictly forbidden. His *raki* table would be laid out for him before noon. Every so often, he would yell "Sevdiye!" and ask for things while he drank.

Eylem had told her sister the other day, "If only he would drink himself to death so that you could be rid of him."

"Don't say that, he is still very young! What would become of us?"

It was as if her sister had unfurled the sails of a compassion she hadn't known about until that day. Perhaps this was what she needed; she was finally living the pleasure of having acquired power, while chiding her husband and grumbling occasionally.

Such men didn't die easily; they suffered and made others suffer.

They had been evicted from their previous home because they hadn't been able to pay the rent.

They were managing to get along when he was in the drug business, whereas now her sister went to clean houses several days a week. However, the little boy was a problem. It was his father who had to keep an eye on him half a day while Merve was at school. But as the man was in no condition to do so, the house was liable to all sorts of accidents. When Seydiye went to work, she sometimes locked the boy into his father's room together with his potty chair.

As Eylem was leaving the room, she remembered the rules and the words which had made her life hell in the home where she grew up. They were flying around her here too, gnawing at the air. There was nobody they could blame for Seydiye's state. In lives abandoned to fate and the easy way out, things turn sour by themselves. With each step you take, mistakes cut your feet as if you have stepped on broken glass.

Her sister had strongly insisted that she should stay with them. Listening to her, embracing her and consoling her were things Eylem could have done, but she would rather sleep in the streets than live in the same house as Şükrü while she watched her beautiful sister wither away in front of her eyes. She could have helped her only if she had some money, but...

While they were having tea, Eylem noticed the long hairs on her sister's legs. Her eyes had sunk, her hands had dried and reddened, her teeth had turned yellow and become shapeless. She was only in her early thirties. Sadness mingled with astonishment stirred inside Eylem. She looked at her sister more carefully. Seydiye was shouting at her child; she was out of breath. Life did not fit her too well anymore. All of a sudden, Eylem felt that whatever she did, she would never be able to help her sister.

If she hadn't resisted, she would have had a similar life. How had she managed to escape that fate? Had she really succeeded, was she completely out of danger? Up to a certain point, yes. And after that, she wasn't sure at all, because she wasn't born lucky. Luck?

It was a white dog with black ears. When Eylem was a child, she would not answer strangers who asked her name. Not because she was afraid, but because she couldn't say "Mutena" and furthermore, she didn't like the name. Even the name of the dog was better: Luck. Her brother – the dead one – had named the dog. He had found it wounded in the street and had brought it home.

The ruling concept at home was that investments for the future were to be made for the boys in the family. Her elder brother hadn't failed this belief; he had become a policeman. The younger one was drowned in the lake of the dam, not reaching the future.

Lately she had been forced to fight to exhaustion the memories that kept coming back without mercy. Her mother, father, brother, grandfather…Although she hadn't seen them in years, they were attacking her with their ghosts. Even her grandmother, whom she adored, appeared to her with her father's face. All of them had rotted like her drowned brother with his bloated purple skin. They still chased her to the ruins in her memory. Each time she had to drive them back to the land of oblivion and nothingness with a new effort.

She quickly added Seyit's face and words to these faces. During the three years she had shared with him, Eylem had always thought – a little more each day – that Seyit was the most difficult type of man ever to bear.

"I love your mouth, I'm crazy for you."

Starting a relationship with a married man was a sin and immoral. But she was so helpless then. She knew it wouldn't last long anyway. Married men were able to make such relationships last, on the condition of paying the price, and only if they were very skillful and very much in love.

"I can't come, perhaps later…It's impossible, my wife is so unhappy…"

She kept her place hidden, she communicated only with her sister. It was she who told Eylem that their father had remarried.

"You're mad, you're crazy, come over here…I never promised you anything…"

Her relationship with Seyit was neither far-reaching nor dependable. To be honest, Seyit made her feel her body, and taste passion and pleasure, dragging her to the reaches under her skin. He taught her to give herself up and forget – even if it was for a moment – all that had happened.

Other than that, their relationship was woven with certain helplessness, plenty of muteness and a dense gloom for both of them. And naturally there was some insincerity on Eylem's side. She would show her gratitude for the man who took care of her with exaggerated hysteria. Was that what Seyit was talking about when in his letter he blamed her with being a whore?

"Don't worry about these things now…I love the way you come…I'm mad about you…"

She remembered those nights. She was writing her thesis. As soon as Seyit was gone, she would sit at the table and would study until the waking hours of the city. She didn't yet know that she would be left high and dry with her dreams, her aspirations and her expectations. She was not going to work for Seyit anymore, because it wasn't an environment where she could make herself a career. She thought of herself as well-equipped and valuable; she had high hopes.

Then she had to struggle for months to find a job. She realized that the bright future people talked about was a huge lie, and all that was said about hopes, goals, passions and walking unerringly toward an aim was only a fairy tale. Even if there was something called the future, it existed for a small, lucky minority. If you had been educated in the States for one or two years, or had certain connections or belonged to a certain circle, then you could advance. Otherwise success was merely a word or an illusion.

There still had to be some other things to be known, to be seen and understood; things which were wider, meaningful, more difficult and sad, things that had not been tasted yet. That was why she continued to read. After a certain hour in the night, letters started dancing in front of her eyes, words hung onto her eyelids. She read with her entire body, her whole being. Reproducing what she had read, turning over each and every word in her head. Books were beautiful things that rustled under one's hand. It was in books that the human struggle, with its great drama, its sacred quest, its fall and its efforts to exist, was presented through endless questions. They were fertile, noble and eternal.

"What a character you are! Are you into archaic, dusty, smelly books now? Are you going be a communist or an anarchist in this day and age?"

How sure he was of himself! He thought he knew everything. He had joined a newly founded rightist liberal party which was rising fast. In a few years, he would most probably take what was his due from the closed circuit fortune offer of power and become rich. Then he would send Eylem packing at the first opportunity and assume the role of the respectable family man.

Yes, but Seyit was right. Times had changed. It was he who found Eylem a job through someone he knew, in an import-export company with good prospects. Perhaps he felt that it was time she took care of herself. Gölba ı Lake, afternoon rains, kisses in the car…tulips, little gifts…a weekend escapade at a five-star hotel in the South…In short, an amusing one-act play which rapidly went back to the point where it started.

Then restless, ambiguous, dragging days…

Eylem was thinking of finding herself a place to live, of going away. Smoke blue, mustard yellow, customary words, cheap parting songs in the dim light…these were all part of the monotony, the unwanted loitering, complicated efforts. A voice in her head kept telling her, "Break the circle, break the circle, don't go back to where you started from." She was stuck with that voice, she couldn't get rid of it, but she didn't know how to go about it, either. Getting rid of Seyit would not save her from feeling like a useless object forgotten on a shelf.

The only thing she could see was that the trade contract between them had been annulled. They didn't miss each other at all, and they didn't call each other as long as there was no obligation. Both had their own problems. The words and accusations they directed at each other had gradually grown heavy like a stone, becoming coarser. Anyway, hadn't the kisses been poisoned, the calls furtive and the laughs false right from the beginning?

A closeness based on bargaining had consumed itself in its nothingness and had ended without leaving behind any tears, bitterness or pain. What Eylem felt – until the arrival of Seyit's message – was merely discomfort.

She had come to Istanbul determined not to get carried away by hopes. She was still in the trial period at the office where she had found a job. She still was not on the official payroll, had no social security. The decision was to be made within a few days, at the end of the one-month period. She felt sure of herself but she would certainly be in a tight spot if she happened to get fired.

She had already taken that risk. She had to believe that she had entered the phase of self-sufficiency. Working for eight hours a day as a third-class staff member at a job she didn't like was eroding her energy, her time, her sensitivity and most importantly, her words which were loaded with poetry. And in spite of all that, it wasn't providing her with the money she needed to survive.

She hesitated for an instant. Had she made a mistake by cutting all ties with Seyit? Wouldn't it have been wiser to keep handy this man who had been at her side in her most difficult days? He was ordinary and his ability to understand fine points was limited. But on the other hand, he was a positive, open-minded man who had the skill to accept life on its own terms and keep his expectation at a low level. He had been very helpful at loosening the rules and the limits she had been imposing on herself, even if he never understood her stormy world of emotions.

Suddenly she remembered the ugly things the man had written. Was she scared of her future? Why couldn't she get rid of her obsession of having to be with a protective man? This was a tendency which had lately resurfaced amongst young women in a more crude, more selfish and calculating manner than that of the conservative concept. It was a plague that was spreading fast. Find a neat man with money and live without having to lift a finger!

And how about love? She hadn't been in love yet; she hadn't loved anyone passionately. But from all that she read, she had learned that love did not obey reason. Furthermore, love could quickly turn into hate if it was forced. Eylem wanted to taste pure, irrational love. She felt she had to be free and independent even if it were only for this.

There had been stages in her life. Nothing had been handed to her on a silver platter. On the contrary, everything simple had been turned into something more difficult, more complicated, full of obstacles. She realized something about herself. When she was in a tight spot, when her emotions came into prominence instead of her intellect, she could be as cruel and mean as she had wished to be some time ago. She could give up what she possessed without hesitation.

"*I owe you nothing! I don't owe anybody anything,*" she had shouted at Seyit on the last day she saw him. She was filled with the unquestionable force of anger.

"You are an egoistic, calculating person devoid of love! What a fool I have been! I'm telling you, you won't go far being as evil as you are!"

"You were using me!"

"You were the one who was using me!"

Whatever the sort of contract, most of them were annulled with words like this or of this kind, anyway.

The rim of the tea glass in Eylem's hand was broken. She placed it on the side table with disgust. She promised Merve she would buy her a new pair of shoes when she got her salary. She was going to bring Özgür a red truck. With a faint smile on her face and a dizzying feeling of fantasy, she sat a little longer with her sister.

She walked back home. It was a warm day almost like summer. The streets were crowded, the sidewalks full of people. Men with nothing to do were standing around in front of shops and in doorways or playing cards in stuffy coffee houses.

She bought a few literary magazines and a newspaper. The racks were full of women's magazines. With their pages on how to hook and keep men, recipes, fashions and expensive cosmetics, they somehow had to appeal to women, otherwise there wouldn't be so many. They provided information on problems of love and how to have sex, beauty and orgasm techniques. What was strange was that they seemed to assume you made love all the time. They suggested lots of clothes to buy; they gave "fantastic" examples and ideas about how to organize parties and how to decorate homes. Naturally for those who had money…for those without any money, it was impossible not to feel unhappy, dissatisfied and miserable while looking at these magazines.

When she came home, she arranged her kitchen. She didn't have too many utensils. She wiped the interior of the cupboards and arranged them, lining them with clean pieces of paper. Her mother had done her best to make her into a good housewife. She had given her daughter torturous tasks ever since she was a child. Eylem wasn't one of those dainty, clumsy girls who didn't know how to cook, although she would have liked to be one. She found it smarter not to have the soul of a cleaning woman. Not to know, or pretending not to know, was the right attitude, a novel outlook that separated womanhood from being a domestic slave.

She went to bed early and she glanced at literature periodicals. If she could improve the poems, she would send them to some magazines. But she still wasn't satisfied with them. Her world of emotions was becoming shallow because of the worries of daily life. She would be able to write better and stronger poems if she was in love, she knew that. Sometimes she missed the frenzy of love's pain, be it only for this reason. However, she was very far from this possibility; she felt a strange draught, an inexplicable oppression in her soul.

There were noises upstairs again. The floor was shaking under firm steps, the window was rattling with the dissonant voice of a man shouting coarsely, wildly. There was a violent blow, followed by the crash of an object falling and shattering on the floor. The woman's voice was now more dolorous and imploring and that of the man, more ferocious.

She wouldn't be able to sleep. She was cold all over, and trembling inside. She went to the kitchen and made herself some herbal tea. Mint, camomile and hot water…she smoked a cigarette. In her youth they had frightened her so much, that the fear of being raped had turned her life into a nightmare. The number of sex maniacs had increased lately; lots of women who lived alone were being raped in their own homes. When she went back to the bedroom, she looked at the garden door, holding her breath. Was it strong enough? "I must keep a club by my bedside or an iron rod to smash brains with a single blow," she thought.

She remembered with pain and shame. She was beaten very badly once by her brother Mustafa, the one who was a policeman, and a few times by her grandfather. Her grandfather was bad enough but her brother had almost killed her. A boy who worked at the gas station had written her a letter which he had put into a matchbox and thrown through the window, and her brother got hold of the matchbox. The boy had written things which gave the impression that there was something going on between the two. He was suggesting they should meet. She couldn't make her family believe that she was completely innocent.

She had tried to wipe out that evening, but it always came back in fragments. Out of time, far away, foreign…without thinking as if drugged, she sometimes dreamt about her brother's blows, his banging her head against the wall, blood running from her mouth and her nose, then dragging her by her hair out into the garden where he kicked her body and broke her arm on the frozen ground.

They had to take her to the hospital.

She was silent for days, whispering, talking very little. After being released from hospital, they closed her up in the back room of the house. She couldn't eat; she lost weight and become a bag of skin and bones. She didn't look at the mirror or at anyone. Only her elder sister spoke to her who always cried when she came to Mutena's side. Her parents' faces wore the darkness of being cross. Their accusing looks gave her more pain than her beaten body.

The incident was not mentioned at home. That is, as if it had happened but not happened, as if something would suddenly rot and disintegrate if they were mentioned. With a horrible feigned ignorance, they took refuge in the disgrace and suffocation of things they knew. She waited for her mother's embrace and consolation. She desperately wanted her to shed at least one teardrop. That was the first time she felt the desire to escape from home, and she carried this for years like a pain postponed.

She never spoke to her brother again. Their paths crossed several times in Ankara, but she walked past him without looking at his face, as if he was a stranger. Once, he came to Seyit's workplace and threatened her. That time she locked herself up in the kitchen.

Oblivion! An ugly seal embedded in the frayed cloth of memory.

To get away from the past and to need it less...

Now she noticed something which seemed very strange to her. She had never been able to put this incident down on paper; not the incident itself but the pain etched in her soul. She had wanted to but she couldn't. She wasn't able to write anything about her body, about the pain, the yearning, the changes she had lived through. She had kept it away from words like an unnamed taboo. Perhaps her shame would be purged if she could write about it. In fact, all words that came from the heart were about the body. They were the voice of the body, they were born out of the body. They were as visible as the body but subjective, as free and as prohibited as the body, as secret as the body.

She had written pages and pages, but she had always skipped abuses or memories of her body, taking the easy way out, pretending they did not exist. That was why she hadn't been able to produce anything but lifeless, abstract, flimsy empty poems. Her writings had remained dull because she was forced to forget about her body when she wrote.

"*Nobody*" was actually her body.

7

In the morning Volkan left home very optimistically, thinking "All is well." The road to the airport was empty, as there wasn't much traffic yet. It was a beautiful gray blue, cloudless October morning. A thin mist lay over the city like a silk shawl. The trees were still green challenging the autumn which seemed reluctant to show it. Both sides of the road were full of huge office blocks, construction scaffoldings and giant billboards that attacked people with messages. Gradually the buildings grew less and less. Beyond empty lots covered with weed, far away, one could see rows of ugly gray apartment buildings and roofs full of dish antennas. Ugliness had spread like an epidemic to the outskirts of the city.

He had listened to music for hours the night before, killing time while contemplating whether to call Melike or not. It was now ten days since he had met her. He had waited long enough to see how she was; there was no need to drag on any longer. The conversation would flow by itself anyway. Besides, they would feel more at ease on the phone.

However, if daring steps were taken without abiding by the rules, every game ran the risk of turning into a sudden fiasco. He was a master at the game but he didn't know what kind of a player Melike was.

On the other hand, she didn't seem to be the sort of woman who would coyly wait for the man to call first. Naturally she might not have liked him, not found him interesting; there was no need to feel hurt. She might have come to him only to claim her meager treasure and acted affable just to ensure she got back her goods safely.

She had definitely been affable. Her looks, her gestures, the way she talked, that sweet tension between them, leaving the door open as she left, everything indicated that he had made a positive impression on her. In that case, why should he hesitate? He should offer his friendship, make an effort to win her heart. In his social environment, such relationships could be established in a moment. But this time, he was faced with a different, mysterious woman and that was what made it exciting.

He wondered what she was like naked.

He had gone to bed late and slept well. Then, at dawn he had woken up suddenly with a disturbing feeling of anxiety. He had wrapped himself with a blanket and sat on the terrace. The damp smell of pines from the forest mingled with the calm, iodine-laden breeze of the sea and filled his nose. The sky, the hills and the sea were enveloped in a fog with saffron yellow glitters. The rising day was slowly opening up as if wanting to shed light on all the ambiguities, secrets and formations, turning the beauty and all the eternal splendor and squalor of the city into gold. Dawn was a repeated rejuvenation, a touching, warm and powerful renewal. A divine inspiration, an open road was needed, but even with a superficial glance, that process indicated what would follow.

His intuition was strong. Having sobered up with the cool of the morning, his childish excitement of the previous evening seemed quite arid. It was unacceptable that an experienced, fastidious, mature man like him, so good at conducting difficult negotiations, should be obsessed with such an absurd fantasy. It was most unbecoming of him to have his eyes on an unpretentious and modest woman, pouncing on her like an old lecher. He didn't need an ordinary love affair. Neither did he have time for being troubled about desperate fantasies. Life and love had to be much more dramatic and intense.

It could be, why not? But he wasn't going to be in Istanbul for at least three days. He couldn't suggest a meeting on the telephone. All the same, he could send her flowers to remind her of him. Wouldn't it be better to close the matter after this attack if necessary?

What would he lose if he wouldn't get a response, if he was left alone in this game? There had already been a beginning and it would be cowardly to leave the story midway. He wasn't complicated by nature and he knew how to protect himself. In spite of all that was negative, even if all was a lie from the beginning to the end, he needed a new woman in his life. This could be Melike or someone else as long as she was outside his social environment.

He could love passionately someone genuine, someone sincere. He could undertake impossible things, wait for telephone calls with agitation. He could shout into the void, talk to himself or send love messages full of crazy words.

Perhaps before long, all these would be boring repetitions of past experiences and turn into a past to be remembered with a smile. So? Catch that lively, bright flame inside you, take it and put it in your palm, keep your eyes on it, kneel before it. Come on, once more, forward for a last try!

"Mehmet Bey, I want to send flowers to a lady today. You will have to take care of that," he told his driver.

"Yes, sir. As you wish."

Why should it be absurd? A man can send flowers to a woman he likes. This is a sign of interest. He wrote the address on a piece of paper and gave it to the experienced, white-haired driver.

"What kind of flowers would you like?"

"White orchids; or let's leave it to the florist."

"Shall we add a card?"

"Er, yes, let's."

He took a card from his briefcase, wrote "I miss you" on the back and held it to the driver.

"Don't worry, sir. I shall have them make a nice arrangement and I will deliver it myself."

The car stopped in front of International Departures. As soon as Volkan had gone through the security check, Ferdi ran to him and took his briefcase from his hand. It was evident from the helpless expression on his face that something unexpected had happened. His eyes were hesitant, his looks worried. He held the briefcase against his belly like a shield and waited for a moment, trying to gauge the effect of the news he was about to break. Then he took a couple of steps without direction, as if pushed backwards.

"Your plane has been delayed for two hours, sir. Apparently there is a technical problem," he said as if moaning.

Volkan stamped his foot on the floor, "Dammit!" he shouted.

No, he wasn't expecting this, especially not today.

So much effort has been made, all is prepared, and on the very day when you are to reach your goal, some trivia forces you into a position where you can do absolutely nothing. No, he couldn't go on taking public flights. It didn't work anymore, it just didn't!

"That's enough! Why don't we have a private plane at our disposition? Why don't we go with our own plane? Private plane, yes, I want a private plane!"

When he heard the voice, it had to be his own voice, he covered his mouth with his hand as if frightened from his own fury. The voice quickly went back in but its echo remained in his ears. I WANT!...Who? Private plane? Private plane ...private ...

His foot remained where it had hit the floor. Was this really his own voice? "My voice! Me ...Who am I? Private plane. Why not, there could have been one, but there isn't. What should I do now? What would be the best thing to do?"

The lounge was crowded with morning passengers and confusion. There were long queues in front of the ticket counters. He looked around to see if there was anyone he knew. Had anyone heard him shout? No, the humming of the crowd was loud.

Take a deep breath, count until ten. Private plane! Absurd, yes, but Geneva today, Dubai tomorrow, Brussels three days later, Berlin, New York, Rome…it wasn't easy to keep up with this pace. Even if I travel first class, how can someone in my position work efficiently while being dragged about in ordinary public planes which arrive and depart as they wish, where the narrow seats behind are filled with people who smell of perspiration, where ill-natured children shout and babies cry, turning the trip into torture?

Of course a private plane was necessary. Special escorts. Comfort. A desk, a bed…other delights he couldn't think of at that moment! Someone in his place and position should not take a step anywhere without these things. I…

Who the hell are you? Pull yourself together.

All of a sudden he felt dizzy with intense distress and estrangement. He opened his mouth to say something but no sound came out this time. The same questions were turning around in his head: Who am I? Where did I come from? Where am I, what am I doing? Who am I to want a private plane?

They were standing in the middle of the hall, blocking the way. As they moved toward a corner, he looked at his watch out of habit: seven-twenty. Even if the plane left by nine-thirty, it was most unlikely that he would be able to make it to Markenis' appointment.

He asked Ferdi, "Where is Tuğrul?"

"He went to see if he could change your ticket for an earlier flight."

Why wouldn't that damn voice inside him shut up? Who am I? Where did I come from? More importantly, where do I want to arrive at? Where the hell am I running like this?

He took off his jacket and loosened his tie in preparation for an approaching panic attack. The armpits of his shirt were wet from perspiration. His loose, well-cut brown serge trousers were scorching his legs.

"It's so hot! Doesn't the air-conditioning work here?"

"Let's go to the cafeteria. I'll call the others to inform them about the situation while you have some breakfast and relax, Volkan Bey," Ferdi said. "We'll postpone the appointment until tomorrow if necessary. There won't be a problem, don't worry."

"What do you mean there won't be a problem! I waited ten days for this appointment."

Ferdi touched his shoulder affectionately, leading him toward the cafeteria. Volkan let himself be guided gently. Tuğrul came back, dejectedly buttoning his coat, empty-handed.

"Good morning. What news, Tuğrul?"

"There are no other planes. There is one over Athens but that one arrives even later. I think…"

"What do you think, tell me?"

"We could inform them of the situation and ask to postpone the lunch by one hour. These things always happen, Volkan Bey. I think Mr. Markenis would understand…"

"Let's hope so…"

On such occasions, these young men who were Volkan's apprentices acted as if their most important duty was to pacify their boss. Actually he had chosen them for their cool-headedness. They sat down in the cafeteria. The seats were very narrow; he had a hard time fitting in. He had started to – or was about to – feel the depression of this unfortunate incident which was not his fault. He asked for some water. He took out a tranquilizer from his shirt pocket and waited, undecided whether he should swallow it or not.

He had lost control and drunk too much the night before. If he took a pill on top of that, he would feel even worse. He had lost hope of making it to his appointment, so he put it aside. It was impossible. He should have left one day earlier. But how? Wasn't he in Moscow the morning before? Luckily the most important meeting was the next day.

He put back the pill, drank the water and took a deep breath. They could manage Markenis but his anxiety increased when he thought of the crucial meeting of the next day. Otto Sperber was a man who could read the mind of his opponent at one glance. He was a former leftist whose old fox face was continuously being polished by fame and money. His face always wore an expression of someone who always expected his opponent to say "yes," of someone assured that all would be very easy for him, a merciless, grinning expression. That's why there were many people who didn't want to see him even in their dreams.

Volkan reminded himself that he had to be strong.

He hadn't had any breakfast at home. He had taken a handful of vitamins and drunk a large glass of orange juice. Tuğrul asked the waiter for some pastries that he knew his boss liked. Volkan approved by nodding his head. He couldn't manage to control his appetite in moments of stress.

He saw his face shining like the moon in the large, shiny crystal of his watch. Who am I? It's me, I'm Volkan, Volkan Kuman, the handsome, successful, romantic man! Or rather, the one who used to be!

He wasn't feeling very well at this moment.

Melike might have found him too fat, bulky. He had to lose weight as soon as possible. He had some training devices at home but he was too lazy to use them. If he started right away, and with the support of a strict diet, he would lose four or five kilos before their next meeting. There was no need for pessimism. It was still too soon to say all would be well. There could always be fresh starts, and it was quite possible that the question of what it would develop into would be answered very soon.

But orchids were not the right flowers. It should have been something more modest. She had admired the chrysanthemums. No, lilies or yellow roses…women adore yellow roses. There will be difficulties, I may suffer. That's all right. I have to live a love affair that will make me jump in the air or make me crawl; it would be death not to live it through.

To love again is the hope that it will be different this time, isn't that so? Isn't love getting carried away hopelessly, knowing it won't work? Love. A very pretentious word…I should say "perhaps." That is the key word! One mustn't underestimate or skip coincidences even if it is a state of enchantment with no future. What is the future? Isn't it something that overshadows the present? Live the day! Let yourself go with the flow of the moment. The world is so small and life so arid!

This Yellowspot…the child poet…This was what he should have written the other night instead of those convoluted, unclear words. Dear Yellowspot, don't worry about the future, live the day, my child! He could still write this, of course. He felt a brief remorse. His head was so empty, so hopeless that night, he had written depressing strange things to the poor kid. Naturally, one can become more sentimental when one is lonely. What's more, it was easy to address the void. If you don't like it, you just pass through, he thought in consolation.

"Where are the pastries?"

He should have written a more meaningful message on the card that went with the flowers to Melike. No, it was fine. Short and to the point…orchids were fine, too. He knew the driver would buy the freshest and the most expensive. Naturally he could have written something grandiose such as "*Thanks for the spring you have woken in me.*" Perhaps such a card would have been more impressive. Perhaps she would have laughed at that stale, clichéd love declaration. Let her laugh…Melike! Melike Eda…what a beautiful name this was! It was ringing in his head. It had suddenly, irresistibly come forward from amongst millions of names!

There was no need to be hopeless. The world wasn't really such a bad, dark place. It had its stars, dawns, mornings, beginnings and women. There were songs, poems, smells, butterflies, flowers and seas. Yes, he shouldn't forget the irregularities, the confusion, the hypocrisy, the ambition and the evil; but there was also love making, tears and innocence.

Yes, there was. You, hopeless child, Yellowspot, raise your eyes and have a look…

There, everybody was going back and forth in a flurry and in hope. Things worked amazingly well in spite of all the chaos. People loved each other and then they grew apart. Problems arose and they were solved or not solved; but all the same, life continued.

I exaggerate everything; I've become too soft lately. But the truth of the matter is that I'm not so special, he thought.

I, he had been saying, always I, for years...who was this I, what did it mean? Someone who was tired of running frantically toward an unknown future, one who had hit the bottom. An idiot who had reached the point where he didn't know what to want from life because there was nothing left to want; a fool who had accepted to live as allowed by others, while his emotions and thoughts had stepped away from all things normal. Actually they were both the same thing. It was most probable that there were other potholes to fall into ahead of him.

His head was aching. He was no longer going to ask himself questions. It was neither the time nor the place to volunteer to sit in the chair of the accused. He put two small pastries into his mouth and ate them heartily, with pleasure. He lighted a cigarette. No matter what, it was still a lovely morning.

He should have been sorry for having missed his appointment with one of his most famous, most prestigious supporters and customers, but it was possible to look at the situation from another perspective. Was it clever to consider it an honor to be in the same place – at tables overladen with all delicacies imaginable – with people wheeling and dealing to wrap up contracts which would harm the helpless, hungry populations of the third world, and be against the interests of young people qualified but jobless?

Well, well! When did I reach the stage of thinking about such niceties? Or is it my suppressed and shrunken class consciousness which is acting up?

Had there been some changes in him or in the world within the last two or three days? No, certainly nothing had changed. His eyes were still looking in the same direction. However, the world was slowly rotating in front of him, and sometimes his eyes suddenly caught something. Even if it was as pale as the moon in the daylight, the truth could be seen when one raised his head and looked around.

He remembered Yellowspot's article once again. This was such a strange world that, sooner or later, both success and failure led people to disappointment. It wasn't possible to understand the reason of this without getting to the bottom of things. One had to study each link in the evolution of man in order to reach the final result. But perhaps nothing had that much importance anymore.

If you had made your choice about which side you were on, you advanced without bumping into this or that, without getting bruised or wounded. The important thing was to make the right choice at the beginning. Yes, but it was still difficult to be sure of the thing defined as "right," because that too varied greatly. Perhaps the question which interested him now, this very important question which had suddenly appeared out of nowhere, "Where am I going?" had something to do with the transformation of his concept of right and wrong.

What had changed? Let's try to think with a clear head. What changed and made me like this?

People loaded the two words "human being" with a myriad of meanings every moment. On the other hand, enmities and ambitions never ceased. People talked endlessly about justice and liberty, but continued to drag their fellow human beings into hunger, bondage, death and savagery, while others continued to stay silent in the face of such atrocities. "Great humanity" was only on people's tongues and in laws which were never enforced. What a shame!

Sometimes Volkan felt embarrassed as though he had a part to play in all this hypocrisy, this brutality. He was searching for himself in some corner of that dark well. He was tired of indifference, of showing silent respect to things which were not to be explored, of walking with vanity as if he were someone important. His business had taught him the power of money; but more importantly, how difficult it was to possess money, and as in some cases, how incredibly easy. And the worst thing was how dangerous it could be according to who possessed it.

These were important experiences but what good were they, what was he doing with them?

Noise, announcements…the flight to Hamburg, number six-zero-eight…last call…London, two hours' delay! No, it wouldn't do, all this confusion…he had to think about this matter seriously when he had more time.

A wave of anger rose inside him. Let Markenis wait, he thought. Those who have something to gain have to wait, and those who don't want to wait, don't. Was there a reason to take it to heart so much? Why was he making his life so difficult? In any case, this job…

Volkan had hinted that Harun too had to be informed about the backstage of such secretive, dubious transactions. But as always, Harun had passed over the subject. The sale was almost finalized and needed utmost confidentiality. At this point, they would be discussing only some details. Unless proven otherwise, they had to trust the customer to be honest and without ulterior motives.

"What! What honesty? There are rumours that the intermediary company representing the opposite side has connections with a Moslem terror organization!"

"Don't mess things up, Volkan! Let it fall!" That was what Harun had said. Even if it were so, he was sure the buyer was not involved. And which buyer is completely innocent in international negotiations?

What bothered Volkan was the boring, condescending air of Markenis' unfriendly, ostentatious men with whom he would be bargaining. The faces of these types seemed to be made of plastic as if to safeguard important and crucial information, and their brains were too shallow to dig. They told lies, they created all sorts of obstacles and they used a sharp language even when discussing the technical details of the contract. No doubt he would have to be alert and secretive like during the Israel deal last time. He needed two days to feel safe enough to take off his protective mask. That was all right. After all, the men were not a private gang waiting with their hands on their guns. To start with, the strategic value of the merchandise was an advantage for Cosmos. Everybody had a weak point. Still, it wasn't going to be easy, this time it wasn't going to be easy at all.

So be it! It never is, it shouldn't be…A quick, hopeless, uneasy feeling stirred in him. How long would he be able to stand this business, this crazy pace? What would be missing in his life if he didn't go to this meeting, if he gave up everything, if he completely withdrew from this environment? Nothing. On the contrary, if he considered the matter from a personal point of view, he would begin to exercise and lose weight, stop smoking and regain his health. He could fall in love again, go to Cape Hope, even get married and have children.

A child! That would be wonderful, but first, a mother had to be found.

Anyway, we'll see. I haven't reached forty yet. Dreams of a happy family can still be put off like many other things. His business was always urgent, but his private life seemed like a tangled thread ball made up of postponements. My boy, you are the no-good addition of all the dreams you have put off into the future. What future? The future is a fairy tale, and it can never be a comfort for exhausted people like me who have run off the rails.

Did he have a dream worth making an effort for? No. One who didn't master his own life could not have any dreams concerning the future. Could someone who thought he experienced everything have a dream to nurture? His was a life bought and run by others. Perhaps he was running at full speed toward death.

His pulse quickened, I'm dying, he thought. He gulped down the orange juice. Nobody was going to reward him. He didn't need it, either. He had earned enough money and could make more if necessary. What he didn't want was to rush from one deal to another with a burdened conscience and hating every minute of it.

"Are you all right, sir?"

"I'm okay, Ferdi. May I have a dark coffee, please?"

Tuğrul got up with respect. "Would you like to see some newspapers?" he asked.

"That would be good."

Volkan called Harun. The phone rang but nobody answered. He must be sleeping; God only knew where he had been till morning.

"The boss isn't up yet."

"We'll take care of everything, sir," said Ferdi.

What did these two young men dream about their future? The usual...to get ahead in life, to make more money, to rule and to live well. In people's dreams of the future, the good, the bad, the easy, the impossible, the most beautiful and the ugliest could coexist, but in the long run, all lead to the same thing. Volkan wondered why that beautiful tissue woven with the altruism of his youth dedicated to the future had unraveled in such a short time. He didn't know and he was panicking. It was impossible for him to think clearly, simply. He had to keep cool. As always...It was wrong to add fuel to the fire.

He went through the newspapers Tuğrul had brought.

As always, he carelessly glanced at the headlines and then the economy and sports pages. The papers, it seemed, had found nothing important and noteworthy to report. Paris Hilton had arrived and she had displayed her buttocks. The wine and champagne cellar of a bankrupt industrialist would be auctioned off. American soldiers had been photographed while applying inhuman torture to Iraqis.

The news was stale, the commentaries incomplete and one-sided, and the points of view narrow. It was not much fun to have first-hand information about what was going on, and to live in the midst of secret relationships and shadowy deals. That was why the third-page news had been drawing his attention for some time. Attacks of madness and murders, traffic horrors, fatal illnesses, rapes, children who were lost or had turned into snatch-and-run thieves...He read these incidents without skipping a line, as if they were mystery stories. All these news gave more clues to what was going on. As he took a look at the latest escapades of half-naked girls in the magazine pages, he thought about sexuality which was now dominating everything and everywhere. That dark, intense, prohibited sexuality running underground had somehow spurted out like wild lava, enveloping everything, and this one and only and limitless freedom had started flowing freely in the streets and slums of the city.

In one of the newspapers, they had put a few pictures of a man the police had captured; the man had put a knife to his son's throat threatening to kill both the boy him and himself if he wasn't given a job right away. While reading this news, he felt a tension mixed with weariness, something like impatience before an explosion. It wasn't because he was directly moved by the story. Thanks to similar incidents that one saw on television everyday, such threats had stopped being interesting a long time ago. The thing was that unexpectedly, he felt he could identify with that man. For some reason...finally he too could do something like that one day!

He got up and went to the men's room. "I don't really know what I want," he thought. He wasn't so sure now that he wanted this Melike woman either. An antique smuggler, the so-called maker of bangles and baubles! Always the same decay! What he needed was an intelligent, conscientious woman. He felt like a needy idiot who thought that the first woman he met was an angel without wings. The world was full of tramps. If the woman made a pass at him, he could sleep with her a few times, that was all.

Melike's image appeared before his eyes. Her calmness, her elegance, her mystery...suddenly he felt close to her, as if she were his sister. And to think he had tagged her as a smuggler and a tramp a moment ago...

No, there was no need to fool himself. He was alienating himself from people because of his job. Lately, he had started feeling extremely suspicious of all he did, all that he madly ran after. Feelings of guilt were bearing down on him almost all the time. He had been trying to silence his consciousness, to ignore it, but his innate righteousness was constantly calling out to his conscience to return.

He looked in the mirror while washing his hands. For a moment, he felt accidentally trapped in someone else's shape.

"Hey, you, fatso," he said to the man over there. "Instead of going to meet a crooked money dealer, a vile moneylender, you could go wherever you want, or even better, you could do completely different things for the good of humanity."

Fatso? No, it was impossible to find a word which would describe him the way he looked. He couldn't see himself as he actually was. He saw only what he wasn't, what he lacked and his defects. He saw himself through the eyes of others and that created a feeling of inferiority. He was totally confused. Perhaps it was because that morning, a little while ago, he had come face to face with a stranger whom he had been thinking was himself and he had been terrified.

What was happening really?

Hadn't he been thanking God for his luck only a short time ago? He had risen rapidly, and as a young man he had attained many things people struggled for all their lives and never had. A glamorous, abundant life, a good job, respect, money…

He was not proud of thinking about it, but he looked at losers his own age with the condescending look of those sure of their abilities. He secretly blamed them for being clumsy and lazy. Many people of his generation with the same qualities as he, and those maybe even more brilliant, were helplessly trying to adjust to being out of jobs, to the difficulties, the confusion, the ambiguity and the lack of security in their lives, all the while blaming bad luck for all their misfortunes. Well, people had different levels of education and abilities. Their power to make money was also dissimilar. More was demanded from those who could, and their price was paid. That was why his road had always been radiant and cheerful, whereas others looked hopelessly and anxiously at the darkness in front of them which gradually got darker and made it impossible for them to see the future.

Though even small children – Yellowspot – were aware of the truth now. They could soon corner him somewhere and spit in his face. What did this yellow spot mean? All those things s/he had written about stock brokers, the devil! Yellowspot? Of course, this name had to do with seeing. So, yellow spot!

He shuddered. What's wrong with me? he thought. Did his eyes open the moment he stamped his foot on the floor in anger? Perhaps. With a feeling of pain and loss similar to hunger, he realized he longed for all that he had lost but didn't miss, or perhaps preferred to think he didn't miss. His life was only a mistake, even a denial. Astounded as if he had suddenly fallen into a vast void, he stared at the hole of the washbasin.

He had to leave his job. I'll first go someplace, he thought, try to pull myself together. He could do it. He was free! No, he wasn't. His was something like hidden slavery. He was a living dead in the command of those who tried to scare the world with their roars.

For some time now, he no longer believed that his life was continuing in a brilliant and glorious direction. He was traveling between cities of the world, meeting bankers and brokers of global fame in international money centers, negotiating and bargaining on the international level with financial organizations, but constantly feeling restless. Being entertained in private clubs by Wall Street brokers and being invited to the best restaurants in the world were things many people would envy. But after some time they made one feel like a machine. Everything was empty, absolutely empty!

In time, one got fed up even with sleeping in super luxurious hotels with second-rate Playboy girls presented as hush-up compensation for dirty deals. As one secretly accumulated anger and anxiety and fear of getting stuck in the mud or falling into an abyss in a work environment geared for continuous rise, one realized that the crown placed on one's head was actually made of barbed wire. The anticipation of something more beautiful and more meaningful became a heavier burden with time.

One could not hide his unhappiness from himself forever. When he looked back, the exchange boards looked ugly, and all those tensions and shocks seemed unbearable. So did economic crises – sudden or long expected – and conceited men behind wicked money games…

He was going to give up. There was nothing to be afraid of. He wasn't going to be a wretched man who had sold his soul;

someone who couldn't go back although he was squirming helplessly.

When he was adjusting his belt, he realized that his hands were shaking. Perhaps he had been waiting for a small spark which would bring him back to his normal self. He had not analyzed the word transformation either from the angle of meaning or of necessity. He certainly hadn't given it much thought, it was only an interpretation.

To be honest, he hadn't shown the dexterity – or perhaps the strength – of saving himself from the muck at the beginning. However, he was in a position to do so now. Certainly he wouldn't be able to free himself from the albatross around his neck all at once. He had to have a plan. He had to calculate his deeds and withdraw carefully, without haste.

So that was how it was going to be. His victories would suddenly come to an end at an unexpected moment; victories he had won trying to stand on his feet in spite of knowing all along that every single road was crooked.

Two...four...one...last call...

No, his transformation had started quite some time ago. That moment when he froze and asked himself who he was after stamping his feet and shouting those strange words, was only a very powerful moment of discovery and it was the end.

The end of a period.

The metallic sound of the loudspeakers was echoing in his ears. Two...four...one...last call...

This was the end. He wouldn't have to hurry from now on. He hadn't felt so peaceful in a long time. He could still smell the bad odor that had settled on him but it would soon pass. Very soon...

8

Melike walked toward the entrance of the gallery, doing her best not to show the guests her growing discontent. Standing there in the gallery were young girls who had come in just for fun while passing by and they were hiding their curiosity behind serious, courteous masks; there were overdressed women with exaggerated makeup; a few badly dressed middle-aged couples; people on the gallery list who were regular customers of free drinks, an old collector, and some shrewd jewelry copy-cats. It looked like it would be an unexceptional opening.

The artifacts were exhibited in glass-covered modules scattered around the small room where the dominating color was white. Gold and silver jewelry of various sizes looked attractive under the bright lights. There were mythological figures, transformed plant shapes, abstract fish-bug shapes, pins, necklaces and bracelets with precious stones.

The sweet scent of lilies – sent for the opening of the exhibition – had spread all over the room. In one corner, a trio of violinists was playing chamber music. As it was Melike who was paying for the opening, there were plenty of drinks and titbits to eat. Her purpose was not so much to make money but to feel and to show off her pretension and her difference from the rest.

After trying on different things at length, she had decided on a long flowing black skirt and a narrow, saffron-colored silk shirt with buttons on one side of the neck in kimono-style.

She had tied her hair in a knot, and her swan-like neck showed itself in all its beauty.

For a while, she walked around talking to the people she knew and enquiring after their welfare. She answered people who were asking questions in the name of small talk. At about 7:30, she completely lost hope that the opening of her exhibition would be as she had imagined. It was dull, very dull!

Come on now, can't somebody come to cheer me up, to make me feel comfortable, she thought.

Her uncle was going to stop by, he had promised. He probably wouldn't come alone; perhaps Hayali would be courteous enough to come, too. It was her uncle's business who he would allow to spend his money or get hold of his property. The more she thought about it, the less interested she had become. She would be the last person to question Hayali.

Melike remembered Aysevim. She was her uncle's other inheritor. If she would hear what was going on, she would go crazy; only Aysevim could beat that man. No, it wouldn't at all be wise to bring in that witch at this point.

In the days following her talk with her uncle, Melike had thought about Hayali a lot, trying to analyse her feelings objectively. The truth was that it was always difficult for her to be alone with him in the same room and to start a dialogue easily. She always became extremely tense and didn't know why.

What was even stranger was that his homosexuality affected her immensely. She had finally been able to confess this to herself. This was a complex feeling, it was as if she wanted to acknowledge that difference and at the same time, penetrate into Hayali's mystery to remove that difference. Perhaps what she really wanted was to see her own image in Hayali's eyes and make a headstrong move to remove the sexual similarity. This way, she thought, she would be able to dig into his shield.

She remembered Hayali's arrogant eyes, his frustrating self-confidence and his mocking jokes. She got angry. No, that fox would not fall into that trap. Furthermore, there was no way of giving him a lesson as long as her uncle was between them.

Come on, let someone interesting come!

She took a glass of white wine from the tray held to her. She was wearing a ring with a large sapphire stone on her finger; it was one of her own creations. A white-faced girl with dimples in her plump cheeks bent over and examined the ring. Melike smiled and turned her eyes toward the entrance.

The week before, she had thanked Volkan with a short sms for the saffron yellow lilies. It was obvious that he had sent them to entice her and she couldn't say that she hadn't been pleased. It was a beautiful bouquet, almost the embodiment of the interest he felt for her. His driver had brought it to the shop. That elderly, courteous man seemed to be a faultless helper and his thoughtful eyes faithfully watched where his master was looking.

The young man had responded immediately, saying that he might drop in at the shop on Saturday. And he had come. It was a pleasant visit. He seemed to be a careful, gentle homebody. He looked thinner, and he was wearing fine casual clothes. It was obvious that he had made an effort.

Melike had shown him her studio upstairs; they had exchanged glances several times and had had tea together. Unfortunately the shop was never free of clients that day, and the shop assistant was a curious girl. They had talked about general subjects in a choppy conversation. Melike had decided that the man could be a good friend, a good husband and even a father but she had struck off his possibility of being an ardent lover. An intuition, naturally it was only an intuition.

"Volkan Kuman," she repeated silently. She wished he would turn up that evening. Yes, a little excitement wouldn't be bad in this stillness. If he did come, she was going to be very nice to him and look at him carefully once again. She would then decide whether he was worth seducing or not. Actually she had felt energetic and strangely happy since the day they had met. Perhaps it was the joy of having finally met the right candidate for fatherhood, who knows? A lovely, intelligent child from an intelligent father, why not?

She saw her uncle come in – swaggering a little – with I ık at his side. They kissed. Hayali had an important appointment with someone. Good thing! Melike didn't have the patience to watch him play the leading role to draw attention to him, not for even half an hour, not this evening! If only this girl hadn't come either. She was wearing tights with horizontal black and white stripes under her very short, torn denim skirt with threads hanging from the hem, and a long, black admiral's coat with shiny metal buttons and epaulets, an outfit fluctuating between the ridiculous and the absurd. Well, maybe it wasn't really so bad. It fitted teenage fashion standards.

She looked at I ık with a touch of jealousy. Why did her uncle have to drag this girl with him everywhere? Was it to show that she wasn't his girlfriend but his secretary and a close friend, or was it because he needed to be pampered? But how? The girl looked so serious that she gave one the impression of ill omen. She had no makeup; her face was expressionless and stone-like enough to show that she had come out of obligation. As long as she hasn't come to kill me, thought Melike. She was still young, very young. She hadn't yet learned that it was hypocrisy which made people civilized.

"I won't stay long," said Niyazi Bey, putting his arm on Melike's shoulder. "You know I don't come to openings. How is it going?"

"I was excited for no reason. There isn't much action," said Melike.

"It's good to exhibit, it is necessary. What's more, you look very beautiful tonight." He laughed as if he wanted to give her confidence and his approval. They went through the exhibition together.

"My congratulations, I like your show," I ık managed to say. "I would like to buy this bracelet."

"I will reserve it if it isn't sold in the meantime," said Melike.

Niyazi Bey put on his glasses to have a closer look at the silver bracelet which looked like three intertwined snakes and was decorated with colored stones.

"It really is beautiful," he said. "Don't sell it, we've bought it, all right, my dear?"

For a moment, Melike became angry but she got over it quickly.

"Of course Uncle, it's yours."

She thought her uncle's love for this girl was understandable because of his nature. She was the personification of an undeniable beauty both feminine and masculine, and of lust which was not intimidating. The double-sidedness of this child whom he had taken into his protection was the ideal figure of human history and mythology. Sensitivity, delicacy and hidden desire were feminine traits, whereas aesthetics, nobility and courage were masculine, and the characteristics which symbolized the union of these two were divine. One had to avoid underestimating this little girl!

Melike tried to imagine her uncle's serious air which formed a contrast with the youth and the slimness of the girl, his protective fatherly manner and the sexual power of the other one over someone like him. She quickly put Hayali next to them, and she felt a jolt. This was a relationship with deeper roots than she had initially thought.

"Seeing the whole of your work like this is most exciting, Eda. You are a true amateur, and I mean that as a compliment. These are daring designs. You have a lot of taste and this strengthens your ability to feel."

"Thank you, Uncle."

"Now with your permission, we better go."

"Won't you have a drink?"

"No, dear. We'll be out and our night is long."

As Melike was seeing her uncle off, she caught a glimpse of Volkan's driver in a dark blue sedan stopping in front of the shop. Unexpectedly her heart jumped. She watched as Volkan got out of the car. He was attractive, very attractive! She relaxed. With a fresh wave of excitement, she reached out to her uncle and gave him a kiss on the cheek. She had cheered up as she called out playfully to his bodyguards, "Protect him well!" Then she stepped aside to make way and held out her hand to Volkan.

"I'm happy you came. I didn't think you'd be able to make it."

"I almost didn't, Eda." He looked at her for a moment as if enchanted. They smiled at each other. He was wearing a light yellow shirt under a dark brown herringbone suit. Melike smelt a whiff of the light, distant scent of the man. A familiar yearning woke up inside her. Yes, everything was as it had been before. The same scent, the same optimistic amber eyes that gave one a sad feeling of loneliness. Meetings, excitements...moments that came back within a perpetual chain of repetitions. Those illogical, fiery joys...

It was almost nine o'clock; very few people were left inside.

They walked toward the module in the centre. They were both a little awkward. Excited too, as though they didn't know where to begin...they looked silently at the pieces under the glass for a while. It was as if they were afraid of saying the wrong thing or searching for a logical base to their words. Melike felt as if she had predicted this situation that seemed totally coincidental, and that she was the one to direct it.

"It's lovely to hear your voice, to be with you," Volkan said. "I'm not boring you, am I?"

"No, what makes you think so!" said Melike with feigned surprise.

"I don't know. I haven't been sure of anything for some time..."

He took another drink. Volkan...he saw his face reflected in the glass case, an indistinct image...his eyes caught Melike's ring unconsciously. He realized she was looking at him, waiting for him to finish his words.

"It was a difficult day," he said. "Too agitated...I had to escape from a meeting to come to you. It looked like it would continue until morning."

For an instant, Melike stopped at his expression "to you," and she looked at him with curiosity, but his eyes were elsewhere. The roots of his hair were wet, he looked shaken, his face was pale. Suddenly she felt a deep compassion for him, a strong desire to protect the young man from his problems unknown to her.

"Did you lose some weight? You look thinner," she said.

"I have a strange life," answered Volkan. He paused. "I am beginning to find it difficult to carry the duties and the responsibilities. I don't have a day to myself; monotony, schizophrenia; there's nothing else." He paused again. "It's not something I can explain in passing."

"If you wish to share..."

"Yes, I think I specially need a sister at this point."

"I understand," said Melike and smiled. Actually it wasn't understandable at all. A sister?

"Will you have dinner with me tonight? Are you available?" asked Volkan suddenly, looking into Melike's eyes. They were imploring words.

"All right," said Melike, nodding her head as if she was faced with a helpless situation and added, "It might take about half an hour to get out of here. Is nine-thirty all right?"

"Sure. Thank you. I'll make a reservation."

They silently went through the exhibition. Volkan had calmed down, he had relaxed. He praised Melike's imagination and craftsmanship. Was there a danger of copying and even industrializing these beautiful pieces?

"Of course there is," said Melike. "Some of the people you see in this room are here for that purpose. Sooner or later there will be those who will come to take photographs, too. But when you think about it, even works of art which are protected in museums are open to such dangers. All the same, the copies which everybody can buy do not decrease the value of the originals."

"You are right, the most valuable thing is being one's self," said Volkan.

They left at 9.30.

"Shall we walk? Where we're going is not far from here," said Volkan.

They walked along the Bebek coast; it was a five-minute walk to the restaurant. Volkan showed Melike his home, the penthouse where he lived, which was along the way. They passed through the night which was dense with the humidity of the sea and through the lights of multicolored neon signs. Men at restaurant doors were calling out to them inviting them in. The air was clean, relaxing.

Volkan turned and looked at her. Her elegance, unpainted lips and makeup which accentuated the beauty of her eyes made the young woman very charming. Her reserved docility awakened a feeling of friendship and the longing for an amicable chat rather than a feeling of desire.

"I'm fed up with everything," he said. "I've even started to hate people because of my work."

"That's sad. What are you planning to do?"

"Going on a safari in Africa to get new strength."

Melike laughed.

"Will you come with me?"

Melike thought of the images of Africa she had seen in documentaries. She remembered the lions proudly displaying their power. The big cats and the jackals hunting, the wide open spaces…

"I'm very serious. Would you come?"

"I'm thinking, please let me think. This is the most daring and the most interesting proposition I have received from a man I hardly know!" She laughed again. Was this serious? No way, just some light-hearted chatter, she thought. Well, she too could go along with the joke.

"Why not, let's go! Yes, I'm coming. When?" She looked at Volkan with a challenging expression on her face. One or two locks of hair had come loose and fallen onto her face. Her eyes were glistening as though filled with water, but they were inflexible.

"Fine. I'll arrange everything and I'll let you know," said Volkan. Although he normally liked light-colored eyes, he had never seen such beautiful black eyes before, he thought.

When they sat down facing each other at a table on the second floor overlooking the road, they felt they had already known each other for a long time. They were content being together under the dim lights, smelling the odor of the sea, hearing the traffic's hum coming through the open window. Melike remembered the word "sister." Or had she met this man at the wrong time? Sister? She thought of their previous meetings. No, he had been very different. Volkan had to be in a depressed mood, temporary, special to tonight.

Actually, it wasn't so bad to be a sister. Until now, whenever there was a man next to her, the story always ended in bed. And after that…emptiness. Although, this kind of closeness would keep one away from all the pitiful circumstances of being in love.

"Yes, my brother Volkan, I'm listening to you…" she said laughing. They clinked their wine glasses.

Volkan talked about the issues that had been suffocating him during the last few months, he was feeling like a wolf in a pack of wolves. He didn't want to bore Eda with the details but the country was being dragged toward dark spaces by blind, corrupt people. He did not want to be a part of all that or to serve as an instrument. He had come to know that one couldn't be happy with money, or by arriving at the position he had dreamt about while he was young. He was the son of an honest middle class civil servant. His parents were idealistic people. He had to go back to his origins, naturally as much as he could.

"I'm sorry," said Melike. "I don't want to be rude but nowadays it is a great luxury for people to be able to think about giving up their job. I understand that you have guaranteed your future. Think about those who haven't been able to do that in spite of struggling for years; those who have to keep a job they don't like although they have never climbed higher than the lowest rungs of the ladder."

"I sometimes wish I were one of them. Then I would be closer to life."

"I don't think so, you wouldn't want to be so helpless. You would be very unhappy."

"Yes, but why can't I be the master of my own life even though I have all the means?"

"You can. Today, the most important asset is money. Most people think 'I'll wash my hands once I hit the jackpot,' but they can't get out once they are in. A thief also says 'I'll rob a bank, secure my future and I won't do it again,' but once he does it, he can't give up."

Volkan was dumbstruck. He looked at her as if he were insulted; he perspired heavily.

"I'm very sorry you interpret it that way," he said, "whereas I needed to be understood."

"I don't think I have completely understood your problem," said Melike.

There was a short silence.

"Actually I don't clearly know it myself. My head is full of questions. I don't know how I will explain myself; how I will manage to understand myself first of all, and then make someone else understand."

"Try it, I'm listening."

"I mean I don't want to stay in neutral territory which everybody defines as happiness. I am on one side, and there is a terrible drift on the other side which blunts my senses. Look, I'm a mathematician and I love mathematics. It's pure and it's clear, but I think I've made a mistake somewhere."

"When you think about leaving your work, don't decide with your heart; you may make a mistake," said Melike.

"I never consider it a failure to renounce those things that I can easily do without. I'm not afraid of searching again, finding, losing and even not finding. Because in spite of everything, I know that my soul is profound and pure."

"Rilke says that everybody is born with a letter inside, and that only those who are candid with themselves can read it," said Melike. She lit a cigarette, blew the smoke into the air and assumed her listening position.

"What a wonderful statement. I think I want to read that letter now," said Volkan excitedly. "Sometimes I feel like a character in a novel, someone who is not real, someone fictitious. The same goes for my social environment. I am tired of short-lived, shallow relationships. I will need to learn everything all over again, but I need the help of something or someone who will give me a hand, who will guide me."

Melike looked at him with sadness; no, she looked at him with downright pain. She couldn't be the right woman for this man, because she herself was rootless. An ordinary flag which fluttered with every gust of wind…she wasn't at all cut out for the constructive role this man expected from a stable woman. Any closeness between them could not advance along this line.

Furthermore, she couldn't tell him that she too was in a similar environment. The only difference between them was that Melike was watching things from a higher position compared to Volkan. Once again she felt the incomprehensible sweet agony of the impossible.

The fish they had ordered arrived. They waited till the waiter left.

"I think you are exaggerating the problems, my brother," said Melike. "There is no need for you to be so hopeless."

"Believe me, I'm not exaggerating."

"According to what you say, you have been living in some kind of an emotional deception. Many people live that way, many more than you would think. Actually, you can't call it deception; it's a form of hiding, an escape, even an attempt to stand on one's own feet. In a way, I live like that, too. What's more, this way of living is spreading fast. That's how things work and we perceive this as the normal way; we join the crowd quite consciously. I think this is an inevitable collapse, a situation special to periods of disintegration. What seems strange to me is that those who cannot keep up are questioning this development. The ones who are involved in one way or another don't seem to mind. How do you …"

"I care, because the circle is getting smaller and smaller," interrupted Volkan. "I say this as an insider, basing it on reality and not on the fears of the generation before us. I refer to concrete facts. Should I call you Eda or Melike?"

"You can do both, whichever is easier for you. You know, I'm impressed with your approach or perhaps your explanation. Someone I loved ten years ago carried similar anxieties but nothing changed. The milieu of disintegration and chaos continues to exist with newly added lies all the time."

"Precisely. I've understood that while some people use hollow words and concepts for playing the role of disciples of freedom, democracy and the ideal model of society, others get away with the loot. Perhaps that was a bit crude. Let me put it this way, while some people lay idle, or even play unintentional accomplices, others display disintegration on an international scale. There is no place here for the human element. This new chaos will try hard to get through."

"I know this idea and I'm not as pessimistic as you are. This is a stupid game. Those who are really disintegrating are the ones who think they rule the world. The Roman Empire also ruled the world but it finally disappeared in unsubstantial vulgarity."

"I would have liked to see that. All right, that's enough of politics. I've probably bored you."

"No, but I want to ask you something else. Although this is the first time you and I have a proper conversation, you didn't hesitate to reveal your world and yourself as you are. Why?"

"I don't know. Perhaps I wish to show you that I am aware and open. But naturally it can't be only that. I haven't talked about such matters to anyone, especially to an attractive woman like you, for a long time. Perhaps that's why I'm uncomfortable with everything except the truth."

"From what I understand, you trust truth too much. You should think twice about that."

"I've observed that you are not an easy person. You are challenging me."

"No. Since a very long time I haven't met someone like you, a sincere but earnest man. To tell you the truth, I'm a bit astonished," said Melike. "I must have missed refinement." She bit her lip. She put out her hand and squeezed Volkan's with a quick, soft touch, then drew her it back. They looked at each other unreservedly.

They ate their fish in silence as Turkish music played softly.

"Now it's your turn to talk. Tell me about yourself," said Volkan.

"What do you want to know?"

"I would like to know everything about you."

"If I can be your sister, you will learn in time. One can't get near the truth when talking or making comments about oneself. This is quite acceptable, even necessary."

"You said sister? No, I don't think I can suffice with that, Eda."

Melike raised her eyes and looked directly at Volkan.

"So what are you going to do? Do you think we shall stay perched on the line like two loving sister and brother doves?"

"We can make wars of emotions," said Volkan. "That is the period we are in now. This is a kind of war unknown to those without emotions, those who have lost their feelings, and to the thick-skinned. Actually we have already started the war and I like it very much."

"Be careful, you may become a martyr!"

"So be it! With pleasure."

They exchanged a long look, as if enchanted by each other. Melike was feeling the thrilling excitement of the desire to fight a powerful adversary. This was what she had been anticipating for some time, what she had secretly been dreaming of. Winning or losing was not important in this battle; she only missed and wanted the pleasure of combat.

Volkan lowered his eyes, letting the challenge in Melike's eyes fill his soul. He felt an unpredictable desire to bite her long and elegant neck, and to make her blood run. His body was burning in flames. The passion which he had imprisoned inside him for such a long time had freed itself of its chains.

When they left the restaurant, they walked back along the coast to Bebek. They took Melike's car from the parking lot. She was going to the other side of town.

"You still have a chance to think about it, don't forget," she said to Volkan before stepping on the gas pedal. "War after war may tire you."

"What every man waits for is to be finally defeated and forgiven by a woman," said Volkan.

He felt as sturdy as reinforced glass, come what may.

9

Eylem went to work in a worried state of mind on Thursday morning. She felt cold inside even though it was a warm day. The sun and the sky shone brightly outside the windows that were always shut. She talked reluctantly, wearily with a few customers on the phone. It was the end of the month. She was to learn about her fate that day.

The young man who sat at the table opposite – she hadn't been able to learn his name yet – lifted his head and looked at Eylem; he pointed in a somewhat rude manner, to the ringing telephone on her desk.

"Yes, I hear it. Do I have to answer it immediately?" Eylem scolded him.

The man took a long look at her with condescending eyes and slowly shook his head and put his hand to his ear and removed it as though saying "are you deaf."

"No, I'm not deaf but you seem to be!" said Eylem. All heads, frightened eyes turned to where Eylem and the man were. Finally someone had exploded! The fun was beginning. But no. The man lowered his head and stared at the screen. Eylem looked at the phone which had stopped ringing. The chief appeared at the door and withdrew. Dammit! That was not necessary. She didn't answer the telephone right away, she would let it ring four or five times; she couldn't work because of all the incoming calls.

There were about twenty young men and women in the partitioned office. She raised herself a little and looked around. These idiots talked barely audible with low voices, even to the customers on the phone. They also closed one ear with their fingers not to hear the loud hum of the printer in the office. In the next cubicle, there was an arrogant man with a shaven head and a face the color of sawdust. Next to him, there was a girl whose small head looked bigger with her red, puffy hair, and a little further, a tiny man with beady eyes who looked as if he had trouble breathing. Some were in this cage for ten years, others five or three. They were tense or angry, feeling that they were condemned to stay behind those desks no matter how hard they worked. The ambitious ones must have stopped caring or maybe they were tranquilized consciously or unconsciously. Their common trait was their hopelessness.

What was their life like, she wondered. Without doubt, some ran home as soon as they left this place, others were furious at their children who were born before their sperms dried out and some went to take alcohol or to let their troubles disappear in other ways. There might also be some psychopaths who made murder plans, all kinds of perverts ...What a waste, thought Eylem. They could very well do other things. For instance, they could sell lemon or simits in the market, play the mouth harmonica in the metro, start working as a barman, sell soccer tickets at the black-market, or something like that.

What did they think about? Their holidays? The seashores where they would oil their bodies and doze in the sun? The instalments of the car or the credit card payments? Were they happy? What was their concept of happiness? Didn't they feel the need to express in words what they considered right? Then why did they settle for only body language? Actually there was no need for them to obey rules so strictly. If they wanted they could easily destroy the established order altogether. That was nothing to be so afraid of. This much pressure was classified as abuse, and these people became more and more intimidated instead of revolting. Poor things ...not only them, of course ...there were millions of people in the world who couldn't talk freely and didn't have the chance to express their thoughts and feelings.

Toward the end of the day, she was called by the section chief. Dora Waller was a woman in her thirties. She had an unsympathetic long face and thin lips with a malicious expression. She offered Eylem a seat. A secret smile flashed over her face for an instant, and then she decided on an expression of artificial sorrow. After dallying for a while pretending to study the file in front of her, she raised her head and looked at Eylem. Her limpid blue eyes seemed to be the only innocent aspect of her. Perhaps she had hardened herself on purpose in order to survive, to manage and to succeed in business. Eylem smiled cautiously.

"I'm sorry, but we won't be able to work with you, Mutena Hanım."

There was a long silence. What the woman had said was merciless but definite.

"Why not?" asked Eylem, as if making a futile request.

"Your experience is insufficient. We have observed that you make a lot of errors in the documents."

"I always take great care..."

"Your job demands more attention and flexibility. And most importantly, your colleagues have said that you are not suitable for teamwork. You may go to the personnel department and collect your accumulated pay. Your job is terminated as of tomorrow." She put down the pen in her hand on the desk.

"Flexibility?" said Eylem in a somewhat condescending tone.

"I'm very sorry. Discussing won't change the result."

A simple statement. A clear and undisputable decision. There was nothing more to be said. Eylem got up with the dignified silence of the loser. Then she murmured something as if to hear the calmness of her own voice,

"Yes, good bye, Ms. Waller."

"Good luck."

Good luck...how kind!

As she walked in the corridor, she felt pain spreading through her whole body. She stopped at the fixed window and looked down wondering if everything outside had burned down and shattered. No, everything was in place, was impervious and cruel, everything was the same. The Bosphorus, the bridge, the passing cars…pretty *yalı*s and houses amidst greenery…the coastal road, the boats, a tanker…

She wanted to cry. Her future had once again been struck by a blow. Not suitable for teamwork? Yes, but she wasn't offered an environment where she could know her colleagues and start collaborating. They hadn't yet given her time to understand how things worked, what the communication possibilities were. She knew that she was among the most methodical and diligent people in working life. She was realistic and cool-headed. Perhaps she lacked creativity; that she reserved for writing. Doubtlessly, her biggest fault was that she had principles, a definite personality and experience that gave her an aura of arrogance. People felt this and became pitilessly jealous. She simply couldn't manage to act like a half-witted, docile boot-licker.

After taking her money and leaving the workplace, she went to a park on the shore. She sat on a bench and looked at the sea for a long time. When she would find a new job and start working again, she had to follow a different path. Even if her feelings were hurt she would overlook the things which were not revealed to her; she would believe everything she was told and act as one of the flock. She would be aware of everything at night but live as a complete idiot during the day. Like someone cheerful, capable, carefree…

The seagulls were drawing circles above the sea; the long white streak left by an unseen airplane had cut the sky like a knife. Eylem heard the humming life of the city flow behind her, throbbing like a pulse. Life was continuing, but not ahead, not toward the future; it was accumulating, piling up where it was. She suddenly remembered the rule: *something whose existence is not imagined cannot exist.*

She stayed at home for a week, spending almost all of her time at her computer. She browsed the head-hunting web sites and left her CV in all of them. She went through ads for human resources and business ads and made applications. There weren't too many suitable jobs for her. The effects of the economic crisis were still continuing. Thousands of people were jobless and the wages were very low. If she was careful, she would be able to manage for two or three weeks at the most. She was also going to lean on her credit card a little, but the amount due was already quite substantial.

An ad had drawn her attention; she reread it and noted the telephone number.

Looking for women employees with university degrees!
Cultured LADIES between 18–25, successful in human
 relations.
If you work with us, you may make 500–750 NewTL
 per séance.
(Those who are interested may call the telephones
 below:
Tel: 0212 3...)

They were probably looking for natural faces to use in television ads or as models for third-rate textile firms. Yes, but why should culture be necessary for such jobs? They probably included fashion or advertising within the definition of culture to define the job to some extent. There were lots of girls who put aside their university diplomas and were making good money in jobs like these. Eylem would like to try but she didn't find herself beautiful; what was more, at 168 cm she was not tall enough.

She thought a while; there was no mention of height in the ad. What's more, professional makeup experts could make the most ordinary faces look beautiful and photogenic. The important thing was to have a bone structure which looked good under the lights, and she was lucky in that aspect.

She stood in front of the mirror and examined her face objectively as if it belonged to someone else. She had a nice, impressive face. It could look much better under the right light. She decided to call and find out what the job was.

She visited the web site where she had written on "the future" under the pen name "Yellowspot." There were a few more replies to her article. Someone had sent a bad poem. Someone else was asking her permission to use it in her/his thesis. Somebody with the pen name Saffron Yellow had sent her an interesting letter. Saffron Yellow wanted to establish direct contact.

Yellowspot,

On some nights, a person stands at a dark seashore, looks at the endless sky and feels happy to see that all the familiar stars are in their usual place. Then suddenly, he notices that another star farther away, not as bright or as large as the others, is winking at him. He feels curious, is this a meteor?

I'm curious about you in the same way. I was impressed by your courage and by what you wrote. I felt that it was I who had called you. I'm in another story, and it is difficult to explain how one situation can include another entirely different situation.

It has been a long time since I heard a voice like yours. Perhaps I had temporarily lost my hearing. I have finally met in these surroundings someone with a clear spirit. I don't want to pass you by.

I would like to write to you individually.

Man or woman, whoever it was, seemed to be calling from another planet. S/he seemed to be somewhat haughty and had a feminine style. The fact that the pen name started with yellow had to be a reference. She used her own pen name referring to the sensitive spot which provided the eye's focus. And what was the meaning of her/his name? Saffron yellow was an agreeable color. It symbolized the sun, wealth, the awakening of the earth and fertility, it fitted the concept of illumination, it indicated renovation, attraction, joy and harmony, in short, warmth and fertility. It was most probable that the person who wrote to her was a woman. She wanted to express her loneliness and at the same time her joy of life.

There was no need to reply immediately. She was going to write privately in a few days. Of all the answers that had come, hers/his was the one she liked best. She felt a slight joy. Yes, she was going to enjoy corresponding with this person. Who could s/he be? To be curious about each other, to prolong the curiosity for a long time without the risk of disappointment...that alone was beautiful. To extend your hand in peace to someone you don't know felt good. To wait in a state of happy consciousness in the place where the waters of dreamland mingled...

I'm in another story...another story. Nice. Perhaps entering some other story would change her own.

Before going to bed, she looked at the mirror again. There was a small, sad void in the place of her face this time. It was as if her image had become foggy to protect her from the harms that could be inflicted on her by the world. Harm? Nobody could harm her. What did she need other than a blanket in order to stay alive? Maybe it would be better to give up everything she was attached to. Then she would be rid of this painful struggle she was fed up with. She would be able to live without having to open her palm and cringe, without shuddering, without getting wounded.

She looked around her. This ramshackle furniture, these rickety cotton curtains, the dim light bulb hanging from the ceiling at the end of a cord, bare walls which seemed so repulsive...in such a place, it was very easy for a person to lose her control over things that made one a human being. In that case, what did she own that she would be sorry to lose? It wasn't so difficult to see something that would feed the intellect, to feel pain and to touch life. But if there was a future, it had to be a future worth this self-sacrifice.

She drank a glass of milk. I wish I had a bottle of wine, she thought. She had learned to drink wine with Seyit. Sometimes her childhood fears recurred, and she jumped off – without any fear – the red hot cliffs where demons sauntered, falling into the depths of hell. Her crime sheet was closed. The angels of sin no longer had their eyes upon her for some time now; just like the angels of mercy and benevolence...the thick rope which connected her to God had not completely broken, but that part of her consciousness no longer believed in forbidden tales, and it defied those who placed obstacles between her God and herself. She now spoke to Him without knowing – and without caring much – if He heard her or not. With her own voice...

Not to concern oneself with being, only to be...this was the important thing, this was where she stood.

She puffed up her pillow and went to bed. She abandoned herself to the soft embrace of her quilt. The nights were getting cooler. Soon she would have to heat her place. A butane stove was the easiest solution. How much would it cost, she wondered. She remembered the ad. Five hundred liras for one séance...In any case, they wouldn't find her interesting, so they wouldn't give her seven hundred fifty. Never mind, five hundred was very good, too. Naturally, first she had to find out what these séances were about.

The next day, she called the phone number given in the ad. She made an appointment and got the address. Friday at fifteen hundred hours...the day after tomorrow...the place she was to go to was on the second floor of an apartment building with a clothes shop on the ground floor in Maçka.

When she put down the receiver, she felt excitement mixed with impatience. She had woken up with a panicky feeling that morning. The inside of her head felt soft and sticky like a bread pan full of dough. What was she to wear to look acceptable? She ran to the cupboard, she slid the hangers one by one trying to find something appropriate. Shapeless, cheap clothes...she hadn't been able to buy herself anything new for a year.

First, she thought of wearing trousers, and then she decided a skirt would look nicer. She had lovely legs, she should show them off instead of hiding them. On the other hand, she shouldn't look pretentious, either. She was going to do all she could to take this job. Wasn't it ordinary people who played in commercial films? Were the girls used in the promotion of detergents, diapers, sanitary pads and food any better than she? She put aside a black skirt and a bone-colored tight body with a square neck. The heels of her shoes were frayed; she had to have them repaired.

That night, she plucked her eyebrows, removed unwanted hair from her body, took care of her skin and made herself a honey-and-lemon mask.

On Thursday morning, she prepared to go to the hairdresser on the main road. Should she have them bleach a few strands? No, it was better to stay natural. When she walked along the street and reached the road, she remembered Seydiye saying "One door closes, another opens." She looked at the sky; gray cloudy world, she thought.

Until now, she had always lost when many girls her age were constantly pocketing things. She silently thanked the people who passed by without bumping into her and the cars that drove along without running her over in the crowded street. Every step she took was awkward. She felt weightless, as if about to fall off a cliff; she felt that she could be very clumsy today.

She thought about the models who put on airs with their voluptuous presence or their suspicious absence, drawing everybody's attention. Surely she had to gain some experience, look more lively, more charming and attractive. She had turned into a sulky, cold and dull person after all that she had been through.

She stopped in front of a shop window. That rose-colored blouse didn't look bad; but no, she wasn't going to dress from slummy shops anymore. Yes, but…what if they didn't like her? She was rushing into daydreams. It was too soon to be hopeful, much too soon!

She left her black high-heeled shoes to be repaired. She had neglected her hair since weeks; the tips were all frayed. She entered the hairdresser's, settled into a chair and looked at herself. The lights on both sides of the mirror made her face look a little pale and drawn. It's from worry, she thought. After all, she had had a bad week.

"Your hair tips are frayed, shall we cut a little?" asked the hairdresser's assistant.

"Do whatever is necessary. Let's shorten it a bit. I'd like a natural hairdo. I also want a manicure."

She stopped by her sister's before going back. She wasn't home; she hadn't come back from work yet.

She spent the evening in preparation. After watching a film on television, she browsed the internet aimlessly late at night. She reread the reply Saffron Yellow had sent her. She was going to answer calmly, in a roundabout way. She started a few times, each time differently, then she wrote this:

> *Saffron Yellow,*
>
> *It is very nice of you to wish to know me and to correspond with me individually. Your message was very kind and your words refreshed my spirit.*
>
> *Are you sure it's a good idea to correspond? For my part, I have some doubts. I don't know if I need a stranger.*
>
> *I'm not as brave as you think. It is very difficult not to feel helpless while time flows, changing all the time, continents slide and stars are born and die. I'm hopeless, because in this pitiless world where billions of objects and human beings are continuously marketed, I may not be able to accomplish anything other than ceasing to exist.*
>
> *A cold, rainy evening. I don't have a stove, I'm a little cold. On evenings like this, I miss not being born with a smile on my face and lately I see things that I wasn't able to see clearly before.*
>
> *If I tried to tell you about my life, it would be an ordinary chain of unfortunate incidents to be condescended. But still, I know that if there is a listener, even the most ordinary person can enchant him with his/her secrets. That is why I'm using the instrument on which I call out to you as a writing board and as I'm writing, I'm thinking that life is not an adventure but a silly parody.*
>
> *I should tell you about myself in order to stop you from making assumptions about me. I'm a stranger in town. I have no job, no money, no address book. There are no regrets in my past, but all the same, it is tiring to remember.*

If you are a woman, unfortunately so am I. If you are a man, keep it in mind that I'm not writing to you to have fun or to open the door to virtual lovemaking. Love acquires a meaning only within the perspective of the past and the future. It turns into a strong, integrating force and helps us find our way. Everything else is a naked alienation.

We might be able to communicate if you give up your somewhat haughty manner.

Eylem

The next morning she woke up very early. Her dreams had been complicated and dark that night but she didn't remember any of them. All the same, they had left in her a blind fear, a groundless pessimism. She looked at the mirror while brushing her teeth. Her skin was as smooth and luminous as that of a baby. It had been nourished with deep cleansing and cares, had become silky.

Outside, a docile sun was shining as it sprinkled soft shadows on the pale autumn weather. Feeling cold on such a beautiful day reminded Eylem once again that she had to heat the house. She put on a thick sweater and quickly had breakfast. She hadn't liked her hair the day before. It was too exaggerated so she combed it again. She changed the color of her nail polish to a natural one, taking off the dark burgundy which had been put on the day before. I still crave for certain things like a peasant, she thought. Luckily, she sobered up quickly.

She had never paid much attention to her beauty before. Perhaps she hadn't felt the need because she had never loved anyone. With pointless pride and fear, she had hidden the beautiful parts of her inner world and her nature. Perhaps the failures in her professional life were due to this. Her lethargic timidity, her dullness, her indifferent manner must have repelled the people she worked with.

She now had to change in order to pay the price of her failure. She was forced to bring out her secret femininity. The femininity she had offered only Seyit until now. This was what counted; beauty was the most important thing in her social environment. The values she considered sacred at one time had lost their validity. She had to adapt herself to the world instead of lamenting over hopes come to nought or unrealized promises.

She got dressed and stood in front of the mirror and opened her legs slightly which looked even longer on high heels, taking the classical position of girls in photographs. She looked at herself and could not find any fault. On the contrary, she was glamorous. She looked so attractive that her body did not match the dullness in her soul.

Her heart beat fast and she felt a great fatigue. She threw off her shoes and collapsed on the side of the bed. No, she couldn't fool herself any longer. She was aware of what she was preparing for.

She wasn't that naive. Things could develop toward something she could no longer control. If everything that happened was trickery, never pure, if the bushes had become so tangled, she had to confess to herself what she was preparing for.

Her face contracted, she felt hopeless. Don't go, you know what will happen if you go, you mustn't go! No, you've been through so many disasters there is no reason to panic, come on, go, go and see!

She found the shop after some searching. It was on the ground floor of a whitewashed, five-storey apartment building. It was long and narrow with a simple window. There were everyday clothes for young people which were different and tasteful. On the side window, she read Modescort written in gold letters. She went in and asked for Jale Hanım. A young shop assistant made a call, then she led her to the elevator at the back of the shop telling her to go one floor up.

Eylem looked at herself in the dark mirror of the elevator cabin. To look younger she hadn't put on any makeup. She wished she were wearing some blush on her cheeks. As soon as she got out of the elevator, she found herself in a large room where one wall was covered with a mirror. It immediately struck her as a gorgeous place. She took a deep breath, put a smile on her lips and waited. Suddenly she remembered that she hadn't found herself a different name. God, how inexperienced of me! Eylem wouldn't do, no! Elvan? Yes, that's good.

A young, tall, fair-haired woman smiled at her and took her raincoat. She asked her to sit down and wait a little, then disappeared through a door. The only place to sit was an elegant Chinese couch with dark red upholstery. She softly perched on it. Light classical music was playing and the ceiling spots were illuminating the room softly. A few impressionist reproductions hung on the walls. There were bolts of multicolored silk or brocade spread on a table, their loose ends came down to the floor intertwining harmoniously. On the coffee table in front of the couch some dried flowers in a crystal ashtray caught the eye. A short evening dress in bright pink chiffon was put on a mannequin without legs or arms, next to a screen decorated with Japanese figures.

The floor was covered with a thick, beige carpet. It made her shoes seem cheap and very ugly to her. She looked at the only window in the room which was behind thick tulle curtains and she noticed the artificial eye, the camera under the thick plaster moulding along the side of the ceiling. She glanced around; there was another eye in the corner across the room. She was being watched!

At that moment the fair-haired woman reappeared and asked Eylem to follow her. They passed through what seemed to be an apartment entrance, went along a short, dim corridor and came to another door. The woman gave Eylem a large smile, as if wishing to encourage her, and opened the door.

It was a spacious, bright room which was flooded with light through the large windows overlooking the street. Eylem softly closed the door and waited. This room was decorated as neatly as the previous one. A woman with brown hair, large green eyes and thick lips, who seemed to be about thirty-five years old, was sitting behind the desk next to the window. Eylem saw her stand up and come toward her. She was slightly plump but tall and wearing black trousers hiding her weight and a cinnamon-colored jacket. Eylem observed a diamond brooch on the collar of her silk blouse. She was attractive.

"Let's sit there," she said, indicating the comfortable looking white couch on the other end of the large room. On the wide couch earth-colored cushions were piled up. A smoky mirror covered the entire wall on the opposite side. Once again, Eylem thought that she was being watched. Feeling the woman's eyes on her – and probably those of others – she walked toward her. They shook hands.

"I'm Jale," the woman said, as if waiting for an answer.

"Elvan Özgül…"

Eylem very erect, the woman sprawling, they sat at two ends of the couch.

"You seem timid, relax honey," said Jale. Eylem noticed that one of her eyes was blue and the other, green. She felt dizzy for a moment as if she had lost her feeling of depth.

"I came to apply for the job in your ad but I didn't quite understand what it was," she said. "That's why I may be a little tense."

"There is nothing to be tense about. We are a publicity and escort agency which gives service to upper level people. What was it that you studied?"

"Economics. If you should need my CV…"

"It's not necessary. You can tell me about it, darling. What have you done so far?"

Eylem felt levity, a slight vulgarity in the woman's general behavior, but she didn't let on.

"I worked in several small firms and then in a large American insurance company. I have been without a job for a while."

A dauntless pigeon was sitting on the windowsill and was cheerfully walking around with short, weak chirps. Eylem first looked at the bird then at the woman's face. Her slightly cynical, questioning gaze tightened Eylem's heart. For an instant she could feel it beating in her stomach.

"A business life from nine to five is difficult," said the woman.

"It's not because of that, there were problems that had nothing to do with me," explained Eylem. "Crises, getting cheated, jobs way below my abilities, having no hope for the future...Were I living in another country, I might have had a chance to advance. It is most disheartening to know that you are condemned to be stuck behind a computer in some office for years."

"Are you living with your family?"

"I'm alone. I just came to Istanbul, I was in Ankara before."

Jale got up and rang the bell on her desk. Soon a woman, apparently a house-help, appeared.

"Bring us some tea, Mercan." The woman respectfully bowed her head and went out.

Jale was looking at something on the computer screen. Her white forehead, framed by her tightly drawn-back hair, shone like a little snow-covered hill in the light that fell through the window. Eylem now found a chance to study her objectively. She seemed to be showing off authority. There was something about her that made one think of the manager of a brothel. An undeniable sensuousness was depicted into every line in her face. She raised her head and looked at Eylem with piercing eyes.

"There are many young girls who work with us," she said. "The sort that go ahead and do what they have set their minds on. They left their pasts behind and succeeded in building themselves new lives because to attain their liberty they risked stepping outside the conservative rules of our society."

"What kind of new lives?" asked Eylem, feeling bolder now.

"How old are you?"

"Twenty-three."

"Now, honey, you are not a child. Let's talk frankly. Here we give service to the crème de la crème, rich people, high society. These people need the company of young, beautiful and cultivated girls. They come to us for companions with whom they can travel, have fun or go to parties. These can be people of all ages and positions; businessmen, artists, sportsmen. They are all people we know and trust. I don't know if I have made myself clear."

"That is, friendship and intermediary services."

"Yes, that's right," said Jale with emphasis.

"I thought it would be something like modeling or acting in commercials," said Eylem, her voice sounded weighed down as if she was offended with the nature of the work offered.

"Do you have any experience in this business?" asked the woman. She sounded serious.

"No, but…"

"Yes, first of all, you have to form a substructure. Don't take that too lightly. Most of the girls and even the boys in show business have come into prominence by having someone important backing them. First, you have to be seen in nightclubs or bars with a famous television producer or people who are considered powerful in the market. You have to draw attention to yourself so that you can find a job. It's very difficult if you don't present yourself properly; nobody would even know about you. Naturally being with such people requires general culture as much as a good looks. How's your formation, honey?"

Courtesan, thought Eylem. She wasn't surprised because she had come more or less prepared. At least, the anxiety gathering in her formlessly for the last three days had finally taken shape. She felt she was being drawn into a dialogue developing in a direction she couldn't control.

"I read a lot and I write some poetry; it wouldn't be an exaggeration to say that I am well educated."

"Do you speak English?"

"Yes, quite well."

"Any other languages?"

"Some Arabic…"

"Well, it's you who has to decide. By us, the main thing is willingness," the woman interrupted. "We are very selective and we try to secure the most appropriate and best relationships for our staff. Would you believe it, they have all bought their homes, their cars, secured their savings. One of our girls is an actress in television serials; another one is a very popular commercial star. There are even those who got married. Naturally our customers are more interested in the ones who are seen on the screen. For instance, a man calls and says, "I want that beautiful girl who is in the milk commercial."

"I couldn't quite get what the working conditions are," said Eylem.

"There's nothing to understand. The addresses, the licence plate numbers, the distinct characteristics and the psychological states of our clients are registered with us. We are a new establishment and already have a prestigious place in the market. When a customer calls us, we study his data and give him services accordingly. The limits of the job are precisely stated beforehand. There is a certain tariff and the responsibility of obeying rules mutually. Naturally, developing personal relationships is imperative to enter the show world. This depends on your ability."

"Are the fees in the ad valid?"

"The amounts we have announced are minimum and for an hour. It changes according to the program and the period. We get 30 per cent."

Everything was open and clear.

"I would like to know about possible disadvantages," said Eylem with a thin voice.

"No disadvantages. Our boss is an ex-police officer. I used to be in the security business myself. Our network is large. There are some people we know amongst politicians, we know lawyers, doctors. Absolute security…health checkups are done regularly. We control each séance; we bring the girls there and back. How long you stay with us is up to you. One who has made enough savings can say 'That's it' and leave at the end of her contract."

Tea was served. Jape came back to the couch and sat down. What harm is there in trying, thought Eylem. Wasn't this what she had done with Seyit? Being ignorant about dirt was not enough to be protected from getting dirtied. To put it in a place that belonged to others, to try to keep it from coming close was of no avail. What's more, it was no use trusting in God and taking refuge in prayers. You couldn't survive with them.

"I understand," said Eylem.

"Now go to the secretariat next door and talk to the employee there. You have to fill in a form."

"I want to think until tomorrow."

"Of course. But you can still fill the form. You have to write your real name."

At that moment, Eylem could almost see a baby lying on its back in the dark, crying her heart out and thrashing about, waving her arms and legs as if asking for help. The only thing that pierced the darkness was Jale's porcelain-covered teeth.

"If you accept, you will go through a training period of three weeks. There will be people who will look after you. You will get into shape in our gym. We shall change your image and we will have you looking much more attractive and beautiful. We will take care of everything about you from A to Z. Where do you live?"

"In Kağıthane."

"You must move to a more appropriate place."

"I don't have the means right now."

"You will soon."

"I'll think about it, I will let you know," said Eylem.

"Secrecy is most important, what we have talked will remain between us."

"Naturally…"

"You are a beautiful, attractive girl. It'll work out fine."

Eylem went out. As she was crossing the corridor, she realized that the two apartments were joined together. Just then, she thought she heard a sound. A sound of suppressed laughter that she thought came from behind one of the doors. Or was it a sob? Something in between … She drew back; in that voice, she could detect the echo of a sob hidden in laughter.

When she went back to the large room, she was met by the same young woman. She was very plain, without any makeup, her blond hair in a pony-tail, and she seemed very cheerful. She took her to a room which looked like a large secretariat with two glass tables, file cabinets and other details. On the walls there were beautiful black-and-white art photographs of women. Another girl was talking on the telephone.

"Blond. Er, about one eighty. New. She stars in the stocking commercial. For three hours it's one-thousand-two-hundred, sir. Did you say 307? Yes, sir. Er, about half an hour. It depends on the traffic."

Eylem filled the form which was held out to her.

When she went out, she saw that the sky had clouded over again. Jale Hanım's explanations and her effusive parse of Eylem's beauty were ringing in her ears. She hadn't been able to say "no" to her. She had wanted to but she couldn't. Sometimes the word "no" could be very difficult, and sometimes it was totally useless.

One had a sense more than just knowledge, and it was called intuition. It was rooted beyond consciousness, in a deeper place. It was born out of the sum of all the experiences and emotions during the flow of one's life, mainly from the reason and result relations. Her inability to say "no" had to do with this. She knew her inclinations. Until then, she had spent all her energies for an internal and external control she thought was suitable to her situation. She had tried to prevent herself from slipping, but she had finally lost control.

She walked slowly along Rumeli Street passing the shiny, glamorous shop windows. All she wanted was to walk. To put one foot before the other and go...she knew her future would be shaped by this walk, the brave steps she took and the distance she covered.

She didn't realize she had already arrived at the dolmu stop. Perhaps she did, but she continued walking toward Ni anta 1. It wasn't possible for the world in one's mind to come to terms with the real world. Therefore, the only thing to do was to try new ways of perishing within a great deterioration, within the ever-repeated circle of deterioration and corruption.

10
Winter

Volkan was going through the newspapers as he listened to his mother's tinkering in the kitchen. Gülsen Hanım had arrived the night before; they hadn't seen each other since June. When she told him she had missed him very much, Volkan insisted on her coming to see him.

"Mother, I'll be eating something small, I'm on a diet," he called out toward the kitchen.

"I'm only preparing soup and salad."

Volkan had lost three more kilos running on the treadmill for an hour and a half every morning and eating like a child; he was in a good mood. As he would be forced to drink less while his mother was there, he was planning to lose two more kilos that week.

When he was with his mother, he felt as if he were still a small child. It was a reassuring, affectionate feeling. The short moment between the times he heard her voice on the telephone and when she said her first word were filled with distress, with small and large incidents, passions long forgotten, stories written on the spot or later. The image in his eyes was of his mother as a young woman and himself, still a child. A sweet, blond, rosy-cheeked boy who looked at the world with large eyes full of hope and joy...

He had to dig very deep to find happy memories.

Kindergarten...pictures made with grains, plasticine figures...The days when he refused to eat, being forced to say he was sorry...primary school, the chart of seasons on the classroom wall, spring, summer, fall, winter...the chart of poultry...the ruminators...having a cold all winter...the colored world atlas...Lego toys...

A dim street full of trees...houses one after the other...he doesn't like playing out of doors. He is afraid of the urchins in the street but he knows all the holes for marbles. He is sovereign in his own room. He shuts himself there and dreams. Perhaps he is a child who is not capable of being a child. He makes models and puzzles from chocolate wrappings. His father says he has character. It is as if he had grown up and then became a child again.

To grow...his clothes shrink fast...his body turns into a pale, heavy cocoon. To perceive himself as himself. To see himself as a cowboy, a boy hero who is capable of overcoming all difficulties...

He was eleven years old and they were in Ankara. His father was private secretary to one of the ministers; they lived in government lodgings in the Saraço lu neighborhood. It was a difficult time. Dozens of people were dying every day in street battles; there was shortage of fat, kerosene and petrol; long power cuts were disrupting life, and the black smog which had settled over Ankara was making it difficult to breathe. His father would come home around midnight, preoccupied and worried. The Ecevit government was living its last days.

The lodgings all in a row were very old and shabby. What remained in Volkan's memory were the gray inlaid concrete steps of the building and the floor covering, the high ceilings, the ochre paint on the window frames which had thickened and blistered, the two rooms and the narrow kitchen that opened into a hall, and his mother's complaints about the smallness of the house. They had shivered day and night, as the radiators were of no use, because the heating system was installed in the first years of the Republic and the pipes were clogged with lime, and to top it all, there was the fuel shortage.

As soon as he came back from school, Volkan would shut himself up in his room, writing terror and murder stories for long hours and illustrating them afterward. Even if his subject matter was rather worrying, his mother was happy with her son's interest in writing. It was a sign of his sensitivity.

At the end of that year, 110 people according to official records, and hundreds according to his father, died during the incidents in Maraş. His father didn't come home for days, and this incident hovered over their lives like a nightmare. Volkan drew for months the horrible scenes, the blood, the fire and the corpses he had seen on television and in the papers.

Then the government fell and his father was appointed as consultant by the Demirel government known as the Second National Front. The country was drifting toward the coup of September 1980.

His mother had prepared dinner. The dining corner in the living room was a smart alcove decorated in the Far Eastern style. There was a wide, low table surrounded by a low sofa with cushions. Japanese lanterns, plants with wide green leaves and wall ornaments completed the picture. However, Gülsen Hanım could not sit there comfortably.

He looked at his mother putting soup in his plate. She looked serene and was smiling. Her smile was still beautiful but it was somehow bitter, even if it still kept the traces of a young woman's smile of a far away past. She was someone else now, so was Volkan. Nobody could stay as himself for such a long time.

This new flat with a view, which he had recently bought, had made his mother uneasy. She was disturbed right from the beginning by the sudden rise of her son. After each of his accomplishments, she first rejoiced, then immediately after, she was afraid and doubtful; she remained silent with worried bewilderment. Now the thought crossed her mind that perhaps he had unintentionally taken some false steps just to get hold of a place like this. Any other mother would be happy and proud of the success of her son but she only felt fear and suspicion. No doubt the reason of these feelings was her old-fashioned notions of candor and honesty. How could he make her understand? *"But Mother, I can't live in the slums!"*

When Gülsen Hanım came to visit her son early in summer, she observed sadly her son's life, his extra kilos and the riches he had acquired without striving too hard. Gülsen Hanım wasn't a woman of set opinions but according to her, the whole country was tragically drifting rapidly toward destruction with its politics, its people, its nature and everything else. It was certain that Volkan's situation was closely related to this aimless, unprincipled and negative change which wasn't being taken too seriously.

To soothe his mother Volkan had to assure her that he hadn't changed, that he was still the same person. After a while you get used to having money. When he told her that he was a partner in the company with a 12 per cent share in the profits, that this meant having an income which would keep him in welfare all his life, the poor woman opened her eyes wide and asked him what price he had to pay for this.

His mother…The delicate, dedicated, modest teacher of the Republic…disappointment with a bitter world was waiting patiently in her dark blue eyes. She was a member of an extinguishing generation and she would stay that way to her dying day. It was natural for her not to conform to the changing world and the spirit of the times, and even to oppose them. Especially after the 1980s, everything seemed false, illegal and corrupt to her. Since some time now, something as sharp as a razor separated her from the rest of the world.

He couldn't share her fears and loneliness, because he had his own loneliness to think about. He loved her, her slender build, her straight posture and her smile. Her worried hands that caressed his hair, the clarity of her words that stood for justice; her eyebrows raised in fear when she heard words of banking, stock markets, commerce and large sums of money…

She still lived in Ankara. She was a retired philosophy teacher. She had found her real identity and got to know herself better when she divorced Volkan's father years ago; she had never remarried. She was working for some nongovernmental organizations and seemed to be happy.

She was going to visit a friend in Erenköy that day and go shopping afterwards; the driver would be with her. She left after lunch.

After lingering a while, Volkan decided to call Melike. They had met twice after that evening when they had dinner together. They had sat in a café the first time; they had gone to a concert at the AKM on the second meeting. However, no feelings were stirred, not an attraction that resembled love, no physical intensity that would impatiently insist on their being together. On the contrary, they were getting further away from each other at every meeting. That was why they met less and less. Perhaps that was how this adventure was meant to be and there was nothing to be done.

Melike probably lived like him, too. She seemed to be a powerful, domineering woman. So, what's wrong with that, thought Volkan, nothing. There was no logical explanation, really. At one point, she had said, *"Men know a lot about the world, but they know nothing about themselves."* Then she had said something like, *"We all have secret sins."* At the end of every meeting, she was anxious to get back home. For some reason, she did not want to prolong her meeting with him. And the most important thing was that she criticized Volkan rather than understand him; this was unpleasant and disturbing.

He still enjoyed being close to this woman or to keep the fantasy alive in his head, although it was obvious he wasn't going to fall in love with her. Perhaps he subconsciously applied the best approach when he used the word "sister." Was there any point in knocking about with a know-all woman when he could be enjoying himself with someone younger and more docile?

On the other hand, it wasn't right to decide hastily, to give up on the girl before they even got to know each other and before they had made love. Even if it was a loose relationship, they were still at the beginning.

He postponed calling Melike till evening. He might have a drink after his mother went to bed, then he might gather some energy and be able to tell Melike a few nice words.

He had been home for four days; he hadn't even shaved. He felt a sweet, melancholic pleasure from letting himself go; he enjoyed going around in worn-out sweaters and corduroy pants with knobbly knees. Harun had told him, "You are on leave. Don't come back before you pull yourself together." This was a forced leave but he had already benefited from the repose.

He watched a basketball game on television, dosing every now and then. It was evening. The weather had been bad for days, but the sun had finally shone that day for the first time. He got up and looked at the sea.

As the blue of the sky got darker, it gave the air a pink hue and sprinkled silvery spots on the sea. With modest helpless assent, the Bosphorus reminded the spectator of the city's heritage of intrigues, its glory and many more things, savage and beautiful, shy and grand, forgotten and turned to fairy tales as if it never happened.

He heard the soft mist of his childhood and adolescence dreams vibrate in the air. As a child, he had dreamt of becoming a captain and going around the world in a big ship; a short-lived wish, devoid of expression and nondimensional like a photograph. This might be the reason why he had started writing strange, savage stories when he was twelve and when his mother was in prison. Although he was afraid of policemen and military officers at that time, he thought it was adventurous to be a detective. It should be fascinating to try to find the real criminals instead of taking in those who weren't guilty at all; to solve mysteries slowly, cunningly, and then go back to peace, order and happiness.

When he was in high school, his favorite subjects were math, art and Turkish. Numbers, colors and words would go around in his head when he wasn't at school. His mother wanted him to be a doctor, but he had decided to be a pilot. He would stare at the sky for a long time, envying the birds. His fascinated eyes were fixed on birds with tired wings as they glided with patient pride toward solitude. Then just as they were about to fall, they would compose themselves and take wing again.

He had a headache. He had drunk too much at the club the night before, and his flu had gotten worse. He was in no mood to develop new thoughts or a new point of view. All the same, hoping for silence and serenity consoled him.

Different thoughts were racing through his head. Man was a continuous being dependent on a variable past within time. The past was scattering its seeds everywhere, grass was turning green, growing and spreading continuously until it became a forest. Then unknowingly, one also became a part of that large forest and that continuity. The indifferent hands of time tied everything together, and at some moments the future could turn into the past.

He heard the painful cry of a kestrel in the grove.

He returned to his childhood. Their lives had become very complicated at a certain time. Straight after the coup, they had left their lodgings and moved to a house in Bahçelievler. In those days, his cousin on his mother's side, Sergen, whose family lived in Izmir, came to stay with them. His father had opposed this long visit and there had been violent arguments between his parents, disturbing the peace at home. Sergen kept to his room most of the time trying not to be seen by anyone. Volkan liked him. They listened to music, played games and joked with each other. He was happy to have found the older brother he had always longed for.

His mother had warned him emphatically not to talk to anyone about Sergen.

That was what he had done. They now spoke almost in a whisper at home. They had taken refuge in a silent, fearful anticipation to protect themselves from the violence and the horror that was taking place outside their home; to have a normal existence at least within their four walls. His parents were struggling to defeat the confusion using patience as a shield. They no longer argued, but accumulated their anger against each other in a durable composure.

Nevertheless, his mother was taken away with Sergen in the middle of the night a few months later, with the accusation of "hiding, aiding and abetting a fugitive in her home although she knew that he was wanted."

Volkan had just entered adolescence. His emotional world was turbulent, his body ached. He had become even more introvert upon seeing his mother punished that way. He was learning what it meant to long for somebody. He was also learning other things. He had got to know his mother's courage, her pride and her bravery. He didn't know who to blame.

He couldn't forget those days when he was stifled in an indignant unhappiness born from disappointment. Those were frustrating, frightening times.

He spent that period at his uncle's, trying to understand for a long time what had happened and feeling as if he had suddenly fallen flat on his face; all alone in a darkness oozing out of every stare he got, every secretly sarcastic remark, every pitiful smile. Then one day, he unwittingly heard his aunt's words and came to know that his father was having an affair with one of the secretaries in the office. He was devastated but still didn't believe what she had said. In such instances, words which seemed harmless contaminated the truth so far unknown as soon as they were spoken. They usually rose from nothingness, were constantly repeated until they fell down a dark abyss. And if you are weak, it gets even more difficult to defend yourself.

When his mother was released after about a year, the atmosphere at home still hadn't changed. There was a strange gloom, a new kind of silence. Her parents felt almost pushed out, exiled from society in some way. It was as if everyone was watching them, their lives were blocked. They divorced six months later. Volkan felt that the reason for the divorce was what they had gone through. Those days when fear and frustration suppressed people's lives were a period of great stress and personal reckoning for everyone; loves were exhausted and marriages ruined for no reason.

When he asked his mother about the divorce, her answer was simply "We couldn't get along together." His father later married that secretary, and Volkan grew apart from his father. He lived in Izmir for years and they seldom met each other.

He had hardly felt the absence of his father. Actually their closeness as father and son had always been partial, so the removal of a father figure from his life had made him feel relaxed and free. His mother was everything to him; there was tranquillity at home. He had lots of friends at school and was appreciated as an intelligent, lively, warm person. He felt like a child running joyfully toward the sunlight. What made him interesting and attractive was that he was deep, impressive and not devoid of a sense of humor.

Throughout his education, he had been led to believe in happy days awaiting the country, a bright future, and that he too could – and that he should – have a place among those who would build that bright future. Those were the days full of enthusiasm when the wall came down. Youthful days when one naively believed in happy endings, when it was easy to imagine living for universal goals and values and to dream of a world where there were no more boundaries.

Once upon a time he had looked at life with this childish excitement. Until he realized he could go no further. Until he realized that time was not an element that belonged to him, one that he could shape; but on the contrary, that he was a tiny particle of time with limited function. Life continued flowing under the surface with its whirlpools and eddies not secretly but visibly, openly and simply.

His phone rang, it was his mother. Her friend wouldn't let her leave, so she was staying overnight. He hung up and suddenly felt relaxed. It was good to have his mother there, but he didn't feel at ease when she was around.

He thought of Melike again. He wondered if she had ever married. She never said a word about herself, and she cleverly evaded his questions. While Volkan threw up all that he kept inside, she just watched. Obviously he was the one who started the game handicapped; that is, if there was to be a game.

Why shouldn't there be a game? What else was there to do? He called Melike. He felt strangely restless when he heard her voice.

"Hello, how are you?" He could love her just for that voice.

"I'm better. I couldn't call you, because my mother is here and I had to take care of her. Where are you?"

"Don't worry about it. I could have called you too, but I just couldn't get around to it. I'm at the exhibition, in the gallery."

"And I'm just a few hundred meters away from you."

"Are you home?"

"Yes, I'm on leave. Why don't you come over?"

"I'm busy tonight." There was no intention of an explanation in her voice. It was harsh, nervous and definite.

"All right. Well, I'll see you later."

He put down the receiver angrily. What indifference! He aimlessly walked around in the flat. It was six o'clock and the evening stretched in front of him; empty, without anything to do. He could go and see her, at least find out what business she had. Why shouldn't he have the right to expect sincerity? And Melike might change her mind if they were actually facing each other. Perhaps he could even bring her home. He decided to walk toward the gallery.

He aired the flat, changed the sheets – just in case – and tidied the study. He was shaven, dressed and ready by seven o'clock. He left quickly. As he walked, he felt uneasy about the discrepancy between his thoughts and actions. As someone used to success and power, he couldn't help feeling that he wasn't appreciated, that he was actually hated.

The neon signs had started glittering. There was a light cold wind, and the sea was softly lapping against the quay. Boats docked in a row and the shadows of an embracing couple sitting on a bench were drawn on the sherbet-colored evening. The world was beautiful; it was definitely a place to enjoy living in.

His body felt lighter, as if gravity had grown less, so he quickened his steps.

All the same, when he arrived at the door he disapproved of what he had done. He hoped that Melike would be gone. On the side window, there was an exhibition poster he hadn't seen when he was there before. The background was not a photograph but an enigmatic picture which looked as if it were reproduced from a painting. In this picture which somehow resembled Melike the lady had beautiful hands with rings on her fingers.

He entered shyly. Melike was at the back, talking to a middle-aged man of middle stature, with a short, trimmed beard. They were standing. Melike looked very attractive in her jeans, a Russian-style shirt, a red wide belt of soft leather which she wore over her shirt and a black cashmere shawl over her left shoulder. The toes of her short-heeled boots showed under her trousers. She was wearing a thick, ebony bracelet.

When she first saw Volkan, she was surprised for a moment. Then she quickly got hold of the situation and gave him a daring look from under her long, black lashes. She nodded reluctantly and gave him a forced smile. Then she started to walk, her heels clicking on the stone floor. That lovely walk as if she was bouncing...at that moment, an elderly woman waiting by one of the stands halted her and asked a question. Melike stopped to answer her. She had put on the air of an experienced saleswoman with feigned affection, a disguised excitement and stereotyped words.

Volkan forced himself to stay calm and not do anything rash that would hurt his pride. He took a glimpse at the man she had been talking to a while ago. He had an over-confident air and he was talking on the mobile. One of those pseudo-intellectuals, a so-called artist, a stupid show-off, thought Volkan.

Melike left the woman and approached him. The expression on her face was one of hurt, and she seemed tired. Volkan felt a great temptation to embrace and kiss her. It was almost like a command he could not defy.

"Welcome. What's up? We just talked a little while ago."

"I felt a sudden urge to see you."

Forcing herself to stay silent, Melike took a look at the man who was still on the phone.

"Who is that?" asked Volkan.

"A colleague."

The man had finished talking and was coming toward them.

"Hello," he said, his hands in his pockets.

"Hello, answered Volkan coolly.

They looked at each other. The man was wearing a pair of tight black trousers, a tobacco brown velvet jacket and a striped shirt. He was bald on top and had a ponytail. He was wearing an earring in one ear. He looked at Volkan as if trying to figure out what sort of a relationship he and Melike had. Then he turned to her seeming to have lost interest in Volkan.

"Aren't you going to introduce us?" he asked.

"Metin, Volkan," said Melike without enthusiasm.

"What is your profession, sir?" he asked Volkan.

"I'm a football player," he answered. Metin looked at him doubtfully from head to toe.

"Pity you've become a bit old for that," he said.

"Yes, but I'm the Goal King of the Year."

"You are very funny!"

"Metin is a well-known photographer," Melike explained, in an attempt to improve the atmosphere. "And Volkan Bey is a stock broker."

"Well, darling, are you ready, are we leaving?" asked Metin, nonchalantly.

"We'll leave in a moment," said Melike uncomfortably. She seemed oppressed, dominated.

Volkan moved away so that the others could talk in peace. He pretended to study the jewelry. It was obvious that this man was a disturbing part of Melike's life of which he knew nothing. Melike walked over to him with quick steps.

"I'm very sorry, I have to go somewhere with Metin tonight; I told you on the phone."

"Please relax, I'm leaving right away," said Volkan with a low voice. He looked into Melike's eyes. The girl answered his look with a short, hopeless glance as if asking for help. Metin made a grimace and looked arrogantly at Melike and then at Volkan. There was a touch of aggression in his glance. His mobile started ringing and he walked toward the door, to answer it.

"I'll be waiting outside," he said and went out.

"I'm happy to see you. I've missed you, and I wish I could have passed the evening with you," said Melike.

"Who is he?" Volkan asked again.

"Not someone worth talking about," said Melike. There was a moment of silence. "Don't think I'm emotionally involved. He is an old friend. I'm sorry, I didn't want to distress you." She seemed humiliated, as though one of her secret weaknesses had been discovered.

"It's my fault, I am the one to apologize. I shouldn't have come suddenly like this."

"That's all right. We can meet tomorrow evening. My uncle is celebrating his birthday tomorrow. I'm going there, and I'll be very happy if you come with me. Will you?"

"I don't know…" His voice was broken, hurt.

"You can come over to my place in the afternoon. We'll have a drink first and then leave at about ten. All right? Come on, say yes! I'll send you a message with the address tomorrow morning." She was looking at him with a sincere and imploring expression.

Consolation prize, thought Volkan. He felt himself advantageously poised.

"All right then," he said, almost whispering.

Melike went to the glassed separation at the back of the shop and said goodbye to the girl who ran the gallery, got her coat and bag and came back. They went out together; Metin was in front of the door.

Melike embraced Volkan warmly and kissed him on the cheek.

"Good night, sir," said Metin with a triumphant air.

The wind had gotten stronger, and for a moment Volkan didn't know where to go or what to do. He felt both hurt and guilty. He had shown unnecessary courage and had been stood up, even cast out. What's more, he was left high and dry for another man.

Obviously Melike wasn't the woman he had imagined. The woman he expected her to be, hoped her to be … perhaps there was no such person anymore. The woman he was longing for seemed to be much more difficult, mischievous and dangerous. On the other hand, it wouldn't be right to be narrow-minded about the situation. Melike was a businesswoman. It was natural that she should have a circle of know people. And she had told him beforehand that she wasn't available that evening.

He didn't want to go home. He just couldn't bear to spend that night alone. To hell with Melike! There were many women he could be with. First, he thought of calling Nilhan, but he couldn't go to bed with her. He needed to have a little fun, make love, relax. He dialled Fundi's number. She was home, and she was thinking of going to the club. So she was free.

"I want to come to you, Fundi. What do you say?"

"Great! I've really missed you. Grab two bottles of wine and come right over."

11

Volkan got a little closer to Melike and took her hand in his palm. A slender hand with long fingers … was this the hand in the exhibition poster? No, that was the hand of a model. And how about that blurred picture?

"That was a portrait I made at the academy. It was Metin who took the photograph of the hand. He made that poster."

They were in Melike's home, sitting on the couch. Volkan was relaxed. He had had a great time with Fundi and had regained his self-confidence. Life seemed to be easier, simpler. What he and Fundi were looking for was passion; the effortless, temporary excitement of existing.

The pursuit of satisfaction was like a circle; it had to be repeated. It ended and started all over again. Actually, it wasn't a difficult journey even if it sometimes seemed like a prison.

"I'm full of contradictory feelings," he said to Melike. "I'm far away from you one moment and close the next. Perhaps I'm afraid of being disappointed, because I don't know you at all."

"I have the same feelings, but that has nothing to do with you. You are open and sincere, whereas I'm never sure of anything that I consider to be right about myself."

"That's difficult to believe."

"More than ten years ago, a man that I was in love with wrote a novel about me.[1] I tried to read that book with an impartial eye and I admit I had the chance to look at myself from the outside for the first time."

---

[1] *Green*, İnci Aral

"Fascinating. I'd like to read that book, too."

"It has long been forgotten. The writer was tragically suffering from schizophrenia when he wrote it, and the result was a confused text. Although he used my real name, the woman in the book is not entirely me. She is an interpretation, a point of view, because I never told him anything. All the same, there were some correct observations and they impressed me.

The writer later told me that I had overidentified myself with the character in the novel, and he dismissed my objections. However, it was a good approach which carried certain clues."

"That's how novelists seem to be. They first reveal people and then they tend to deny it. I don't read many novels but that's what people say." They laughed.

"By the way, Metin is also in the book, and with almost one hundred percent accuracy. If you read it, you will find out who he is and what he is."

"I'm thoroughly confused," said Volkan. "I'll read it at the first opportunity and we'll talk about it at length afterwards."

It was a pleasant living room. Two armchairs, a couch, a rather high rotating bookcase full of books...Statuettes on the mantelpiece, two books on the side table by the couch, with bookmarks in them...The one on top was Proust. Paintings and drawings of different sizes on the walls...there were too many knickknacks in the room but all of them had been chosen and placed with care. Her home was unpretentious; it had a pleasant, warm ambience which reflected the character of its owner.

As they were having their drinks, Melike asked Volkan if he had married before, and he told her about Carol. Even if theirs wasn't a marriage, it was close to it.

"How about you?" he asked.

"Once. I was nineteen and I was a student. It didn't even last two years. For one thing, marriage was the wrong thing to cling to, and I wasn't able to become domesticated."

"This Metin, is he from those days?"

"You could say that. At that time, I was a child and he was the devil. Later, I always had irritating people like him in my life. I witnessed their drunkenness, their loneliness, their obsessions. With the exception of the writer I told you about, they were all so hollow, one like the other, that I felt as if I were experiencing the same man over and over again. I would leave them then because I felt that they didn't deserve me." There was hopelessness, a distinct pain in her voice.

"I understand," said Volkan.

"What do you understand?"

"That you have lost hope and don't consider me an option."

"You misunderstand. You are a very attractive person but I'm not the woman you think I am." She laughed nonchalantly.

"What is it that you expect from life, from the future?"

"To suddenly learn what it is that I expect."

"Maybe something will happen or someone will come along and you will say 'There, that is exactly what I wanted,' is that so?"

"No, not at all. I'm quite aware that there is no such guarantee. Whatever…I will now prepare you something to eat. Cold cuts and salad?"

With his head full of questions, Volkan watched Melike as she went to the kitchen. He was glad she hadn't told him not to come. He had suddenly found himself in the role of the caring and protective friend with a kind heart. Although this role implicated a certain amount of disappointment, he was happy with it. He knew the risks of such closeness. A docile, understanding and sympathetic brother meant the extinction of the excitement, of the wild desire to discover the other, in other words, of sexuality. He watched Melike as she walked to and fro preparing the sauce for the salad. She poured the rest of the wine into the glasses. He couldn't understand why their relationship had developed in this direction. He never had a sister or a brother. He was never forced to love a woman without desiring her, longing to touch her; he had never known that taboo.

They were going to eat in the dining room. They took their plates there and sat facing each other. Volkan looked at

Melike's beautiful face and suddenly understood. This woman preferred a sincere, easy, assuring closeness and relationship to a disquieting and doubtful estrangement and uncertain future. At that point, love and passion became inappropriate. This meant helplessness for a man, utter humiliation.

"You may find my uncle somewhat odd. He lives with a young man," said Melike suddenly, putting down her wine glass. Volkan shuddered for an instant. Then he scolded himself, go hang out with her, be brave, act like a man!

"Wouldn't your uncle mind an uninvited guest?"

"No, he would like it, but the people he is with may shock you."

"Why would they? Do you think I got this old at the hem of my mother's skirt?"

"In general, heterosexuals approach those with different preferences with a subconscious feeling of pity. And they themselves are the first to be disturbed by this."

"I find that their disturbance is not directly related to those people. Their suppressed, secret dreams surface through them in a sophisticated way, and their own insufficiency turns into erotic anger."

"I don't think it's that simple. There are darker aspects in society's outlook toward the marginal."

"The instinct of the majority is to eliminate, even annihilate what it finds to be contradictory. It tends to iron out everything, to create monotony, to equalize things."

"I can't agree with you totally," said Melike. "If variety frightened human beings as much as you say, we would be living under more equal conditions in a world which was more just."

"That's another matter. At that point, the balance of power comes into the picture; those who rule, and others who are ruled. How in God's name did we come to these subjects now?" Volkan suddenly became silent. They spoke too much, drowning their chances in unnecessary talk. He stared at Melike, but their eyes didn't meet. She smiled sweetly, as if telling him not to try in vain.

They cleared the table. When Melike went to bathroom, Volkan poured himself a double whisky from the bottle on the side table. Wake up, man, come to your senses!

He stood around with his drink in his hand. A couple of nude marble water sprites on the mantelpiece caught his eye. It was obvious that Melike was very experienced in the subject of men. Contrary to women's general approach to the subject, she had told him that quite openly. Her honesty was probably due to her self-confidence.

He thought himself to be the last link in the chain for the time being; however, this didn't frighten him. It would help him take a conscious attitude. It was better to enter the relationship with open eyes rather than dealing with unexpected confessions that might suddenly appear out of nowhere one day. Who Melike had been with other than that drip called Metin, Volkan wondered. Whose bodies had she visited? And how about you? What strange thoughts were these! He was almost forty and she was about thirty-five. He remembered the night before and Fundi. He might say that he had already been unfaithful to Melike.

The drink had taken away some of his tension. A cheerful optimism was budding in his heart. Nevertheless, he was still confused by not knowing how to behave with a woman for the first time in his life.

Melike came back. She had put on makeup and gathered up her hair. She was wearing a short, tight black dress with thin straps and a silver necklace decorated with pearls. She looked magnificent. Volkan couldn't take his eyes off her for a while. Melike put on a new CD and came and sat next to him.

"You look very beautiful," said Volkan. Everything about this woman creates a devastating feeling in me, discourages me at every step, Volkan thought. Melike thanked him with a soft voice, smiling encouragingly.

They looked at each other with a gentle understanding. Volkan realized that he had started feeling a desire similar to what he had felt as he ran to the gallery the evening before. It was exciting to sense Melike's warmth, the closeness of her body, to inhale her scent. Right from the beginning, everything she said had confused his mind and his feelings, yet here he was in her home, next to her.

He had been chosen. He was feeling proud, frightened and victorious as if this was the start of the adventure he had been longing for forever. On the other hand, there still wasn't much meaning in their relationship. He could easily be sent off like the other men.

There was no need to turn his back to reality, to focus so much on a passing fancy. Once the interest of this know-all traveler of hearts was over, no doubt he would find himself amongst the other victims. Oh, what the hell, he thought, and tried to concentrate on the girl.

"I have been thinking about that game of emotional battles you suggested," said Melike. "To tell you the truth, I am not a player. I am as I seem. I don't see much talent in you, either."

"That was just something said in passing," said Volkan.

"I don't want to fight," said Melike. "I don't want to hurt, wound or defeat anyone. I just want to love. I'm very late for that. I wasn't able to enjoy anything deeply for a long time, even with the man I loved. Then he died, I understood how much I loved him only after I had lost him. But the pain I suffered taught me how to feel. Now there is something else waiting for me, something quite different. I long for a long-lasting, trustworthy, permanent relationship. And what do you feel?" There was a bitter, negative timbre in her voice.

"You talk so much, I can't get hold of my feelings," said Volkan. "At this moment I feel like laughing and crying at the same time. I'm thinking about all that I'm missing in the confusion in my life and…I want to abolish this unpleasant sisterhood-brotherhood pact between you and me." He leaned toward Melike and looked into her eyes, then he embraced her and felt her naked arms around his neck. They kissed. It was a sensitive and loving kiss, but it lacked the tempting sexuality, the real warmth.

This is our first touch, it is most normal, thought Volkan. For a moment he felt he was going back to the adolescent fears when he had thought that he would be scorned for the lack of sexual strength. Then he remembered the ridiculous, unpleasant, aggressive young boy who yet hadn't been able to know his emotions. He was no longer that boy. He had to check himself for the time being, because of this woman...

"You are still able to love," said Melike, her arms still around him and her cheek against his. She was warm and had a lovely scent; she was just wonderful.

"Why did you say that?"

"Because you didn't try to challenge me, to put on a show," She gave Volkan a light kiss on the cheek. Volkan thought about how dull passion could be when it was needlessly fiery and commanding; that it made people lose hope of love right at the beginning of a relationship. Perhaps this was what Melike meant to say, but did she have to put everything into words?

"I feel I'm in trouble. You are very outspoken," he said.

"I think that's a good thing," murmured Melike.

"Not always."

They listened to the vibrant, sad crescendos and the brilliantly soft passages of Callas as they talked about love, and how at the beginning of each love affair, one got the feeling that s/he met with her/his future, that her/his life finally balanced itself and didn't need another chance. Volkan took her in his arms again. This time their kisses were more passionate, more fiery although Melike was checking herself.

Volkan enjoyed Melike's candor, but her being in charge all the time made him somewhat angry. It seemed to him that each word she uttered, each movement she made was a part of her resolution. Why this? Why did she need something to guide her? She probably did this so as not to leave things to chance, but in doing so, she broke the spell and paralyzed Volkan.

Ever since the day they met, she had been bolder than him, maintaining the leader's position. That was why Volkan felt awkward next to her, and couldn't help thinking that his image was getting damaged. What was to happen if the closeness he felt for Melike turned into a burning self-abandonment before long? His weakness would make him ill, and he would become even more vulnerable in front of this difficult woman.

He looked at Melike. She had told him that she had been in love with a writer. Had she been able to love him unreservedly? Or had she wounded the man's ego with her dominant character?

"The man you loved, your writer, why did he die?"

Melike's face twisted as if she was in pain. She put her head back on the couch to hide her face, now she was out of the lamp's light.

"He didn't think anybody heard him." She waited. "And when he believed that the world was not his world anymore, he gave up living."

"Did he commit suicide?"

"It was revolt or suicide." She looked at her watch. "We should go now," she said, getting up quickly as though closing the subject.

We will fight whether she wants to or not, that's how it seems to me, Volkan thought. No love could be faultless. He saw himself swimming in deep, rust-colored waters. He had started to swim, he was on his way. There was a tiny lighted window on a distant shore, and he wanted to get there at all costs to see what was behind that window.

All the lights were on in the mansion when they reached there. Melike joked with the guards at the gate. They walked up to the drawing room on the upper floor where there were dozens of candles of all sizes everywhere, creating a dreamy atmosphere. Inside, there were about ten or fifteen men and women and others that seemed to be in between. Someone was playing the piano and a few couples were dancing. The ones who were sprawled on the armchairs and couches were eating and joking. They walked on between side tables loaded with glasses and plates.

A half-naked elderly man, who seemed to be in a state of lethargy but ready to pounce any minute, was doing an exaggerated tango with a young boy in makeup and very tight trousers. The boy's eyes were constantly peering around. Volkan noticed the boy's attractive body, his strong arms and his smooth back.

Melike went to her uncle. Four or five people were sitting on the rounded corner couch. Her uncle occupied the best seat in the room and looked like a chief protecting his clan. Introductions were quickly made, and Melike and Volkan settled in the small couch facing the corner.

Niyazi Bey had his arm on Hayali's shoulder, and their knees were touching. The man looked tired of lust and of enjoying the pleasure of power. The most striking thing about him was the density of his regard. His green eyes looked around penetratingly. Deep lines ran down from the sides of his nose toward the corners of his mouth. His stance and his way of asking to be served had the air of a mafia boss having managed to rise above his milieu, with more refined manners. After the first enthusiastic welcome, he fixed his eyes on Volkan for a while. Then his questioning gaze turned toward Melike; he finally smiled. This was the carefree courtesy, the artificial half-smile to be shown to someone in passing. Obviously Volkan wasn't interesting enough for him.

Volkan looked at Hayali; he was the most conspicuous person there, the one who immediately caught everyone's attention. He was comparatively short for a man and had an athletic build. His body was young and firm like that of an agile, strong animal. He must be a self-sufficient man who gives pleasure to others, Volkan thought. He seemed to be aware of being number one and didn't hesitate to display it proudly. With his very short hair, his large oriental eyes and his sharp mouth smiling cynically, he was so seductive that for a moment Volkan was amazed. The young man had concentrated on the music and was nodding his head to the beat. Then he turned his eyes to Volkan and stared through him as if he wasn't there.

This picture of the happy family was completed by a transvestite sitting next to Hayali. With her exaggerated makeup she looked strangely attractive and repulsive at once. This is a world in itself, thought Volkan. He couldn't understand how the music could be so fast and yet so sad.

He felt uneasy and alone, and turned to look at Melike. He saw that she was looking at Hayali, her whole interest seemed to be focused on him. There was a haughty, vainglorious expression on the man's face; he seemed to be mocking an enemy he had trapped. Volkan felt that there was a problem, an unsettled account between Melike and this man. His sarcastic lips, which gave away his cunning and hedonism, had contracted, and Melike's body had become taut like a cat ready to pounce on its prey. Volkan lighted a cigarette, he was asking himself why he had been dragged there. Rather than following Melike, wouldn't it have been better to offer her his own choices?

Next to Niyazi, there was a tall, strikingly beautiful woman in a low-cut dark red blouse and tight black pants. She was constantly paying him complements with unexaggerated, elegant gestures and words. Melike leaned toward Volkan and whispered in his ear that this woman was actually a *real* man, he was married and had a small child but made his living as a transvestite; he was dressed and prepared by his wife when he left home for work. His nocturnal name was Handan. Poor thing! To be a *real man* and a female prostitute at once…a man, having a prostitute within…

Volkan cast a secret, but intense look at Hasan or Handan. A handsome man who liked the softness of a woman but offered himself to men to gain his living…don't touch him, he wanted to shout to everybody. Don't touch him!

He felt a deep sorrow for *everyone* who liked to pretend to be someone else or was, willingly or unwillingly, forced to do so. Something was consumed every moment, through copulations, being reduced to one single body, separations, roads, voyages, runways, loneliness, silences, accumulations, executioners and victims who took pleasure from each other. He saw two young men standing by the wall and embracing passionately, their hips pressing hard against each other. What was being displayed here was a violence-provoking tension born from the contradiction between the inner and outer worlds.

They raised their glasses, toasted and drank.
Then they drank again.
And again.

Hayali put on a Karagöz and Hacivat shadow play full of obscene dialogues and made everybody double up laughing. The laughter, the shouts, the cheers got quite out of hand.

Niyazi Bey stood up and made a speech about what an exceptional feeling it was to be amongst friends; he seemed to be on the verge of tears.

Dance music was playing; the pianist had taken a break and was having a drink.

Nobody was talking much, preferring instead to make eye-contact and use body language. Volkan caught Melike once again as she was looking at Hayali with a wicked glint in her eyes that reflected a mixture of fury, hatred and desire. He saw a trace of expectation mixed with worry on the young woman's face and Hayali looked at her with pitiless scorn. Volkan was devastated. Melike was somehow smitten by this man.

He felt a cracking in his head as if a high-tension wire had suddenly broken, followed by an irreparable, melancholic rupture.

Why on earth had he come here? No, actually it was good to come. In this carnival, true, hidden feelings had broken free of confusing clever talk and the control of the mind, and they had been reborn in their simplicity.

Which real feelings? Volkan put his hand on Melike's back, grabbed her shoulder and squeezed hard, hurting her. Melike threw back her head and gave him a sharp look with a moment's glitter of fury in her eyes and her nostrils flared in anger. A sly, rebellious look ...there were shadows under her eyes and a fiery flush on her cheekbones. Turning roughly, she freed her shoulder, got up and pulled Volkan by the hand.

"Come, let's dance."

"Let's not," responded Volkan, feeling like a machine suddenly broken down. Who was this woman clinging to his arm with a strange frivolity, acting like a spoilt teenager? What was happening, what play was this where he was a walk-on like in theater?

"Come on, come on…"

Volkan got up to prevent the situation from turning into a comedy. They started swaying softly at one side of the drawing room. Melike was looking into space as though Volkan's feelings were of no importance. She seemed to be concentrating only on her own passions and dreams. Or perhaps she was displaying her beauty to an unseen mirror. Volkan felt more drunk than he actually was. He staggered for a moment as if hit on the head. Then he pulled Melike close to him angrily and whispered in her ear,

"That man, Hayali, are you in love with him?"

Melike's arms fell suddenly, she stepped back. Her mouth contracted as if she was disgusted.

"What a disgusting question that is! He is a …"

Volkan caught her arms violently, and pressed her body roughly close to his again. He only felt anger and disappointment. They started turning with faster steps.

"So what? Isn't it possible? It certainly is; I saw the way you looked at him."

"What look? I would drink his blood if I could."

"Hate, is it?"

"Pure hate!"

"Why?"

"He is an impostor. I am not even sure he is a homosexual. He is playing with my uncle."

"Perhaps it is your uncle who is playing with him. What harm has he done to you?"

"You are forming rough ideas of matters you know nothing about, Volkan."

"They say there is only a thin line between the desire to kill and the sexual desire."

"Something said for the perverse!"

"But it's true that hate is the secret face of love, isn't it so?"

"Isn't it too soon for demonstrations of jealousy, Volkan Bey? I don't like such things at all."

"If I could just understand what you love and what you don't. By the way, why did you bring me here?"

"You are very rude tonight. You wanted to be with me, didn't you?"

"All right, I'm sorry. Let's sit down."

People were either all talking simultaneously or silent altogether, which was more the case.

The music had changed. Arias from Bizet and Verdi filled the room for a while; then fast, noisy rock music started.

In one corner of the big room, people were making love in candle light.

The dominant feeling here was desire, and this was more important than stale words. Perhaps that was why the music was turned loud enough to block conversation. There was no use for words when the aura of desire had permeated the air, the trembling light of the candelabras, the lipstick stains and the finger marks on the glasses, the wine, the clothing, the mirror and the flowers. There was no need for everyday words to express desire. The only language appropriate in such situations was that of poetry, of music.

I must go, thought Volkan. I don't belong here. I'm an underdeveloped, conservative man without any existence, that's all.

"Volkan are you all right? Is something wrong?"

It was Melike. She is trying to protect me, thought Volkan. She is sorry she brought me here. The light that came from behind framed her brown hair. She seemed to be having a very good time. Hayali was standing beside the table. Suddenly he caught the boy by the arm who had been dancing the tango and squeezed his buttocks.

"Hayali is a dangerous man, you'd better watch out," said Volkan without looking at Melike.

"That is what I'm trying to do. You have greatly misunderstood me," said Melike.

She was staring at a transvestite with exaggerated blond hair, in contrast with her rough features, her harsh crimson lips and her fake breasts; she was dancing in the middle of the room, as if in a trance. Volkan's eyes were on two people, one that looked like a woman, the other like a man, embracing each other dreamily, with closed eyes, turning, oblivious of the rhythm of the music, enjoying the "togetherness" they had created. The smell of cigarette smoke, stale makeup, alcohol and perspiration was getting heavier.

He thought that this group of people, who were distant from each other and yet not at all strangers, was not much different from the group where he belonged. They came together at a smaller venue to see each other, to dance and to pair off just like the others. Making a few adjustments in his mind, he tried to accept the situation and enjoy himself. He had a few more drinks. Fortunately, the whisky was good.

A complete pandemonium broke out when it was time to cut the cake. Everybody was shouting, singing "Happy Birthday" to the music, laughing loudly, teasing each other and looking happy amid all this noise. He was the only stranger in every sense of the word.

Melike was leaning over her uncle's shoulder, helping him to blow out the candles. Her smooth naked arms, her mouth, her throat, her waist, her breasts…everything about her was so beautiful! She looked good in this environment. What's more, she seemed very sure of her place, of her brilliance. Those who were here were already in there. If there was one who didn't fit anywhere, who was dark and ordinary, it was himself. Perhaps everyone was looking for their own paradise which would transform their life into a believable lie; knowing that hell would win every time.

When she came back and sat by him, she told him that he seemed tired and could leave if he wanted to; she sounded very distant. She was going to stay a little longer, it wouldn't be right to leave her uncle. Volkan accepted her suggestion with some relief and joy. He felt he had got over a silly obsession of love. Yes, it would be better if he left. He had a headache and was supposed to get up early the next day.

They passed through the crowd and walked to the stairs. They said good night using the usual meaningless, unnecessary words.

That night, Volkan dreamt of naked men and bloody, frightening chasing scenes. The noise of all the vehicles running from one end of the world to the other, and the hum of crowded streets, demonstrations and factory production lines filled his ears. He saw people hurled in the air after horrible explosions, flying pieces of paper covered with illegible writings.

The interrupted rhythm of love songs, resembling one another was pouring over all these things.

12

E ylem took a taxi to go to Taksim. It was against the rules
to get to work by herself, but there was no need to ask
for a car when she was going somewhere so close. Jale
Hanım had suggested that she move in with two girls who
were sharing a flat in Etiler, but Eylem hadn't accepted. She
needed to be independent at all costs.

She got off in front of the hotel. Scared but trying to look
calm, she took the elevator to the sixth floor. Looking at the
room numbers, she walked along the corridor toward room
673. She needed so many words to define her fall, such weighty
excuses to forgive herself, that she had given up thinking. For
days, she had been swimming in a dark haze, approaching with
understanding the object she had been reduced to. She was
trying to believe that her new life, which did not clash with
her conception of the world, would teach her once more – but
this time once and for all – the naked and simple facts of life.
This was a temporary process, she promised herself, it wouldn't
take long.

How many men had she gone to? She had lost count. She had
been with her first client in a three-floored villa – a clandestine
brothel – in a residential complex in Çengelköy. The one who
ordered the girls could choose between a hotel, his own home
or the place provided by the company. The villa had a large
living room on the ground floor, and four bedrooms and a large
bathroom upstairs. With its veranda overlooking the garden,
its furniture, its music installation and all the other details, the
house offered all the comforts needed for this business.

The house was managed by a middle-aged woman of Russian origin who spoke Turkish. She lived in the garden floor flat which had two rooms and a kitchen. This harsh, large woman named Lara, whom the girls called KGB, was in charge of the cleaning, the meals, taking care of those who came and went, keeping discipline and even collecting the fees. The house belonged to a woman called Aysevim who also owned the boutique in Maçka. She was the boss of the company, and according to rumors, she was a former member of the secret police. She had started this business in partnership with a woman from the jet-set called Betül or Beti who ran a fitness and sports center in Etiler. Beti lived with a man who was the manager of a nightclub in Kuruçeşme, a convenient place for showing off and marketing the girls.

The girls generally stayed at Çengelköy if they were to be working at night or if there was to be a group party. Great care was taken not to cause any problems by disturbing the families living in the other villas, and music was always kept at low volume. Lara was an able and probably experienced manager from all aspects. She was pitiless and never conceded, but she did her job faultlessly. The appointments were meticulously arranged by the secretaries in the office under Jale's supervision, and it was made sure nobody ran into each other. On one occasion, Eylem had sat in the living room with another girl for about an hour until her regular client had arrived and she had left. The client was always called a "parcel."

On her first time, Eylem's client was a dark, romantic, courteous young man who was chosen carefully so as not to frighten her. They were together from nine in the evening until midnight and Eylem slept over at the villa that night after he left. The man's father was the owner of a well-known women's shoe shop. They listened to music and drank wine together, chatted even if superficially while they pretended to flirt and later they made passionate love.

Eylem hadn't been with anyone for six months after Seyit. She greatly enjoyed making love to this unexpected man who was perfectly all right in every way and impeccably clean, and she liked him immensely. In the comfort and naturalness of the home atmosphere and with the measured, delicate approach of the man, her body awakened without special effort, and she responded to the client eagerly. This first experience, which had scared her beforehand, went so well that she almost felt surprised, and even a little offended for having to accept money on top of it. It was just as they had told her; there was nothing dangerous or negative about the job, and it was wonderful not to feel contaminated.

Later, she had thought of other things, naturally. Such an attractive man could have had any woman he wanted. Why then did he prefer to be with a woman who was paid for it? Did he have a deficiency in the subject of love? Was he able to sleep only with a woman he bought? Was there a wound behind his faultless image that made him prefer such an obscure relation?

Who knows? There were lots of things she hoped life would teach her, and that included all that she wanted to know about the male sex.

The second customer was somewhat different. He was an imposing, mature man. Jale had said that he was an MP, but during the entire hour he had constantly scolded her saying, *"You don't understand what I'm telling you, do you?"* and had confused and upset her by telling her off with frequent remarks such as do this, do that, what a strange girl you are. And when he ejaculated, he had almost turned into a dog, howling and shouting so much that Eylem had panicked thinking he was dying. She was grateful they were in the house and not at a hotel. When she complained to Jale about the man, she was given as explanation: "He is a very good man, but he was oppressed and finally deserted by his wife. You have to indulge him, go along with his wishes."

At first, she thought that this job had nothing to do with photo modeling or becoming a famous ad face as she had hoped – or hoped not – when she had started. But, there had been some developments in that direction. For instance, she had been with a man in the textile business, who had promised to use her as a model. The main thing was that this was a well-paid job, that was certain, and she needed to work. As expected, she hadn't received a serious, satisfactory answer or offer from any of the other places where she had left her CV.

She stopped in front of Room 673. This was the end of the road. She had been with more than twenty men in two months, but she still wasn't able to shed her fear. She took off her coat and put it on her arm. She was wearing a short skirt and a tight, synthetic pistachio green blouse. She knocked and walked in. She left her coat on a set of luggage. She said hello and smiled at the man who was sprawled on the armchair next to the window, watching her attentively, smiling with a smug expression of superiority. She grinned back with some apprehension and curiosity, trying to look relaxed. Wasn't he going to get up and shake her hand? How rude he was! How and where would they begin? What would they talk about?

Eylem glanced around the room. She looked carefully at the bright colors that didn't go with the gray sky beyond the curtains. She looked at the bed, the cupboard doors, the mirror on the dressing table, the radio playing softly as if she was seeing them all for the first time. She smiled at the man again. The immobility of his features made her lose her courage for a moment. It was obvious that he was used to giving orders from his armchair and being obeyed. So she had to be faultlessly respectful.

"Come close, honey! What was your name?"

Eylem said her name and walked toward the source of the voice with a feeling of flying at a dizzying altitude, as if entering an exam she would not be able to pass. She didn't have to talk to this selfish, cold-hearted man. Anyway, it was difficult to make small talk…just yes and no would be sufficient. The man had opened the collar of his white shirt down to his chest covered with dark fur. For a moment, she tried to think of him as being something close to a human being, some definite concept or something like that but she couldn't do it. A large body, thick lips, saggy cheeks. And in the bulging brown eyes, the conceit of "I know best about all that exists and happens in the world" and a frightening expression of superiority which made Eylem feel helpless...

Poor thing! How unhappy he looked. He had loads of work to do. He was obliged to attend one meeting after the other at the appointed hours from morning till night, to manage lots of people, to take the necessary decisions and to develop projects. This gap between two meetings was probably good for reducing his stress. He was in no mood to chat with an ordinary whore at this hour which he had reserved for escaping from reality. If necessary, not that it was, if necessary, he could buy stupid stuff such as art or poetry in other ways. Look at him, thought Eylem, he is in need of pleasure and yet indifferent to the object of his pleasure. He wants to have an orgasm but he is disgusted at the thought of becoming intimate with the woman he is going to ejaculate on! Without stopping to think about what was lacking in him, he was trying, in the shortest of times, to plod open a way for himself between the legs of a pretty doll. He does everything he can to keep this a secret from his employees, his droopy, reluctant wife, his grown-up sons, his secretary who he is careful not to seduce, and even his God, had it been possible. Unfortunately here he is again, on the crime scene...

The crime scene...a biggish hotel room with yellow walls...closed curtains...a wall light turned on above the mirror...a double bed covered with a honey-colored bedspread, two bed stands, bedside lamps...everything is unfamiliar, so are the forms and the feelings. Words which define all objects are merely connotations, images.

Eylem sat in the armchair opposite the man. She crossed her legs. The room was floating in front of her eyes; it was as if she was drugged, she didn't feel much uneasiness. Knowing that she was somewhere but not knowing where fitted the image of the man's *nobodyness*. She hadn't expected to find a familiar place, anyway. All the same, it would be nicer if they would chat a little, talk about themselves and get to know each other a bit. Couldn't this blockhead open his damn thin crack of a mouth?

Couldn't he talk about the weather, the traffic or the music playing on the radio? Why was subtlety of thought so far away from such people?

Feeling the man's unpleasant gaze on her body and on her legs, she tried to remember what was done to start a conversation, a relationship in such instances. She had learned that some men liked to masturbate while they only watched, others had orgasms by sucking a tit or a toe, some others wanted to be beaten or treated like a dog, and all sorts of other nonsense. She had received training for fifteen days and had shown good progress; she also had some experience...All the same, she was confused. There had been no change in the man's attitude for the last ten minutes.

The girl at the agency had told her that this man didn't like to drink, that he expected the girls to come without having taken alcohol. Actually a glass of stiff drink would have helped to warm up a little. Perhaps they could talk about cars. What for?

"What do you like, I don't know what your interests are; how do we begin?" she asked. At first, this had seemed to Eylem like a general question that was open to all interpretations. However, under the circumstances, it had turned out to be very clear and completely directed at the goal. And actually, that was what was needed.

"Are you new, they said you were new, is that true?"

Eylem blushed and uncrossed her legs. There was no need for an answer.

"As for what I like, let's start with a blowjob," said the man. "Mine doesn't rise by itself; you have to work at it a little. We didn't come here to sit, did we?"

Eylem got up, trying to keep cool. In these first months, they could have arranged for me people who are more civilized, more sensitive, she thought. Yes, because it was impossible for her to feel good between these short hairy legs with this thing in her mouth. There was no human finesse in this body, no chest where she could lay her head, no words in that ugly mouth to comfort her pain. There was only emptiness from beginning to the end, an emptiness which could be endured for four hundred dollars an hour! Well, what had she expected!

"Strip, honey! Just keep the garters, I said it on the phone, you do have them on, right?"

Eylem hesitated for a moment. Right, but she had to take the money first. That was the rule. Rules were important and they were not to be forgotten. And when it was like that, this oaf had the right to see her as a common piece of merchandise. As if he had understood what she was thinking, the man took the envelope from the table next to him and held it out to her. Eylem took it and quickly put it in her bag.

There was no longer any need for useful, delicate words, or a well meaning, understanding approach. Eylem had already memorized the necessary erotic words and how she would take off her clothes, how she would use her mouth, her hands, her muscles. She had committed herself to remember that she was a female mammal above all. She had to obey with docility, to walk on high heels, to offer herself up, according to various tastes. She had voluntarily accepted to stretch herself on the torture rack in a dungeon which would contaminate her soul eternally.

She turned up the built-in radio on the headstand. Pleasant Latin music was playing. She started taking off her clothes, revolving, protruding her breasts, her buttocks, undulating up and down, crouching down with legs apart, twisting her waist, as if dancing. She threw off every piece of clothing one by one except the black garters.

It was astonishing. With every piece of clothing she took off wriggling and twisting, she was getting farther away from the feeling of the 'self,' and conceiving herself as a silent body which consisted of nice-looking organs and a hole to be penetrated. This was because the body was capable of adopting itself and basically it wasn't really such a complicated machine. Very few words could sum it up, and everybody knew this visible, ordinary language; not even a language, it consisted of learned abbreviations and formulas. Under these conditions there wasn't much left to be discovered.

The difficult part was to become herself through the body, to name it and feel it deeply.

She put herself on a *tabula rasa*, a blank page; a faceless body without a name, without a sign, without an identity. Not to be someone who loved in order to be aroused and make love, someone who waited for the caress of the loving hands that felt desire only for the one they loved. It wasn't difficult to parade a body nobody was obliged to have feelings for, to give it the required shapes and make it do the required jobs. It could be fatal in the very end but it wasn't difficult. She saw the man take off his clothes from the waist down moving slightly as he sat. She felt happy thinking she wouldn't find it difficult to obey his commands, to answer his calls. She was descending very fast, and what's more, she was doing it willingly as a sensitive and reasonable being. This didn't feel out of place; she had already been obliged to try this many times. And anyway, everything seemed possible and basic when one opened her eyes, as long as there were no delusions. Her job was to surrender and efface herself, to return to the fertile darkness of her body, to clear her memory and to forget about time.

For a moment she tried to see the man as a father, a brother, a relative, even a husband. She asked him his name. Ahmet Mehmet, cut the man short. No, he wasn't that either, he wasn't anyone who could be named, and he certainly wasn't any of the people who were close to her, one she could imagine him to be. Until that moment, he hadn't uttered any word of affection, any exclamation of surprise, any reprimand. It was certain that he found it difficult to speak about the thing he was so silent about. With shining eyes he had displayed his sleeping dick in front of a girl and that was all.

Eylem felt a sharp pity. This was a compassion which went beyond what she felt solely for the man. It was a regret directed at life in general, at the helplessness and destitution of man. This man needed her for reasons she didn't know but which were very valid from his point of view. So he kept her with him by paying her money. Even if he had factories, workers, plush cars, beautiful houses and a wife, those were not enough for him. There was an emptiness inside him which was difficult to understand, one which could be filled only by a rented girl.

Unfortunately she couldn't give him anything, except this body which was stared at and battered but which could never be reached at. Insipidity was the only thing she could give to those who approached her with nothing but the endless, inadequate hope of naked desire.

She closed her wings and came down to earth. She went down on her knees in front of the armchair, and she let the hand of the man grab her by the nape of her neck and roughly bury her head between his legs.

She was hearing the receding, thundering noise of a passing plane. Her conception of time was blunted. She wanted to get out of bed and go out, take some fresh air, but her body felt heavy, as if glued to the bed. She forced herself to remember where she was and who she was.

It was the same room. She had suddenly found the man on top of her. He had grabbed Eylem firmly almost like a wrestler. His one arm was like an iron rod, behind her, holding her by the waist, and the other one was around her hips. She had pushed him off as a reaction of her pain and anger, but she hadn't been able to resist this rape. The man seemed to be struggling to prove himself, or even to take revenge. It was as if he was trying to eat her up at once. He was testing her, measuring her endurance. He was trying all positions, forcing her, hurting her, making her shout. It was frightening, as if she had been abducted to the mountains!

She opened her eyes. He was standing by the bed with a towel wrapped around his waist, watching over her as if waiting to see her last breath before he left.

"You're very sweet, baby. I'll ask for you again. Come on, get up!"

Finally. A few crumbs of emotion, thought Eylem. She uttered a silent oath.

"You're very rough, you hurt me!" she grumbled. "You can forget about the next time if this is the way you behave! And the agreement was for one hour…"

"I know, don't worry. I'll pay for everything." He was getting dressed.

Eylem closed her eyes. The bandit had taken full advantage of her inexperience. The more experienced girls were sure to have certain methods for dealing with maniacs like this one. She had to learn these things. She sat up in bed and tried to arrange her disheveled hair.

Her mobile phone was ringing, but she had no idea where her bag was. She got up with difficulty and started looking around. The man pointed to the armchair. She went and got her bag, found the phone which was ringing insistently and answered it. It was Jale, asking her if everything was all right. Eylem told her that it had taken long and that she was about to leave. She wasn't going to complain with the man looking straight into her eyes. Did she want a car? No, she couldn't wait; she was going to take a taxi. So they know the man's habits, they sold me out knowing what would happen, she thought to herself. Dammit!

She sat on the side of the bed. Certain words and images were constantly chasing each other in her head, scattering haphazardly and then shattering into pieces. She felt pain in the depths of her body and on her back. Her chest heaved softly like that of a sleeping child. The man took out his wallet from the pocket of his jacket and threw the extra four one hundred dollar bills in front of Eylem who was combing her hair in the mirror.

"Okay? I'm leaving; you should too, don't dally too long."

"That's too little; considering I won't be able to work for some days, that's far too little…"

The man threw two hundred dollars more on the dressing table. Eylem didn't look at him. She heard the door open and close. He had done more than beat her but at least he hadn't tried to bargain, the damn slob. Perhaps this was a test, a test of patience and endurance. Well, it was over. Who knew what else she would have to face in the future.

The room was darker now. The curtains no longer filtered the daylight. She looked at her watch. It was almost six o'clock. She thought about night and the tranquillity of her bed. She got up and went into the shower. She soaped her entire body thoroughly and waited under the hot running water. When she began drying her hair in front of the mirror, she couldn't recognize herself for a moment. It was as if someone else was there. Her lips and her eyelids were swollen and red. There were bruises on her neck and shoulders. She got dressed in a hurry. She knew clients preferred new girls. Novelty was more attractive than beauty; that was why agencies were always looking for new faces and fresh girls, never turning away applicants who looked halfway decent.

Art, culture? Suddenly, these words seemed like a cynical joke to her. Everything was a lie. The company had made them up to have their conditions accepted.

Eylem gathered the bills and put them in the envelope together with the other ones. One thousand dollars for two hours! She had been battered, she had felt terrible, but she had obtained what she deserved. The man had treated her like a common whore. Without talking, without sharing...so be it. One thousand dollars! After she subtracted the 30 per cent cut the agency would charge her, she would still have seven hundred dollars. This was her monthly salary when she worked from nine to five as an insurance employee. The university, professional experience, all the work and the struggle, hopes of a career, they had all been futile.

Honor, chastity...the man of her life, eventually a house, lovely children...delusions...to be trapped, to take the bait...what makes love real is one's purity and sincerity. Being able to dream and being optimistic enough to keep believing in the future. As for me, I lost that purity many years ago, she thought.

It was evening when she came out. It was cold and she was shivering. She pulled her coat close and wrapped her scarf around her head. She wanted to walk a little in spite of the weather. She joined the crowd and turned to stiklal Avenue. She felt that she was drifting in a void. Remembering what had happened was a ferocious, indecent pain. She had been disappointed and hurt that day. She could feel the pain in her nerve ends; still, she was open and empty to what would come later. To the touches and the smells, the meetings and the adventures…to the male figure who waited behind the door every time and who was *nobody*; to jumping from bed to bed remembering she could never refuse what was demanded from her.

She entered a pudding shop and drank a bowl of soup. When she came out, she walked all the way to Tünel.

She hardly ever saw Jale, they usually communicated by phone. Eylem went to the gym three times a week, exercising regularly. Her body was more beautiful and more flexible than ever. She had grown close with Didem, one of Beti's two assistants who took care of the girls at the gym. They had gone shopping together the week before and bought themselves sexy underwear and a few other things. Most of the clients liked simple everyday clothes of good quality.

She decided to call Jale the next day to reproach her a little about the man. She was obliged to swallow such mishaps, to be on good terms with her employer and pull her life together, but surely she had the right not to want this man again.

For the time being, she had solved the heating problem of her flat with two butane stoves, but that wasn't a healthy solution. She had a secret hope like all the other girls: catching the attention of a wealthy man and becoming his mistress. She was determined to show an effort for such a radical solution before she became tired and worn out. But she needed a lot of luck.

When she got home, she tried to heat the flat by turning on both stoves. She and some of the girls were going with Jale to the famous nightclub of Beti's boyfriend the next evening. She would have better days and meet better men in exclusive environments, no doubt. One couldn't bear this life without that hope.

She had a bite to eat and checked her mailbox. There was a message from Saffron Yellow. She hadn't heard anything for some time; she wasn't expecting it and was surprised.

> *Eylem,*
>
> *I haven't been able to write to you for some time. I have no excuse.*
>
> *I have no assumptions about you and I won't have any. I perceive you as a contrary voice; you make me feel the weight of the human spirit. That is what I like.*
>
> *I'm a thirty-six year old, experienced man. I don't want you to think that I am one of those who hunt at random. What's more, the image I have of you is very clear.*
>
> *I am an executive in a financial company. I almost left my job when I read your article about the future.*
>
> *I've had weaknesses, I've made mistakes; the past is formed rather quickly. By trying to see the future, one is dragged into pessimism. Whatever the conditions may be, I feel that we must only want and imagine the future. This is the only way we can hear the song of the world.*
>
> *I'm sending you my photograph. (Volkan Kuman)*

It was a nice photograph. He looked like a famous film star whose name she couldn't remember. Perhaps he had sent her the picture of that actor just for the fun of it. Volkan Kuman was taking her for a ride! Executive in a financial company, come on! Such men never removed their eyes from the stock board to look around them, especially in front of them. He was really shooting off his mouth. *To hear the song of the world!* She looked at the text that appeared on the screen:

ARE YOU THERE, YELLOWSPOT?

It was the first time Eylem had caught him online. She became excited.

E – Yes, Saffron Yellow. I'm thinking.

V – Tell me what you are thinking.

E – I feel that even to want and to imagine would need some support, a hope or some light. I'm devoid of these; apparently you are not. Good for you! I doubt everything that you say about yourself. That's why I'm not curious about you. The man in the photograph is not you, either. Why do you feel the need to do such things?

V – What I write is true, I am who I say I am. I'm trying to get out of the dirty world of money these days, and I'm lonely.

E – I had thought you were a woman! It's not important. I don't need clarity and consistency these days. On the contrary, I feel favorable about chaos and diversity.

V – What are you trying to say?

E – Nothing. Do you know why I write to you? Because just like so many others who are about to drown, there is nothing else I can do other than throwing the scream inside me, or even myself, into a hole, in other words, here.

V – We couldn't get too far in these two months. We are having a dialogue for the first time; I'm finding it difficult.

E – I don't have ready answers, either. I'm more prone to expressing myself by thinking. Boring, isn't it? I wish you were someone who was more of an outcast. Then you would have been different from all those people who bear the same feelings from head to toe, and you would have saved me, even if only slightly, from being so pessimistic.

V – I am who I am, I am only this much. Can you send me a photograph?

E – No, because I don't look like any famous actress.

V – Don't be unfair, that's my photograph!

E – All right. For the moment, I prefer ambiguities to reality. Surprises, deceptions, dreaming about the impossible…I know beautiful encounters can also sometimes happen in this universe.

V – You are too emotional. You can see the colors but you cannot differentiate between them.

E – I'm not like that, but my mind and my life are rather confused these days. I have entered a new path and I am walking fast without knowing where I'm going.

V – I may be able to help if you tell me about it.

E – I don't need any help. Exile would suit me better.

V – What you write seems too enigmatic to me. Perforce I find myself in the same state of inadequacy and artificiality when responding to you, and I feel like a student doing his homework.

E – Perhaps you're right, but I'm afraid of destroying whatever it is between us. For a long time, I lived in hell hoping for heaven. When I looked from there, I saw that there were too many lies in this world. Then I got to know myself and tasted desire, but still I could not go beyond being "nobody."

V – You are not nobody, Eylem.

E – I am. I have nothing except myself. And what I want most at this moment is to become invisible.

V – That's what you are at this moment. If we try to be open and get close enough to feel pain from what we write to each other, we might succeed in talking face to face.

E – I have another suggestion for you: don't write to me. I'm so small, so insignificant that you should forget about me. I will be less sad then.

Eylem turned off the computer and went to bed. She couldn't sleep right away. The worst part of her situation was that, although she was a normal woman, she had to turn her back to a physical relationship in which she could live fully, where she could freely express her emotions including sexuality. As long as she continued in this job, she couldn't have a boyfriend, someone with whom she could get emotionally involved, and not even afterward. Even if she gave up living this way in the future, she would always have an ugly past. No matter how carefully she concealed it, she would always be afraid of having her past revealed. But she had thought about all these things before saying yes to the agency.

She wanted to have a relationship with Saffron up to a certain point, mainly to satisfy her emotional side. She would create a dream for herself, one which would belong to her world, and as she became part of that dream, she would feel the physical excitement that anything could happen any moment in that illusion of deep mystery.

She imagined meeting Volkan in a café.

She was wearing a camelhair coat. He was of middle height, brown-haired and with a somewhat conceited air. Naturally he would be very surprised when he saw Eylem. You only know me by my writings, Eylem would tell him, but I'm another person. Saffron would say, you are more beautiful than I expected.

He would be living in a nice but disorderly home. Perhaps he would be a man slightly wounded, divorced from his wife, his little daughter coming over at the weekends. He would be in search of things. He will get married if he finds someone appropriate. He hasn't had too many relationships with women, he has been cheated at least once. He looks healthy. He is good-natured and means well. He is not too well adjusted. He doesn't feel all right about being with a woman he doesn't love. He has never forgotten his first love. He is a little naïve, excited. He just sits there opposite her. He has advanced in his job, but because of the confusion in his private life, he is no longer successful. He will leave his job if he can find something better. He acts relaxed as if he had all the time in the world, because he has some money.

He likes films, music and football. He says he is picky in love. He wants to choose and be chosen. He doesn't seem to be like his peers. He looks at Eylem with interest as he holds his teacup, as if he likes her. He doesn't think about sleeping with her just yet.

"Do I want someone like that?" Eylem asked herself. Not at all. He is just a common type you see around. She liked to dream. What was important was not the content or the quality, it was the dream itself that was important. Dreams connected and tied together this place and somewhere else, knowing and forgetting, accepting and denying, the past and the future, stopping and running, evading and falling.

This was the only richness, the only consolation we could salvage from resisting, from our fatigue of confronting life.

She slept deeply and dreamt of Saffron. They were walking in a thick forest on a narrow footpath. The road curved softly right and left. The air smelled of linden and there were extraordinarily beautiful mushrooms under the trees. Sometimes the path got narrower and large green leaves brushed against their faces.

They were outside of time. It was like night but it wasn't night. The time of the dream was forgotten. Saffron was saying that they were lost. Eylem didn't care. She felt happy in that environment. They stopped by the edge of a still body of water. A black frog and a green frog were mating. This was a bad omen.

When Volkan told her he wanted to make love to her, Eylem lay down under a bush. Volkan took her in his arms and kissed her. Then he started to ask her questions: how do the other men treat you, what do you do with them, tell me...You mustn't ask me such things, because I am in my deathbed at those times, said Eylem.

She withdrew herself, jumping quickly up, and to her horror, she saw that her legs had turned into frog's legs. She suddenly woke up.

13

Thinking about Melike gave Volkan the impression that time had suddenly grown longer and that he had turned hollow inside, but this was due to the inevitable. He had approached Melike in the hope of entering her territory and taking refuge in her warmth. But suddenly, they had become estranged. It hadn't worked for some reason. His gloom made him feel as though he were covered by a grey cloth woven with sadness.

The car entered a wide lane lined with trees on both sides.

Harun was giving a belated New Year's party in his palatial home on the hills above stinye. The area in front of the garden gate was filled with expensive cars and swanky four-wheel drives. The road that led to the house in the middle of the garden was decorated on both sides with blinking colored lights and flaming torches. The sound of violins was flowing out of the house and the atmosphere was one of majestic and noble celebration.

It was very cold; it had begun snowing. The guests, trusting that it would be warm inside, had come dressed in impeccable, elegant clothes of thin taffeta, silk and cashmere. As they walked with quick steps from the garden to the steps leading to the house, they seemed highly impatient for the warm promise of the night.

Harun was wearing a black suit and a bow tie. He walked uncomfortably as if his brilliant black patent leather shoes were too tight for his feet. He welcomed Volkan with an embrace.

He took him by the shoulders and shook him amiably. Only sixty people had been invited, but the crowd inside gave the impression that more had arrived. While talking and laughing, the guests sitting on leather couches and silk-upholstered Versace labeled armchairs looked with admiration – or jealousy – at the paintings with gilded frames, tall vases, showcases, crystal mirrors and the ribbons and ornaments hanging from the ceiling. The waiters, well-mannered and faithful, were walking with silent steps circulating silver trays amongst the guests standing in groups. There were industrialists, businessmen, a former minister, two or three journalists and many figures directing the money market, all of them subjects of the smile stuck on Harun's face. Naturally there were also husbands and wives, mistresses and lovers as well.

A waiter approached Volkan and asked if he would like a drink. Volkan looked at the multicoloured drinks in the crystal glasses and took a martini. He decided to have wine at dinner. He greeted and kissed Selda who came over to greet him. The young woman was wearing a strapless, mushroom beige silk dress; she had lost a lot of weight since the last time he had seen her. Her dress kept sliding down as she continually pulled at it in order to make sure that she covered her tiny, hollow breasts. She looked aged and ugly. Her makeup was bad and carelessly applied. The edge of one of her false eyelashes had come unstuck. Volkan noticed that she was quite drunk although the evening was just beginning. According to Harun, they had come through – once again – the crisis of divorce. Apparently when he challenged her by saying, "all right, let's get divorced," Selda had developed cold feet. *Sure, where else would she find all this luxury, this splendor, the unlimited credit cards!*

A small orchestra on the second-floor landing overlooking the hall downstairs was playing live dinner music. The lights had been arranged with care. Everything had soft lines and was in yellow and beige tones. The flames in the huge fireplace at the corner of the hall were reflected on the burgundy parquet floors, giving them a crimson hue and illuminating the Moroccan leather armchairs flanking the fireplace along with the mahogany beams on the ceiling. The carpets where the hall led to the terrace had been removed for dancing.

A sumptuous buffet was spread on the table in the dining room two steps down. The variety and sight of the food was royal, and the people trying to help themselves at the table were moving their arms up and down like butterfly wings. Volkan walked over to have a look. Canard a l'orange, various hors d'euvres and cold olive oil dishes, slices of smoked salmon on ice, tiny tomatoes filled with fois gras and caviar, grilled shrimps and so on. The full, bare breasts of women, sparkling jewelry, giggles, laughter, the clinking of porcelain and silver and the harmonious tinkling of thin wine glasses, lights of the Bosphorus far beyond seen through the closed windows of the terrace, everything seemed like a dream one didn't want to wake up from.

He talked and joked with a few people. He listened to the impressions of a woman journalist who had been to the Far East. Amiable, clever, stupid faces…smiling faces of those who believed themselves to be dynamic, rich and lucky…insincere, temporary involvements…

Selda was again at his side.

"You look lovely," he said to make her feel good.

"Lovely? I'm suffocating, Volkan. Look at this stupid crowd! I sometimes feel like escaping to the mountains."

"Come on, don't say that, you're exaggerating. You have everything to feel good about."

"There is everything except happiness and love! You know…"

"There would be no problem if you could be a little optimistic."

Selda raised her hand impatiently, as if saying enough, no more advice.

"It looks very smart, doesn't it?" she said turning her head and looking around. "But this is not a home. It is a house with no personality, no different from any other rich man's house. Plus a lifeless man, a bastard of a husband who cheats on me with whores!" She reached out to the tray of the waiter who was passing by and grabbed a glass of gin. Volkan quickly thought that he had to get rid of this woman before the conversation got out of hand. Let her get divorced, who is stopping her! Harun isn't happy with this crazy woman, either.

"I started taking art lessons; my teacher says I'm very talented. That's the only place where I can breathe, you know…"

"Great! I think art is the best therapy…"

"Can we sit and talk one day, Volkan, just the two of us?"

Harun came close, reached out from behind his wife and took the glass out of her hand. She turned and looked at him with ferocious anger.

"As you can see, I don't even have the liberty of having a drink in this house," she complained. She pouted and looked like she was on the verge of tears.

"You've drunk enough, you're going to pass out anytime soon," said Harun. "Go pull yourself together, freshen up a bit. Lie down for a while and rest if you're not well. Come on, darling."

Selda waited for a moment. Then she moved away quietly, obediently. Volkan was once again assured that in spite of everything, Harun was managing his wife very well. As a matter of fact, nothing could put him in a bad mood tonight. He was happy and excited. Just the day before, he had signed a forty million dollar contract for prospecting gold. This was only for his efforts in obtaining the concession for the Canadian company and acting as its cover.

"What do you think? Everything is perfect, isn't it, my friend?" he asked. "All my friends are here and I'm in great form tonight."

"It's a lovely evening, really well organized," said Volkan.

He looked at the friends, or the honor guard. Bank swindlers, manipulators; those who knew in advance about imminent devaluations, others who ransacked the seashores, the ones who pocketed unearned income from real estate, contractors of inflated state tenders, those who had a good time at the state's expenses; those who charged 10 percent commission for a deal, others who had bought fame from the media, smugglers and elegant mafia dons. Names and names ...the people and the subcontractors of the new order like Harun, and those of even newer orders ...journalists who have become rich overnight, boot-lickers and agitators ...the free, the powerful, the talkers, the insatiable ...

The evening and the conversations were becoming more and more animated amidst smells of leather, cigars and wine. Everybody was talking at the same time, but naturally not about how they conducted business. They never talked about those subjects openly in front of others. Those sort of negotiations and bargaining went on behind closed doors, usually on a one-to-one basis, and the deals were made or broken in a language that only they could understand. When they got together in places such as these, they talked about houses, cars, yachts, receptions and parties, recent dieting programs and illnesses, trips and vacations.

Greetings, casual remarks and short chats over, Volkan went to sit in one of the armchairs in front of the fireplace. He slowly nibbled on what he had on his plate. He had lost eight kilos since October, e had slimmed down a lot and looked much younger. The mirrors were kind once again, and his self-confidence had increased.

He noticed Nilhan amongst the crowd. She was in a far corner, talking to a man in the textile business who produced upholstery fabrics. She and Volkan hadn't been able to get together after the last telephone call. He decided to wait for the moment when she would turn around and spot him.

The orchestra was now playing dance music; it was amusing to watch the people on the dance floor. He could hear fragments of the conversations and laughter of the people in motion. Insinuations deep enough to make one worry, the swishing sound of fabrics, the scent of perfumes ...The images were endless, excessive.

He saw that Nilhan was walking toward him. He got up to greet her, he embraced her, they kissed, and as she was affectionately caressing his cheek, he guided her to the dance floor. She was wearing a long, tight dress of night blue taffeta, a smart evening dress with a collar that tapered at the nape of her neck, leaving her shoulders bare and her back uncovered to her waist. Volkan put his hand around her.

"I can't believe my eyes, you're so handsome, you've become so slim, my love! You didn't torture yourself too much, did you?"

"A little. I've missed you, and I've also missed being handsome to you."

"So have I. How do I look?"

"Unbelievable. Is it love that makes you look so beautiful?"

"Possibly, I'm madly in love."

Volkan put his face against her cheek and closed his eyes. He felt her warm breath, the very slight milky scent of her breasts that perfume could not quite conceal. He felt the calm and hasty femininity of the body in his arms as if he was hearing the echo of a distant past. He saw before his eyes a room that smelt of ocean salt, wine and hyacinths. He ran his hand along Nilhan's tanned back. What they shared at that time was not merely sexual. There was something more than that in the warmth of their bodies, their locked palms, their endless kisses. The world became simpler, more believable when they were hiding in each other's bosoms, skins. Then they lost that purity, clarity and intimacy, never to find it again.

"Do you remember our room on the island?" he asked.

"How can I forget? I was there with all my being and I loved you."

"Are you alone, don't you have a lover?"

"No, I don't. Volkan, something queer happened to me ... No, I won't tell you, you'll never believe it."

"Come on, tell me. You don't surprise me anymore."

"My lover is a woman. Obviously I must have been interested in women and never knew it. I think that's why I was never able to establish a long-term relationship with men."

"And..."

"And... I've never felt anything like this, a feeling as intense as this."

Volkan stopped. His arm at her back fell to his side. This was ridiculous. An affectation, a pretence, a need for change ... Nilhan whom he knew all those years!

"See how surprised you are! Come on, let's get a drink. Actually sexuality is a complex subject. You can be wrong about yourself and you end up losing a lot of time. I wish I could have known this before I turned thirty."

"What can I say, one expects everything from you, but this is a bit too..."

"You don't take it seriously, do you?"

"No I don't. It will pass."

I really need a stiff drink, thought Volkan. They walked to the bar. Harun stopped them.

"Did he tell you?" he asked Nilhan. "Your friend wants to leave me, to quit his job."

"Why?" asked Nilhan, to no one in particular. Then she turned to Volkan, "Are you going somewhere else?"

"No, nothing like that. I just can't continue anymore, that's all." He looked at Nilhan. Her eyes were bright and cold. Her face framed by her brown hair combed straight back made her look angelic and devilish at the same time.

"I don't think it will be very good for you to pull out at this point," said Harun. "We are a family, a dream team, Volkan. If there's a problem, we'll take care of it. I don't want to lose you."

Volkan assumed that the word *we* was an expression of joint fate. It was a pronoun wide enough to contain all sorts of long-term relationships. In Harun's mouth, it had the significance of abstract dependence, and it put too much responsibility on his shoulders. That was one of the reasons why he didn't want to discuss the subject with him. Furthermore, he wasn't sure that Harun would be able to understand his feelings. The discrepancy between them had nothing to do with the difference between their emotions, their intellects or their cultural levels. Harun lived in another world and he had no major problems to ponder upon. This was the source of his power. It was senseless and unnecessary to tell him "I'm a pawn and a nobody in this muck, and I no longer want to waste my time and my future for you."

"Really, what's the problem?" asked Nilhan as she took a glass of red wine.

"I'm tired, that's all," said Volkan. This was the only excuse that didn't need a defense. "I've lost my will to work."

"Talk with him a little," said Harun to Nilhan as he quickly moved away to talk to the British banker.

"It's not right to give up your career at this age," said Nilhan. "You're at the top, you're very successful, you're talented and you make good money."

"This feeling of failure goes much deeper than it seems; it is difficult to explain. I feel a deprivation which cannot be soothed with money or anything like that."

"My goodness, you sound melancholic! Go to therapy, take a long leave, go on a trip, I don't know, do whatever you want but pull yourself together!"

Volkan smiled. He wasn't able to add some meaning to his life, he couldn't see anything of value in himself other than his mere existence, and he was dejected because he felt he didn't know how to live his life. Wasn't this the most frightening of all failures? No, it was time to take control and change the situation.

He thought of Eylem. The name Yellowspot suited her better. They now wrote to each other regularly and chatted on screen. Volkan felt he was being pulled into another world, as if he was penetrating into her mystery. After screening them carefully, he had told her many things that he had never mentioned to anyone, things he hadn't pondered upon, even those he thought he had forgotten. He couldn't do more than that, because the more he wanted to explain himself, the more defects he discovered in his soul, and he couldn't be as sincere as Eylem wanted. On the other hand, while he was battling with her, he was also calming down as he wrote; it was as if he had an orgasm. Sometimes words turned into writing without control, making him feel as naked and defeated as he had never been before. His strongest feeling was an aching, crazy exuberance. Eylem seemed to answer everything he wrote with the same sincerity – was she sincere? – but she was still determined not to show herself to him.

"I've never been so healthy before," he told Nilhan. "Do you know what the problem is? I don't like myself. Perhaps it isn't possible to become someone else, but at least I must try."

Nilhan was quiet as if lost in thought. She had probably realized that she wouldn't be able to convince him. Perhaps she was hoping that he would return to his job after living as he wished for a while. They walked to a quiet corner in the inner hall and sat on a small couch, their knees touching.

"Is there still no one in your life?" asked Nilhan.

Volkan thought about Melike. That was his last, his most tangible relationship. It suited Volkan that their estrangement had come at a period when he was busy traveling. He didn't feel guilty, either. Neither of them had anything to lose anyway.

He couldn't tell Nilhan about Eylem, because he was sure she would ridicule and scorn him.

"There have been a few, but none worked out," he said. "I think I have lost my ability to love. The women I go out with no longer seem interesting and attractive enough to keep me from being bored."

Although he didn't like rules, he had phoned Melike about twenty days ago for the sake of politeness. It was a cold, forced conversation. Then they had met for a drink at a hotel bar one evening. For some reason, he had found the young woman to be ordinary, awkward in her role, tense and unpleasant during that meeting. They had a hard time finding things to tell each other and to talk about; they chatted about trivialities and got up before long. Volkan came to the conclusion that all was finished, and Melike probably felt the same way.

"I was dating someone, but while I was taking my time trying to be reasonable as I tried to solve her dominant character, I lost my enthusiasm and it didn't work out," he said.

"In other words, you waited too long at the door with your foot on the threshold."

"That's right. If we accept the fact that love pushes one forward without control, turning him into an impatient character who can't wait, my reactions remained too calm, too sedate."

"One could very well love a woman with reason and logic," said Nilhan.

"Hearing that from you is not at all convincing."

"You are right. Perhaps you weren't too harmonic in bed."

"We didn't even get that far."

"Well, forget it. Who was this woman?"

"She's an antique dealer. She also designs jewelry and so on."

Nilhan looked at Volkan with a suspicious, condescending expression on her face.

"Or was she playing modest with you? What are you doing with middle class women? What the hell are you up to?"

Volkan shook his head to say no, getting a little angry.

"She's not someone like that. Anyway, let's leave the subject. Do you think it's very clever of you to decide all of a sudden that you are a lesbian?"

"Are you trying to remind me of the past? Is it my fault if I was the victim of a male dominant conspiracy with very deep roots?" She laughed heartily. "If you only knew who my lover is…" she murmured. She gave a sigh and became silent.

"Come on, tell me. You've already mentioned it, so talk!"

"But you won't tell anyone!"

"I promise."

"She's the wife of an energy company owner made rich by the government. He is an Islamist and she covers her head. Don't think she is one of those demure homebodies. She studied law but she can't work because her husband doesn't want it. The man has a second wife in another house, can you imagine?"

"So you couldn't find someone better and became the victim of revenge!" said Volkan. He laughed as if he were getting even. "Are you making it all up?"

"It's absolutely true. You should see the woman…She isn't even thirty. From outside, she looks like an unobtainable virgin. She comes from another world but she hides a volcano inside. A disappointing marriage, a body laden with longing, a reactionary deviation and departing from the straight and narrow road! And naturally choosing the least dangerous one, another woman."

"Amazing. Where did you find her, how did your roads happen to cross?"

"At the office of my gynaecologist. We started to chat while waiting. I fell for her that moment. Oh, Volkan, if you only saw her..."

"Be careful not to get into trouble..."

"Actually you are so right. It would be a scandal."

Fireworks were launched in the garden. Nilhan got up. Everybody had gathered in front of the terrace doors, watching with amusement the glittering lights which shot up from amongst the trees, burst in the sky and rained down everywhere like colorful serpentines. Suddenly they found themselves in the crowd. Volkan quietly walked away from the confusion and approached the bar. Shock after shock, he thought. He felt as innocent as a newborn baby. He had by chance fallen in with these people who were hungry for money and sex, and he sometimes surrendered to his own animal instinct. But such tricks, manipulations, taking and giving by both sides nauseated him at that moment. Luckily, his fate which was not as definite as theirs was keeping an eye on him. He swilled his brandy in a single gulp. He took one of the Havana cigars in a silver box, cut the end and lit it. The atmosphere had cheered him up, making him feel lighter, and had put him in a calm, quiet, painless mood.

His eyes searched for Nilhan; she was playing the superstar for a group of bankers. Wherever she went, she had the knack of forming lively little groups that were constantly renewed, because she was most attractive and powerful in every way. In spite of this, she was condemned to loneliness, and this made it easier for her to waste herself and embrace all sorts of unacceptable people. She is in love with a woman, a knockout in a head scarf! Changing categories like this at her age is a bit too much.

How about me? At least she has listened to her inner inclinations and has shown the courage to step out of line. What am I doing? Based on what fears did I discard Melike? Is it proper of me to be playing at love like an amateur with a woman I haven't seen? What's more, apparently she too covered her head at one time. Why am I searching for my prey in such distant territory? Why do I feel the need to talk about my parents, my childhood and reveal my secrets to someone who could be considered to be of the lowest order in social hierarchy, while I'm unable to find someone who seems logically suitable?

Oriental melodies pervaded the room.

The guests drew aside to make space, and a half-naked belly dancer came into the middle of the room shaking her body amid shrieks of delight. She started dancing to the rhythm of the tabor. Oiled and tinseled skin, crimson lips, bright blue eyelids...slightly muscular arms and legs...beads jumping up and down on her hips...a book where everything was written...

The woman continued to twist her belly as she shook faster and faster. She quickly rotated around the dance floor and pulled a bald banker by his arm to her side. As he tried to accompany her by moving his shoulders, she took him by the necktie and embraced him only to push him away quickly as shouts and yells rose from the crowd. A few women jumped to the dance floor and started belly dancing, and three or four men threw off their jackets and joined them. It was crazy.

Volkan forced himself to look. He searched for one person he liked or admired immensely amidst these arms that rose and fell, the feet that beat the dance floor, the disheveled hair, the belts and suspenders, in all this emulsion of mad joy and delirium. There was nobody. Husbands and wives, mistresses, lovers...there were only those who loved women, others who loved boys, super luxurious prostitutes and madams, and faces that symbolized millions of dollars deposited in banks in Zurich, New York and London.

There were some hurting truths and conspiracies.

The belly dancer had retired. Slowly the confusion died away. The tabor went silent as those on the dance floor got tired. The hum of fast breaths and jokes was heard once more. He barely noticed Nilhan who came to his side, kissed him on both cheeks and said goodbye.

He missed his home. He missed going and chatting with Eylem, pouring his heart out to her. He was going to tell her about that night. His driver had to be downstairs, in the kitchen. He sent him a message with one of the guards. He tried to look for Harun and the way out. His boss was going toward the toilet bathed in sweat. He waved to him, shook his hand hastily, said "see you Monday," and quickly walked out. As he was putting on his coat, he saw the image of a pale man who looked like him in the smoke-colored mirror in the hall.

When he stood outside the main door, he couldn't make out where he was for a moment. It was snowing, everything was covered in white. Cool, clean and healthy. He took a few deep breaths. His driver took him by the arm and helped him down the stairs. They went outside the tall walls of the complex which had been erected to protect the riches, the lustful bodies and the happy homes within, and walked toward the heated car waiting in the street. The attentiveness of this kind man was very soothing, and he let himself go. At that moment, he felt a desire to forget everything forever.

He wrote to Eylem two days later:

Yellowspot, my love,

I have finally been able to leave my job which had been lying so heavily on my shoulders since some time. At this moment, I'm far from that feeling of being ground in a mill whose speed was out of my control. I am now living in an ambiguous piece of time and I'm not afraid.

When I was leaving, I wasn't strong enough to take an open stance against this job which I have been toiling over for years and which I feel has desensitized me by chiseling away at my moral values. However, I'm sufficiently at peace from that aspect. The coming days will be a period of complete rest for me from my professional life and my focus will be on my personal relationships. I shall minimize my expectations and try to focus my attention on the world.

I am closing this subject. But let me tell you only this, together with my job, I am abandoning also the circle I have been part of until now. Naturally I will be very alone for some time. I need you.

Until now, I have tried as hard as I could to tell you about myself. I did my best to communicate to you my feelings and my thoughts without hiding their direction. I think you must have understood that I'm not a member of a secret society or playing some game that is unfamiliar to you. I'm a normal man who belongs to this world.

You too have told me many aspects of your life that you don't want others to know. You gave me the impression that you did not refrain from revealing yourself as you actually are. I thought over the things you wrote, I sincerely felt pain and sorrow at times, and I realized that I was getting closer to you with every letter.

At this point, I don't approve of your behavior which I define as lack of courage. I am closer to you than I have ever been to anyone. And I can no longer bear to have you waiting in my world of imagination like an unsurpassable obstacle. Just to know that you exist makes me feel better, but at the same time, you are the reason why I feel so helpless. Why all this secrecy, so much mystery? There are thousands of pictures in my mind which could be yours, but none of them fits in properly. When I write to you now, I feel as though I'm trying to express myself in a language I hardly know, worried and blocked.

We are at a point where we won't be able to take a single step forward if we continue this sort of a communication. That is why I give up being soft and patient, now I decide to make a radical change in my approach.

I want to see you as soon as possible.

You feel a strong urge to relate, to communicate and to write what you have experienced; you write and you scream. However, *you don't direct these at me, but at something else more superior, something that goes above the individual. I know that every beautiful and correct sound that rises from man increases in endless echoes and finally reaches a certain place. But being the only mediator of an activity which you enjoy — and accept as being harmless — and where you don't need me at all in order to continue is beginning to wear me out.*

I want to know you, to touch you. This is a request which goes far beyond curiosity, it is a necessity. I'm giving you my telephone number once again. I will wait for your call. If you say no, I will lose all my faith in the tangibility of this closeness without a name, and I will stop communicating with you.

You may have reasons you find valid, I will on no account protest, and I will be respectful.

I will cherish your presence within me, but then this will be my last message to you.

Volkan

14

Melike entered Beti's beauty and sports center. She went there twice a week, worked out for a while and then had a massage done. She could have gone to a place on the other side of town, closer to her home. But this center, where Aysevim was a partner, suited her fine and she enjoyed the cleanliness, the decoration and the sympathetic staff. Furthermore, she was given the VIP treatment for being a relative of the boss, and that was a great bonus.

Aysevim didn't come to the center very often. Actually Melike saw her cousin, who was three or four years her senior, every now and then because of Aysevim's irregular lifestyle. She was always busy doing many jobs which were related or unrelated to each other. When she had returned from abroad two years ago, she had bought two large flats in Levent. She had them converted into one and settled in it; and last year she had opened a second-hand clothes shop in Maçka. She had money and a very large circle of acquaintances, although it wasn't very clear how and when she had got to know all those people. Her living room was transformed into a private bar especially over the weekends. This large place where a wealthy, quick-witted and showy group sat and drank, gossiping about all sorts of things from politics to art, having fun telling obscene jokes and eyeing each other, became an amusing haunt after a certain hour. So much so that at a certain point, Aysevim had considered opening a bar because of the interest people had shown. However, she had later changed her mind and decided on the casting agency.

Melike had also visited her living room a few times the year before. But after an unpleasant occurrence, she no longer set foot in the place. It was an incident she didn't want to remember, one that filled her with shame every time she thought about it.

One evening, she saw there a gorgeous young boy whom she found attractive. It was a period when she was about to burst from the boredom and loneliness of the flesh. Then before she knew it, before she had time to understand how it happened, she had dragged the boy home with her. As always, something had pushed her toward a man she didn't know except for his wild smell. Perhaps it was the feeling of hopelessness and the absolute need for having sex, good or bad.

They jumped into bed without any dallying. Melike took control when they started having sex, and exerted great effort to make the game as wild, as impressive and as fiery as possible. She attacked the boy with impatient, passionate caresses and rough moves at breath-taking speed. The boy was defending himself but also obeying orders like a soldier.

After everything was over and the sun was rising, Ozan – that was his name – wanted to get up and leave. He was standing at the door fully dressed. He had fixed his eyes on Melike in bed, as if he was waiting for something. She asked him what he wanted, if he wanted to go, why didn't he? Then the boy asked for money, for his fee. Did he want money on top of it? Yes, because he had spent time, he had rented his body to her. This was his job; it was how he made a living. Melike remained curled up in bed, feeling empty and turned inside out, as she stared at him without being able to move a single finger. She pointed with her head to the bag on the chair and asked him to take whatever he wanted and never cross her path again. Ozan, with a half-rebellious, half-cornered but decisive air, emptied the bag on the bed, took two bills out of her wallet, threw the wallet on the floor and quietly went off.

When he was gone, Melike put her head under the pillow and cried for a long time. She spent that day crying and vomiting. She felt old, slighted, broken like a glass vase. She had used force on the boy though he didn't want it; she had effaced his will, and played with him until he was nauseated. Naturally he had unloaded his shame and arrogance on Melike, and he had gone off dragging her soul and femininity into old age in an irreparable fashion, shutting her there in her own night.

After this incident, she couldn't bring herself to call Aysevim for a long time. Even if she hadn't been involved, Melike felt betrayed by her. That house was a place for losing one's self in unlimited freedom, for amazement, for gushing out all kinds of words and ideas which would go nowhere, for multiple, live, unashamed hunting and improper friendships. Were people having sex in the back rooms? Were they snorting cocaine in the bathroom?

Aysevim…How could she live with all these hitches in her life?

An eccentric mother, even if she wasn't as bad as Melike's, a frail, quiet father who was a fisherman, scorched by the sea breeze and sun. A childhood spent in boarding schools on scholarships given to the needy. An adolescence filled with the proud psychological tremors of being a policewoman. Finally a magnificent career as a whore in the slimy underbelly of the country!

Melike didn't know her as well as she thought. More than anything else, she did see her as she wanted to. They had shared memories of childhood, and they had lived in the same flat when they both were young women. Aysevim had graduated from the Police Academy at that time, and Melike was a student at the Academy of Fine Arts. Because of her stepfather's insistence, she was staying in a stifling, religious girls' dormitory. Her maternal uncle provided her with financial support and encouraged her to leave the dormitory and live with Aysevim who was more than ready to accommodate.

They rented a small flat in Fındıklı and moved in. This change was the start of the road which led her to self-discovery and independence. If for nothing else, it was for this that she felt indebted to her cousin who knew how to hide her feelings, easily adapted to the times and wandered at the extremes perhaps to become free from herself.

Then, Aysevim was having an affair with an important chief of the secret police who was much older than her. He was good-looking with his short black hair, austere metallic blue eyes and an attractive, statuesque body. He had a tense, proud, aloof air, especially when he was with strangers.

Then there had been others. Aysevim was ambitious and greedy. Instead of loving the men she was with, she saw herself as an expensive −even if not very valuable − commodity she could offer them, receiving in return much more than what she had given.

After Melike got married to Yeltekin and moved out, Aysevim started an ambiguous relationship with a handsome high-level bureaucrat called Ekber Gürle who was past his prime − and also a bit thick in the head. After some time, she was transferred to the secret police force where she advanced quickly. She lived with Ekber in Ankara for a few years in a luxurious flat in the district of Çankaya, turning into a brand new woman with the way she dressed and moved and with everything she had. According to Photo Metin, Ekber was using her as bait or reward to approach foreign agents and important persons he was in contact with. If Metin was to be believed…

Following Ekber's disappearance in the US in March 1995, Aysevim lived in Niyazi Bey's house in Notting Hill in London for five years, and Melike stayed with her whenever she went to London on business. The phone rang constantly and Aysevim was out almost every evening; it was a fast, animated life. There wasn't a particular man in sight, but she constantly negotiated with people who dealt with marketing of antiquities of Anatolian origin to certain interested parties.

Melike knew that Aysevim was a partner in the smuggling business of their uncle. Although it was hard to believe, there were times when antiquities were sent to Aysevim in ordinary postage parcels. Sometimes Melike also brought her valuable small items, stones or manuscripts. She carried these items without asking questions, as a silent courier. Her uncle felt that it was safer for her not to know how things worked. In the end, everybody, including Melike, got their share.

Those were years filled with self-conditioning and faintheartedness. Melike was far from making an effort to understand in which set of connections one's judgment of values was formed, and at which level principles and beliefs carried any meaning or were unable to do so. They were the years when she felt weak, believed in the emptiness of life and felt a longing for the simple. Now she found herself much stronger and experienced thanks to what she had come to accept partly consciously, but mainly unconsciously.

There were very few people in the gym. She took off her trainers and got on the treadmill in her shorts and tank top. She set the treadmill to twenty minutes. She started walking fast in rhythm to the machine as she looked at the mirror in front of her. She was attractive and unpretentious; she seemed to belong totally to this world. She did not wish to search for anything in the sky or in the stars. There wasn't anything anymore that she had to learn, to get to know, to seek, to await or to forget.

She could make mistakes every now and then. There was nothing wrong with that. Because of someone who crossed her path or had a tempting voice…that was also part of this world. For instance, letting someone slip through her hands just as she was about to catch him. She would feel pain when giving up someone she considered a proper person, but she knew that the pain would pass quickly. That was her nature, and Volkan wasn't the first.

The treadmill was going faster, she began to run.

Volkan. Even if his body structure wasn't perfect, he had something other than handsomeness. A wide flexibility, a special, restful slowness…a lassitude similar to the life rhythm of a well-fed, somewhat lazy cat…his unhappy eyes and the touching, inaccessible loneliness of his smile made him appear more profound than he really was. Actually he was quite unexceptional. Too good not to be boring in the long run.

We weren't made for each other, she thought, finding her decision to be a cliché, but this was the shortest and the wrong definition. Being made for each other was not so important in theory. As a matter of fact, it was better to lean on opposites. However, things were different when it came to implementation and sexuality.

Melike felt two kinds of interest for men who approached her. The closeness she felt for good-hearted, affectionate, loving men like Volkan didn't go beyond the feeling of peace and emotional satisfaction. She loved them but she didn't feel the urge – or felt very little of it – to abandon herself to them. In that case, she resorted to words for covering up for the insufficiency of her body, and she spoke constantly or started discussions. This was a form of self-defense.

Volkan had tried in vain to keep up with her in hesitant, conflicting desperation, something she had found ridiculous at times. He couldn't be too naïve to know that passion was a wild, lawless, one-to-one relationship which had to be lived naked, chest to chest, screaming. For some reason, he had tried to generate love with an almost idiotic stiffness and with his distressed language as he sat opposite her. Naturally it wasn't easy to seduce a woman who preferred to deny her body only by courting her. A cunning touch or an unexpected passionate kiss was more impressive than ten volumes of words, also easier and much more enjoyable.

Melike found it interesting that the men around her seemed to be growing away from the learned role of the male. They were becoming softer, more affectionate, more respectful and sensitive. As for the women, they were the exact opposite, becoming rougher, bolder and more passionate. Men were shying away, becoming more passive, and women were inevitably taking on a more active role to keep the balance.

She remembered her last meeting with Volkan about two weeks ago. They had met at a bar and sat together for about an hour. He was in such a depressed mood that Melike didn't feel like talking. It was almost a meeting of farewell. He told her that he was about to leave his job and that he would be going on a long trip. Melike was about to ask, to Africa? But she changed her mind. Something had happened at her uncle's birthday party. He had probably concluded that she had a relationship with Hayali. And there were other things too, no doubt.

She thought about that evening at the mansion. Volkan's strange, unbecoming and uncomfortable manners had made Melike feel quite awkward. Moreover, she was so disturbed by Hayali's contemptuous glances and the offensive, scorning attitude he assumed from the moment he laid eyes on Volkan, that she badly regretted having taken the poor man to the party. She was now sure of one thing; to those who didn't know him, Volkan seemed like an outdated, nitpicky man, old in soul, someone who thought that everything was made up of the three basic elements, someone who had a hard time defining disparities.

The alarm of the treadmill went off and it slowed down. She stopped it and stepped down. She saw Aysevim coming in. She was walking with her back straight, sure of her power and her beauty. She was wearing a violet blue suit, and had gained some weight since Melike saw her last. She had let her hair grow and dyed it red and she was wearing it in a chignon. She was the perfect picture of the boss. Melike called out to her. They kissed.

"I've missed you, darling, and I just couldn't come to your exhibition. I was told it was beautiful. I have so much to do, I don't know where to begin anymore," said Aysevim.

"Why do you work so hard?" asked Melike. "Uncle was asking about you the other day..."

"I'm busy with delicate matters, dear. Difficult matters..."

"What are those delicate matters, I'm curious to know?"

"You don't want to know, darling. I'm marketing women to sex-hungry capitalists!" She gave out a laugh. Melike stared at her with her mouth open in amazement. The towel she used for drying her perspiration almost fell out of her hand.

"It's a joke. That is only a general definition. You know, that's what they really do in show business. The main artery of the business opens to the capillaries by nature..."

"What a fright I had," said Melike. "Being a madam was probably the only thing you haven't tried yet."

They sat on a weightlifting stool.

"Intermediary services is a sector which is ready to get out of hand any moment; it isn't easy to control, to apply limits, Melike. And it has become even more difficult these days. There is the agency and then there is the shop. It's true that I have employees but all the same, I have to take care of things on a one-to-one basis."

"I'll go and take a shower," said Melike, giving up trying to understand what Aysevim's words meant. "Let's sit at the café for a little while if you have time."

"Go take your shower, honey, and I'll talk to Beti."

In the café-restaurant, there were a few women whose photographs often appeared in the social columns of newspapers, five or six lovely girls, an elderly man with carefully dyed hair and mustache and two playboys. The broad windows with wooden shutters looked onto a large garden full of pine trees. Even though the weather was overcast, it was a pleasant winter day. There were comfortable armchairs in the café and a large screen for watching sports. The dining area had impeccable tables with white tablecloths.

Melike sat in an armchair and started to wait for Aysevim. She couldn't decide whether she should tell her that Hayali had become part owner of the *yalı*. Aysevim was liable to exaggerate the situation and create confusion, and that would jeopardize Melike's relationship with her uncle. On the other hand, Niyazi Bey was in such a precarious situation that he could lose the house altogether. Let them do as they want, she thought, I don't mind.

No, she did. Why should they allow that racketeer to appropriate such a valuable asset? To be ignored, to be cheated counted very much. Hayali seemed to have started a battle of power, and Melike would not let him get away with it. She felt a strong urge to knock him down, make him kneel before her, then kick him about. She trembled with the desire to take him by the shoulders and shake him, to fall and drown in the well of his dark, sparkling eyes, to bite his full lips that were always slightly open and to make them bleed, to hurt him and more than that, to tear him to pieces.

She imagined that threesome in a huge bed making love passionately. She saw Hayali one moment in the shade, one moment in the light, on top and underneath, inside of one and then the other. She saw his golden arms, his back, the masculine curve of his legs. He was pressing the girl, locked onto her body. He grasped the girl's small, round, boyish buttocks, who looked as if her head and arms were torn off, and who struggled and wriggled on top of the old man. The images changed from moment to moment. They were wrestling like hyenas, losing each other and then searching and finding one another again. Forming a whole with arms and legs hanging down from all sides, they were tearing the silence into pieces with their murmurs, pants and howls, then piling on top of each other.

Melike felt a burning jealousy as if her groin had been stabbed by a blunt knife covered with the rust of the past. She was startled. She felt herself to be weaker than she had ever been before. Her temples were throbbing. What was beginning to develop between Hayali and her remained outside logic or will. Or were they both being burnt up by the instinct of self-defense and combat which was inherent in their animal origins? Yes, there was no doubt that the challenge, reproach and scorn in the way he looked at Melike triggered the angry longing hidden in her being.

The body's defiance was damaging and it was always the same. She couldn't feel pleasure if a man didn't possess her with unbridled violence as if he would kill her any minute. Her sexuality could be activated only at the moment when she felt to be dying, that everything was finished. This was the reason why she had an affair with Metin at the same time when she was in love with Nedim. She had denied everything when Nedim had confronted her, and this had made him even madder. She quickly removed the past from her mind.

Now she wanted her enemy, that Hayali who was devoid of love. No matter how much she tried to ignore the fact, her new obsession was Hayali. The forbidden Hayali, because he felt her inclination and scorned her for it. Just to make her suffer, he let her feel his distance and his inaccessibility each time they met, he even enjoyed this.

It was true that hate was the unseen face of love. Even if she turned to stone in front of him, the need to pass from this side to the other was waiting in her like a deadly desire and was expecting to be fulfilled.

Aysevim arrived, and they went over to the dining section and ordered steak and salad. They chatted about all sorts of things: the shops, business, the whims of customers, the fluctuations in the rate of foreign exchange. Melike found it difficult to speak. Words were sticking to her throat, melting on her tongue.

"You don't seem too well, what's wrong with you?" asked Aysevim. How healthy she looked. How carefree she was with the usual crazy glitter in her eyes and her manicured hands which were insensitive to pain and open only to cheap thrills. She was dating a man who was in the hotel business. He had just been divorced. He did everything she wanted but he wouldn't have guests in the house. On evenings when he couldn't come to her, she said, she sat in front of the TV with her cat in her lap.

"There is something I want to tell you, but I'm not certain whether I should or not," said Melike. The words had poured out of her mouth of their own accord.

"Tell me if it is important."

"You could call it that. Uncle told me that he gave 50 per cent share of the house to Hayali. I think he is under pressure."

Aysevim smiled with a condescending, unconcerned expression on her face.

"Would you say our dear uncle has gone senile, Eda?"

"No way, he's completely agile."

"What he did is unacceptable. Well, if it is, let's hope for the best. Why should we mind? The uncle takes good care of himself, he is fit as a fiddle, and who knows who will live and who will die. So, why did he tell you this?"

"Aysevim, how should I know? Perhaps it's because the other half may go, too."

"Apparently Hayali has sold his precious ass for a lot of money. That *yalı* is worth at least three or four billion liras, Eda."

"I have a feeling they aren't on very good terms. Uncle was quite concerned."

"Well, in that case he is expecting our help. If Hayali manages to get hold of the place, he will either throw him out or kill him. We must take measures."

"What can we do?"

"I know the uncle better than you do. He probably did it to keep that faggot from leaving him. We might have to get a senility report. Naturally first of all, we must intimidate Hayati a little to remind him that he is not totally free to do as he pleases."

"I wish I hadn't told you! What do you plan to do?"

"Leave it to me."

Melike spent the next afternoon in the shop and in the studio upstairs. The shop assistant took care of the visitors. Business hadn't been too good lately. The market was in panic due to the constant rise of the foreign exchange rate.

She liked her place. It was rather secluded but pleasant. At the back of the shop, there was a small kitchen and a hidden room where she kept old stuff. She marketed not only jewelry but also old antique pieces. There were vases, little bronze statuettes, porcelain knick-knacks, glass essence bottles and antique decorative pieces displayed in old walnut cupboards. She had placed two winged armchairs in one corner with an old lion-footed tripod in between. When she was organizing the place, she had taken care to turn it into a well-decorated, smart room and not just a space where old pieces were thrown about. It was necessary to have good taste in order to display diverse pieces in harmony, forming a whole.

The studio upstairs was decorated with stuff which she hadn't taken to her new home when she moved out of the shop. With its few pieces of furniture, a few valuable antiques and a drawing board, it had the atmosphere of a somewhat untidy but romantic living room.

The little bell hanging over the door rang, and a lovely young woman walked in. She hesitated slightly when she saw Melike and gave out a small exclamation of surprise. She looked familiar but Melike couldn't recognize her at first. As she got up from her table and walked over to the smiling woman, she suddenly remembered.

She had seen her four or five years ago at the hotel of her relative, İlhan Ağabey, at the first birthday party of the son he had by this woman, on that awful night of the murder. For a moment, she saw İlhan Sacit's bullet-riddled body by the pool. The poor man had died for nothing because of this slut.

"Do you remember me, Eda Hanım? I'm Renginur."

"Of course. How could I forget," Melike muttered.

Renginur held out her hand. Melike shook her hand without enthusiasm. The bitch has become even more beautiful, she thought. She looked very smart. Naturally, she was a rich woman now. Three-fourths of İlhan Ağabey's estate now belonged to her, or to be exact, to the child she had borne him.

"How are you, Eda Hanım, what a coincidence. I didn't know this place was yours."

"Yes, for a long time now."

"I've been in Istanbul for two years; I was in Izmir before, as you know."

"Yes, I heard that you married, congratulations," said Melike with a bitter voice.

"Yalım needed a father. I didn't want to remind you of that horrible event, I'm sorry." There was infinite grief in her eyes but an offended resignation could be detected in her voice. She must have accepted the fact by force of reality and only in her mind, not in her soul.

"You weren't to blame," said Melike, half-heartedly. Actually that was the truth.

The case had lasted a long time; the shooter had not spoken, not betraying those who had hired him to kill. Actually the perpetrator was quite obvious: İlhan Sacit's sister-in-law, Fikran. But there was no evidence. Melike had learned from İlhan's brother, Armağan, that a year later Rengigül had married a young man who was in the leather business.

"Do you ever see Armağan Ağabey? How is he?" asked Rengigül.

"He moved to Antalya. I hardly see him anymore. He and Figen divorced two years ago."

"I'm sorry. They were a lovely couple."

"The self-sacrifice of donating life to others never goes beyond being a sad effort. One is always alone," said Melike.

"I loved İlhan. I suffered a lot; naturally it's not important whether others believe this or not."

"It was a great pity. I sometimes think that ours is a cursed family."

"Oh, no, how can this be true? Anyway, I'd better go, I'm in a hurry. I'll come back some other time."

"If you would like to look at anything…" said Melike.

"I was going to look at that brooch in the window but I don't feel like it anymore. I'm a bit upset."

"I understand, my dear. How is your son?"

"He's just fine. He's in kindergarten now."

She has matured, Melike thought, she has found peace. She is definitely no longer striving for recognition. Melike watched the young woman who was walking away into the gray darkness of the street under the softly falling rain. Perhaps a curse was a negativity or a contradiction that grew in one's being. A civil war, a chaos, the more ignored the more it gets diffused in our lives, flowing over and turning into fate.

It was almost six o'clock. She sent the shop assistant home. The girl lived in Maltepe; she had a long way to go. Melike was going to close the shop in an hour. She went to the kitchen at the back. There was a small counter and a sink there. A miniature setup for tea and coffee. She made herself a cup of tea. When she heard the tinkling of the bell on the door, she hurried into the shop and saw Hayali coming in.

They stood face to face for a moment, looking at each other silently.

Hayali had never looked at her like that until then. He radiated arrogance, a tension full of anticipation and a wish to play games. Melike didn't turn her eyes away from that look. She let loose her desire which she quickly hid, and in return, she received a smile from him.

Hayali hardly ever came to the shop. He had dropped by at the most three or four times in two years. Melike felt time was like a sieve which had sifted all the truths she had known or had foreseen.

"How are you, Madam? We have missed you," said Hayali. His courtesy implied the usual subtle irony, his arrogant distance. A general contemptuous outlook on life rather than coolness...

"I am honored," said Melike. "To what happy occasion do I owe your visit?"

"Does there have to be a reason? I was passing by, and I just dropped in."

"Why don't you sit down?" She showed him to an armchair. Hayali didn't sit, he went over to the glass-covered counter. He waited in thought as if looking at the pieces inside. Melike was leaning against the table with the cash register, watching him as she tried to be calm.

This young animal with a rugged beauty, this unknown tramp, slighted by her uncle who had given him his ridiculous nickname, could not have come without a purpose. She was sure that he had a problem. Friendship was out of the question. He was wondering around the shop in an insolent manner with his hands in his pockets with an evil, foggy look in his eyes. These could not be good signs. With an instinct of self-defence, Melike looked out at the street. The rain had turned to sleet. It had grown dark, the lights were on. A steam cloud was hovering over a manhole on the sidewalk; a whiff of sponge cake had drifted into the shop through the door which had been opened and closed a little while ago. She felt Hayali looking at her, and she turned toward him.

"What is your problem with me, Eda?" His voice was soft, almost affectionate. "What is it that you want from me?"

"Problem? What problem? Wrong question."

"Don't do that. Don't act as if you don't know. That will make me mad. This is not you."

"How can you be so sure you know me well?"

"You can't hide your feelings. One has to be an imbecile not to know what you want."

"And what is that? Tell me so that I know."

"You're crazy about me, aren't you?"

Melike froze for a moment; her head was burning inside. She stared at him as if she couldn't believe what he had said. The enemy was constantly advancing toward her, opening and bleeding her childhood wound caused by docility and obedience, turning it into anger and rebellion. This time it wasn't her *uncle-dad*, but this bastard whose body she desperately craved for, his irresistible eyes and mocking mouth. She forced herself with all her strength to put on an indifferent air.

"I consider your words as a rude attack on my personal territory," she said. "Did you come here to tell me this?"

"Actually I was going to suggest that we bury our hatchets. Let's talk openly and end this tension. This is of no good for either of us. We must compromise."

"Hatchet? I don't have anything like that. Furthermore I'm extremely calm."

Somebody was standing outside, looking at the jewelry in the shop window. Then she came in. She was a rather elderly woman and she had some lettuce in the plastic bag she was carrying. She asked Melike if she could show her the silver spoons in the window. In the meantime, Hayali had started giving the woman information about the spoons, explaining how valuable they were. They were expensive, yes, but they were old, and there were some spoons in the Topkapı Palace Museum which were very much like these.

As he was talking tenderly to the customer, Melike thought how kind he could be if he preferred. His voice too, it was like water. So much so that Melike heard him but didn't feel the need to know what he was saying. She was watching the movements of his lips, longing for the language of his hands and feeling all this in an astounding dizziness. The woman bought the spoons and left. Melike put out the light of the shop window. She turned the key in the door. The only light in the shop now was the night light on the table in the corner. She had decided to listen to Hayali and find out what his intention was.

"We can talk if you'll be reasonable," she said. "Let's sit down. I'll bring you some tea." She went into the kitchen. She pressed the button of the electric kettle. A compromise? What sort of a compromise? No, that wasn't possible; it would be more pleasant to fight with this man. She thought about the phrase "increasing the tension." That was a kind of progress, too. She put a tea bag in a mug, poured the hot water in it, took the mug in her hand, turned and came face to face with Hayali.

The first thing she felt was a sharp fear. His face was swollen and taut, his mouth was contracted as though it was about to shout or bite; he was looking at her with a naked, piercing look that reached her heart. In that tight space, Melike tried to step back from him. Hayali had opened his arms to both sides and he was holding the frame of the door, blocking the way out.

"You are in my way," said Melike. "I've prepared you some tea. Step aside so that I can pass."

"Come on, don't play games with me. You would jump on me if you were strong enough, wouldn't you?"

"You faggot, you liar! You disgust me, disgust me!"

Hayali made an angry dash toward her, and Melike threw the tea and the cup in his face. The young man's chest burned and he charged at her in a frenzy and attacked her.

Melike pushed him off, as they struggled. The jars and the drying rack on the counter toppled over with a loud crash. They looked as if they would strangle each other, tear off each other's heads. Hayali took Melike by the hair, roughly pulled back her head and bit her throat. Melike gave a cry, and tried to attack and scratch his face like a cornered cat but he grabbed her arm. At the same moment, she felt a hard slap on her face and she staggered.

The young man pushed her back against the wall. His arms were strong and tight. He closed his mouth on hers and kissed her furiously, as if to make her bleed. Melike let herself go as if she were shot; her will to defend herself suddenly disappeared, and an earnest urge to reciprocate took its place.

She resisted that furious, beastly attack very little, only just enough. Without it, she had been nothing but a barren existence for some time. Her voice was muffled in her throat. Hayali was caressing every part of her body so vehemently as though he wanted to tear it apart; no part of her body belonged to her anymore. Her hands furiously took hold of the man's face, her mouth searched for his lips again and found them of their own accord. If it was to happen, it should finally happen and that would be better than uncertainty. And why should it not happen? A person, a man or a woman, gender uncertain, but no, it was of no importance.

Her arm was around his waist, was it her doing this, she wasn't certain, but that was the way it was. The other one, who was he? That wasn't certain, either. Their bodies went through a shadow. At one time, when they were watching and longing for each other, they knew this would happen someday and they knew how their war would come to an end. They both knew that the long anticipated single combat was inevitable.

They just ignored it.

Everything was burning and the flames were illuminating their faces. All the same, the world was beautiful, very beautiful. It was beautiful with its darkness, its winter, its rain, its snow. There was no problem. There were no glances. Their hands moved, they locked together and then let go, knees were bent, eyes were closed. They were sinking together. Their kisses were perfect, their lips parted and closed upon each other again. The darkness was short, and yet it was very long. What they had learned till that moment and what they would never learn wasn't important at all.

Humidity. Rubbing against each other and being dragged. Defeat and fiasco on all fronts. So be it. There was no logic anymore. A weak word, murmurs. A hand that remains in the air, clenched fists, and then small screams followed by a strong final thrashing movement…that magnificent and blurry feeling of death…

They fell to the floor in front of the counter. There was nothing to say. It was a moment when even the slightest word would have been too much. They covered each other's faces with kisses. Hayali pulled Melike close with his arm as if he was afraid of being abandoned. A small murmur came from Melike's mouth. Short, unconnected words were going through her mind. Guilt. Silence. Shame. I'm not afraid. Love. Childhood. Orgasm. Dream.

Her back was icy cold from lying on the stone floor. She didn't know when and how they had undressed. She turned to her side.

"Say something," she said.

"That's how it is," said Hayali. "What else can I say at this moment?"

He got up and put on his clothes quickly. He seemed to be in a hurry to run back to the others.

Melike felt pain, she was hurt and disappointed. How could she have made the mistake of surrendering to him so easily? They had barely conversed until then. There was a silent war between them, but their emotions had not surfaced, were not revealed.

No, they were close and at the same time strangers. It was a mutual cognition and avoidance that came from sensing and reading each other's minds; a secret desire which had reached the point of loneliness, anger and hate. Had it been Hayali's intention to destroy this desire? Did he want to get rid of it, of this burden, to tear it apart and cast aside?

"Why did you come?" asked Melike. "Why now out of the blue?"

"I don't know. Suddenly I found myself here. Perhaps it was to give you a chance or that we would share a secret that would reconcile us. It was not planned."

"A chance? What a ridiculously arrogant ..."

"I thought we could come to better terms."

"Don't go just yet, stay with me a while."

"I can't."

Melike put on her clothes. Hayali had passed into the shop and was standing by the door. It was almost nine o'clock. The rain had turned to snow, and the narrow street was dark and deserted.

"Why do you always hide behind yourself?" she asked looking at him.

Hayali looked at Melike with eyes shining with concentration, with eyes that could see but not feel. Then he lightly caressed her cheek with the back of his hand.

"I was hiding behind the person you were trying to imagine, but I was also watching you carefully, Eda. You were more than ready. That was why you made yourself so unattainable. Try to understand, I could postpone acting only so far."

They looked at each other. For the first time, Hayali's face was free from that mocking smile. Melike saw once more that there was no outlet for her feelings. If she gave him a chance, he would take advantage of her hate to the end.

"You only taught me the beauty of hate," said Melike. "Don't ever think of this as a victory."

"I think I'm the one who has lost," said Hayali. "All the same, what I'm looking for is not love. Forgive me. We may be much more distant from now on. Try to keep yourself afloat, will you?"

He looked at Melike for a second with a stony expression, then a barely perceptible mistrust appeared in his eyes. He suddenly opened the door, turned up the collar of his coat and walked away under the softly falling snow with quick, sure steps along the sidewalk toward the main street.

It's over, thought Melike. He will never step in here again and nothing will remain behind. She tried to detect in her soul the hate she felt for him. She couldn't. As she remembered the union of a little while ago, she had a pleasant, languid sliding feeling in her belly. She burned inside with the desire to run after him, to beg and make him stay.

She wanted to cry out loud, to scream and shout, but she couldn't.

No, the battle wasn't over yet. All the postponements had only been put off once again with a majestic ceremony.

15

Tatula Mix Restaurant Bar, *with its menu offering different tastes from various parts of the world, and its renovated Chalet-style decoration, is one of the popular venues of Istanbul that has made itself a name as one of the coolest spots in the city.*

There was a large blazing fireplace in the most attractive corner of the room where patrons sat in armchairs and ottomans, sipping hot wine. All the tables and the long bar were occupied. The light from tiny lamps, candles and the fireplace gave the room a dreamlike atmosphere. The sound of the saxophone and the piano from downstairs, where there was live music twice a week, could not completely drown the hum and the laughter inside. Music played in a melancholic tone like a sound that came from afar.

Everybody was in dazed contentment, because everything here fitted down to the last detail the rhythm of the time, of development, of being in a world city.

The women, *in their jeans styled by the avant-garde trends of the day, tiny balloon skirts, sparkling, low-cut tops, stiletto-heeled shoes or Marc Jacobs boots, looking like they had popped out of some foreign fashion magazine or an Anna Sui show,* were in harmony with the spirit of the venue.

The menu, which was full of strange words, seemed to Eylem like a witch's recipe. She left it on the table and looked at Jale. They had been seen in less trendy clubs before but it was her first time in a place like this.

They were four at the table; there were two more girls besides Eylem and Jale. One was Sumru, an archaeology student. She was a baby-faced, innocent-looking blonde. She too could be considered new; some time ago she had appeared in a carpet advertisement. The other girl, Aytül, already had some experience. She was a tall, breathtaking brunette. She had graduated from an exclusive high school, and although she came from a well-off family, she had serious problems with her father. About ten days ago, Eylem had been obliged to go with her to an appointment with a man who had asked for two girls. Jale and Didem had had a hard time in convincing her to go. They had told her that most men made such demands, that she would be double paid for such an appointment and she would have to get used to the idea if she was to continue working there.

It was bad. The man was young, cultivated and polite but Eylem froze the moment Aytül touched her. She somehow managed to fill the hour with Aytül's guidance, and later avoided looking at her and at mirrors for days.

A waiter came and asked what they would like to have. They weren't hungry, and it was almost past dinnertime. They would only have something to drink.

Jale asked the waiter, "Is Aydo Bey here?"

"Yes, Madam. He will be with you in a minute."

Yüksel Aydolar was Beti's boyfriend and the owner of the restaurant. He came and stood by the table, greeted Jale coldly and took a quick look at the two girls. His gaze stayed longer – even if somewhat furtively – on Eylem's face, which was under the light of the lamp on the table. His mouth contracted into a forced smile.

He had an artificial tan. He seemed to be an athletic type, sensible but also conceited. He quickly looked around at the tables and the bar. It was a quick glance as if he had discovered his fly was open and was looking around to see if anybody had noticed. He was probably content with the turnout in the club, because he turned to Jale with an optimistic gesture of the head.

"Okay," he said. "Did you bring the pictures?"

Jale took out a thick envelope from her bag and held it out to Aydo. He took it and went away.

The month before, Eylem and Sumru had their photographs taken in a studio. Separately, in different costumes … dressed in bathing suits, half naked, on their knees, on their backs, on all fours … from the back, bending down, straight or curly hair, with pouting or half-open mouths … photographs which could be considered half arty, half erotic; most of them black and white, some in poses and atmosphere reminiscent of the postcard beauties that were circulated in Istanbul at the turn of the century …

These had probably been useful, because when Eylem used to have two or three customers per week before, she had begun to take two or three per day. Aytül had told her the best of these photographs would appear on a web site, but Jale insisted that this was not the case.

Eylem wasn't thinking of moving to another place yet. She sometimes stayed in Çengelköy for days, because it was a cold winter, and the villa was nice and warm. Food was no problem; Lara always cooked something to eat. Eylem read when she had time, or she flipped through fashion magazines or women's monthlies.

Three weeks had passed since Saffron's last message where he had insisted on seeing her, and she still hadn't written back. He seemed too real for the virtual world, and unbelievably naïve for the real world. The things he had written had made Eylem strongly, disturbingly curious but she couldn't decide what to do. The most practical solution would be to stop writing. On the other hand, she had started to feel some kind of love for him while she wasn't writing. If she pushed him out of her life, she was going to feel alone and empty inside.

One needed love to perceive the world in the right way. When you were alone you would not be able to observe certain aspects of life from where you stood. If alone, you would also doubt the reality of dreams, because dreams had no witnesses.

However, it didn't seem quite normal to her that a well-off, mature, sensitive man should be searching for internal calm and freedom which he said he missed, by communicating with someone he knew nothing about. Neither was it easy to believe that he was longing for someone sincere to whom he could pour out his heart. Eylem sometimes imagined him as a man of a certain age who still hadn't grown up. And sometimes she wished she could see him, stay close and hide in his lap. To be protected from the world, to offer herself only to him, to be free of the strange, surreal situation she was in and to stay put like that as long as possible.

She was afraid of meeting him socially, of losing control. They were continuing their relationship with letters as they had done right from the beginning. This romantic tie which she couldn't underestimate gave Eylem a break from her depression and helped her to write. However, Saffron had refused to make do with that much and now he was keeping quiet.

At one point, he had even written to her that he could find her a good job. He was giving her a chance to start all over again. He promised her a new life. Promises…men's promises…gratitude and flattering delusions…she was beyond the age of depending on that enticing male fantasy of saving a woman. She knew that men prepared themselves for this role through idols, not reality.

To seek and to find…to be dependent or independent…all these were concepts pertaining to a future that would never come. It was too late, much too late…

In the beginning, situations which she used to consider taboo or sinful were giving her great shame. Then she crossed the line between shame and shamelessness, and started seeing herself not as a victim, but a laborer who did the job she was obliged to do. There were crimes uglier, heavier and more unforgivable than earning money by using one's sexuality. Genocide, wars, injustice, exploitation, torture, even bigger evils…what's more, those who suffered these evils, or opposed them, or at least condemned them had no place to escape to. If giving up your beliefs and your values, keeping in step with the world was considered as losing – according to some – then losing was the only way out.

Anyway, nothing much had changed since Seyit, except for the variation of faces and bodies. What was defining and unbearable at this point was that she lived not as a simple being but by being conscious of her own complicated existence. She suspended her consciousness whenever necessary, stressing her impervious self. However, her make-believe did not save her from feeling that her *self-awareness* was at her heels.

Every so often, she heard the coarse words she used to hear from Seyit. Sometimes she was even obliged to repeat these out loud to certain perverts who enjoyed hearing her confess that she was a prostitute. As the price was generously paid, there was no problem. Also, when playtime was over, she could depart easily, without leaving behind anything. Then she returned to her own self, and she closed the door from the outside insensitively as if she had not been involved in anything, hadn't lived through anything, hadn't uttered a word. Even if it was nothing but a sad denial, this was the easy way out. No matter how attractive it was, there was no need for an emotional bond which would cause conflict between herself and her *self*, resulting in their estrangement.

She had to end her relationship with Saffron. There was no reason to bring a custodian into her life, to offer herself to him for free, to live with fears that would paralyze her soul as she tried to hide the unsavoury secrets of her life. But most important of all, she was in no condition to spare time for a relationship that was sure to end in heartbreak.

"Come on, come to life. There are people looking at you," said Jale.

"You want to make whoopee? Then tell us something funny, sister."

Aytül lived with her parents so she usually worked during the day. Eylem was at least free. She didn't have anyone who would track her, ask for explanations, to whom she would have to justify her conduct.

In spite of the pitiful hideousness of their situation, they were forcing themselves to laugh and be joyful during the night, amid the lively human tide and the music. Sometimes, Eylem imagined that some of the words they spoke were of a precivilization language; nonetheless she didn't mind. The wounds didn't look fatal as long as they didn't bleed.

"I've had enough of that regular parcel of mine. He tried to wear my underwear the other evening!"

"My mother is out hunting these days to find a suitable husband for me."

"You owe me 180 dollars, honey."

They weren't friends. They were allies in a dark world.

"I'll pay you, honey. I have it on me."

Their conversations were about money, dicks of the customers, new shoes, sales at this or that showroom. They had effaced their previous lives. They were live engines sought by those who wanted their fantasies and sexual desires satiated, in exchange for green bills. A thing…an object…they were porcelain dolls with painted smiles on their faces that belonged to the world of men who liked to flaunt their power to buy everything and everyone, including their miseries and misfortunes. They did this to enjoy the power of their money, while pretending not to attach much importance to this transaction.

"I feel hot. Are we going to sit here as if waiting for husbands? Can I have another drink?"

"Why don't you walk over to the girls' room, darling?"

"I'll go in a while," said Eylem. She had to get up and show herself to some people. She took a sip from her drink and looked around discreetly. Aydo was talking to a middle-aged man who seemed somewhat bedraggled, with a bohemian air. He turned around and looked toward the corner where she was sitting. She had two parcels the next day, and this one would probably be the third one.

Jale winked at Eylem. She had been telling her from the first day that she had to confront her obsessions if she wanted to get rid of them. It was difficult to resist the determined optimism that radiated from her face. She was strict and yet affectionate; she made a point of getting along with everybody. She was the right hand of the boss, and she always said that the protection of the girls was what she cared about most. Eylem had seen the woman called Aysevim once in the café at the gym, but they hadn't talked. Although she had looked at Eylem with piercing eyes, she wasn't interested enough to approach her. From what Eylem understood, this woman preferred to seem uninvolved in this dirty business. She was the brain behind this shady business and also the one who established important contacts. But she preferred to stay out of the limelight.

"Eylem, go to the bar, honey. Aydo is beckoning."

Eylem got up. She walked with careful but lively little steps on her high-heeled shoes. They had prepared her for that night. They had chosen from the boutique a tight, flaming red dress with a frilled, low-neck collar, exposing most of her breasts. She couldn't help wondering who the previous owner of that dress was. They had made up her face and styled her hair with great care. She certainly looked very beautiful in the mirror. Sometimes her beauty bothered her, seeming to her like a curse, and she wished she could cast aside this shell of hers.

It won't be long, she thought, as she settled herself on the bar stool Aydo had shown her. She looked and smiled at the tall man with the round face covered in stubble and a protruding belly. *How are you?/And you?* She had already saved up 14,000 dollars in three months.

What would you like to drink?…/ I won't have anything, thank you. She helped her sister and supplied the children's small needs. Of course she hadn't told her sister what she was doing. She thought that Eylem had a good position at the company, that her salary was increased. *I have an advertising agency. My name is Sezgin. You have a lovely, original face./And I'm Elvan. How do you do?*

If she could continue this business for a couple of years, she would be able to buy herself a small place. Then she would return to life, find an ordinary job and work. Her escape plan was ready.

We are preparing a special catalogue. We could put your picture in it. What do you say?/Oh, why not? What sort of work will it be?/ We'll talk about it. Naturally I'd like to know you better. Shall we spend the night together?

It was most obvious that the woman in the pictures would be someone entirely different, definitely an illusion. That is, if he still remembered Eylem when he sobered up. Just now, he was either very drunk or he had taken some drugs. His eyes were closing, he seemed to be far away and he couldn't control his mouth. No, there wouldn't be any photographs. There was no longer any art, beauty or love. Everything had lost its value. Even happiness was sexual fulfilment only, a momentary explosion based on pleasure and imagination, a cold, random deal.

She wanted to forget everyone and everything so that she could embrace nothingness better. She wanted to forget again, once more, countless times. She wanted to reach oblivion itself and its unending, clean, pure shores.

On the way to the house in Çengelköy with Sezgin, she silently sat at the back seat of the car wrapped in her coat, her face turned toward the window. It was midnight. The man was holding her hand. He was wearing a wedding ring, she touched it. *Does that bother you, darling? My third wife. She's eight months' pregnant. We can't sleep together anymore. Would that bother you?/No, it doesn't...* Whereas it actually did. She felt like a sad child. How awful it was not to be loved, only to be desired and having to endure it. Why was this man holding Eylem's hand and not the hand of the woman who was going to bear him a child?

But his palm was warm, patient. He may get rough later, she thought. He had almost passed out. Suddenly everything seemed very complicated. Where was she, where were they going?

They were crossing the bridge, driving through the familiar streets under the cold, pure night lights. The sea seemed to be holding its breath, waiting for the moment when the scream it had been storing reluctantly would burst through the ground and be free.

This city, she thought, even its soil, its cobblestones are filled with infidelity underneath. This is the city of pitfalls. It is the easiest thing to lose one's way, to get lost here. This is the city of the lost and the dead, an amazingly sad refrain. A memory that is continually bleeding as it slides back to the time and its own space. The destruction deepens as we look on and the city angrily plants itself in front of its past while turning into a fairground.

She pulled back her hand. The man's hand had grown heavy and limp and his skin had turned cold. The desire which had been waiting in his body a while ago had inconveniently withdrawn from his instinctive animal memory and it was sleeping. Eylem woke him up when they arrived at the house. *I must have dozed off, sorry. /It's not important, just relax.* She should finish her business one way or another and get rid of this corpse quickly.

Lara was waiting. She had been informed. They went upstairs to one of the rooms. Eylem tried to take off the clothes of the man who was like jelly. *My love, come on make me hot, what was your name, what a gorgeous ass you have, baby…*She laid him on the bed. *Speak, tell me what you want.* She propped him up on the side of the bed like a sack. *Do you love me? Tell me you love me. Don't lie.* He was in no shape even to move. Desire was only in his head, in his mind; his organs were not obeying him.

Eylem pushed him over on the bed and lay beside him. The smell of alcohol was oozing out of every pore of the body which was trying to embrace her muttering unintelligible words. His hand stopped short as it tried to caress Eylem's breasts. The idiot! He was going to spend the night there and pay for "the whole night." Eylem took the man's arm off her breast and placed it by his side. She pulled herself to the far side of the bed and closed her eyes. She walked toward her own fairy tale. It was a tale she enjoyed. It was a lullaby she sung to herself.

Whenever she closed her eyes while she was with someone, she found herself in the forest of souls in the land of nobodies. There she felt that she belonged both to this world and to the other. She sometimes hid in a secluded corner and sometimes walked on footpaths that went up and down the hills. Her body usually traveled in a horizontal position. That way she could see the blue lace of the sky in the openings between the thick foliage of gigantic trees, and she felt relieved. When seen from below, the universe took shape according to the forest. Colors, lines, labyrinths, rustling of the trees, the sound of a stone toppling into the water, the crackling of the bushes and the whisper of the wind were in complete harmony. Plants and animals existed alone, and yet they formed a beautiful and magnificent union while staying true to themselves.

This environment was good for Eylem. Murmurs, loud panting, insults no longer existed then.

When she was in the forest, she felt that her body was lost but not touched. It was the only place where she didn't feel devoid of locality, where she didn't feel that she was dully repeating herself or someone else. She sometimes felt as if she was searching for something unknown as she walked along lanes covered with blackberry bushes, lanes that could be left behind only by walking. Then she understood that she had taken her soul to the forest in order to forget how defenceless she was. Even if she felt breathless in the arms of an unknown man, she didn't feel the urge to pass over softly, convincingly.

She only felt quick expanding motions inside her, and she patiently waited for the moment when a low-flying bird would come and flap its wings on the water. This way it became much easier for her to continue her obligatory labor than it actually was in reality.

She liked to jump from branch to branch and swing amongst the trees, to rest leaning against a fence when she became tired, to look at small forest insects, to watch this chaos of life in which she too played a part. There were certainly other animals in the forest. Birds, bees, dragonflies, mosquitoes…foxes, beavers, porcupines, tortoises, fish-like creatures, moorhens…the quiet ones, the noisy ones, the discontented, the obsessed. When Eylem closed her eyes, she saw all of these with their general features, usually in the coital moment of four-legged animals, and she conceived herself as a huge yellow eye.

When she woke up, all these images became one mingled fleeting memory and her own image, rapidly spinning as it fell into the darkness, disappeared in the pupil of her eye.

After taking two more customers the next day, she returned home in the late afternoon. This place, where she didn't spend much time, was her last resort and her poetry house. She no longer complained like she did at the beginning. She managed to warm it up when she paid for fuel. The only thing that softened the harshness of her life was reading, as always. Books refreshed her, gave her a confident joy. There were times when she read for hours wrapped up in a blanket or worked on a poem all night. She no longer wrote to Saffron because he never replied. She missed the nights she used to spend writing to him.

She had told Volkan about her childhood, her parents, how she grew up, what she read and what gave her pain. Even if she hadn't described to him her entire life, she had told him about important milestones, the shadowy world of her own internal courtyard, her brief and emotional impressions of the present. Volkan knew her as a virtuous, sensible little woman. Someone pure, consisting of breezes, life worries, insignificant emotional complications.

The best thing was to be quiet, because she had been born sinful, ready to be torn apart, to be used, and she had been hurled into the hell, that is, this world.

However, she still had water, light, bread, and best of all, money to buy as many books as she wanted. Books helped her feel cool inside and warm outside.

She wasn't going to work over the weekend. She would see her sister, read and do some cleaning. Then she put the finishing touches – for the time being – on the poem she had been writing for some time.

I'm a spotted butterfly
Born from its own color
In the forest of souls
Scale by scale I shed my skin
I'm a coin in circulation
Afraid to slip
Out of one's hand and
Into the dark gutter
I lay myself
At the first stop in hell
Under bushes that smell of fire
For scavenger birds to pick at my body

She was excited to see that there was a message from Volkan in her email. There, he hadn't been able to keep his word and he had written again!

Eylem,

You wrote me that some people conducted their relationship with the world with their head, and some with their hearts. When considered with the head, with logic, it is inevitable to seek a relationship of reason–result. Whereas love cannot become true before it defeats reason.

I still want to see you but I no longer make it a condition. I accept defeat and I retreat.

When I left my job, what I wanted most was to go as far as I could from the point where I was at that time. You were the moving force of that process. I approached you with a childish optimism and madness. I was nurtured by your sentimentality. Now I find it difficult to cope with your silence, your absence.

I have been without a job for a month now and I'm not at all bored. I have taken pleasant short trips, gone on hikes. I have been to the cinema, the opera and concerts. I have watched the tapes of the best music performances, dance groups, theater companies, seen my childhood friends. I have gone shopping to my heart's delight, I have read and slept.

But all the time, I had the impression that I was missing something.

We share a past where we confided in each other. Even knowing that the other one is there at the end of the line is a comforting thought, something like a promise of eternity. I love you hopelessly like I love the people I love most.

Will you write to me again?

Eylem read these lines over and over again with trembling hands. Suddenly she felt a strong urge to call him. Her heart tightened with the pain of losing something beautiful. She walked to the window hoping for some relief as if she could see something other than the concrete buildings in the darkness and the rain. She lifted the curtain by the corner and looked outside. She saw the shelters of those who scrambled underfoot, as they continued to live their ordinary, difficult, small lives; dirty and dark under the cold blue street lights, a few lamps here and there, balconies full of litter.

Could there be a way out of here?

She remained standing by the telephone. She could take the way out if she wanted, even if it were only for one day, one night. Why should she deprive herself from the tiniest hope? Only momentary pornographic pictures were what remained in her memory of the men who had entered her life until then. Volkan could be a mirage in this merciless desert. A supportive friend who would help her stand on her feet…a distant joy…

It was almost midnight but it was all right, she could wake him up. They were close at that moment, very close.

She opened a bottle of wine with trembling hands. She sat by the telephone and drank a glass of wine, then another. She looked for a long time at her hands holding the stem of the glass. She agreed with Volkan; it was not at all rewarding to tell someone certain things only in writing, and to love him while remaining only within the limits of writing, because writing meant hiding one's self to a certain point. It was not at all possible to be one's self without touching, tasting, seeing and hearing.

She pulled the telephone close and dialed the number she knew by heart. The phone rang four times. She waited, her heart pounding, hoping for an answer and yet dreading it. Then an anxious "hello" was heard.

"It's Eylem. I was moved by what you wrote."

There was silence at the other end, then a surprised, excited answer.

"I wasn't expecting it," said Volkan. "No, I did expect it, but I didn't have much hope. I'm very happy."

"I just couldn't decide. I didn't want to leave you hopeless like that." She gulped, I'm the one who is hopeless, she thought. She sighed and shifted her weight from one leg to the other. As she stood there by the window, with the receiver in her hand, and her heart beating fast, she felt for a moment that some things were changing, that she was stepping over the threshold and entering another space.

"I don't know what to say," she said with a trembling voice. "I want to see you now."

"Why was it so difficult for you to decide, Eylem?"

"I don't know. Perhaps because I was afraid everything would become mediocre."

"If you hadn't called everything would have turned into nothing."

"I realized that tonight. No matter what, there had to be a voice, a face."

"Absolutely. When can we meet?"

"An afternoon early next week would be fine."

16

It was seven o' clock in the evening. Volkan was waiting for Eylem in the lobby of a hotel in Taksim. The moment and the place he was in seemed to be a limitless "space–time" which was composed of all the places he had been in, including all the moments of his life and the ones he had forgotten. A transparent continuous time which came into being by itself…a bright, breakable glass globe which could slide from his hands and shatter into thousands of pieces any moment…

There was a fluttering feeling in him, light and heavy at once, a vague rebellion. He hadn't thought that she would agree to see him. They had reached the peak very suddenly. He tried to remember what he had written to Eylem. He was very sentimental and slightly drunk when he wrote to her. He felt that way then and he was feeling very lonely. His present reality was somewhat different.

Here he was, all excited and waiting for a small, unimportant woman found on the Internet. This was a deprived position for a man. Had he come down in life? If not, why did he feel the need to include this ghost woman in his life? After so much experience, had the map of his inner life changed completely, reaching the point of collapse? If not, why was he doing what an oppressed, lost man without identity would do? Why was he taking shortcuts?

And whose thoughts were these? What was there to be ashamed of in his situation? Shame, he thought, a feeling we are taught to have when we step out of the usual path of behavior and belief, becoming visible. What creates shame is the judgment and the eyes of others.

As someone who tried to reject that judgment and those eyes, he had ended up here on his own accord and in a most natural way. He had learned about life by experiencing its different aspects in an environment which glorified sexuality and sexual liberty, scorning and ridiculing romantic feelings. He had been afraid that such a life style would destroy him, and he had decided not to abide by anything in his past. After having pushed all these thoughts aside, it was stupid now to look down on himself, to think just like before.

It was as if Eylem had woken him up from his hibernation at the start of a new season. He had poured out his heart to her continuously for three months. This momentary alienation had to be due to the anxiety he was feeling. Who would he find in front of him? An obstinate young woman who hadn't matured enough, who could express herself only in writing? A shriveled spinster or a firebird? Considering that dreams and imagination were hardly ever compatible with reality and that coincidences could not be prearranged, the woman who would arrive would probably not be the one he had imagined.

Eylem, when her name became integrated with what she wrote, made him think of a thickset woman who was sentimental and totally feminine, and yet also cold and slightly neurotic, in constant denial and defiance. A misfit who walked in the front line in street demonstrations with a flag in her hand, who was quarrelsome and harsh in bed…However, the most important components of this image, which were color, light, texture and smell, were missing and the picture did not go beyond being a pattern.

As for the name Yellowspot, it created the image of a petite young girl, amiable, warm, docile, lonely and in need of protection. A sweet hope sprinkled amongst the shadows of a half-formed dream, something like a yellow shooting star.

Which of these two pictures did he want? Neither one of them. A blend of the two would be ideal, and that was what he expected. Perhaps he was here just to live that moment, this present time which was open to surprises.

He was sitting at a seat close to the entrance and watching those who came in. He suddenly had the feeling that he had fallen into a black and white film. Such things used to happen in old Turkish films. After all, their starting point was true life, so why not, maybe he would soon meet a woman who resembled Nurhan Nur whom he liked so much.

The mean girl had not only hidden herself, she hadn't even sent him a photograph, making sure he was completely in the dark. Was she afraid that she would be leaving nothing to Volkan's imagination if she destroyed that precious distance and filled it with her being? He remembered her timid, soft, childish voice on the phone. That voice did not quite fit her rebellious nature.

Yellowspot had said, "I will be wearing a black coat and a yellow scarf." A very general description ... All the same, if he wasn't totally wrong, he was sure he would recognize her with an entirely different aspect, the one that reflected doubt and distance.

He didn't disdain her. It went without saying that it took strong will to keep suspense so masterfully for months, making it possible and necessary to establish indirect contact. It was true that they had reached a point where they didn't know what to write to each other anymore. She seemed to be closing herself, growing more distant. This had awakened in Volkan the will to cross the boundary and the wish to beat the master at her own game.

For the first time in his life, he was feeling a disturbing attraction and a downright sexual desire for a woman he hadn't seen. A strong impulse to seduce and possess ... For a long period when he lived without really knowing himself, he had made love to many beautiful women who came his way, and he had forgotten about them the next moment. They had left nothing behind, not even any crumbs.

He wasn't hungry for love. He and Fundi had lived a four-day escapade in Cyprus, having fun in the casinos all night and making love as much as they wanted. What he felt for Eylem was something different but he didn't quite know what it was. What was this violent, heartrending longing? Was it because they had met in the deep innocence and measureless daring of writing? Was it the flexible, wide open, uncontrollable richness of words which made it possible for one to face his estranged self without being shaken or intimidated?

There were very few people in the hall; a middle-aged couple huddled together, a fat woman busy with her little daughter and an elderly gentleman. Volkan glanced at his watch. Yellowspot was already twenty minutes late.

He looked at the slender young woman in a black coat. He recognized her by the way she hesitated at the entrance of the hall and the yellow scarf she had put on. He couldn't believe his eyes.

Eylem's glance settled on him and she walked over to him. Volkan got up, as they greeted each other, shaking hands somewhat awkwardly.

She took off her coat, put it on the chair next to her and sat down. She was wearing a wide black skirt, an open-necked, narrow black sweater over a thin, white tank top which accentuated the beauty of her figure.

"Even if it was a little difficult, we finally managed to come to the meeting stage," said Volkan. "But your scarf isn't yellow, it's saffron yellow."

"So that you would recognize me more easily," said Eylem laughing. "I got it for you; I had to search hard for it. You know, your pen name was enticing as a name as well as a color. I was impressed."

She raised her eyes and looked at him. Her look was distant, heavy and hopeless, but she was very attractive. Hers wasn't a striking beauty, but it was a mysterious, different kind of charm far from the current concept of doll-like beauty. An unhappy beauty that was reflected in the hidden look in her large, hazel green eyes...In amazement and dizziness as if he had been offered an unexpected treasure, Volkan took the scarf Eylem had held out to him, wrapped it around his neck and asked, "Do I look nice?"

"Yes, it's lovely."

"You're very sweet, Eylem. It's a good thing I forced you into meeting," said Volkan.

"I had no choice. Only death could keep me from coming."

Volkan had naturally thought that the girl's reluctance to meet could be due to her physical shortcomings. He hadn't dwelled upon the idea too much, provided she wasn't an extreme case. He knew that what drew one person to another was the meaning lying behind the general attitude created by a glance, a stance and behavior, something which the person who was locked in the body could not see for himself.

"But why did you hide for so long?" he asked. His voice was muffled.

"I may have waited for our closeness to mature," said Eylem. "And also the way we met…" She sighed as if that natural grace, that softness had been shaken for an instant. There was brilliance in her eyes and a slight hesitation. For a moment, her anxious, slightly bitter glance stayed on Volkan. Then with a quick, abrupt movement, she turned her head and looked around the room.

"Has it matured, do you think?"

"I don't know. It was something like a game in the beginning. I'm surprised that we have come to this point." She was excited and tense, but she was doing everything to conceal it. Volkan looked at her with an affectionate, light-hearted smile.

"We won't stay here. We will go to have dinner somewhere nice in a little while."

"That's not possible. I have to go to my sister's tonight. I can stay only for an hour."

"But we had agreed to be together the whole evening."

"It's an emergency, I apologize."

"I'm very sorry."

"Let's leave it to another evening," said Eylem. "We will get used to each other better, spread it over time." She tried to explain her unease.

"This is an interesting experience for me too," said Volkan. "Something different. I wasn't expecting someone like you. I feel as if I've been punched in the face." They laughed.

"So what did you imagine me to be like? Haughty, bald, blind…"

"Oh, no. At least I had your photograph. I really did you injustice by not believing you."

Volkan looked at Eylem's face. He saw the distant look that had settled on her face, a mixture of timidity and exigency. He found her even more attractive. He went back to that afternoon when he had pressed his lips passionately on the mouth of the first girl he ever loved. He was living that mysterious happiness once again, feeling the endless excitement of not knowing, of innocence. His numbed spirit had awakened and seemed to be blessing the adventure he had been longing for.

Due to the boldness of her writings, he had imagined Eylem to be a daring woman. However, what he faced at that moment was a well-equipped, impressive innocence which could be cast off easily when the time came, and this made her even more alluring. This little woman seemed like a fresh page for him where he could write anew correctly all the relationships he ever had with women, one which would absolve him of all his past sins. He felt great pleasure in burying them all, and especially his latest flame Melike, into the past.

During the period when he had turned to Melike, his interest in Eylem had faded, almost disappeared. Then their correspondence had become more intimate and more frequent, flaring up his interest again. Volkan was sure that this was not an investment toward his own quest, but rather a basic feeling of wellbeing and a wish for approval that he needed on the road to renewing himself. Eylem had told him such interesting things about herself that, in spite of all the risks, his curiosity had been wrapped up in a feeling of affectionate intimacy.

They ordered coffee. Volkan thought about the possibility of her becoming his lover soon, and he was filled with pleasure. As far as he knew, there was no one in her life. She had written him about having a long relationship with someone while she stayed in Ankara, explaining that it hadn't been love and that it was completely finished. When they were addressing each other from a distance, from their private domains, they had opened their hearts to each other sincerely with the confidence and boldness of being far from each other. Now they both were feeling quite awkward face to face, having to appear informed and yet ignorant. Perhaps, the real reason for their uneasiness was that everything was extraordinary and absolutely perfect at that moment.

They quickly took to each other. Whatever obstacle there was between them disappeared while they had coffee, and their conversation took a natural flow.

"Where do you live, Eylem?" asked Volkan. For some reason she had never told him.

She explained that she was living below Kağıthane, close to her sister's, and that she wasn't very happy there. She had told him a little about her sister, the children and her paralyzed brother-in-law. She briefly mentioned them again, without much enthusiasm. She was convincing and modest as she described her world as a small, narrow place.

"The ruin you mention, the new road you have taken, what are all these things?" asked Volkan. "I have been thinking about it."

"Gloomy, empty words…I sometimes become overemotional," said Eylem blushing slightly as she tried awkwardly to brush aside the subject. "It's difficult to stay in balance. It's been six months since I came to this city. I still haven't been able to grasp its soul and I feel a little lonely. Life is very fast here. Sometimes I feel as though I'm not keeping up with the turn of the hours on the clock and I'm constantly falling behind. Can you understand that?"

"I'm trying. I know a few things about you but these are reflected from your point of view. People can get to know each other only by talking," said Volkan.

"But you have to understand in order to know."

"You are right. That applies to both of us. As a matter of fact, it applies to everyone. One's perception of himself, of the world and of others is changed forever when one can understand and interpret what one has experienced."

"This may be the death of reality or what is known as right. Well, I should leave now."

"I can drop you off wherever you are going."

"Thanks but I'll take a taxi."

"It was a very short meeting. Let's have dinner tomorrow. Would you be available?"

"I don't know, it depends on my sister and brother-in-law. Let's talk tomorrow."

"Have you found a job? I had written to you that I could be of help."

Yes, she had found a job right away. She was working in the accounting department of a textile firm. She liked her job and had a satisfactory salary.

"Aren't you thinking of going over to a job where you can make a career for yourself?" asked Volkan.

"No, economics wasn't what I had wanted to study anyway. And when my work experiences ended up in disappointment, I realized that I wasn't very gifted. Now I want to earn enough money to support myself and concentrate on writing."

Together, they went out, to the evening full of lights and noise. Eylem hailed a taxi, as she seemed to be in a hurry.

"It's been a pleasure. I'll be seeing you," she hurriedly told Volkan and jumped in the taxi as if running away.

She is timid and sweet, definitely very sweet, and I'm in no mood to think about what love is and what it isn't, thought Volkan. Love is love and it makes one do crazy things. As Nilhan said, you waited all your life with your foot on the threshold, sonny boy! What a coward you are!

The next day, he tried to reach Eylem on the phone many times. Her home number didn't answer and her mobile was turned off. Perhaps it had been cut off because of an unpaid bill. He finally managed to reach her in the afternoon of the second day.

They met in Ortaköy the next evening and went to a quiet, pleasant restaurant.

The waiter guided them over to a secluded corner and lit the candle on the table. Eylem was happier and more lively that evening. She seemed even more beautiful and relaxed after a few glasses of wine. Her serious, sad expression had disappeared. Her glances were excited and furtive but full of smiles. She was trying to avoid clichés when she spoke, choosing her words carefully, and yet she did not sound artificial. She was so natural and laughed in such a lovely way that Volkan felt relieved as though he had just passed a tough examination. His eyes met Eylem's gaze, and what he saw was the gleam of a curious child and affectionate interest rather than sexuality.

"Do you like this place?"

"I'm glad that I answered you when you first wrote to me; and I'm happy we are here together at this moment. This is real happiness," said Eylem. She had propped up her head with her palm and she was leaning on her elbow. Her wavy, long black hair fell onto her neck.

"Why was your phone dead the other day, Eylem?"

"Let's agree on one thing. I hate being controled and having to account for myself, because my best years passed doing exactly that. I've grown weary of it," said Eylem straightening up. "If you ask me too many questions you might tire me."

"It was just interest and some curiosity on my part. I didn't think you would react so much."

"I can be harsh when it comes to protecting my freedom. I'm very sensitive on this subject, I'm sorry."

Volkan imagined seeing a theater stage. The back room of a shanty house...A world full of depression; attempts to make it bearable with embroidered pieces of cloth on the furniture, local television series and arabesque cassettes...An actress in the role of a young girl who works in a textile factory at an overlock machine...What had gone wrong? He didn't know what kind of a smell or a sign had set her off, but a tiny line of separation had suddenly appeared between them.

"I know, but I have been thinking about you for three days. Naturally I was worried. I kept calling you to hear your voice, to tell you about how I feel. I panicked thinking I had lost you."

"Oh, Volkan…I understand. I should have called you but I had…so much work. Meetings all the time, all those conceited idiots!" She took a big gulp of wine. Her ornate bracelet rattled on her arm. Then her eyes settled on her thumb with a distant gaze as if she had slipped over to a moment of immobility in another world.

Volkan watched her expression. No, there was nothing to worry about. It was normal for one to lose control over the things that made her who she was. After all, the world would always be a foreign place for people like her.

He raised his head and saw that Eylem was studying his face with a detached frankness while she waited. Her dark green woollen dress decorated around the neck with a wide black ribbon framed her face and neck like the leaves of an unfamiliar plant.

They waited, hesitating quietly. Then Volkan spoke to break the silence, "Who do you look like, your mother?"

"I don't know. I probably don't resemble anyone. At home, we never spoke about our physique, our bodies. The subject was totally ignored."

"You have a very expressive beauty, Eylem."

"Thank you. I believed for a long time that I was ugly and I was, too. Can you imagine what I looked like in that outfit, covered from head to toe?"

"No, I can't."

"I was able to write you only a fraction of what I lived through."

"It must have taken great willpower to leave all that behind."

"I don't know if I have been able to do that. I still have problems in my relationship with my body. I still have a broken heart and…I'm angry."

"I know."

"That's why I want to write. I understand everything better when I write, and understanding eases my pain."

"You mean a lot to me. Please let me help you to recover."

"I'm not worth the effort. I'm just an ordinary woman trying to stay on her feet one way or the other, someone who could easily be a thief, a killer or a prostitute."

Her voice was harsh and bitter, like a scream. Volkan was shaken to the hilt. The girl was looking at him directly, with her head raised, her eyes dark, as if challenging him. Cold, her mouth tight, with a condescending air...

"What strange things you seem to say! Come on now..."

He looked at her in amazement, curiosity and pity. She seemed to be very sure of who she was. He remembered how innocent she seemed on the day they met for the first time, and he felt a slight fear. The expression on Eylem's face slowly softened. She took a cigarette out of Volkan's pack and waited for him to light it. Then her eyes met his; the darkness had disappeared, they were now full of light.

"This is the feeling I get from my life and the world we live in," she said softly. "It is the essence of what I say, no matter how unreal the rest may be."

She lowered her eyelashes and waited like a naughty child expecting to be forgiven. She seemed so docile that Volkan felt a tremor inside.

"You don't seem to turn your anger to the right direction," he said. "I understand from what you have written that your effort to find yourself is without aim, left to roam."

"It's no use to run after shadows. Someone of the *nobody* class has to believe in chance, to depend on it. We do not possess the freedom of shaping our own path for better or for worse."

"Do you mean to say you believe in fate?"

"No, I'm talking about the system, not fate. The order which offers virtual freedom, forcing one to make marginal decisions."

"You were so brave in your first message. Why do you yield now?"

"I no longer find that attitude realistic and logical. You come to the crossroads one day, and something totally unpredicted suddenly appears before you."

"Abandoning yourself to chance takes you nowhere. I do not deny the value of small surprises but freedom without will is dangerous."

She looked at him for an instant with a scared look. Then she turned her head toward the window, implying she did not wish to continue the subject.

"You wrote me that you have never been in love. This seems incredible to me, Eylem," said Volkan.

"I believe that love is a real feeling but at the same time temporary and difficult to reach. You first come together with a great attraction, then you become wounded and you part. I don't like the nature, the design of love. That is longing first and rejection in the end."

"It doesn't always have to be that way."

"I wouldn't know. For my part, I believe that I have missed all my chances forever."

It's very difficult to communicate with her at this level, thought Volkan. He quickly changed the conversation to more amusing daily subjects.

They were laughing as they descended the steps outside the restaurant. It was very cold, an oppressive, dark, icy winter night in March. Volkan put his arm around her shoulders and pulled her close. He felt he wouldn't get to know her unless he saw her naked, until their bodies were united. To be embraced, to be loved would comfort this fiery creature and give her back the initial goodness of her being. Wasn't there serenity in the depths of one's body?

"Will you come to my place?" he asked. "I live close by and it's still very early. I'll take you home later." He was tipsy; they had eaten little and drunk a lot.

"I better not," said Eylem hesitantly. "I'm tired, I have to go home. Not tonight."

"You must come. I want you to come so much. Come on, trust me."

His request was simple. A man and a woman…All the same, he didn't want her only as a woman. Although he had been disappointed with Melike, he wasn't hurt when it was over. But Eylem's image which he had saved in his mind seemed like an endless fairy tale at that moment. A world to live in and discover…

"Please don't insist."

"In that case I'll drop you home."

"No, no. I'll just take a taxi." She was watching the street uneasily, waiting for a taxi to pass. Volkan's car was right in front of them and his driver was waiting.

"No way, we'll take you home. Why do you behave like this, Eylem?"

"I don't want to drag you into narrow, ugly streets. This car can't go to those parts."

"It can go anywhere. Come on, darling."

Volkan almost pushed Eylem into the back seat and sat next to her. It was pleasantly warm in the car and the driver was going slowly.

"My hands are frozen," said Eylem. She looked at Volkan but she didn't smile. Their eyes met. Her presence was like a soft breeze. She was complex and difficult, but she was like a breath of fresh air, a deep breath. Even if he wasn't aware of it, this airiness gave him the hope of finding again a forgotten song, the warmth he missed, a dream he had lost. He took her hands in his and warmed them. Eylem closed her eyes and lay back.

Volkan was touched by the expression of sadness in her face. The need to kiss her, to console her, to take care of her wounds passed through him like a jolt. He was hooked, mixed up with her. He was a little scared, but then all love affairs were scary in the beginning, that is how it should be. He felt Eylem's hand come to life, as it became warm and held his hand tightly.

"Do you think I'm a woman with a complicated soul?"

"No, darling, you are an orphan."

There was a short silence.

"Let's go to your place," said Eylem. Then she added with a barely audible voice, "I need you." She opened her eyes and looked at him hopelessly for a moment, and then she closed them again.

The living room was gloomy. The light by the door of the terrace filled the room with soft shadows. Eylem was still in a melancholic mood, she was sitting quietly on the low couch, watching the weak flames struggling in the fireplace.

Volkan brought some coffee and two glasses of cognac and sat in the armchair opposite Eylem.

"Drink this, you'll feel better."

"Your home is lovely, peaceful." Eylem took a sip from her drink, left the glass on the coffee table and leaned back. "My home is sordid. I've always lived in miserable homes. This is the first time I have a place of my own but that too is miserable. I bought my furniture from second-hand shops."

"I'd like to see it anyway."

"I wouldn't want you to. It would have been too embarrassing. What I want to tell you is …" She stopped.

Volkan saw her sit up and gulp in an effort to say what she had to say. He waited.

"Our social backgrounds are very different."

"No, they aren't. We can smooth out our small differences."

"You don't understand, there is a class difference between us, a deep crevice."

"We are from the same class, Eylem."

"It doesn't seem so to me."

"Look here, you think too much. Why don't you try to let things take their own course? Live the moment. Isn't it beautiful? Isn't it exciting?"

"It's very beautiful. I feel as if I've known you for years. I'd never want to give you pain…"

"Why should you give me pain? We've just met. We are adults, we are free people. We can experience some beautiful things together. This may be a streak of luck for us. You have to approach it positively."

He got up and put on a CD. He went to the study and came back carrying a large teddy bear with a missing ear. His mother had brought it from her home, his childhood toy. He put it in Eylem's lap. They laughed.

"This is my sleeping companion from my childhood. I'm giving it to you."

"Why didn't I meet you before?" said Eylem. Her eyes were full of tears.

"It's not late..."

"It's too late. Believe me, it's much too late."

"No, it isn't. What's more, I am not addled with what I feel for you."

He looked at Eylem. Her eyes were glistening with tears, she seemed to be enchanted. Her fingers which had been caressing the bear loosened. Volkan leaned over and kissed her softly, as if asking. He got a passionately positive answer. He pressed his hands to her cheeks and continued to kiss her until she was out of breath. Her body was melting, coming undone in his arms. Then suddenly she pulled herself back tersely, as if startled. She buried her face into Volkan's shoulder and started to cry silently.

Volkan knew these tears, that bittersweet pain. He kissed Eylem's wet face with a feeling other than desire, a feeling full of a past with heartbreaks, an unknown future and endless promises. He caressed her back, her hair, her shoulders. He kissed her again and again.

"I'm frightened, hold me," murmured Eylem.

"What are you afraid of?"

"Everything, the future..."

She got up pushing Volkan away slightly. She went and sat on the ottoman in front of the fireplace. She pulled her knees close to her belly and wrapped her arms around them. The fire was making reflections on her face, her chest. Suddenly she seemed to have gone very far away.

Volkan sat next to her. They silently watched the fire together, with resignation and understanding. It was sad to have lost desire. He looked for the slightest change in Eylem's face, a warmth that would reach him from her distant smile, but there was none.

"This is an illusion," she said after a while. "Dawn will come and all will be over. Then you will see the ash on my skin." She turned and looked at Volkan with sadness and anxiety.

"What are you talking about, Eylem? What's wrong?"

"Can you call me a taxi?"

"No. I can't let you go at this hour."

He picked her up and carried her into the bedroom.

They sat on the bed in the dim room. They undressed each other. Volkan saw her full breasts with pink tips, the shadows in her armpits, her navel buried like a ring into her soft flesh, the promising silence between her legs, and he trembled. She was very beautiful. Her hair melted in the light, tiny glitters vibrated in her eyes like the wings of a beautiful leaf bug. She was the picture of delicate spontaneity. The way she parted her elegant, glistening, well-formed legs and stretched them to support her body was exquisite. Volkan felt a maddening desire to love her, protect her, own her and take her as his own.

He caressed her silky skin, her soft curves. He abandoned himself to the pleasure he felt when Eylem's sensitive hands moved over his chest, his groin, his shoulders. They closed on each other with astounding desire. They made love with a warm, mysterious, shared feeling, with candor and abandon. With desire and with compassion...Being both themselves as well as the other...Wanting to understand who they would be if they hadn't been themselves, wanting to renew the world with brand new emotions...

Then they embraced and lay in each other's arms. Eylem had pulled her knees to her chest and she was crying with small sobs. Volkan pressed her against himself and felt that delicate, vulnerable body undulate in his arms. He said her name over and over again. He kissed her face, her tears until her head was tilted back. Eylem gave a forced smile, put her hand on her breast and lay on her back. Volkan put his head on her belly and let her hands caress his hair.

They didn't speak. Their emotions were so intense that there was no need for the gilding of words. They kept silent as though every word they would utter would remain inadequate, ordinary and cheap. Their bodies were constantly repeating every forgotten word.

Volkan felt that the body in his arms was growing heavier, becoming more distant. Their hands met every now and then in a desperate caress. They were tired; they were at the point of breaking away from each other against their will. Then slowly they were defeated by time, the enemy of love and to the night and sleep.

When Volkan woke up at about seven o'clock, he saw that Eylem was no longer in the bed. He got up anxiously and looked in the bathroom and the kitchen. There was no sign of her or her clothes. He found a note on the bedside table.

"I took your bear. I will keep it as a memory of our encounter. I will always miss you and this night. Thank you for your closeness and your compassion.

With all my heart…"

17

Melike woke up to the sound of a banging door. She was lying between soft, white satin sheets. There was a faint smell of wood and polish. At first she didn't know where she was. Then she recognized the wooden ceiling painted white, the doors of the old-fashioned cupboards, the smell of the sea, and she remembered she was in the *yalı*.

Her memory was full of short, broken images. Her uncle's phone call, asking her over to the *yalı*. Her fear ...she had drunk too much the night before. She couldn't put the events in order.

Lately she had been drinking too much, walking aimlessly for hours, crying without reason. Drink soothed her pain, dragged her into a carefree lightness, turned her into a vagabond, but only for some time.

After the night at the shop, she didn't see Hayali for six weeks. Sometimes she doubted whether that night had ever happened. There was nothing between them that warranted such intimacy. Furthermore, she had been shamefully dumped at the end. This was the only truth she couldn't bear, no matter how hard she tried with undue cool to cleanse her memory. She phoned Aysevim the day after that night, trying to find out discreetly if she had made an effort to intimidate Hayali.

"*Stay out of this*," said Aysevim. "*I'm taking care of it. Why, did something happen?*"

"*No, I just asked. He hung up on me the other day.*"

Naturally this was not true. They hadn't communicated at all.

Once the masks had fallen in a most unexpected way, what could they say to each other, how could they look at each other?

Melike felt most confused in the days that followed. It was as if she had been left with a sad, unbearable burden. The pain of love flowed in her veins as blind desire when she thought of Hayali. She pushed aside her wounded pride and her trampled emotions and wanted him again. Her hate had lost its vigour and her anger had turned into the mourning of being deprived of him. Now she was dreaming of abandon rather than war and making an extraordinary effort to maintain her hatred.

Their intercourse had been an exaggeration entirely devoid of love, a callous roughness which carried no hope, a momentary rapture. But it was beautiful all the same, as beautiful as the impropriety of a magnificent accord.

This was what she longed for every moment, day and night.

She got up and went out to the hall. She walked to the bathroom, washed her face and brushed her teeth. She returned to her room and got dressed.

She had arrived at the *yalı* the evening before. Her uncle's voice on the phone had been a little cool, anxious and hurt. He was telling her they had to talk. Melike had imagined Hayali to be the reason of this coolness and she had come running, frightened and worried. She felt trapped, restless, tired and ill when she sat opposite her uncle.

Niyazi Bey didn't look too well, either. He was pale, weak and pensive.

"There have been some negative developments, Eda. Hayali has been in London for two weeks. We had to get him out of the country because some people are making life very difficult for us. We were getting critical phone calls threatening him with denouncement or death."

Melike felt an infinite relief. So that was why he hadn't called.

"Is it known who these people are?" she asked, her voice was calm.

"There is a big shot involved. We had a disagreement about the price of an invaluable piece he wanted to buy a few months ago. When Hayali went to talk to the man, he apparently put his gun on the table and told Hayali he wouldn't leave the room alive if he didn't accept the price the man gave him. Naturally our man didn't accept the offer because it was about one-tenth of the value of the piece. As we knew it was going to take some savage bargaining, Hayali had gone with a bodyguard who was waiting outside. So with the confidence of having him there, Hayali played the hero. He showed the man his chest and told him to shoot. Quite incredibly the man stepped back but turned very angry and now he bears a grudge."

"So what's going to happen now?"

"I feel I've been beaten this time, Eda. I'm trying to come to an agreement, to meet him half way, but the whole thing has gone beyond just being a price dispute. The man lowered his price even more. He turned it into a matter of obstinacy, a fight for power. The son of a bitch wants blood money. Hayali will stay in London in the meanwhile. The situation is critical and it may take some time. We need you again, my dear."

"Uncle, you know that I no longer …"

"I know, but I'm anxious and alone at this moment. There is no other sure way."

"Am I supposed to go to London?"

"Yes, dear. Hayali will wait for you at the airport and watch after you. We have taken all the precautions. I warned him, he will treat you well."

Melike felt remorse at fooling an old man, but the feeling didn't last long. Her joy, her excitement was stronger. The simple truth was that she wanted Hayali, she missed him terribly and she could even throw herself into the fire for this. And what was Hayali's role in this arrangement? Was he calling her to the place where they would be free? She wondered. What optimism! She could never be sure. On the other hand, she knew that if she went, their relationship would continue where they had left off and it would remain secret. What harm would that do her uncle? She cruelly thought, we are young and he is old, as if trying to justify herself.

"Did Hayali go with Işık?" she asked cautiously.

"Of course not, why should she go, what does this have to do with her? I need her here; she is the one who does all my work."

Then it's worth the effort to go, Melike thought with joy and pleasure. She felt a restless desire to see Hayali and to be alone with him.

"I can't say no to you, you know that, Uncle."

"I know, dear. Thank you. You can be sure that what I'm doing is serving a passionate minority in finding the joy of possessing the most exclusive relics of history and rebuilding the past by owning these. This is an expensive and dangerous illness, whereas I'm getting old and I feel that I'm declining. However, I won't give up this job until the day I die, because I can't live without secrets that give me pleasure. In short, I need your help more than ever, Eda."

"What's to be taken to London?"

"Small but very valuable Assyrian pieces from the looted Baghdad museum. They reached us somehow, and we paid a fortune for them. We definitely can't keep them here. They've to get to London as soon as possible."

"You're putting me at great risk …"

"It's not like that. There's no danger of a tip off; we are protected. Some small pieces will be sewn onto your daily clothes. Some of the others that need to be hidden will be thoroughly camouflaged. You will be travelling with plenty of rubbish and you will be dressed as an ordinary laborer working abroad."

"When?"

"In two days, with the evening plane. Your seat has been reserved. Hayali is staying in Notting Hill at the house where Aysevim used to live. You will be staying there, too."

Melike was silent. She thought, he trusts Hayali so much, he can't even begin to imagine what happened between us. She looked at her uncle with an expression of patient loyalty. She was sure there would be no danger in any way. Suddenly she started. Hayali's coming to the shop, what happened there, had it all been a set up? Not her uncle's but Hayali's plan! If that was the case, the matter in question had to be a very big one. Her uncle? No, he would never sacrifice her. But Hayali could. She imagined Baghdad Museum being ransacked. She became even more confused.

"Let's go and open a bottle of good wine, have dinner and talk about other things."

She had drunk too much, wrestling with hundreds of questions and doubts. There was a young Iraqi named Aziz at the table. He spoke some Turkish; his uncle was very interested in him. Who was he? What was he? Was he going to take over Hayali's place, she wondered.

Niyazi Bey had told her that the problem was due to a disagreement in price. Why? What was it that made it impossible to make an exchange according to the rules of equivalence? Or was this some plan of Aysevim? When she thought about Aysevim's environment, her high-level circle of connections, she knew it could very well be. These people owed each other in all sorts of different ways. She could have arranged for the intervention of someone capable of putting Hayali in a tight spot. The threat of denouncement was the most feared trump in the world of smuggling.

Işık wasn't present at dinner. She had gone to see her aunt. That was another mystery altogether. Why was everything so complicated? Why couldn't it ever be simple, open and obvious? Why was truth turning into an ever-deepening dark hole in front of her? She had been born with a certain amount of intelligence like any ordinary person who was not an idiot, and she had had enough education to develop her ability to understand. In spite of this, she just couldn't grasp what was going on.

She was in no shape to go home when they got up from the table. She collapsed onto the bed adan Hanım showed her.

She went home after breakfast. There was a message from Aysevim on the answering machine. She was telling Melike that she would be coming for dinner. Why, when she had so much to do? Melike called the shop to tell her assistant she wouldn't be going in that day; the girl could lock up and leave. She cooked one or two dishes, looked at the papers and fed the cat. She would be leaving it with her uncle; it was used to the *yalı*.

She had read in one of the social news pages that the CEO of Cosmos Holding Harun Baylan had been divorced from his wife amicably in one hearing, and that he had paid her a hefty alimony. There was a picture of the couple dancing in their happier days.

Had Volkan left the company? At their last meeting, he had told her that he was about to quit his job. He had probably found peace. "I could have given him only pain," she thought. At all events, he didn't deserve that.

She felt a commotion, a pleasant movement inside. Two days, only two days later she would be seeing Hayali. Even the thought had an enticing glitter. Theirs had been an incomplete union. The exciting part was yet to come. God, please don't let there be a hitch.

She put her feet up on the ottoman and sat there for a while, trying not to think of anything. For a moment, she considered closing the shop. She had been thinking about this for some time now. What she earned wasn't worth staying cooped up in the shop all day. It would be more profitable to move the workshop somewhere else, and rent those two floors. It was very generous of her uncle to have given her that property. Once again, she thought the price had been paid. She hardened; one couldn't feel gratitude for a favour forever.

Aysevim came at about eight o'clock. She hadn't been to Melike's home for a year. She embraced her with a happy airiness. She hadn't had lunch, so they went to sit at the table right away. They talked about daily matters for a little while.

"What's going on between you and Hayali?" asked Aysevim suddenly.

Melike looked at her for an instant, trying to understand what Aysevim wanted to know, but fearful of giving herself away, she quickly averted her eyes. Her face felt flushed, she was embarrassed as she groped for words.

"Nothing," she said with a raspy voice. "Why did you ask? You know I don't like him."

"That's not how it seems to me, but never mind. Hayali Efendi was obliged to escape."

"I know. I went to see my uncle yesterday."

"Is the old man happy?"

"He doesn't seem to be. What happened?"

"The *yalı* problem has been solved. Hayali gave back the share he had borrowed and he turned it over to my uncle once again. Needless to say, he didn't do it voluntarily. He was forced to sign the paper that was put in front of him. Actually, his thing should have been cut off to give him a lesson!"

"What are you saying!" said Melike in astonishment. "Tell me what happened."

"There is nothing to tell. Money can change its appearance, if it is used as barter for mutual interests or an object of pleasure depending on the situation. I have very important friends and protectors. Nothing would get done in this country if there weren't laws above laws and those who apply these skilfully, darling. Some people may see me as an ex-intelligence officer or even a high class prostitute who saunters around, but they would be underestimating me greatly."

Melike didn't say anything. She leaned back. It felt as if she was leaning against barbed wire, whereas Aysevim seemed to be in a very good mood. After all, with her complex, fascinating games, she had succeeded in transforming a boring and vulgar life into an extraordinarily attractive one.

"My uncle told me that a businessman had pulled a gun on Hayali."

"It's possible. And the price has been paid."

"I hope it didn't cost you too much."

"Not at all. In such instances, the best present is a live chick, cheaper than water!" She gave out a laugh.

"I'm stuck with my uncle's business again. He's sending me to London."

"Look honey, forgive me but couldn't you find someone other than Hayali?"

"I don't understand how you jumped to that conclusion."

"You're not interested in money or the *yalı*. He is all you want. Don't forget this favour I'm doing you, okay?"

Melike fidgeted uncomfortably in her seat. Things had got gradually worse, losing their shape and going beyond the limits of her perception. Or perhaps she didn't want to understand and was pushing away the facts. It was safer not to know. That was how she had always looked at things. It was easier that way even if it turned her into an even more inconsistent, insatiable and lonely woman.

If somebody had seen Melike at the airport as she waited for the London plane, he wouldn't have known what to make of her appearance. Contrary to her usual style, she was sloppily overdressed. She had carelessly gathered her hair with a large, metal hairgrip in the form of a tin eagle. She was wearing a large, short, red jacket and blue jeans. The buckle of her belt was worth a fortune, and her arms were covered in bracelets. She was carrying a large suitcase, a dirty fabric bag and a gigantic package wrapped in plastic and secured by packing tape. It was full of all sorts of old clothes, shoes, towels and other junk that she could find in the house. The artifacts had been placed between the folds of the old clothes, in the lining of the jackets, in her toilet case and the shoes in a way that wouldn't show up on the screen of the security check at the airport. The alarm went off as she passed through the magnetic gate. She showed her bracelets and laughed playfully. They searched her but there was no problem.

She was experienced. The important thing was to seem calm, sure of herself. Furthermore, there wasn't much risk unless there had been a tip off. All the same, she had become excited and short of breath at one point. She was most afraid of Hayali, and it was he who quickened her heartbeat.

The plane was crowded. As holidays were about to start, the majority consisted of workers' families. When they landed in London, she went through the checkpoint without any problem. She relaxed and admitted to herself that she actually enjoyed this excitement. She loved to live on the edge. This wasn't how she had been born, but it was the way she had grown up. During those six years when her *uncle-dad* would come into her bed while her mother slept downstairs – from eleven to seventeen years old, she had lived through similar fears, she had been trained like an animal and she had grown accustomed to being slighted and hurt.

Hayali was waiting at the exit. They looked at each other for a moment. He was tense; he had lost weight and looked haggard. He coolly kissed Melike on the cheek. He looked serious, and that arrogant, sarcastic smile he bore on his face had disappeared. They got into a car and went home. They were quiet and distant as if nothing had happened and uneasy as if full of regret. The night at the shop seemed to be hanging in the air between them, and Hayali let her feel that he knew who had tripped him.

The lawn in front of the house was unkempt and muddy. The house that used to be gray had been painted light blue and decorated with white stripes. It was a small, narrow, two-floored, turn-of-the-century building. The cherry tree in front had not yet blossomed. With its impersonal interior, it seemed quite different from when Aysevim lived in it. It had been neglected for a long time; the curtains had faded and some of the furniture was no longer there.

They spoke casually. *No, I'm not hungry, I ate on the plane. / Are you cold, shall I light the fire? / That would be good.* I wish I hadn't met him, thought Melike. I was just about to find stability, now I'm lost once again.

When she came back from after a shower, she saw Hayali taking the antiquities out of their hiding places one by one with great care. He seemed to be in a trance, as if he no longer knew where he was. Two extraordinary tablets, a small metal statuette, some jewelry and a few seals. A total of nine pieces.

She watched him wrap the artifacts in a soft, thin cotton fabric, rewrapping them in onionskin paper or putting them in wide boxes filled with packing fiber and then finally putting them away into a cupboard's secret compartment dug in the wall. She looked at his hands; those hands which had torn her skin that evening and shattered her soul, were soft and gentle as they caressed the light of the dead. These lifeless remnants were symbols of the longing felt for what was lost. Each one a corpse filled with myths and past lives.

The windows looked out at the misty darkness. Melike remembered that there was a park opposite. The old fireplace was fitted with a gas burner, its flames visible through the glass doors. Hayali came with two glasses and a bottle of wine. He sat in the couch close to Melike. He lit a cigar. Nothing would ever happen to him, thought Melike, he can adapt to any environment.

"We must celebrate your success, it was very important. Thank you for taking the risk of this trip, Eda."

With their glasses in their hands, they looked at each other for a long time without moving.

"I was sure you would come," added Hayali. "You gave me a guarantee that night."

"Did I, I wasn't aware of it. How can you be so sure of yourself?"

"I'm not. On the contrary, I'm afraid."

"My uncle told me what happened, I'm sorry," said Melike.

"It isn't because of that. What makes me sad is that my self-respect has been hurt."

"A nice parody of sadness. Very impressive. You are a good actor."

Melike lit a cigarette without taking her eyes off him.

"Do I hear sabers rattling?" asked Hayali.

"I came for you, because you wanted me to."

"Did you miss the hate you feel for me?"

"Absolutely. Because hate decreases one's self-control and I need that, just like you do."

She bent her head toward her wine glass as though she wanted to hide the words that were falling out of her mouth and the flush that descended on her face. For a moment, she pitied the mad warrior inside her. She was talking nonsense.

"Whether one likes it or not, one can experience love and hate only in his or her own way," said Hayali and went quiet. Phil Collins was playing.

"Why didn't you practice medicine, why are you in this business?"

Hayali looked at her with a crooked smile and didn't answer.

"Please, I'm curious."

Hayali smiled again. This time his smile was tense, bitter. For a moment, she saw that ironic, provocative, fiery look in his eyes. Melike couldn't take her eyes off him. She didn't understand the meaning of that flame in his look. Anger, desire, desperation, pain…What was it?

"You're not going to answer, is that it?"

"Not now."

"All right, what do you feel right now? How do you look at me? What do you see?" she asked, her heart tightening.

"I have always tried to form a center within myself," said Hayali. "Because I'm not a lovable person."

Melike drank her wine silently. She was hearing the music. She no longer saw herself as someone sidelined by love. She was at the climax of a dark and crazy dream.

"Why did you come to me that night?" she insisted. She brought her hand to her chest as if checking the amazement, the clashing emotions, the violence and the gratification which remained from their lovemaking.

"Which night?" asked Hayali with feigned indifference.

"I want to know, please, I need this," said Melike, almost imploring.

The air in the room was pretty warm, a little smoky and dim. Hayali leaned forward, putting his elbows on his knees.

"These things happen in life, and there doesn't have to be a reason. Perhaps it was to overcome my anger."

"Are you talking about the anger you felt for me?"

"How stupid you are! The silliest thing that ever happened to me was to fall in love with you at first sight. Do you know what it meant for me to have betrayed myself, that free-spirited, precious ego of mine, in such a disgraceful manner? You got stuck in my throat."

Melike got up, went and sat next to him. She took his hand and kissed it. Their eyes met.

"You were a great blow to me, you were danger," said Hayali. "All the same, you were irresistible." He seemed surprised at what he was saying.

He roughly reached for Melike and kissed her. Their mouths met furiously.

It was a longed for reunion. They both wanted to die from the poison of betrayal, by each other's hand, happy to give up their lives. They knew that whatever they did, they would remain nailed to that night for a lifetime, because love was the most desperate secret ever created by man.

Time was endless, priceless, and their battle was reckless, fearsome. There wasn't only sex in their lovemaking; there were taboos, sins, madness and savagery.

The night was bleeding quietly, without complaint. It had abandoned itself to their mercy.

It was the morning of the day before Melike's departure. They were in bed. They had greeted the new day by making love. The gray light that came through the window poured over them. They could hear the birds outside. What sort of a dead end had they entered? What was to happen?

"I will try to spend this year here in London," said Hayali. "And you will come and go."

"How about my uncle?" asked Melike.

"He has sensed the attraction between us. We hadn't been on such good terms for a while anyway. I was in a bad mood and he was weary. Your uncle must always have novelty for excitement. He seems smitten by a young Iraqi lately."

"I saw him at the *yalı*."

"All the same your dear uncle is in no condition to manage things by himself. I'm the one who conducts his affairs. He won't give me up."

"What's that *yalı* business? My uncle mentioned something."

"I'm already wealthy enough and I'm also a proud man. It was your uncle's idea. He owed me money, so he suggested the *yalı* and I didn't refuse. Then for some reason, he changed his mind and backed out. He is the one who pulled all sorts of tricks to send me here."

"Yes but I couldn't understand why. What sort of a partnership is this?"

"All partnerships are dangerous and not to be trusted at all in a business like ours. Your uncle tried to turn you against me when he felt you were interested in me."

"He must have imagined what could happen when he sent me here."

"He must have. I'm sure of that. He has given up on me."

"Isn't this an ugly situation? So complex, so unethical…"

"What ethics? People like us cannot do without escapades, rare things, pleasure and money. Me, you, your relatives, we are all bandits, a band of bastards."

"You're being very offensive."

"Stop playing the fool, Eda. Don't you see we are thrashing about in a putrid morass? Our business is to rob graves, to rise above the dark!"

He turned on his back and clutched his hands over his belly. Melike leaned over him and looked at his face closely. "I won't forget this morning," she thought. She smiled. So she was a thief. Perhaps she was, but it hurt when it was said out aloud. It was a long time ago that she had missed the chance of living a smooth and noble life. Even if she made an attempt, she would have to isolate herself from all that she loved. She had started a free-fall together with this man. She couldn't give up this beautiful body, this handsome face, this fire, this complicity. She laughed, mocking herself and the man she loved, her uncle, small ambitions, idiocies, egotisms. She felt sad for those who were defeated today and had to worry about tomorrow.

"Why did you get mixed up in this business, why did you give up being a doctor, come on, tell me," she said sweetly.

"It's a sad story. I performed an abortion and caused the death of a young woman because I couldn't stop the bleeding. I felt that I could no longer practice medicine after that."

"Was that why you hated women?"

"I became estranged after that incident."

"I'm very moved," said Melike.

She placed a light kiss on his lips as if to console him.

This man was hers. Whatever happened, she would stay with him, and she would not leave him to anyone else. Suddenly she felt a burning suspicion. One couldn't be sure of anything in the darkness of the grave the young man had talked about, but she felt she had to ask.

"That girl, Işık, I was wondering…" she said, turning sideways and looking into his eyes.

"Işık? Wondering what?"

"You were a threesome and she was your sex toy, wasn't she?"

"Nonsense! How did you make that up? That girl is pampered because she compensates your uncle's longing for a child, that's all. You certainly have a wild imagination.; What perverse scenarios you seem to have written!" He started laughing, "You really are something!"

"Is it something so impossible?"

"No, but the figure is wrong. A handsome boy is always more preferable to that skeleton and is very easily found."

"Then why do you now prefer a woman, me?"

"I have never limited myself. Humans are bisexual."

He doesn't take anyone seriously except himself, thought Melike. He was ready not to love me, to sacrifice me right from the beginning. And now all he is doing is offering his body as a bribe. Once again she felt herself to be within a game she didn't know, a wicked plot. So be it, she thought. She was determined to go all the way. Everything was beautiful at this moment.

Grab whatever you want, scatter it, toss it about, throw it away, live your life, she thought, because there is no meaning wherever you hope to find it. Even when you think there is, it won't be the right one for you or it will quickly disappear. Don't think about the future because the bottom of this world is hell, a night dark as ink…

18

Eylem was looking in amazement at her artistic, half naked pictures which had been published in a men's magazine, wondered how they managed to make someone ordinary look so beautiful. The pictures had been taken by a woman photographer who worked for Sezgin's advertisement agency. She was a soft, understanding person and there had been no problems when they worked together. According to Eylem's wish, the woman had left her face in the shadows, bringing forward only one of her features at a time – lips, eyes, neck – giving her an even more mysterious air. The beauty in the pictures was so innocent and yet so sexy and magnificent that they didn't seem to have anything to do with her.

And they actually had nothing to do with her. These were the images of her absence. They had isolated her body as a form, turning it into an object of fetish.

"You are on the rise," Jale had said. "Beautiful things will happen because you are different."

"What kind of difference is that?"

"You are not like anyone else. Your figure is very proportionate and you are photogenic. What's more you are natural and intelligent. These photographs will push up your price even more, honey. You may find yourself in the black market! Oh, yes, they called from an advertisement agency this morning. They want you to play in an ad for biscuits. You have finally succeeded in drawing Aysevim Hanım's attention."

They were in the office on the second floor of the boutique, waiting for Aysevim who had wanted to see Eylem. They went downstairs and chose a few pieces for her to wear. Jale knew what would suit her and what won't. My taste in clothes is improving, thought Eylem. She had developed an aura of class, a distance full of pride.

She had been with the same businessman three times in the last ten days. They had had dinner and then gone to his bachelor's pad twice, and once they had been at a nightclub until morning. The man was about forty-five years old, plump, carefree, a hedonist, but he was also most amiable. He loved to talk and to discuss matters. He had become very interested when he found out that Eylem wrote poetry and he insisted on seeing what she had written. On the first night when they had dinner together, they had constantly talked about the meaning or the meaninglessness of life, and whether money alone was enough to have a beautiful life. On their second meeting, he had candidly told Eylem that he had ended his marriage of fifteen years, that he separated love from sexual hunger, that there had always been other women in his life because he didn't feel any excitement when he was with his wife. One had to have a variation of pleasures, try new tastes to add some color to the emptiness of life, but that alone wasn't enough, of course. For some reason, he had lately been feeling in pieces, consumed and lonely.

She had a wonderful time the night they went to a nightclub. They had danced a lot and laughed a lot. He was very agile for his large body. They had talked about interesting things when the subject came to politics. He had said, "The government turns a blind eye to the mafia because it is the government that creates it." The power of the state wasn't enough to deal with everything and the laws never met the needs. The important thing was to accept the developments and possess the dexterity to manage them.

He was a surprising man with his cheerful alertness, his coherent talk, his intelligent questions and especially the loving way he looked at her and the compliments he paid her. When she was with him, Eylem felt as if she had more qualities as a woman. She felt that she wasn't just a doll or a prostitute, but an intelligent, mature, experienced and most important of all, an honorable woman again. Almost. As much as one could be in that environment.

The last time they were together, he had suggested going to Paris for a weekend, and Eylem had accepted with pleasure. She had never been abroad, so it was going to be an exciting trip. It was nice for a woman to feel safe and content with such a strong and balanced man. And if he were to take her under his protection completely, most of her problems would be solved.

Aysevim arrived with the air of a businesswoman, sat at her table and ordered coffee. Beautiful but cold, forbidding, even frightening. Eylem felt fear as if she could easily be strangled by this woman if it suited her one day.

"Look, darling, at the moment you are one of the most popular girls in our agency," said Aysevim. "You have a bright future."

Eylem waited, listening carefully.

"You know that you have a two-year contract with us. But the main goal of the agency is to make everyone happy. In the meanwhile, we suggest to our girls not to enter a romantic relationship with anyone."

"I know, you are right."

"They will suffer and they won't be able to concentrate on the job. There's no need for someone who will get in your way, trip you up, isn't that so? If you only knew how many girls lost everything that way."

"Don't worry."

"Yes. However, this is a different situation. I understand you have gone out with Harun Bey a few times and apparently he was enthralled by you. To be frank, he is obsessed with you. He happens to be a very dear friend of mine. He went wild with jealousy when he saw your pictures in the magazine yesterday. I don't know if it is jealousy or if he has a high opinion of you now, but he has taken on a monopolizing air. He is a classy, generous, pleasant man. Apparently he offered to take you to Paris and you accepted."

"Yes. I suppose he will pay for it."

"Don't mention money, I will take care of that, all right, dear? Now, he will send a car for you tomorrow noon. He might want you to be only with him. What do you say?"

"What do you think?"

"It's you who has to decide. He might suggest living together. You can never know, it might last a long time or it may be short. This depends on you, on both of you. I think you have nothing to lose. You would have a more orderly life. He will be generous. If you use your intellect you can save your future."

"How about my contract?"

"We'll settle that. Harun Bey and I have known each other for a long time so it won't be a problem. We look after each other. The money of some, the friendship of others...people need people. I'd be pleased if you make him happy."

"He is an amusing, pleasant man. I'll try."

Eylem returned home late in the afternoon after walking around Nişantaşı, shopping. She had put Volkan's bear on the table. The poor thing had a shaggy, forlorn look. His owner could be in the same condition. She hadn't seen him since that night they were together. She had shut down the telephone and the Internet connection as soon as she returned home, changing also her SIM card afterwards. She was determined to do everything she could to keep Volkan from finding out what she did and where she lived.

She still became excited when she remembered that night. Being with Volkan was a reward as well as a punishment, a happiness she had never felt before and an ever painful wound...she knew almost everything about the young man. He was like an open book in front of her, but he knew nothing about her last six months, and he never should. This situation was upsetting the balance, the principle of mutuality between two people who had been so close. Eylem knew she won't be able to protect this weak structure which would come crashing over her at the first blow.

That was why she had run away. She would always bear the pain of helplessness. No doubt Volkan was feeling jilted, abandoned half way. For a long time, he had probably put together over and over again the words and images, the emotions and actions of that night, undoing them one by one in trying to reach a conclusion, going from the feeling of failure to incredulousness, from hallucination to reality, just like she had.

She felt she was exaggerating a little. He had probably suffered for a while and then found someone new, because the phase of reality had lasted only a very short time. On the other hand, he had succeeded in making Eylem believe in his sincerity. She had felt this with her flesh and blood. In that very short night, their intense feeling of belonging and their lovemaking so close to the language of the wind made it obvious that they would not be contented only with sexuality. This was the feeling which made her leave Volkan, never to return.

In the note she had left him, she had wanted to say "the most beautiful night of my life" but then she had changed her mind. She wasn't sure he could understand the sadness of their lovemaking which had turned into tears. During the period when they were writing to each other, she had accepted Volkan as someone unreachable, someone who could only be loved and desired from afar. It was a pleasant fantasy without basic details, an agreeable theme of spiritual satisfaction.

Then it had changed direction under the warm weight of the young man, diving into the depths, burning, drowning in kisses. She had slept on his chest like a passionate lover and a defenceless child, as her fleeting joy had turned into fear and pain.

She missed him for a while. At times she felt the urge to run to him and tell him everything, ask for forgiveness and take refuge in his arms, stay with him all her life. But she could feel that even if it would be easy to forgive her at the beginning, forgiveness would not be enough to dispel the feeling of disgust in the long run. She knew that her past would continue to haunt them like a frightening ghost. How could someone who lived her life as a favor, as an endless penance share it with someone else? There was nothing to be done. Just like many other beautiful things, she had been denied love right from the beginning. She wrote Volkan a few letters but she didn't think that any one of them was good enough to send. It was inevitable that the words of someone who didn't have wings to fly, or a voice to speak with, would fall into the void.

Like Volkan, Harun also dealt with money, but from what she understood, his business was bigger and more important than Volkan's. Aysevim's position was clear, she approved. It was most probable that she would be earning more money from this relationship than what she was already getting out of Eylem. Perhaps her price would be paid not with money but with other kinds of aid. Eylem had felt happy after talking to her, even joyous. This was what she had been waiting and hoping for and luck had smiled on her this time. She would be serving one person and generously getting what she was due. She didn't have to love the man; she would keep him happy and do as he wanted, that was all.

A strong, steady man who wasn't disturbed by her past could give her the willpower that was missing in her life and teach her brand new things about life. This relationship would also give her the chance to enter a certain social environment and provide her with security. Although the blessings were plenty, it was also possible that she might be devastated, but she wasn't afraid anymore. In any case, all the stale excesses and everything ordinary, vulgar and disgusting was transformed under the magic hands of money and took on the air of nobility and magnificence.

I must be optimistic, she thought, as she spread on her bed the new underwear she had just bought. How beautiful they were, frothy, magnificent, enticing! She too was beautiful, seductive and fresh. She was worth all these expensive things. She was happy at that moment and desirable. It was more logical to think about the future in the future.

She imagined sumptuous shopping centers, shop windows where expensive clothes were displayed and sweet smelling perfume shops. The tempting weight of brands, dreamy shoes, shawls, tulles. Eye shadows, lipsticks...They were all there to replace what had to be forgotten.

It was impossible to stay the same in this world where everything changed meaning, dimension and quality. That was why she too had changed. She now had to abandon all her old worries and banalities and transform her conscience into a counterattack consisting of the sum of illusions.

19

Early Summer

It was a Saturday afternoon that fitted the end of May; breezy and white like a seagull's wing. The Bosphorus stretched like blue satin between its shores. The noble beauty of the trees decked in thousand shades of green on the hilltops was reflected on the blue of the sky dotted with fluffy white clouds. Nature did not heed the cruel and unpalatable order of the world; instead, it offered mankind wonders every moment.

Happy with this invigorating view, Volkan looked at himself in the full mirror in the bedroom. He had regained some of the weight he had lost in the winter, but he didn't worry about it anymore. He worked out at the gym and swam in the stock exchange pool three times a week. He was in good form all around. He read, he listened to himself, he went to the cinema, to the theater, to concerts. He was rediscovering small pleasures and things that gave him a feeling of space and happiness. Peace, order, being settled…he had given up his business at a mature age, showing an integrity which was surprising even to himself. This was the main reason why he was so happy with his life. It was not a whim nor his destiny, but a serious and voluntary choice which provided him with the enjoyment of life.

He was going to Harun's for dinner with Yasemin that evening. He knew Harun would suggest once again, and even insist, that he return to his job. Harun called him frequently after he had left the job, keeping up his interest in him. He had first suggested meeting at the club, but when Volkan told him he had a girlfriend he was thinking of marrying and asked if he could bring her along, Harun invited them to his house. He too had a relationship which was fairly new; it was more agreeable to be at home. It would be a special dinner party just for the four of them.

The week before, they had gone to the opening of Selda's new art gallery in Nişantaşı and her first exhibition. Volkan hadn't seen her after that New Year party. When Harun was caught by the paparazzi while embracing a well-known actress, Selda had filed for divorce. The story was picked up by the tabloids and they had got divorced quickly, without too much ugliness.

Volkan hadn't been too interested in Harun's affairs at that time because of his own problems. Those were the days when Eylem had suddenly disappeared, and he was walking between the ground and the sky. He and Harun had got together in the club once while the divorce proceedings were going on. His old boss had constantly talked about things like the house, the car, the money Selda was asking for in exchange for divorce, boring Volkan to tears. He had become so agitated that he had barely stopped himself from hitting the man with an ashtray. You've got loads of money, give some to the woman, let her go, have some peace, both of you!

Harun had inevitably given her money. After all, it was easy come, easy go.

Selda had discovered herself after the divorce. She had put on some weight and become attractive. But it was difficult to say the same thing about her paintings. The whole lot were clumsy attempts which didn't go beyond being bad copies and sketches without character, dominated by dirty smeared colors. The painter who gave her lessons was also present at the exhibition. It was quite obvious that there was an intimate relationship between Selda and this heavy-set country bumpkin who was trying to climb up the social ladder.

Selda had shown a suffocating interest in Volkan right from the beginning. This was a hopeless, morbid inclination that came from her longing for a kind-hearted man she so badly needed. The poor woman had looked for solace in everyone.

Volkan felt happily peaceful for having taken an affectionate, fraternal attitude toward her. He certainly wasn't going to flirt with his boss's wife. It wasn't worth it and in principle he was always careful to stay away from married women.

He went to the kitchen and started the coffee machine. He smelled the spring air coming in through the open door. He felt free of all his burdens, liberated.

The memories he still had of Eylem were the physical ones. He had spent only one night with her. He had felt the bridge between his soul and his body, a tangible rapport he would never forget for the rest of his life.

He remembered the bewilderment and grief he felt when the girl suddenly disappeared. His effort to find her was an obstinate passion that made him live in misery for days and nights. Not being able to reach Eylem shattered his feeling of reality, making him think he had lived through a storm. A strong, sudden hurricane which had blown away everything and then subsided. In the confusion, the earth had opened up and swallowed Eylem.

When he was looking for a reason for her disappearance, he had also thought that she could be married. Married or not, Eylem had to have an obligation, a very important reason. That was why he couldn't feel anger or resentment. The fire had raged, turning into glowing red embers which slowly blackened and finally turned into ashes. Eylem had thus taught him how to forget without hate.

Fortunately he pulled himself together after a short while; perhaps he had matured with this devastation. He had been seeing Yasemin for some time. Even if she wasn't very beautiful, she was sensible, intelligent and full of life. They had made love a little while ago, happily playing with each other. Yasemin was a woman who could understand what was expected from her every moment, who knew how to make her man happy. She was in the shower just now and he could hear the water running in the bathroom.

He turned on the music channel of the television. They were playing Mozart. One had to be open to all things that life had to offer, both happy and unhappy, and live it up. Resistance required courage and sacrifice.

It looked as if Yasemin would take a long time to prepare but they were in no hurry. The sun was just setting. The sea was flowing toward the Marmara with golden glitters under the indigo blue sky. The seashore seemed to have the taste and color of cherries. The trees, the awnings, everything looked new. He wouldn't be alone that summer; he had already started making travel plans with Yasemin.

He remembered the past autumn and winter. How hopeless, lost and spent he was then. It was difficult for him to understand now why he had moaned and suffered so much in those months. Now his worries seemed to have cooled down and become distant. I was in depression, he thought. He had been living with the feeling that something had been taken away from him. That was why he had depended on coincidences until everything came crumbling down on him. Both Melike and Eylem were attractive women. He did not consider them adventures that ended in disappointment, and he didn't regret them at all. Eylem had gone through his life like the evening sun, leaving behind beautiful images and memories. And a saffron yellow scarf…*Saffron yellow*…He hadn't thought much about the significance of the color when he was choosing himself a nickname to address Eylem. But the thought had later visited his subconscious quite often. It was an emotional choice; there was a wish for a soft, sweet light in this word. A more mature image and tone than the sharp light of yellow. He looked through the fog of his reality of that time toward where he was standing now. The future could be full of situations one could never imagine.

He was still resting; he wanted to plan well what he would do. Whatever happened, he would not accept any offers from Harun. His preference was to make an investment in art or culture. Yasemin, whose domain was business administration, was a faculty member in a private university. She had suggested starting a special tourism company which would serve special people and work on a closed circuit basis. They were working on different projects together.

How lucky he was to meet this girl! As soon as he pulled himself together after the disappearance of Eylem, the urge to go to Africa had returned and he had started travelling, opening a new door in his life.

He and Yasemin were in the same safari trip. The special camp where they stayed was a very interesting, luxurious and romantic place hidden in the wild. Yasemin was a warm, talkative, friendly woman. Be it art, philosophy, theology, they could talk about everything. She was the daughter of a well-off family from the Black Sea and she was in love with nature. She had told him that her childhood was spent on boats. She had gone to university in England and had a master's degree in business administration from the United States. Volkan liked her for her amiable nature. He admired that she had rooted her freedom on a solid base and that she was unpretentious. It wasn't crazy passion or love that gave one palpitations. It never would be, and there was no need for it, either. Love was temporary and destructive. The moments when two people were together seemed like burning flames, and yet what was left of them was a cold, black ruin.

His friendship with Yasemin was very rewarding. The joy of life of this woman who was over thirty was extraordinary. She wanted children, one, two, three if possible. Sometimes Volkan thought that she was downright ugly but that was not important. As a man who had been attacked by the world, he felt that the desire to join the current of tradition was growing in him, and he didn't mind seeing himself as husband, father or grandfather. He even missed the warmth of a family, the monotonous happiness of fidelity, the tiring pleasures of fatherhood. With her large nose, her deep-set eyes, her plump short figure and her slightly bow legs like those of a naughty child, Yasemin could not be considered a beautiful woman. But she had short, honey colored hair, bangs that fell onto her straight eyebrows and strong teeth that overlapped a little in front, and she was a sweet, capable, faultless candidate for motherhood. There was no trace of spiritual carelessness, secret emotions, traumas and scars that paralyzed women. She was like a safe, open port. These were things that made someone seem beautiful. Furthermore, their sex life was great.

It was very easy to be with her and to love her.

Eylem sometimes passed through his memory as a childish sadness, an image, a picture, a spark of emotion. The fact that he had learned to forget didn't necessarily mean that he had forgotten her. He couldn't, because she was like a dream of flying and he had tragically crashed as soon as he had taken off.

Naturally it was a serious accident and he had been seriously wounded. He shuddered with a slight pain. All his dreams of Eylem were cut off before they could be finished. Evidently his wound hadn't completely healed yet; he had only got rid of the bandages.

It was still fresh, but he knew that it would pass, even if it left a scar, just like the other ones.

Actually time had made all his women look alike. He couldn't differentiate their faces, legs, tongues and laps. What had remained from them was a burden, a considerable but vague sum of deductions. Certain mysterious, illusive and useless personal regrets and broken memories buried in the darkness of the past, becoming incomprehensible and obscure ...

He went in. Yasemin was sitting on the bed in her bathrobe, drying her feet. She was sweet, definitely. She had a nice home in Ortaköy, but they preferred to be together over the weekends since the arrival of spring. His need for her presence sometimes seemed to him like a form of exhaustion; every now and then, he felt stifled and even felt like going back to his old life. He had no doubt that this was because he had lived alone for such a long time. But he knew that whatever happened he no longer wanted to live a life of inconsistent solitude. Even if making love and small joys were not always enough to disperse one's loneliness.

"Well, my lady? When do you plan to be ready?"

"I didn't wash my hair, I won't be long now. I'll get dressed soon. Hey, put out that cigarette right away!"

"It's my first one in three days! What's more, the door is wide open."

"How about your lungs? Do they have doors, too? No smoking Volkan, no smoking at all, my love. All right?"

"I can't promise anything."

"But I don't want a man with a cigarette."

"You're very boring, darling."

They were at Harun's house shortly before nine. The pink and white villa amongst the foliage resembled a raspberry cake. The evening air was slightly humid and cool; the soft light of the windows was pouring warmly onto the garden.

They entered the imposing hall decked in marble and full of golden shimmers. Then an old butler took them into the living room. There was no change in the house. The same ostentatious wealth, the same furniture, paintings, lights ... The pale soft colors of an old dream evening which had turned into a nightmare seemed to appear before Volkan's eyes. Evidently Selda had left with only a few suitcases. Harun had given her a villa in Kemerburgaz. The boy was also with his mother.

The dinner table had been prepared in that part of the dining room which opened onto the terrace. It was decked with candles and flowers, creating a harmony of white with some dark green. The doors were open, and the delightful smell of the newly mowed grass was drifting into the room. Yasemin was wearing a smart dark brown dress cut on the bias, with an asymmetrical skirt, and a string of pearls around her neck. She looked attractive. Volkan looked at her with affection and smiled.

Harun came in with fast, enthusiastic exclamations of "Well, well!" He was wearing informal clothes, and seemed to have lost some weight. He looked at them with a skeptical bewilderment, as though he hadn't found Yasemin beautiful enough, then he shook hands with her and embraced Volkan.

Over Harun's shoulder, Volkan saw the woman entering the room through the door at the back. He froze. The woman lifted her head and looked at him for an instant, turning away her eyes timidly.

It was difficult to believe but it was her, Eylem!

Volkan shuddered. He staggered as if he had been attacked and his knees had given way. He felt like the victim of a practical joke. Scrappy lights were flashing in his mind, making him think of strange coincidences. He had thought about meeting her again in very different places and circumstances. An encounter of this quick, simple and ordinary kind he had never thought.

Harun was introducing his new girlfriend to them. He was saying nice words as a hospitable, cordial host would, and he was preparing the background for a pleasant evening. Volkan shook Eylem's limp hand. She did not answer his questioning look. She had the air of being in a completely different world, a strange world where she didn't belong. She was a woman he didn't know, she wasn't the same Eylem. At least, her presence did not fit the reason for her being there. Then as she shook Yasemin's hand, she smiled like a child who had been caught in her hiding place. It was a somewhat forced, implied smile, but friendly all the same.

"How do you do?"

Volkan watched her self-possession in amazement. Her movements, her naturalness were not affected. She was the image of serious elegance without seeming to notice it. Her face was a meaningless, creaseless mask, as if she had frozen her expression in order to overcome the difficulty of that moment.

She was wearing a sequined, saffron yellow sleeveless top with a deep V-shaped neck and tight black trousers. Her shoes were elegant with very thin high heels. She had on a necklace with a strikingly large diamond. Her hair was in a bun at the nape of her neck. Her air of the beautiful, elegant, proud lady was unbearable.

Harun was asking them what they would like to drink.

They sat and got their drinks. Volkan concentrated on talking to Harun without looking at Eylem – Harun had introduced her as Mutena – while trying to hide his confusion. Yasemin had immediately started talking to Eylem in all friendliness and warmth. Volkan listened to this useless chatter with patient anticipation. He noticed that Eylem was asking short questions to which she hoped to get long answers.

The right kind of jazz music was playing at the right volume. Flowers, reflections, dangerous longings intermingled with past images. At this moment, to retreat is the only thing the body can do against the underground labyrinths of memory, thought Volkan. He wished with all his heart that they had met somewhere else, at some other time. He wondered if he would be strong enough to live through this evening without making a blunder. There were only a few steps between them, and yet they were miles apart. All the same, he felt he was being pushed toward her as if he were caught in a wave.

His memory drifted toward those magic moments they had shared. How incredible that night seemed at that moment when they were side to side in silent despair. Suddenly he felt a burning jealousy. He looked at Harun with fury and a scorn he could not hide. He felt disgusted with him in the name of this woman who had cried in his arms that night, and he cursed Harun's power.

They sat down to dinner. Volkan's movements were faltering and awkward. He spoke with difficulty as if there was some kind of stopper in his mouth. They talked at length about general subjects, art, business and social gossip, new nightclubs and restaurants. Harun was jovial and Eylem was a little pale. She watched Harun as though she was afraid of saying or doing something wrong. She mostly listened and did not talk more than necessary. She carried the unfamiliarity of having recently joined the social environment and the somewhat forced attempt at *participation*.

After a while the conversation drifted to politics. Who was obliged to answer Harun's questions, thought Harun, everything was getting worse. The situation was tense; the economic and social conditions were as worrying as the negative developments within the country and abroad. Harun violently opposed his pessimism. The economy was improving. They were about to leave behind the difficult times.

Not only a liar but also a parasite, a loudmouth who thrives on the misfortunes of the people, thought Volkan in anger. Yasemin was afraid of social upheaval. The unrest of people who worked merely for their keep, those who lived on the brink of hunger were increasing. The population which had lost perspective of the future was waiting, worried but passive, in quiet acceptance of their fate.

"Conception of the future calls for foresight. And that necessitates knowledge and experience," declared Harun. "You can't expect good sense and vision from the mobs in the street. Most of them live for the day. They calm down and come over to your side when you throw a few bags of food to them and hand out some alms."

"I sometimes feel that those who can't choose the right people to govern them deserve what they get," said Yasemin cruelly. She gave up quickly, but with her casual air, her energy and her talkativeness, she was excellent at conquering the social environment she was in. She was the one who was saving the evening and Volkan was grateful to her. Harun had liked her very much also. He was in a good mood, joking and telling stories.

Dessert was baked apples with ice cream. The ice cream balls were decorated with green leaves and a red sauce was poured in circles over the apples. Volkan felt as if he was sliding over to another plane, as if he was there and yet not there. He was there but he was also looking at himself from above. His passion for Eylem had ended in such a bizarre way that it now seemed foolish to him in spite of the pain he was feeling.

He was dying to draw Harun aside and find out where and how he had met Eylem. It wasn't possible for him to understand why she had left him and was now with a man like Harun. He tried to imagine where their lives had intercepted; he was burning as if he had lost a limb.

Volkan could see that Eylem too was badly shaken. She couldn't have been ignorant of who had been invited for dinner. Nevertheless, she had faced meeting him, most probably not to cause any doubts in her lover, her master. Perhaps she had wanted to be seen by Volkan, come what may, and to put an end to a love affair which was over before it had begun.

He was dizzy. He felt an overwhelming urge to get up and walk through the dining room with funereal steps, leaving quietly without making any explanations. He would have been quite capable of doing this if Yasemin hadn't been there. But he couldn't leave her or explain the situation to her.

Where did that name, Mutena, come from? Was that Eylem's real name? Or had it been chosen because it fitted better her present social standing? He suddenly asked in his unhappy drunken state, "You have a unique name," he said, turning to Eylem. "As far as I know, it means 'chosen,' is that true?"

"That's the name my family gave me. My friends also call me Eylem," said the young woman. "Harun likes Mutena."

Harun quickly added, "It also means 'created with love and care.' My beloved! She is so much like her name, isn't she?"

He seemed to be madly in love. For the moment…How long would it last? This was still an unfinished story. For it to be an adventure with a proper beginning and an end, it had to take place somewhere in space, not in this world where the only signs of humanity were the half-burnt, half-moldy remnants of a once superior civilization. It was gradually becoming impossible to form different things for men and women unless a new human race appeared and rediscovered the world.

Volkan looked at the burgundy colored silk curtains, the moldings over the windows and the large diamond on Eylem's neck. There is nothing to be done, he thought. If she can accept selling herself, there is no problem. She would soon find out Harun's personality, his endless faults; she would see his infidelity and learn before long. The man's glitter had probably turned her head, but she would understand with time that it was nothing but worthless gold colored sequins and fancy reflections. He had shared his boss's secrets and he had been the partner of his hidden sins. If he knew Harun at all, it was certain that he would hurt the girl and break her heart. He felt sorry for Eylem as if she had died.

"You really are a lovely person. Do you work, do you have a job?" asked Yasemin, turning to Eylem.

"I studied economics, and I did some modeling at one point, but I gave it up. I'm not working at the moment," said Eylem.

"Business life is difficult, it exhausts women," said Harun. "Mutena is a poet. She has written some beautiful poems; we are thinking of compiling them in a book."

It must have been fairly easy for Eylem to put her alternate life into use when even passions, ambitions and sorrows have become elective, values to be bartered, thought Volkan. The poignant classical music in the background suddenly sounded metallic to his ears.

"Would you read us one of your poems?" asked Yasemin.

"I don't think so, I would be too embarrassed," said Eylem. She laughed and shook her head. Her lips twitched slightly as if a secret button had been touched.

"Please, don't refuse us," insisted Yasemin.

"Later perhaps…" She bent her head. She dipped her spoon into the apple and then suddenly looked up at Volkan. There was a very pure glitter in her eye. Her lips were trembling slightly. They were fresh and lively, as if wanting to be kissed. For a moment, Volkan almost forgot about his crashed hopes, being betrayed and abandoned. He felt a desire to push her into a dark, quiet corner and kiss her furiously.

"She'll read something in a little while, won't you, darling?" said Harun. "I too want to hear you, please."

Volkan had never seen Harun in such an abandoned, tender mood. He had never seemed so defeated before a woman. Volkan suddenly felt himself tricked and excluded from the position of being Eylem's steadfast, secret ally. He wanted to shout "Fool!" into the night, the laughter and all that seductive shimmer. But he wasn't quite sure to whom he should address that word.

With great pomp and show, Harun popped the champagne which the waiter had brought, and he explained that the bottle had been bought at the auction of a so-called bankrupt industrialist. It was forty years old. They raised their glasses to the ladies and to friendship. It really was extraordinary.

Volkan looked at Eylem's elegant hand holding the champagne glass. He secretly studied her once again. She looked pitifully fragile. Proud and docile, captive and timid...He missed her skin with an insatiable longing. He felt a mad urge to take away this delightful creature from Harun, to lull her to sleep in his arms, to melt inside her. He imagined upsetting the table, jumping on Harun, bringing him to the ground with his fists and continuing to kick him with fury when he was down. He wanted to create a scandal. If only he had come alone!

How had this scoundrel bought her, what tricks had he pulled? He remembered the word "model." The mystery was beginning to clear up. His mind was trying to put together the bits and pieces. What had happened was beginning to take shape in fragments amidst the laughter and the tinkling of plates and glasses. Still, this scenario was not enough to dispel the feeling of having been struck by lightning.

"Now ladies, if you allow us, we will talk some business in the next room while you continue to chat here," said Harun.

"Talk all you want, we'll be fine, I really like Mutena Hanım," said Yasemin.

The two men went over to another part of the living room.

"How do you like my girlfriend?" asked Harun as they sat down.

"I'm sorry for the girl. She seems very fragile. You'll soon get tired of her and shake her off."

"No, this isn't just another girl as you might think. She is very intelligent, extremely cultured, she is just something else."

"Where did you find her?"

"I took her out to dinner one evening, and everything happened so quickly. I must have been looking for a woman like her. I rented an apartment for her close by. Your girl is also very intelligent, very lively. How did that happen?"

"We met in Africa. There was a shortage in Istanbul!"

"Well, sonny boy, you never know with these things. Anyway. Now I have a proposition for you. Would you go to Switzerland for a couple of years? You know we opened a liaison office in Zurich. I want you to manage it."

"Impossible."

"You don't have to answer right away."

"I don't want to return to the past. I will try to do something else."

"Look, my friend. I really need someone like you very badly. You will have a quieter life. Just tell me your conditions, and the job is yours."

"Believe me, I'm not interested at all."

"You're very tough, my friend. Don't decide right away, there's still time. Think about it."

"I'm sorry, I can't do it."

"I'll keep hoping all the same. Think carefully, okay?"

Volkan remembered the years he had spent with him. They were over. The past and the future had separated never to meet again. They hadn't disappeared but they had drifted apart, the way it was in real time and in life. This was the basic rule of separation. The stars were also drifting apart until eternity. Everybody's fate was the same at the beginning. Then, according to the decisions made, the roads chosen, coincidences, undertows and currents, people ended up in different places. But certain separations lived in one's memory and continued their existence as if they were not separations.

When they were getting up, he jumped as if he had been pricked by a needle and darted out to the terrace. He was feeling nauseated. He took deep breaths and looked into the darkness. The city seemed devastated to him as though it had been bombarded by tons of bombs. He thought about the silver stars which were like pinheads in the dark blue summer sky and how they drifted aimlessly in space, without dreams, without tomorrows.

"What's wrong, Volkan?" It was Yasemin.

"I feel a little dizzy. I'll be all right in a minute."

"You drank too much, darling. Have some mineral water. Then we'll go, if you want."

"I'm fine. I'm all right now."

Harun came and put his arm around Volkan's shoulder. Volkan shuddered, bent low and freed his shoulder. They went back in together. Eylem was standing, watching Volkan apprehensively. He looked at her, not thinking for a moment about what he should do to remove the great ruin she had left in his soul. He inhaled her beauty, her elegance, her confidant and noble air, which she had somehow attained, and buried it all in the most secret part of his memory and then he carefully covered everything.

Harun was piqued at having been refused. They lit a cigar each. Yasemin tersely turned her head toward Volkan and looked at him reproachfully, but he pretended not to see her glance. To get away from the smoke, the young woman got up from her seat and went over to the far wall and began to study the painting hanging there.

"What lovely paintings you have," she said to Harun.

"Come, I'll take you around the house," said Harun. "I'll show you the ones upstairs first." They walked toward the stairs; Volkan's heart started beating faster. He suspiciously looked right and left making sure he was alone with Eylem. They could hear laughter from the second floor. They were alone. They looked at each other for a while.

"It is very difficult for me to accept the situation, Eylem. Why did you run away from me?" asked Volkan in an imploring voice.

"I'm not the right person for you. You couldn't have loved me." She bent her head.

"I feel cheated from the beginning to the end."

"No, please don't think that," said Eylem. "It wasn't easy for me, either. I learned only this morning that we would be meeting here tonight. I tried to write you a few things this afternoon and I sent you an e-mail. Please look at your mail when you go home."

"Do you think that's enough? I looked for you for such a long time."

"I'm happy that you've found someone who suits you."

"I'm afraid I can't say the same thing for you. Why, Eylem, why?"

"I'm sure you will understand me when you read what I have written."

"I'm hurt by your choice."

"I had no idea that you and Harun were close. And what's more, we may not have a choice under some circumstances. Sometimes we are forced to consent for the best solution."

Her voice broke in sadness, her face convulsed for an instant. Then she turned her eyes to Volkan. Her look was empty and tired. Volkan was silent. This woman had proven courageous enough to show herself to him that evening. How he craved to take her back and hold her tight in his arms.

"I told you that night that we had met too late, Volkan."

"You couldn't explain why."

"It's difficult to explain certain things."

Yasemin and Harun were laughing when they came down the stairs.

"There are some fantastic paintings," said Yasemin. "A superb collection."

"Yes, I've seen it before," said Volkan. "He doesn't only have paintings; if you only knew…Harun also collects antiques."

"I'll show those some other evening. Now let's listen to some poetry, what do you say?" said Harun and looked at Mutena. "Come on, my love. We're listening to you. Please, Mutena."

There was a short silence.

"This will make me feel like a child trying to act cute for the guests. Would it be all right if I didn't?" asked Eylem, blushing a little.

"Please don't refuse us. We really want to hear you."

"I have a poem called Saffron Yellow," said Eylem. "It's a new one, it's not finished yet…but you insisted so much."

Harun turned off the light on the side table. Their faces were in the shade. Volkan wanted to say an encouraging word but he couldn't. He was curious because although Eylem had told him about her poems, she had never shared them with him. They became silent and waited.

Eylem began to read her poem with a slow, timid but moving voice:

> The evening bleeds in my hands
> With saffron yellow sorrows
> And I am silent like a signet
> Not to talk of parting without farewell
> I was late to learn to fly
> As I fluttered my wings in the bushes
> Facing the shameless eyes of the hunter
> I was trapped before you were
> Love is often helpless anyhow
> And short-lived even when mutual
> Clouds are also without wings
> And cannot carry a soul on their shoulders

There was a long silence. Harun was resting his head on the back of the armchair. Yasemin could have broken the silence but she didn't, she was lost in thought. Eylem leaned back as if she was exhausted. Volkan started feeling a frightening tingling sensation which was gradually increasing; his brain had become icy cold.

"That's how it goes," said Eylem. She seemed ready to cry any moment.

"It's beautiful, isn't it?" said Harun. "Fantastic!" He sat up and looked at Volkan with a challenging smile.

"I'm moved," said Yasemin briefly with a dreamy voice. "A lovely, broken love poem…"

Harun turned on the light again. Within a flash of light when desire and compassion sparkled at the same instant, Volkan saw the lifeless sorrow on Eylem's face. This was all that there was. She wasn't there, she was hiding in a place where she could not be reached, which nobody knew and where nobody could go. She was hiding in words, under her skin, in the darkness of her eyes or in the future of a past anguish.

"Does anybody want a drink?" asked Harun enthusiastically.

Nobody answered. Volkan felt himself spinning, rising higher and higher in a void. He wasn't so drunk that he couldn't see that the lines of a poem which had fallen from the stars were floating around. But he was surprised to see how far his head was from his feet. He felt that nothing was as it should have been, that errors and disorder reigned supreme in the world. He listened to the humming silence in the house with so much velvet, illuminated with crystal lamps, polished like a mirror, and he heard his heart throb in his ears.

He looked toward the darkness beyond the open doors of the terrace. He was completely exhausted. He felt a slight pain creeping up his spine. He wanted to say something but changed his mind. It was useless. The past was in pieces. There was no present. Only the future was certain, a line of ordinary possibilities.

They left before midnight.

"You were a bit strange tonight," said Yasemin as they were going home in the car. "Did Harun annoy you or did you upset your stomach? You didn't eat much but you drank a lot."

"It's not important, I'm a little drunk and I'm sleepy," said Volkan. "I want to get to bed and sleep as soon as possible. Shall we give you a lift home?"

"That would be good. I have to get up early tomorrow."

Volkan took her hand and squeezed it. She had understood immediately that he wanted to be alone. He loved this girl and he had made the right choice. He needed a woman like her, that was for sure. No, he couldn't carry Eylem, because he had no wings.

"When are we getting married?" he asked Yasemin, and at the same moment he realized what an unnecessary question that had been.

"In July, that's what we decided, have you forgotten?" said Yasemin and she laughed.

"Let's talk again tomorrow. Okay? Maybe we'll bring the date closer."

The car had stopped in front of her home. "Okay," said Yasemin as she got off the car.

Volkan continued toward Bebek. He was looking at the back of the driver's neck. No doubt the man was aware of everything. He had met Eylem on that March evening when they were together, and now he had seen her in Harun's house as she saw them off. What had he thought, Volkan wondered. The rules had been broken, the line had been crossed. He thought about apologizing to his faithful old friend. He wanted to say, I'm not a scoundrel, please don't misunderstand.

He was drunk, and yes, he was talking nonsense.

He walked along the garden path flanked with bushes, and entered the elevator. He hid his face from the mirror. He knew what he would see. He quickly walked over to his computer as soon as he got home. He waited impatiently to be connected. Yes, Eylem had written to him again.

Yellowspot, Eylem, Mutena…which one? None of them! This time it was a different name.

Saffron!

> *Dear Volkan,*
>
> *I will not write you desperate sentences. I just want you to know this: I'm no different from others. I'm a woman who hasn't had a chance to be different. Even if it wasn't voluntarily, shortly after I wrote about "the future" and started communicating with you, I chose a shameful life style or the easy way out. You don't have much choice when money becomes a vital problem.*
>
> *It's been eight months since I came to Istanbul. When I realized how I had changed, I understood that it was too late to go back. Because the change I went through was not about earning my keep by selling my body to others, but with the diversion of my consciousness.*
>
> *Sometimes I feel the presence of an immense, old and heavy grief, with which I don't know how to cope. I am the only reason*

of this, I can't put the blame on anyone else. But neither can I say that it has nothing to do with you.

We, human beings, gain meaning through our relations with work, family, friend, lover and the world. Just like the words in a sentence. Your friendship, your interest consoled me. I slept in your arms with a self-confidence I had never felt before. It was bliss to be with you.

Everybody is to blame in the face of guilt. But everyone has to carry the guilt of his own life and there is nothing to be done about this.

I loved you and refrained from making you a partner in this.

I'm not worried about the future anymore. It has lost its meaning, or perhaps the future that I long for no longer exists.

I'm keeping your childhood friend, the teddy bear that you gave me. I shall always remember its memory.

I hope you will be very happy.

Eylem

Volkan felt his heart was being squeezed. He walked around from room to room for a few minutes, morose and dejected. Then he dashed out of the building. He quickly found himself in the street. He started walking along the coast with quick steps, erect and looking forward. He seemed to be trying to make his way toward the iron heart of the city

The summer night was tender and calm, the sea was salty, dark and lonely. He heard a muffled scream from afar. He shuddered and stopped, he looked at the rippled surface of the water. He saw a small white hand quickly disappear in the water far away, where the faint light of the quarter moon was pouring. There was an ill-omened ripple in the water, a trembling yellowish spot went on and off for a moment. Then the black water settled once again.

Volkan was filled with sadness. He held out his hand to the sea and said her name.

The poignant sound of a violin drifted from somewhere.

Life continued. It was not a one-page puzzle; it was a gaudy dice game which included innumerable sorrows and stories, a huge dice whose color and winning number changed according to one's point of view, choices and strength.

He wiped his face with the back of his hand. Was he crying or was that the humidity of the sea?